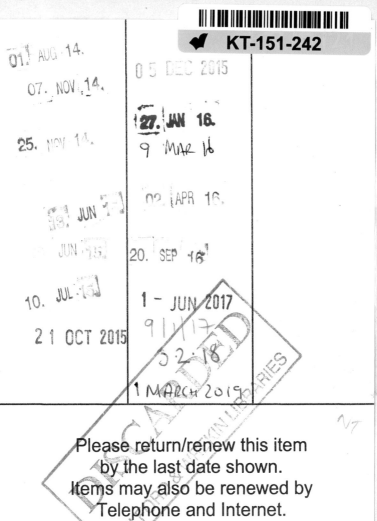

Also by Natasha Solomons

MR ROSENBLUM'S LIST

'Prepare to be seriously charmed' *The Times*

'Delightful . . . Solomons's narrative has shades of both PG
Wodehouse and Isabel Allende . . . There are also echoes of
Jez Butterworth's play *Jerusalem* in this whimsical novel's
deep seam of inquiry into the nature of Englishness' *TLS*

'The light yet poignant tone makes for an unusual, richly
comic novel . . . a treat of a book' *Guardian*

THE NOVEL IN THE VIOLA

'A deeply touching and blissfully romantic elegy for a
lost world' *The Times*

'Solomons's confident timing means that we sense what is
about to happen only moments before it occurs, and are
compelled to read on, not as one might expect for the frisson
of a new event, but for the thrill of having our
intuition confirmed' *TLS*

'A vivid and poignant story about hope, loss and reinvention'
Psychologies

THE GALLERY OF VANISHED HUSBANDS

Natasha Solomons

SCEPTRE

First published in Great Britain in 2013 by Sceptre
An imprint of Hodder & Stoughton
An Hachette UK company

First published in paperback in 2014

1

Copyright © Natasha Solomons 2013

The right of Natasha Solomons to be identified as the Author of the Work has been
asserted by her in accordance with the Copyright, Designs and Patents Act 1988.

A CIP catalogue record for this title is available from the British Library

ISBN 978 1 444 73637 3

Printed and bound by Clays Ltd, St Ives plc

Hodder & Stoughton policy is to use papers that are natural, renewable
and recyclable products and made from wood grown in sustainable
forests. The logging and manufacturing processes are expected to
conform to the environmental regulations of the country of origin.

Hodder & Stoughton Ltd
338 Euston Road
London NW1 3BH

www.sceptrebooks.com

For my parents, Carol and Clive, with love.

And for Luke with thanks for delaying his arrival
until the manuscript was (mostly) complete.

'The map of a face expresses things from which geography might learn.'

Patrick Hayman, *A Painter's Notes* (1959)

CATALOGUE ITEM 1
Woman with a Bowl of Apples (a.k.a. The Fridge),
Charlie Fussell, Oil on Canvas, 26 x 46in, 1958

I T WAS JULIET Montague's thirtieth birthday. This did not worry her unduly, although she conceded that other women in her position might well be disconcerted. She examined her feelings with her usual frankness, but concluded that she felt just as befuddled sliding out of bed at half past six as she had the day before, and when she dressed the children for school she felt no sudden urge to reach for the cooking sherry. Thirty, Juliet decided, was the point in her life when a woman is at her handsomest. She might not have the flush of her teens or the swagger of her twenties, but at thirty a woman has a direct-ness in her eye. Juliet Montague did anyhow. She knew exactly what she wanted.

She wanted to buy a refrigerator.

That morning was wet and unseasonably cold, but Juliet tried not to take it personally. It seemed unfair to have rain on one's birthday, and yet she supposed every day was some-body's birthday and if it never rained on birthdays England would be a desert, and Leonard wouldn't have anywhere to sail his model boat. Resigned, she buttoned her mackintosh, fastened her scarf tight about her throat and darted around puddles the colour of milky tea as she hurried to the station, uncertain as usual if she would make her train. Juliet lost time, mislaying minutes and even the odd hour, the way her father spilled loose change from his trouser pockets. The freezing rain sliced against her cheeks and in half a minute the wind blew her wretched umbrella inside out.

Yet by the time the train was pulling into Charing Cross, the winter's morning had been transformed into a spring afternoon. The laundered sky stretched a taut blue above Trafalgar Square, while shuffling pigeons lined up along Nelson's outstretched arm to dry out in the sunshine like so many pairs of socks. The high puffs of white cloud looked just like the ones Leonard drew in the pictures that Juliet pinned to the corkboard in the kitchen. She glanced at her watch, wondering whether there was time to slip into the National Gallery and visit a few old friends before her shopping trip. The last time she had visited, she'd been caught by a sunflower and misplaced the rest of the afternoon. She'd watched the canvas until the yellow paint began to vibrate and tremble in waves like liquid sunshine, falling out of the frame and spilling onto the gallery floor. On the way home she'd bought sunflowers and sat with Frieda at the kitchen table for nearly an hour watching them in their glass vase to see if all yellow shook if only you watched for long enough.

Feeling her resolve weaken, she jumped on board the first bus going by – which turned out to be going in exactly the wrong direction, but it was such a lovely afternoon she didn't mind in the least. The prospect of a walk beside the park was just right for a birthday. She pictured the neat pound notes and tumbling coins inside her purse and felt a tingle of exhilaration in her chest. Twenty-one guineas. She'd not had that much money to spend since George left. That had happened on her birthday too. And, she thought, as she dodged the spray thrown up by a rushing taxi, at first it had not even been such a bad birthday – she had not known then that George wasn't coming back. She'd only been irritated he had forgotten it was her birthday. Not a card, not even a bunch of flowers from the garden (he'd given her one the year before and she'd been touched by the bouquet of black tulips, pleased he'd remembered they were her favourite, until she'd looked out of the kitchen window and seen he'd lopped the heads off all the flowers in her pots by the back door). Her mind tripped down familiar lanes. If only he'd left a note. He could have written it inside a birthday card, killing two birds with one stone: '*Darling, Many Happy Returns. By the way, I'm off* . . .' Juliet smoothed the silk of her scarf to soothe her thoughts and determined to think of other things; nothing must spoil today. She'd saved so carefully and at last she was going to be a thoroughly modern woman, or at least one not quite so far behind the times. No more fussing with the stupid icebox or leaving bottles of milk on the windowsill outside to chill on winter days and having to buy fish or meat on the afternoon one intended to eat it. She knew how Leonard longed for a television set – for a while now he'd been cultivating friends who possessed one, and when he returned from their houses his cheeks were flushed and he was very quiet, polishing his little round spectacles on his school tie even more than usual, silently rehearsing the wonders of what he had seen. Juliet remained resolute; however enthralling the television might be, it was a luxury and a fridge was essential. Frieda and Leonard watched with fierce solemnity as at the end of each week she dropped another handful of coins into the old custard tin stashed on the top shelf of the larder. They'd not been terribly excited at first: Leonard puzzled that anyone should save for anything other than dinky cars or televisions and Frieda, who spent all her pocket money in the sweet shop the afternoon she was given it, thought of the tin-money in terms of penny sugar mice queuing nose-to-string-tail – she was quite certain it could buy enough mice to stretch all the way to Bognor Regis (a place she could not point to on the map, but which signified an almost infinite distance from Chislehurst).

Frieda was right – the money in the custard tin represented all sorts of pleasures not taken. They had bought cheap seats behind a pillar for *Peter Pan* and Juliet had nearly cried when Leonard had slumped with disappointment, unable to glimpse Peter swinging across the stage, cutlass between his teeth. For a month they had had meat for supper only three times a week (twice at home and once at Grandma's on Friday night). Juliet had tried sneaking into the ordinary butchers on the high street to buy the not-so-dear, non-kosher kind, but Mrs Epstein had caught her coming out and told Juliet's mother, who'd been so upset at the thought of her daughter risking her soul for scrag-end of mutton that Juliet had promised never to do it again. Frieda and Juliet each needed new clothes, though not underthings as Juliet had decided she could endure all manner of privation as long as her knickers were pretty, even if no one would see her in them again. She refused to be one of those women whom the Mrs Epsteins of the world stared at and shook their heads at, muttering with a twist of satisfaction, 'Ach, she was such a lovely thing, but didn't she let herself go after the business with her husband?' Now, at least, when they glared at her with hostile pity, she could think of her silk knickers and smile back.

Her parents had given her the last ten guineas at dinner on Saturday night. Mr Greene slid the notes across the table to Leonard ('Keep them safe for your mother now . . .') while Mrs Greene watched her daughter a little unhappily and wondered between mouthfuls of chicken, 'Are you sure you wouldn't prefer to buy a nice bit of jewellery for your birthday?' Juliet shook her head, determined to be sensible. She knew that her newly minted practicality made her parents sad. On the one hand, they were terribly proud of the way she

4

managed. 'It's not easy what you do, Fidget,' said her father, toasting her with his weekly schnapps. On the other, she knew that they missed the decidedly impractical girl who yearned for tennis lessons one week and a vegetable patch in which to grow rhubarb the next. They wanted her to be showered with golden trinkets and not scrimp for fridges. One Friday evening Mrs Greene confided to Juliet that she believed herself responsible for what she preferred to call 'the unfortunate business'. She confessed, after drinking an uncharacteristic sherry, that she believed it was entirely due to Juliet's name. They had intended to call her Ethel, a good sensible name for the sort of no-nonsense young woman who liked to weed and wore brown shoes and never forgot to telephone her mother before *Shabbos*, but bobbing amid the flotsam and jetsam of good feeling following the birth of her only child, Mrs Greene had an attack of romance (the only one she ever suffered in her life, if truth be told) and found herself naming the baby Juliet. Somehow a girl called Juliet seemed destined for that particular type of drama, what was it called? Iambic. Yes, Juliets were destined for iambic dramas in the way that Ethels were not.

The Bayswater Road was one of Juliet's favourite places. The old iron railings provided an enchanted dividing line – the road on one side and Hyde Park on the other, with green tangles of leaves reaching through the railings like fingers and the birdsong swelling out into the city streets. In the days when there was still a George and free afternoons were ordinary things, Juliet liked to bring the children here in their pram to this rectangle of hush within the clatter of London's streets. Even now Leonard loved the Peter Pan statue concealed in a huddle of ash trees. He liked to pretend he'd forgotten it, for the joy of stumbling across it once again. Men in suits hurried back to offices, dusting sandwich crumbs from pinstriped lapels, and typists in neat wool coats ambled back arm in arm from paper-bag luncheons in the park. The girls were of an age when all money is for spending, friendships are for ever and every girl still believes that she will be the one to marry Cary Grant. No. That was wrong, Juliet realised. That was when she was eighteen. Nowadays the girls dreamed of Elvis Presley and James Dean.

Juliet's favourite time on the Bayswater Road was Sunday afternoons when the railings were transformed from dividing line into destination and festooned with paintings of every colour, style and skill. She never minded that some of the artists were bad and that the landscapes were usually muddy pastorals under mislit heavens, stars overlarge and moon too blue, or that the nude beauty was in fact ugly. There was always something good to find among the more ordinary pictures and whenever she spotted it, Juliet felt she had uncovered a secret that belonged to her alone.

She hadn't had a Sunday afternoon on Bayswater Road for years. Not since the unfortunate business with George. Now Sundays invariably seemed to be filled with the debris washed up from the rest of the week: laundry and half-finished spelling tests, dishes abandoned in the sink, mournful as a shipwreck. She was about to indulge in a few moments of rare self-pity (it was her birthday after all) when to her delight she noticed that further along the road a stallholder had started to fasten canvases to the railings. This was an unexpected treat for a humble Wednesday and she hastened along the pavement in happy anticipation. She found a series of watercolours of London streets, dreary renditions for tourists, but she examined them anyway, enjoying the lazy pleasure of recognition. The stallholder thrust a hurried sketch of the Houses of Parliament into her hands but Juliet had been distracted. Fifty yards away a young man was propping canvases against the base of the railings. She drew closer, stopping before a portrait of a young girl with cropped brown hair and wearing a full primrose-coloured skirt, which caught in the sunlight rushing in through an open casement window. The girl's legs were tucked up beneath her in a pose of child-like ease as she leaned forward, immersed in the pages of a book. The picture pulsed with light. It looked to Juliet as if the artist had snatched handful after handful of morning sunshine and spread them over the canvas. How had he managed to get them to stay in the picture and not dribble away? She glanced at the pavement, half expecting to see puddles of sunlight lying at her feet.

'I'm going to call it *Privilege at Rest*,' said a voice, and Juliet turned, noticing the painter properly for the first time, taking in his pale indoor skin and the faint whiff of turps. He exuded an air of contrived decadence; a cigarette dangled from his unshaven lips and he sported a pair of faded denim jeans, torn at the knee and artfully smeared with paint.

'No,' said Juliet. 'It's called *A Study in Sunlight*.'

She felt him examining her, his eyes narrowing like two little letter boxes, and her cheeks grew warm until she almost regretted speaking. But no, she had been perfectly right. Whatever his intention, this was not a political painting of the kitchen-sink school. The picture had declared itself and taken life beyond the painter's brush. If he hadn't realised this, then somebody needed to tell him. Suddenly he smiled; his frown vanished into an even white grin and Juliet realised just how young he was, not more than nineteen or twenty, probably still a student.

'Yeah, all right. All right,' he nodded at her, throwing up his hands as if he'd been caught filching apples. 'Thought I'd try something different. Didn't really work, did it?'

Juliet smiled back. 'No. I'm sorry. But it's a wonderful painting.'

The young man nodded, attempting nonchalance, but the pink tips of his ears betrayed him. Juliet peered at the signature on the canvas.

'Charlie Fussell? Is that you?'

He held out his hand in answer and Juliet shook it, feeling the calluses and hard skin. A painter's palm.

'Juliet Montague.'

'It's a pleasure to meet you, Miss Montague.' Charlie held onto her fingers for a moment too long and Juliet firmly withdrew, removing her hand to the safety of her handbag strap and suspecting he was laughing at her and her prim middle-class manners.

'It's not . . .' She was about to correct him, to tell this boy that she was *Mrs* Montague, when she remembered that she wasn't really – only sort of. And what did it matter anyway and why would he care?

She cleared her throat. 'How much is the picture, please?'

'Twenty-one guineas.'

Juliet felt the Bayswater Road dwindle into silence all about her, as though someone had lifted the needle off a gramophone record and it kept on spinning but making no sound. Her mouth was dry and her tongue stuck fatly to the roof of her mouth. Twenty-one guineas. Juliet did not approve of fate. Chance was an untrustworthy thing that led to gambling, and then George pawning her fur coat and the little sapphire earrings she was given for Hanukkah and all manner of unpleasantness and yet, and yet, this painting was hers. It was clearly supposed to be hers. She had tried to be dutiful and sensible and everything she ought to be and she tried to aspire to new refrigerators and live only for her well-mannered, messy-haired children but it was no good. She wanted this painting. This was what a birthday present was supposed to be, not a stupid refrigerator.

8

'I'll take it.'

Juliet's voice was no louder than a whisper and her hand trembled slightly as she reached into her handbag for her purse. She did not notice Charlie's eyes widen as she accepted the exorbitant price – having never bought a picture before, she did not know that she was supposed to negotiate.

'Will you wrap it, please?'

'I'm not selling,' said Charlie.

A trickle of anger ran down Juliet's spine like perspiration.

'If you want more money, you're sadly out of luck. This is all I have and I was supposed to use it to buy a fridge.'

Charlie laughed. 'A fridge? You think art is interchangeable with household goods? Now I'm certainly not selling it to you.'

Juliet sucked her lip and frowned. She decided that this was some sort of game she didn't fully understand.

'You don't want this picture,' said Charlie.

Still Juliet said nothing.

'You want a picture of you. A portrait. I'll do it for the same price. Twenty-one guineas.'

Juliet glanced at the young stranger, uncertain if he was teasing her, but he watched her steadily, head tilted to one side as though he was already assessing the pigment he would need for her lip, her eyes. Did she dare? She thought back to that empty wall in the cramped little house in Chislehurst and considered for the thousandth time that she might have come to forgive George in time if only he hadn't taken the painting with him. In the one before her, the girl studied her book in the morning sunshine, oblivious to Juliet's disquiet.

'I want to paint you. You've got a good face. Not beautiful. Interesting.'

Juliet laughed, aware she was being flattered. She closed her eyes, and tilted her face up to the warmth of the afternoon sun, conscious that he was looking at her in that inquisitive painter's way, pondering her face as a puzzle to solve. She found that she liked it. After the business with George, the rabbis insisted that she must become a living widow. He was the one who had vanished but to her dismay she found it was she who had been quietly disappearing piece by piece. At that moment, on her thirtieth birthday, she decided that she wanted something more than fridges, more even than paintings of girls reading in sunlight. Juliet Montague wanted to be seen.

That Friday evening, Juliet sat in the kitchen with her mother, watching the wobbling tower of dirty dishes beside the sink. She knew better than to wash them. Nothing must be touched before the Sabbath ended. Washing-up was work and work was forbidden. Smoking was similarly taboo. She really wanted a cigarette but Mrs Greene would have palpitations if she dared to light a match.

From the living room Juliet could hear her father patiently explaining to Leonard for the umpteenth time why he could not go upstairs to the spare bedroom and play with his Hornby train set. This was a shared passion and through it Mr Greene seemed to discover in his eight-year-old grandson the son he'd always hankered after; hours were lost to signal changes, laying new tracks and the repainting of engines. Fridays, however, were contentious. Leonard couldn't understand the point of being with his grandfather and yet unable to race trains. His grandfather's patient explanations about moving parts and work and wheels meant little to Leonard, who simply concluded that God must dislike public transport.

Juliet knew that her son's confusion was entirely her fault. Shortly after her marriage, she'd discovered that she did not care to keep the rules of Kashrut in her own home. The first time she had accidently eaten a bowl of strawberries and cream out of a chicken soup bowl, she had buried it at the bottom of the garden as was expected. The second time, she rinsed it and placed it back in the cupboard. Nothing happened, except for the merest flutter of guilt. The third time she broke the laws even the guilt disappeared and Juliet quietly exchanged the Jewish standard of one set of crockery for milk and one set for meat for the middle-class standard of one set for ordinary and one set for best. No wonder poor Leonard didn't know how to behave.

Juliet glanced around her mother's kitchen: the cramped stove with its single electric ring and the rickety oven that had to be cajoled (by Mrs Greene) or kicked (by Juliet) into action; the faded curtains fluttering in the evening air that had been green and yellow during Juliet's childhood but had now been washed to a nondescript grey. The evening was cool and cloudless, a string of early stars across the sky. A breeze ruffled the leaves on the apple tree, yet still they sat in the hot kitchen with the back door firmly closed and drank their too strong tea without milk because they always had.

'Mum, we could go and sit in the garden for a minute.'

'Best not.'

Mrs Greene shook her head and gripped her cup tighter, offering no explanation. Juliet frowned, seeing her childhood home properly for the first time in years. The kitchen was fusty and dark and smelled of stale dishes and old soup and she wanted to sit in the starlight and breathe cool, fresh air.

'Come on. It'll be nice.'

'Your father hasn't mended the bench.'

'He's never going to mend the bench. We can sit on the back step.'

Mrs Greene recoiled. 'We can't do that. It's common.'

Juliet stalked to the sink to hide her irritation, adding her cup to the heap of dirty crockery. Mrs Greene cleared her throat, a habit when she was nervous. 'Your father thought that maybe he's gone to America. Many of them do, you know.'

Juliet said nothing. She didn't want to think about George. It was too nice an evening to spoil. Mrs Greene, mistaking her daughter's silence for distress, reached out and clasped her hand. 'Don't you worry, my love. This'll be the year we find him. We'll fix this unfortunate business once and for all, and get you married again.'

Juliet glanced down and saw that she had gooseflesh threading all the way up her arm, although she was not cold.

A month later, Juliet found herself sitting on a vast and broken sofa in a bright attic flat – no, not flat, *studio*, Charlie insisted on correcting her.

'I want the deck of cards on the table. They're symbolic.' Charlie's voice took on a petulant tone, which Juliet recognised as the one Leonard used when declining to eat his spinach.

'Not to me they're not. I don't play.'

Charlie stopped sulking for a moment and glanced at Juliet in mild surprise. 'Don't play cards? Everyone likes cards.'

'Well, I don't. I hate them. And I won't have them in my painting.'

Juliet was taken aback by her own vehemence. Embarrassed that she had betrayed too much of herself, she tried to soften her outburst with a smile, pretend it was a joke. 'Since I'm paying you the princely sum of twenty-one guineas, I get to decide. Goodness, I'm bossy. I suppose this is how rich people are all the time.'

Charlie laughed and Juliet closed her eyes for a second, shocked again at how young he was and a little frightened at her audacity. She was supposed to be at work, busy answering telephones and filling out order books and bills for spectacle lenses at Greene & Son, Spectacle Lens Grinders. There was no son, Juliet being an only child, but Mr Greene assured her that the words '& Son' evoked the necessary impression of an established family business. It nonetheless caused her a pang every time she saw the shop front, a reminder of how her father's disappointment in his daughter had begun with the mere fact of her birth. That afternoon, instead of sitting with the other office girls (always called 'the girls' even though Juliet was the only one under fifty), she'd feigned a dentist's appointment. Unsure if it was guilt or liberation making her heart pound and her blouse stick underneath her arms, she'd taken the train into London and sought out this drab flat – no, *studio* – in Fitzrovia.

'Well, there needs to be something on the table, otherwise the balance is wrong. I want a flash of colour.' Charlie stood back from the canvas he'd set up beside the window, assessing the composition.

Juliet glanced round the small room. Pictures covered every surface – walls, doors, bookcases, even the sloped attic ceiling was adorned with charcoal sketches of dimple-thighed swimmers at the seafront. Three washing lines zigzagged between low ceiling beams, flapping watercolours and pastels pegged to them like knickers. There was little unity of style – this was the hideaway of several painters – and the pictures were all at various stages of completion, from preparatory pencil sketches to finished oils stacked against the walls. A series of gouache seascapes fluttered on their drawing-pins like stuck moths. The floor was bare where it was not heaped with pictures, the boards stripped and planed to reveal smooth, white wood. The

13

ceiling struts had similarly been exposed, the wood sanded and whitewashed. Despite the smallness of the room it breathed with light, and Juliet felt almost as though she was drifting above London in a bright, wooden ship. She inhaled the smell of turps and oils and beneath that the distinctive note of the old building itself, a scent of earlier lives, of paraffin and beeswax, sweat and smoke, dust and deathwatch beetle. It was unlike anywhere she had ever been and the stillness and the sense of quiet industry filled her with a wordless content.

'That's it. That's the expression I want,' Charlie cried out. 'No. It's gone. You smiled. Never mind. I'll remember.'

Juliet stretched out on the sofa, drawing up her stocking-clad toes and watching as he pulled out brushes and a palette of watercolours. She frowned, but didn't like to complain until she remembered the princely twenty-one guineas.

'No thank you. I don't want to be painted in watercolours. I'm not a watercolour woman, all soft pinks and gentle yellows. I need oil paint and definite colours.'

Charlie glanced at her in surprise. 'The watercolours were just for a sketch, but I won't use them at all if you mind that much.' He tucked a brush behind his ear and studied her again. 'You paint too, I take it?'

Juliet chuckled and shook her head. 'No, I'm not a painter, I'm a looker.'

'A what?'

'It's a knack, like the way some people can do the cross-word in ten minutes flat or make the perfect apple strudel. I can't draw or paint but I can see pictures. Really see them. It's not the most useful of skills and both my mother and my chil-dren would much prefer that I had the gift of making apple strudel.'

Charlie continued to stare at her, thick brows creased. Juliet sighed and tried to explain.

'I'd always loved going to galleries – that was always the treat I'd pester my mother for, but I didn't realise I saw differently than other children until I was about ten. At school we were set the task of drawing our favourite toy. I suppose the mistress wanted something cheerful to decorate the rather dreary schoolroom. I don't remember what I drew. I know it wasn't very good. We all pinned up our drawings which were ordinary, not worth a jot, all except for one. Anna's rabbit. It was a perfect portrait. I couldn't look at anything except that drawing. I listened to the other girls and watched them glance past Anna's rabbit, oblivious to its particular beauty, and I understood. Unlike Anna I couldn't draw or paint, but I could see.'

Juliet's stomach grumbled, she'd been too keyed up to eat much breakfast and it was nearly half past one.

'Do you have anything to eat?'

Charlie nodded towards the makeshift kitchen, a sink filled with brushes and a solitary kettle. 'There might be some apples.'

She padded across the floor, picking her way round the piles of paper and canvases. On a rickety dresser rested a bowl of Granny Smith apples. They were a bold, primary-school green amid the bleached wood and subtle painter's tones. She seized the bowl and set it down on the table, dumping the deck of cards onto the floor.

'Here you are. Colour. And besides, it was an apple that brought my family to England.'

'An apple?' asked Charlie by rote, already lost in thoughts of his painting. 'Brush your hair back. Behind your ears. Yes. That's it. And you can keep on talking. I like it.'

Juliet settled back onto the sofa, absently shining the apple on her skirt, watching as Charlie prepared the canvas, mixed paints and then, with broad sweeps of a sponge, marked out

15

the floor, the triangle of light from the window, the yellow-white of the ceiling. Juliet spoke, realising that Charlie was not really listening. She found his half-attention oddly soothing. She could say anything at all – be utterly outrageous, shocking, obscene even, and no one would ever know. With a sigh, she decided that nothing she had to say would seem terribly wicked to a young student. She wished she had something truly despicable to confide, some desire or story to make his eyes widen as the rabbi's had done when Mrs Greene forced her to recite the business with George and the rabbi sat twisting his beard around his finger until Juliet forgot what she was saying, so mesmerised was she by the purpling of his pinkie. She gave a little laugh. She might tell Charlie about George. Would he find it funny or only sad?

'Tell me the thing about the apple,' said Charlie.

'All right,' said Juliet, grateful and disappointed to be saved from her confession. 'Well. We came here from Russia because of an apple. My grandmother Lipshitz was a terrible flirt, but really she'd always loved one boy, a Cohen. I like to think he'd always loved her back but that part of the story was always rather vague. Once I asked my mother to clarify but for some reason she never seemed to think it relevant whether the love was requited or not. My mother is not a romantic. Anyway, when Grandma Lipshitz was about twelve she was dozing in the sunshine in an orchard beside the village and teasing some local boys playing ball among the trees. The ball landed in Grandma Lipshitz's lap and she held onto it, refusing to give it back. A boy pleaded with her but – and you must remember this bit – the boy was not the Cohen. He said something like, "Go on, be a doll and I'll marry you in a moment." Grandma Lipshitz never lost an opportunity to flirt and replied, "If you're going to propose, do it properly with a gift." The boy plucked an apple from a tree and tossed it to her, reciting the

16

Hebrew marriage proposal. When Grandma returned home that evening, she told the story to Great-great-grandfather Lipshitz, a learned rabbi. He became very grave and consulted the other learned rabbis who all agreed: my twelve-year-old grandmother and the-boy-who-was-not-the-Cohen were married. He had recited the holy words before witnesses and offered her a gift which she'd not only accepted but eaten. There was only one thing to be done: the boy must divorce her. Then came the hitch. The boy did not want to divorce her. It turned out that he'd secretly hankered after Grandma Lipshitz but always thought she'd marry the Cohen. Now he wouldn't give her up. She pleaded and raged and threatened to starve herself and hack off her hair but nothing worked. This is where romance gives way to practicality. Deciding that she didn't really want to starve herself to death, Grandma Lipshitz chose to make the best of things. She agreed to settle down with the-boy-who-was-not-the-Cohen if he took her far away across the sea to where she wouldn't have to look on her true love every day. Her husband, realising he was onto a good thing, agreed and they sailed away to England. A few years after they left, the pogroms reached the village. All Grandma Lipshitz's family and the Cohens were murdered. Meanwhile on the other side of the sea, Grandma Lipshitz went on to have seven children and a terraced house in Chislehurst. So you see, I am here because of an apple.'

And a man who would not divorce his wife, thought Juliet, though she did not say this aloud even though she could tell Charlie was no longer listening.

As he paints, Charlie hears her voice as though from under-water. The picture pulls him on. Dark hair but with flecks of red from days in the sun, eyes not quite green, not quite grey. She is trying to be still, but she betrays her restlessness in the wiggling of her toes. She talks and talks but the sound of her voice is wordless, like the tumble of water. Juliet Montague. Charlie doesn't know girls – or rather women – like her. She is not like his sister's friends who are part of the smart set and speak on the telephone in loud whispers, desperate to be overheard. She's younger than his mother and not a bit like her tennis pals with their cool white dresses and endless fretting about the help. He realises that he's trying to paint her but he doesn't really know her at all. She's an assortment of parts, pale hands, blue dress, tiny mole on her left cheek, a bold cupid's bow. He watches and watches her, trying to see. On the table rests a bowl of green apples all the way from Russia.

Years later, when Charlie Fussell is an old man, he sees his painting hanging in a gallery. He makes a beeline for her, eager to make her acquaintance once again, but when he reaches her, he's struck by his own shabbiness. Back then she'd been older than him but now they've swapped places and time has run away from him and stopped for her. In age, he examines youth, hers and his, up there on the canvas. He's filled with sadness (which he expects) and irritation (which he does not) and realises it's quite clear that in a career spanning many decades he painted his best picture one spring in 1958 when he was not yet twenty-one. Nothing he has done since is as good as this dark-haired woman with her bowl of apples.

The summer was drawing to a close. The plum tree in the back garden had discarded its fruit onto the browning lawn faster than Leonard and Frieda could gather it up, so the small yard now smelled sweetly of rotting plums. It was a Friday and the children drifted around mournfully, conscious that Monday was the start of a new school year and that this last, precious weekend had an air of sorrowful finality, like the last penny sweet in a paper twist. They remembered all the things they had planned to do with the endless weeks that were now ending, and regretted the bike they had not learned to ride (Leonard) and the pocket money that they had not saved for the fancy new school bag (Frieda). Leonard perched on the swing his grandfather had fixed to the tree. It was wonky and he slid down to one end of the crooked seat, swinging half-heartedly and lopsidedly. Frieda lazed on the grass, sighing and sucking on sugar-cubes filched from the pantry. Leonard wondered whether if he hid in the abandoned privy / tool shed at the end of the garden, they would find him and force him to go to school. He concluded with regret that they probably would. He slithered off the swing and slipped out of the side gate. As he crossed the scrap of lawn with its pair of flower-pots that passed for a front garden, he noticed with interest that a large van was attempting to steer down the narrow suburban street, collecting snatches of twigs and leaves in its wing mirror like a jaunty buttonhole. His melancholy forgotten, Leonard scrambled onto the low wall between the garden and the pavement. To his intense excitement, the van shuddered to a halt right in front of him. The Montagues never had deliveries. The neighbours did, almost every week, it seemed to Leonard, who always came out to watch from his spot on the garden wall. He had observed with palm-tingling envy when next-door had their new television set delivered. It was so big and so heavy that it had taken three men to carry it up the front path. Leonard closed his eyes and, turning his face heavenwards, muttered one of his grandfather's grace-before-meals prayers, willing his own prayer to become a grace-before-television. His supplication was disturbed by a loud honk of the horn, and his mother emerged from the front door, wearing lipstick in a glossy post-box red. Leonard understood this. If he had known that a television was arriving, he would have combed his hair and put on his Saturday trousers in its honour.

Juliet hurried along the path, calling, 'Darlings, come and see my birthday present.'

She reached for Leonard's hand and drew him round to the rear of the van, where two stout men bundled a rectangular wooden pallet onto their broad shoulders. Leonard eyed them with suspicion. Televisions should be handled with more reverence. Frieda joined them in the garden in her socks, also intrigued by the commotion.

Juliet hustled the children into the house, following in the wake of the deliverymen. Vibrating with excitement, Leonard padded into the living room as the men began to lever open the pallet. Frieda lingered in the doorway, hands thrust deep in her pockets.

'I thought your birthday present was going to be a fridge.'

Juliet flushed. 'Yes. It was. But then, well, I decided that was really rather a horrid present for a birthday.'

Neither Frieda nor Leonard spoke. They had always thought that refrigerators were horribly dull but believed them to be one of those things grown-ups term 'an acquired taste'. They were surprised but intrigued to discover they had been right all along. As the deliverymen finished prising open the packing pallet Juliet, Frieda and Leonard stepped closer.

'Oh,' said Frieda. 'It's much better than a fridge.'

Leonard felt a sharp pang when he saw the object inside the pallet was not, in fact, a television and then a ripple of wonder. He knew somehow that his mother had done something unexpected, something marvellous and something that Grandma would not approve of. He looked at the woman in the crate who was his mother but transformed into some familiar stranger. He turned back to Juliet who stood behind him, head to one side as she surveyed her other self, and at that moment she was a stranger too.

Kneeling, Juliet eased the portrait out of the box and then, slipping out of her shoes, climbed onto the sideboard and hung it on the wall.

'Is it straight?'

'No,' said Frieda. 'That side is lower. The left. No the other left.'

Juliet jumped down and stood between her children. 'Do you remember when another picture used to hang here?'

Leonard shook his head.

'I think so,' said Frieda. 'It was a girl.'

'It was me.'

It was me, thought Juliet, and he stole me when he vanished.

Whenever the opportunity arose, Leonard liked to describe his father's death. He bestowed on him a different one every time, each more wretched than the last. But he knew his father wasn't really dead only gone and *never-coming-back-into-this-house-so-help-me-God*. He heard the things the grown-ups said when they thought he couldn't hear – 'George Montague was a swine' and 'a good for nothing' and a 'coward and a wretch'. Leonard couldn't even remember what he looked like. Sometimes as he fell asleep he saw a picture of a very tall man and he wondered if this was him but there were no photographs to check; not any more.

A week after the portrait arrived he sneaked into his mother's bedroom and pulled out her shoebox of pictures from its hiding place at the back of her cupboard. He emptied the contents all over the floor, searching for photos of his father. He'd rummaged through it many times before but only ever found snaps of his mother standing beside a scissored hole. '*Honeymoon, Margate, George and Juliet, 1947*', it said in pencil on the back, but there was no George, only Juliet and a gap through which Leonard could see the swirl of the carpet. Tonight was no different and he sighed and started to shove the photos back in the box, wondering why his mother bothered to keep them and why he kept on looking, and then for the first time he noticed something else. A scrap of paper was tucked into the lip of the box. He glanced over his shoulder. The door was safely closed. From downstairs he could hear voices on the wireless crooning softly.

He drew out the sheet of paper:

Certificate of Naturalisation:
George Montague formerly Molnár, György

Leonard understood what this flimsy piece of paper meant. His father was a spy. George Montague wasn't his real name, it was just one of his identities. This paper was proof that George Montague – aka Molnár György – had to leave them. He must have put up a fight – Leonard pictured the tall man from his dream declaring to his commander, '*I won't do it. I won't. I will not leave my son . . . or,*' Leonard made him add, '*my women.*' The argument went on and on in Leonard's head, but in the end he saw his father go quiet, saying in a whisper as he wiped away a single tear, '*This is the worst sacrifice a man can make. In all my years of service, I never thought I'd be forced to do this. Only for Queen and Country and for my son, Leonard.*'

Leonard slid the paper back into the box and replaced it in the wardrobe. When he came downstairs his mother had abandoned the ironing and was now folding shirts into jumbled piles. She looked much happier in the painting, he decided. In the painting her mouth twitched with a smile, the one when she knew a really good secret, one she wasn't going to tell you, not yet.

Juliet wondered that her parents' house could contain so many people. She understood how they had once folded into the *shtetls*, sleeping ten to a room. The garden was even busier. Uncles Jacob and Sollie Greene attempted to prop up the left side of the *sukkah*, which was threatening to collapse, and the three Uncles Lipshitz herded more children than she could possibly count, filing in and out of the *sukkah*, in and out, as though practising for Noah's ark. It made an odd sight, the tottering shack of leaves in the middle of the square lawn of Number Twenty-Six Victoria Drive. The *sukkah* was a mass of wild things, twisting stems of willow, hazel and snatches of creeper and the frenzied play of the children. They caught the whiff of the wild and careered and yelped.

'Goodness what a racket,' complained Mrs Greene. 'Here, take these trays. Perhaps if we feed them, they'll lose a bit of their savagery.'

Taking the plates of chopped fried fish, pickled herring and baskets of golden *challah*, Juliet approached the shack, squeezing past Uncle Ed who held a pair of hazel switches to his head like antlers, and chased the children around the flowerbed, his bad leg forgotten in the carnival. For most of the year these were indoor folk who might venture into the park if it was particularly fine, but who were infinitely more comfortable in a neat front room with a nice cup of something hot. Good weather could be conveniently admired through a window and a pot of geraniums was usually considered plenty of nature. But on this night everything changed.

Juliet stepped back to avoid being skewered by Ed's makeshift antlers or trampled by a pink and puffing Leonard.

'How are you managing, my dear?'

Juliet turned to see Mrs Ezekiel arranging a line of marrows stuffed so full that the meat dripped onto the plate.

'Very well, and yourself?'

'Can't complain. Can't complain. But you, always so brave. We all think it's wonderful how you manage.'

Juliet said nothing, long resigned to being a popular topic of conversation among the women, along with the price of lamb chops and the length of Rabbi Weiner's sermons.

'Ah, Brenda. I was just telling Juliet how much we admire her,' called Mrs Ezekiel to a woman who was piped like a sausage into her winter coat.

'Oh yes. An inspiration,' said Mrs Brenda Segal, hurrying over and setting down a dish. 'I was telling my Helen. Don't you complain that it's hard with little 'uns. You've got Harold, whatever his faults. Think of poor Juliet Montague.' Mrs Segal started to carve at the fat grey tongue roosting on her dish, making it wobble. 'Those daughters of ours, always complaining. And they've got no right. No right at all.'

'Spoiled. That's what my Sarah is. Doesn't realise how good she's got it.'

'It's terrible,' agreed Mrs Segal, happily.

The two women smiled at Juliet, their heads cocked to one side like a pair of chaffinches. Juliet was exhausted by their pity, sickly sweet as marzipan. She'd found herself longing for a helping of old-fashioned condemnation.

'Excuse me,' said Juliet, escaping across the lawn. 'Frieda!'

A reluctant Frieda appeared, cheeks shining.

'What? I'm busy.'

'Put on your coat, love. You'll be cold when you stop. No, I won't have that face. Go on.'

24

As Frieda tore into the house, Juliet leaned against the fence, savouring a moment alone. Perhaps she could remain in the shadows for the rest of the night. The children were happy. That was enough. If she kept very still and quiet and didn't glance at anyone, then maybe, just maybe she might be left alone. She muttered a prayer through her teeth.

'Hello, doll-face. Looking fine as ever.'

'Thank you, John.'

John Nature had once been the catch of the community – blue eyes, a handsome face, a smile that made girls smile back. Ten years ago he'd placed third in the Bromley Amateur Wrestling Championship, a feat that caused assorted knees to tremble. Since then the strong jaw line had been blurred by a decade of *schmaltz* on toast and *lokshen* puddings, and now he only wrestled with the straining buckle on his belt. But the eyes remained as blue as ever and he twinkled them at Juliet.

'Lovely kiddies you've got there. But that's no shocker. They're yours after all.'

Before she'd met George, John had tried to take her out on several occasions and she'd always turned him down. She knew he believed that she regretted him. Men like him always believed themselves to be regretted by the women they didn't marry. Now he looked thoughtful and bestowed on her his famous smile, accessorising it with a wink.

'What a wonderful night. Surrounded by family. Friends. Pretty women.'

Juliet was quite accustomed to the charitable flirtations of the husbands of Chislehurst. She knew that they liked to believe themselves to be doing her a *mitzvah* but they always remained slightly anxious, as though, starved of sex as she was, she might leap on them at any moment. Even John, for all his smiles, kept a careful distance between them in case sheer physical proximity to him might overwhelm her self-control.

'I understand your wife's made her celebrated cinnamon slice.'

'Ah, yes. Quite a cook, my girl. Alas, my downfall,' he said patting his belly with benign affection. 'And you? What delight did you bring? I'm sure you're a beautiful cook.'

'I'm afraid not. That's my downfall.'

She spoke with such seriousness that John's face fell and Juliet knew he was considering whether this was what had caused the unfortunate business with George. She smiled to signal it was a joke, and he laughed, relieved.

'What does it matter if a lovely woman can't cook? That's what restaurants are for.'

Juliet made no reply. He knew perfectly well that she couldn't visit a restaurant with a man. A chained woman must stay at home. She imagined the scandal if she were caught sharing a schnitzel with a man not her husband and wanted to smile, but found she could not. She caught herself thinking of Charlie Fussell. He didn't see the stain. She hadn't told him, and yet she suspected that even if she did, he wouldn't see it. He would not speak to her with the wariness of these good men, apprehensive and privately delighted that they, however fat or balding or tedious, had become irresistible to her. Charlie would not study her, wondering what concealed defect had made George Montague disappear.

At last they sat down to eat. Juliet waited until everyone else was settled, before quietly slipping into the last empty chair. Otherwise she knew that everyone would avoid the seats on either side of her – the women preferring to avoid her, and the husbands afraid of her and even more afraid of what their wives might say. She ate in silence, speaking to no one, bathed in the concert of other people's noise. Every now and again

Uncle Sollie shot a wink of camaraderie and her father smiled and sighed.

After supper the women made their expedition to the kitchen, conveying between them the ruins of the feast in a great gaggle. It occurred to no one that the men should help. They gathered instead at one end of the table in the *sukkah* around an ancient bottle of schnapps, which Mr Greene measured out into eggcup-sized goblets dusted off especially for their twice-yearly outing.

The children congregated at the other end of the *sukkah*, the younger on the ground, the older seated playing grown-ups.

Leonard sprawled on the damp grass, staring up at the sky through the lattice of leaves. The weak city stars blinked, faint as torchlight beneath the bedclothes. He licked the slick of grease on the roof of his mouth and closed his eyes, secure in the blanket of the others' chatter.

'Good *sukkah*, this.' A delicate boy sat down beside him, tapping the canvas walls with his finger, an inspector making a survey. His pale skin was peppered with golden freckles, earning him the unfortunate nickname of Cornflake.

'Thanks.' Leonard hoisted himself onto his elbows. 'I made it. Well, Grandpa helped. A bit.'

Kenneth from Number Twenty-Four slid in between them. Leonard did not like him. He was a boy who believed *The Banana Bunch* superior to *Dan Dare* and therefore could not be trusted. Above Kenneth's lip was the thought of a moustache, no darker than pencil shading, but it gave the boy a swagger.

'Didn't your dad help?'

Leonard wound a long strand of grass around his finger. 'You already know my dad's dead.'

Kenneth nodded. 'Right. Yeah. How did he die again?'

Leonard might have said, 'He got sick,' or 'It was an accident,' but he didn't. He could almost bear Kenneth's stupid
smirk, but not Cornflake's look of curious sympathy. Leonard
Montague, son of George Montague, spy hero deb-on-air,
would not be pitied by Erick 'Cornflake' Jones.

'My dad was a pilot—'

'What did he fly?'

'Spitfire. Supermarine,' answered Leonard, quick as a flash.
'My dad was a great hero during the war. You can look it up if
you don't believe me.'

He glared and held his breath, daring Kenneth to challenge
him. There was a second taut with uncertainty and then
Kenneth shrugged and Leonard continued.

'After the war they kept him on as a flying detective. He's
not really dead. He's running missions. Top Secret ones of
National Importance. He's rescued other agents. Bulgarians.
That's why he's not here. It's not safe.'

'That's bloody Biggles!' roared Kenneth. 'Leonard thinks
his dad is bloody Biggles!'

'I do not,' said Leonard, trying to get Kenneth to lower his
voice but the children were all looking round and the laughter
was spreading like whooping cough.

'I don't. I don't. I don't.' Leonard kept talking to stop from
crying but still the tears tickled the back of his eyeballs like the
smell of onions.

'Leave him alone. Our dad's dead.'

To his great surprise, Leonard saw his older sister looming
over Kenneth, hand on her hip and fury in her eye, a harpy in
pigtails.

'You're a nasty boy, Kenneth Ibbotson. Always poking your
big, nasty beak about.'

Kenneth was a little in awe of Frieda. She was three years
older than him, four inches taller and, most alarming of all,

she was a girl. However, he had read *Biggles: Air Detective* on a rainy Sunday only a few weeks before and he knew truth to be on his side.

'He said his dad was an air detective. That's not a real job. Only bloody Biggles bloody does that.'

Frieda wrinkled her nose and gave her best impression of Juliet. 'Don't use that foul language or I shall have to speak with your mother.'

'And Leonard was only teasing, weren't you?'

Leonard nodded, too miserable to speak.

'See? If you go poking your nose where it's not wanted, you'll get told a silly answer. Serves you right.' Frieda turned on Kenneth, her voice a schoolmistress blend of triumph and indignation.

Gratitude washed over Leonard in warm waves like bubble bath. Frieda came and stood beside him, her hand resting on his shoulder. Her thumbnail dug into the flesh of his back to demonstrate her private fury. Leonard knew he would get a clout later, but as far as the others were concerned they were united. He glanced around the *sukkout* and noticed with a tickle of unease that his grandfather and the men had retreated into the warmth of the house, whose yellow lights now seemed far, far away. A few of the older girls stopped their chatter, three glossy heads swivelling to focus on Frieda. The smallest of the girls studied her with clever eyes, blue as coloured glass.

'Your dad's dead?' she asked, her voice cherry sweet.

'Yes, Margaret,' replied Frieda. 'My dad is dead.'

'Perhaps. But it's not what I heard.'

Leonard held his breath, wanting to know what Margaret heard; not wanting to know. He watched her pretty face, its china smile.

'I heard that *Juliet Montague can't keep a man.*'

The whooping-cough laughter returned, more virulent than before, spreading through the children. Leonard felt his sister's fingernails dig into his shoulder, leaving little half-moons even through his coat.

'That's not true.' Frieda spoke quietly, her voice barely louder than a whisper. 'You're nothing but a liar.'

Leonard frowned. He didn't understand. *Can't keep a man.* That wasn't a secret. It was a puzzle. But he saw that Frieda knew what it meant. His sister's face turned very white, whiter than when she'd had the flu for a fortnight and the doctor came every day.

'Liar. *Liar*.'

Frieda spoke the word like a curse, but Margaret set her porcelain smile and crinkled her button nose.

'I'm not a liar. You are. Your father isn't dead. He's a thief.'

'He is not.'

'I know he is – I heard my dad say. Your dad owed mine fifty pound when he left. Fifty pound. He was nothing but a con artist, my dad says.'

The hand on Leonard's shoulder trembled and he reached up and gripped it and Frieda squeezed back, all her annoyance with him forgotten.

'I don't believe you,' said Frieda.

Margaret shrugged as though the whole discussion was nothing to her. 'If your dad was dead, your mum would have got married again. But she can't because he isn't dead. And I know what your mother is.'

'Shut up.'

'I know.'

'Shut up. Shutupshutupshutup—'

'*Aguna*.'

Leonard did not know what the word meant, but he felt Frieda start to cry, great sobs against his back, sobs that made his body rattle in time with hers.

He couldn't sleep. Or rather he didn't want to sleep as when he did his dreams filled with puzzles he could not solve. *Couldn't keep a man. Thief.* His father was a spy with two names. Leonard knew that was true – he had the paper to prove it.

He slipped downstairs to the living room and sat huddled in his dressing gown before the portrait of his mother. She smiled but not at Leonard. Without blinking, he crawled backwards to the sofa but no matter how he ducked and wriggled, she would not look at him.

Fifty pounds. My dad says. Not what I heard. Leonard knew his father wasn't dead, so why didn't he come home? If he did, his mother would be as happy as her picture. *Shut up. Shut up. A con artist.*

Suddenly Leonard understood. He stood up and belted his dressing gown. At last he knew what he must do. He must find his father and explain that it was time to come home. And, best of all, he knew how.

At five minutes to seven, Juliet slipped out of bed. At seven o'clock she knocked on Leonard's bedroom door and went inside. At three minutes past she checked the bathroom, the kitchen and then the living room where she discovered Charlie Fussell's portrait no longer on the wall but propped against the sideboard. At six minutes past seven she asked Frieda if she had seen her brother and together they looked in the garden and the small tool shed and the cupboard in the hall and out by the dustbins. At a quarter past seven Juliet realised Leonard had vanished.

'Sweetheart, sit and have this.'

'I don't want to drink stupid tea. I want to find my son. He's eight, Mum, *eight* and he's all alone. Oh God. Oh God.'

Juliet stayed at the kitchen window, watching for him, willing him to appear. Time buzzed in her ears.

Mrs Greene straightened a dishtowel. Wiped a drip of tea from the table.

'Your father, everyone, they're all out looking. They'll find him, love. It might take an hour or two, but they'll find him and bring him home. I promise. He hasn't vanished.'

They both thought of his father, but neither of them spoke his name.

Juliet paced beside the window, unable to leave it, unable to blink.

'Why would Leonard run away? Why?'

Mrs Greene tried to persuade her to sit but Juliet flicked her away, dizzy with fear. It floated before her eyes in red plumes and she couldn't think, she was drunk with it. Her mother was talking but it was an effort to listen to the words.

'We sat here when his father disappeared.'

'Stop that. He isn't a bit like . . .' Mrs Greene shrugged, superstitious about saying George's name aloud. 'Leonard has just wandered off and got lost.'

Juliet leaned against the windowsill, murmuring an incantation, 'Let him be all right. Let him be all right. If you don't let him be all right, I'm going to convert to bloody Christianity.'

Unable to distinguish Juliet's words Mrs Greene was gratified that she still turned to the Almighty in such moments – sometimes she fretted over her daughter's soul.

'He's just taken a notion. You know Leonard.'

'You're right. Of course you're right. I just can't bear . . .'

'I know, love. I know. Don't even think it.'

Charlie Fussell was up remarkably early. Or rather he had not yet gone to bed. He'd been to a party and then drifted back to the studio early, bored by the usual crowd and the usual in-jokes, ones he'd laughed at for so long that he knew rather than felt them to be funny. And he couldn't sleep. He sat up in the quiet dark, smoking cigarette after cigarette, watching the watercolours strung like knickers on a line across the beams. In the gloom he couldn't make out their subjects; they were just a mass of blank wings. He wondered if the others knew he sometimes slept here. Probably. They almost certainly did the same and yet the thought of them here, stretched out on this battered couch in this room, irritated him. That stained cup, the empty window, the city's lull before dawn – they all belonged to him, not to the others.

If he couldn't sleep, he might as well paint. Even after the party, he wasn't drunk. He couldn't bear people who painted drunk or high – it was an affectation of the amateur. An artist must have control over his brush down to the final fraction of an inch, the touch of a hair. The routine of mixing the paints, preparing his brush, priming the canvas gave him a profound, muscular pleasure. It was a process so familiar and yet he never found it dull. Instead it filled him with a wordless calm. The thought of the picture was loose and embryonic, a shadow he must reach for and pull out into the air, a handful of seaweed from water. Tonight, as sometimes happened, his brush guided him around the canvas. It was an odd picture. Not his usual style. More abstract and only the hint of figures, and yet there was something about the colours that he liked. Was it salvageable? Charlie frowned, wishing not for the first time that he could ask Juliet. She'd know straight away:

'The best thing you can do with that picture is paint over it.'

Or: 'Make it about the figure of the boy, the one at the front. It's his picture.'

He hadn't done a portrait since Juliet's and sometimes wished he hadn't sold it to her. No, that wasn't true – he liked to think of it hanging in her house. In her dining room. A pretty dining room with French colonial furniture and a vase of – what were those flowers, the ones with filaments like eyelashes? Anemones. On the dining table a glass vase filled with purple and red anemones. But that wasn't right. Juliet wouldn't hang a portrait of herself where others could see. It was private. She would see those days as belonging only to the two of them. Charlie smiled, pleased with his deduction. It would hang in her bedroom. Nowhere else.

The night before, Leonard had hummed with certainty, but he found that his confidence dwindled with dawn. It was easier to be sure of things in the dark. He'd caught the milk train easily enough and even though there was no one around to punch his ticket, he left money on the counter for when the stationmaster arrived. For an awful moment he'd thought he couldn't open the carriage door, but finally, jumping up and down, he'd managed it. He huddled in the corner of the car, staring out the window, trying to be inconspicuous and prac-tising his story in case somebody asked. *'I'm John. I'm going up to London on a class trip to see the dinosaurs. I like to be on time so I'm taking an early train.'* It was a dull story, which Leonard regretted, but after what'd happened yesterday with Kenneth, he'd decided to be careful. In the end no one asked. He didn't like to think of his mother worrying about where he had gone, but everything would be all right again when he reappeared with his father.

Leonard disembarked at Charing Cross and found a spot under a newsstand to wait. The station was empty save for a couple of tramps snoozing in the doorway to the gents' lava-tories. Leonard hugged his knees and watched the slow jour-ney of the hands around the station clock. Not yet. Bulldog Drummond always picked the right moment, when he had the greatest chance of success. Leonard didn't want to try to find his way in the dark and certainly not without a map. He must wait until the kiosk opened – the awning declared: 'Confectionery, Newspapers, Tourist Map, etc.' The minute hand moved so slowly, slower even than it did in the last lesson before lunch. Still too early. Not yet. And then the first strands of daylight blew through the station, rousing the pigeons who waddled and cooed, flapping nasty grey wings too close to his face. He reached into his pocket to check for the hundredth time that he still had the address. His fingers brushed paper. It was all neatly written out in his very best handwriting, the one he saved for thank-you letters and stories in Mrs Stanton's class.

At ten minutes to six, a man in fingerless gloves arrived to open the kiosk, pulling up the shutters with the raucous noise of a football clacker. Leonard stood, dusted himself off and cleared his throat.

'Please, I'd like to buy a map.'

The man peered over his counter, starting when he spotted Leonard.

'Here, how old are you? Should you be out by yourself?'

Leonard tried to stand very tall inside his shoes. 'I'm nearly twelve. I'm just short for my age. It's not very nice of you to make a comment.'

The kiosk man, on the small side himself, gave a sympathetic shrug.

'All right. A map? What kind of map?'

Leonard pulled out the address from his pocket and handed it over. The man read, his lips twitching.

'You need an A to Z.'

Leonard wanted to ask if that was a type of map but in case this was the sort of thing twelve-year-olds were supposed to know, he said nothing and handed over a shilling. His purchase under his arm, he retreated to the far side of the station, wanting the kiosk man to forget all about him.

He slid the book out of the paper bag and groaned. Another puzzle. It was a map of squiggles, much harder than any of the atlases they studied in school. There wasn't even a proper picture of England. Leonard glanced around and realised the silent station had metamorphosed into a frantic Tuesday-morning rush – men in pinstripes wearing hats, men in blue jeans not wearing hats, women clutching handbags and briefcases and packets of sandwiches. By seven o'clock he was defeated. The map, if it really was a map, remained a worming mass of squiggles. It was time to resort to Plan B. Only he didn't have one. And he had to find his father. He had to.

'Are you all right, son?'

Leonard looked up and, to his dismay, found himself staring at his own reflection in the spectacles of a station attendant. The attendant stooped at an uncomfortable angle so as to be at Leonard's height and addressed him in that special tone reserved for children and the infirm.

'Where's your mother, son?'

'At home.'

Leonard glanced over his shoulder to find the kiosk man watching them. He must have alerted the stationmaster. Leonard scowled at the treachery, and turned back to the attendant.

'My name is John. I've come up to London on a class trip to see the dinosaurs.'

'And you've lost your teacher.'

'No. I came on an early train. I didn't want to be late.'

The attendant studied Leonard for a moment, his face putting on that expression his grandmother sometime wore when listening to him – puzzlement, followed by mild suspicion that Leonard was giving her cheek.

'I think we'll give your mother a bell.'

'There's no need.'

'All the same.'

Leonard considered briefly the merit of making a run for it but he'd never come better than second to last in the hundred-yard dash at school, and even though the attendant didn't look much of an athlete either, he had the benefit of longer legs.

The stationmaster's office was warm and smelled of toast and was stuffed fuller than Rose's Deli – only, instead of jars of *haimisher* cucumbers and saveloys, it contained timetables, loudspeakers, uniform caps on pegs, a dozen telephones and a science board of blinking lights. Any other morning Leonard would have relished the experience.

'Right, what's your mother's telephone number?'

'We don't have a telephone.'

The attendant gave Leonard a stern look, which he met with alacrity.

'You could try my father, though. He should be at work by now.'

The man reached for a grey telephone.

'Right then, what's his number?'

'Oh, I don't know that. But,' said Leonard, sensing a squall of irritation brewing, 'I have the address.' He handed him the paper with the address in his very best handwriting. 'You can look up my father with that, can't you?' he asked, trying to keep the shrill of desperation from his voice.

Juliet hadn't moved from her spot in the kitchen window. She refused to leave it even to dress, and remained in her dressing gown and slippers. Mrs Greene tried to keep up a patter of comfort. 'I wish I'd brought my knitting. There's nothing like the clack of knitting needles for consolation.'

37

'I'm going outside. I need to smoke.'

For once Mrs Greene made no complaint, and Juliet escaped the warm confines of her sympathy. Her hands shook and it took her several attempts to strike the match, and once she'd lit her cigarette she let it burn down between her fingers. She didn't want to smoke, she wanted quiet. Her skull brimmed with the whirring of a thousand insects, all humming and crawling across her thoughts so that she couldn't think. Her father and the others would find him. They would. For all their delicious horror at her misfortune with George, they all came today the moment her mother called. There were no looks of wry curiosity this morning. Husbands vanishing were one thing. Children were quite another. That fear was feral. They'd all marched up to the house. Even the men in their black hats and long silken curls, the ones who wouldn't speak to her, wouldn't shake her hand, were out there some-where searching for her son. Nothing less would rouse them on a holy day but today Leonard had trumped God. God wishes it, they said, the boy must be found.

Juliet walked to the end of the patch of garden and perched on the low wall, Leonard's favourite spot. It was mild for autumn, the morning sun making the poplars lining the street blaze like torches. A scarlet acer leaf landed on her shoulder and she held it between her fingers, thinking that she'd always wanted hair that red. And then she saw them, at the corner where Station Road turned into Mulberry Avenue, Leonard and Charlie Fussell, hand in hand.

Charlie saw the crumpled figure sitting on the wall straighten the moment she noticed Leonard, a thirsty tulip springing up in water. He watched as she rushed at them, purple dressing gown flapping in the sunshine, long hair loose, Rapunzel running along a terraced street. I hardly know you, he thought.

So this is where you live. Until that moment he hadn't been able to picture it. He imagined her coming to life as she stepped into his studio, like the ballet dancer in his sister's jewellery box that twirled round and round when he'd lifted the lid as a boy.

'You horrible, awful thing,' she said, kissing Leonard and folding him into the wings of her dressing gown.

Charlie stayed back, trying to watch them with a painter's detachment. Leonard submitted to his mother's kisses with weary acceptance, meeting Charlie's eye over the top of her head.

'I couldn't call you,' said Charlie.

'No,' agreed Juliet, still not releasing Leonard.

'Please get a telephone,' he said, though in truth he was grateful that she did not have one as it had meant he'd had to come here.

Leonard squirmed and she loosened her hold but would not let him go. She held out her hand to Charlie and he took it, feeling the warm dryness of her skin. 'Thank you for bringing him back.'

An ice-cream van tinkled past them, 'Pop Goes the Weasel' wheezing in its wake, pausing a hundred yards beyond, the tune wafting back towards them. Juliet didn't move, and they remained frozen, an odd tableau in the suburban street. Charlie waited for her to ask the questions that surely must come. At last she stood, and not letting go of either of their hands, she turned to Charlie.

'Let's eat ice cream,' she said.

Juliet waited until the last drip of ice cream had been licked away. They sat in the living room, Charlie on the one good chair, Juliet on the floor and Mrs Greene beside Leonard on the settee, keeping an eye out for chocolate spills on the ancient baize. Juliet felt sorry for Charlie; he had been forced into their family drama, an understudy made to perform in a strange play.

She wondered how he felt seeing his painting in their ordinary front room. The bowl of green apples in the picture was the brightest thing in it, making the walls somehow browner, the heavy furniture heavier still. The Juliet in the portrait was poised, smiling out of reach. She liked how he saw her, and supposed that now he had encountered this dreary weekday version of her, he would paint her differently. She tried not to mind.

'Leonard, darling, we shan't be angry but you must tell us why you ran away.'

'I didn't,' he replied, indignant. 'I went to find my father.'

'Oh Leonard.'

Juliet wanted to pull him onto her lap like she used to when he was little, let down the curtain of her hair and hide them both behind it, but the small upright figure tucked beside his grandmother on the shabby settee gazed at her with quiet dignity. Even if the others hadn't been here, she wouldn't have dared. She wanted to say, 'When did you grow up? I wasn't looking. Bring back the baby who laughs when I sing to him.' Instead she reached for his hand, oddly grateful to find he didn't draw away. 'Darling, no one knows where your father is.'

Even now, she noticed her mother wince, signalling her to shush in front of Charlie – these were private, family things not to be discussed before strangers in un-ironed shirts and none-too-clean trousers.

'I thought Charlie was my dad.'

Juliet laughed at the absurdity of it. 'Charlie? He's far too young. He's a boy himself.'

Looking from one to the other, she realised that she had somehow succeeded in hurting the feelings of both.

'Why did you think Charlie was your dad?'

Leonard said nothing and scrutinised his knees.

'Why, darling? I'm so sorry I laughed. It wasn't kind of me.'

Leonard was quiet for a moment. He picked at a freckle of ice cream dried on his leg. 'I know my father was a con artist. Like Charlie.'

Juliet willed herself not to look at Charlie to see how he liked his new profession. Leonard interpreted her silence as doubt.

'I know my dad's a con artist. Margaret Taylor told me so.'

Juliet swallowed the laughter fizzing in her throat. 'But sweetheart, your father's name isn't Charlie. It's George.'

'No it isn't. It's a lie. I found his secret identity. I know. I know.' Leonard curled his knees up to his chest, and started to sob.

Juliet pulled him into her arms. If only the others would go away. They were intruders here. *Leave us. It's only we who matter.* She remembered when she was pregnant with him. For three months she hadn't told anyone she was expecting again, not even George. He had so many secrets and this was hers. She had drifted through the weeks in a pleasant daze, insulated from everything. Nothing mattered; not even the usual troubles with George. The secret warmed her. Later, when George had vanished he left behind a hole, a round scorch mark across their lives. She tried to ignore it, put one day in front of the other and ignore the saucy smiles and whisper to herself *it doesn't matter, as long as the children are all right*. And now Leonard had run away on a story, his heart broken because it wasn't true.

Mrs Greene settled beside her, rubbing Leonard's back as the sobs ebbed away. 'The others are coming back. What do we tell them? We mustn't set them talking.'

Juliet shut her eyes. She was the snag in her mother's respectability.

'Tell them anything you like.'

'Tell them I'm giving Leonard painting lessons and he couldn't wait until the next one.'

The two women looked at Charlie in surprise, having almost forgotten he was still there, part of all this.

'Yes, all right. Tell them that,' said Juliet.

Through the windows of the living room, she watched the mournful parade of black hats process up the garden path. The kitchen would fill with well-meaning neighbours and acquaintances, all relieved that tragedy had been averted, downgraded to another snippet of tittle-tattle about poor Juliet and those dear kiddies.

In the afternoon Juliet and Charlie sprawled in the October sun. The grass was long and unkempt, sprinkled with yellow leaves. At the bottom of the garden Frieda and Leonard picked apples from a lopsided and sickly tree, pausing every now and again to hurl windfalls at each other, which smashed wetly on arms and legs.

'How did he find me?' asked Charlie.

'Your address label on the back of the picture.'

'Quite an imagination.'

'Yes.'

'After all, I'm just a boy myself.'

Laughing, Juliet covered her eyes with her hands. 'I'm sorry. I didn't mean to be rude. Anyway, isn't it nice to be thought young?'

Charlie did not reply. Juliet lay back, studying the diluted blue of the sky, and listened to Leonard's shriek of glee as he discovered a worm in a windfall and lobbed it at his sister.

'My mother will watch him for ever – terrified he's inherited his father's genes. Vanishing is in the blood, you know.'

'You're not worried he'll do it again?'

She turned her face away to catch the last of the autumn sunshine.

'He didn't run away. He went looking for someone.'

But to herself she said, *'I'm terrified. I'm terrified of going to bed and lying in the dark and remembering how it was when he was lost. I'm terrified of the other children and the awful things they say to him and to Frieda. The lies they tell them. And the truth.'*

Leonard had brought Charlie here but Juliet wished that he had not. She liked Charlie in the hush of his studio. She did not want his looks of kind concern. She wanted to seal up the memory of those afternoons, keep them crisp and safe. The cool, white world of the studio was separate from the cluttered lives of Mulberry Avenue and, like red and green on a paint palette, she didn't want the two to meet and muddy.

'I'm sorry for the worry Leonard must have caused but it's good to see you again.' He hesitated. 'I could come back. Maybe next Saturday. See Leonard. Teach him some tricks.'

'You can't.'

'Who says?' Charlie snapped. 'It would be good for him. Boy like that without a dad, needs to be around a chap from time to time.'

Juliet sat up and took in the flush of indignation on his cheeks. 'We're not like you,' she said. 'Don't be fooled by the electric kettle and the well-mannered children. The modern world hasn't reached us yet. This isn't London, it's a village and it isn't quaint and it isn't charming. You can come and visit and eat strudel and everyone will be terribly kind and they are, they really truly are, but you don't belong. Be glad you can go home to your white studio and your white walls where no one watches you.'

Charlie shook his head. 'You're talking nonsense. I don't understand a word of what you're saying.'

'Of course you don't,' agreed Juliet. 'That's why you can't come here again.'

She saw from his face that he still did not understand, and said more gently, 'I can't have a man calling round here. Be my friend, Charlie. Don't come back.'

The next day Juliet was unsure she had done the right thing. Leonard got into a fight at school and broke his spectacles while Frieda was sent home after cookery class for lobbing wet meringue at Margaret Taylor. Juliet spent a good part of the afternoon combing sticky egg whites out of Frieda's hair. She knew she ought to punish both children but she didn't have the heart. In the evening she discovered every single copy of *Bulldog Drummond* and *Biggles* stuffed into the wastepaper basket in Leonard's bedroom.

The following morning she caught the bus to work as usual. A dreariness hung in her soul as though it had been put through a whites wash with a rogue black sock and come out drab and grey. The walk from the bus stop to the factory seemed to take twice as long as usual and the piles of old fish and chip wrappings and billowing trash bothered her. Greene & Son, Spectacle Lens Grinders was situated down a tight, redbrick alley in Penge. The Victorian warehouses had mostly given way to modern shop fronts taking care of all life's needs; the high street bookended by a shop hawking prams at the top of the parade and an undertakers at the bottom. A single row of blackened warehouses remained. Juliet was fond of the lone cobbled street, which had briefly hosted an unsuccessful fish market (Penge was not noted for its proximity to the sea) and she liked to think that the stones still reeked of cod.

Juliet had officially joined the firm four days after her sixteenth birthday and apart from a brief respite during her marriage to George, she'd worked there ever since. Mr Greene always considered spectacles to be a blessing – not only were they his vocation but they'd also saved the lives of most of his family. Along with his three brothers, he'd been declared unfit for combat during the Great War owing to a strong astigmatism. Forty years on, the firm was filled with cousins and uncles most of whom had reassuringly poor vision ('a blessing, a blessing' they all knew to recite when Mr Greene repeated the results of a poor eye test). Ben Greene ground the actual lenses, Sollie made the frames, Jacob did the accounts, while Ed Lipshitz who, with a squint in his left eye surely must be considered the most blessed of all, went out on the road as salesman, sending Frieda and Leonard picture postcards from places as far-flung as Blackpool and Bournemouth.

As Juliet slipped in the front door to the factory, she tried to be grateful but she knew it would be one of those days when she felt she'd waited through entire lifetimes between arriving at ten to nine and putting on her coat at a quarter to four. During those summer months when Charlie had been painting her, she'd spent the week in furtive anticipation of the fortnightly trips up to town on weekday afternoons. She'd felt guilty as she concocted the first lie, but as the weeks wore on, unease gave way to anticipation. The girls in the office might have pitied her bad luck with headaches and toothaches through July and August, but Juliet had hummed with happiness. Now the days rattled on, empty and identical.

Drearily, she climbed the stairs. In her pocket she had Leonard's broken spectacles. He'd been sent off to school tearful and in his spares. Juliet abandoned the feminine preserve of the back office and braved the hot metallic stink and machine-gun rattle of the grinding workshop. She shouted

45

over the din, waving at her father. Mr Greene grinned with delight as though he did not see her at the factory every single day and this was a treat.

'Hello, my darling,' he said, kissing her. 'How are the children?'

'Naughty. I think Leonard's still rather over-excited after his expedition. I'm afraid he broke his glasses.'

She handed Mr Greene the shattered spectacles, which he examined with a physician's interest. Usually he was severe on those who broke their spectacles, such hallowed items ought to be treated with proper deference, but she was confident that Leonard would be excused. Leonard was at long last the fabled son for 'Greene & Son'. He was a blessing and, to his grandfather's overwhelming joy, he was also very blessed, requiring spectacles from the age of three. 'Ah, these things happen,' said Mr Greene, slipping the frames into a brown envelope. 'I'll get one of the boys to mend them for him today.' He smiled. 'I remember the day I measured him for his very first pair. I helped him to see for the very first time. What a gift for a grandpa! I felt like a conjurer who'd stumbled across a genuine piece of magic.'

Juliet, who had heard this story many times before, kissed him in thanks and retreated to the office, swapping the crash of the grinding machines for the clatter of typewriters. She glanced at the clock. It was not yet five to nine.

The days stretched on, endless and unremarkable. Before Charlie and the portrait, Juliet had been able to accept, if not relish, the quietness of her life. Now she itched, restless. She'd sent Charlie away – did that mean nothing would ever change?

On Friday they went round to Mr and Mrs Greene for chicken. On Saturday Juliet let down the hem on Frieda's school skirt, and Leonard broke the bird bath, colliding with it while chasing Frieda. For tea they had brisket. On Sunday they went for a walk. Juliet was boiling saveloys for tea when the doorbell rang.

'Leonard! Frieda! Can you see who it is?'

She heard Leonard whoop with delight and then a familiar voice in the hall. Without realising what she was doing, she unfastened her apron and tidied her hair.

'Hello, Juliet,' said Charlie, leaning round the door and peering into the kitchen. 'I've got a proposal for you.'

CATALOGUE ITEM 2
Woman Bathing,
Jim Brownwick, Charcoal on Paper, 10 x 12in, 1959

J ULIET HAD NEVER seen a house so vast – not outside the
pictures anyway, and certainly not one that people lived in.
It looked more like a museum or a town hall, albeit one
marooned in the middle of endless lawns and taut green fields.
Even from a distance it emerged from the woods, the trees part-
ing like stage curtains to reveal a curving façade of brick and a
mass of bay windows, the late morning sunlight flaming from
every pane so that it looked as if the house itself was ablaze.
Juliet gripped her suitcase tight on her knees, and willed herself
not to be impressed, not to be overawed. She turned to Charlie,
who was steering the car one-handed and driving too fast.

'And only your mother lives there?'

'Yes. Just Mummy since Sylvia got married last year.'

Juliet couldn't understand how one person could live in
such a house. She pictured Valerie Fussell as a pale Miss
Havisham type, a lace-encrusted echo drifting from room to
room, lifting dustsheets. The wind rushed at her through the
open window, making her eyes water. Wanting to ask Charlie
to slow down but not wanting to seem gauche, she adjusted
her headscarf and attempted to smooth her hair.

'Don't worry. You look fine.'

Juliet ignored him. She looked out of the window to where
scarlet flowers trembled in the long grass and ivy slapped
against a telegraph pole. Charlie swung the car sharp left

48

along a long gravel drive lined with slender beech trees, their leaves sounding like running water in the wind. Juliet closed her eyes for a moment, feeling almost dizzy with nerves. She remembered the anxiety in her mother's face, the sadness in her father's as she kissed them goodbye. She tried to think of other things. At least Leonard and Frieda had only been excited and hopeful of presents.

Charlie drew up before a set of stone steps that led to an elegant portico. Up close the house was even lovelier. Juliet felt she was glimpsing a screen beauty in the flesh, discovering that the camera had not done her justice. Charlie had told her that the house was early Queen Anne and rather grand, but he had not described the warmth of the brick in the sun, the perfect symmetry of the front and the curling balustrades in greying stone above the attic storey, or mentioned that the house was built entirely without corners.

'It's round. There aren't any edges.'

Charlie laughed. 'Trust you to notice that straight away. A quirk of the architect. Obsessed with the Baroque.'

He climbed out of the car, jogging round to open her door. Juliet allowed him to help her out and prise away her overnight bag.

'What about the pictures?' she asked, gesturing to the boot.

'We can get them later.'

'I don't want anyone else touching them. They must be displayed in the right order.'

'I know. I know. And don't worry so much. This is just a pleasant weekend.'

'A pleasant weekend?'

'Yes.'

Juliet snorted. Her idea of a pleasant weekend was a lazy morning in bed and a walk along the river to the Tate, then perhaps an ice cream. She wondered again if this was a mistake.

A woman in a neat woollen dress emerged from the front door. She was rounder and older than Juliet expected and wore no make-up, not even a dab of lipstick. Seeing them both, the woman smiled, holding out her hands to Charlie, who hurried up the steps to kiss her. Juliet allowed herself to feel a trickle of relief.

'Mrs Stephens, this is Juliet Montague. Juliet, Mrs Stephens.'

Juliet's relief evaporated. This wasn't the dreaded Mrs Fussell.

'Is Mummy in the drawing-room?'

'She's on the terrace. It's so warm today, she's got one of her heads.'

Juliet noticed them exchange a momentary glance.

'We'd better go and say hello.'

He drew Juliet inside and into the largest hall she had ever seen – she suspected that her own terraced house could comfortably fit inside. It was three storeys high and a double staircase snaked down from the top floor on both sides, rejoining in a balconied landing at each level. Juliet wondered why on earth they needed two sets of stairs – perhaps one staircase was an up and the other a down. Charlie dumped her suitcase in the middle of the hall, hurrying her across a chequered tile floor. Juliet supposed they never played draughts on it. Leonard would consider that an awful waste.

'I thought you said that only your mother lived here.'

'That's right but there's the staff, of course.'

Juliet stopped and glared at Charlie. 'There's no "of course". I live with Leonard and Frieda. There's no butler who I forgot to mention.'

Something in Charlie's face made her pause. 'There's a butler too, isn't there?'

Charlie reddened.

'For God's sake, Charlie. You could have warned me. A bit grand you said, but nothing over the top. Do I even have the right clothes?'

Charlie reached for her hand, wanting to placate her.

'It's fine. Just a pl—'

'Pleasant weekend. Yes. You said.'

She snatched her hand away from him, folding it behind her back, anxiety making her irritable.

Juliet could not know that Charlie was as uneasy as she. He wished that he didn't have to bring her here. Other girls had been impressed as he walked them over the house, leaning into him as he'd pointed out the portrait of Uncle Frederick in his lace ruff, the girls tittering and nudging him at the likeness. Beside the surprisingly cheeky seventeenth-century picture of Andromeda chained to her rock, a rosy nipple peeping from her nightgown, Charlie often tried for a nuzzle and a kiss. But he'd made certain to bring such girls here on weekends when Mummy was up in town.

Juliet glanced up at the galleried landings above, wanting to find them overly ornate, but inside the house was as elegant as out. The wood of the great staircase was solid English oak honeyed by a rich patina of years, while light poured from the endless bay windows, spilling onto the hall tiles. On a gilt table rested an arrangement of white gardenias, cabbage roses and enormous hothouse lilies, yellow pollen dusting the marble top and the scent of gardenias filling the hall and rising upward like steam. The flowers were arranged in precise disarray and, Juliet decided, needed only someone to paint them.

Charlie led her through a south-facing sitting room, the curtains drawn to protect a crowd of paintings, all warring with the gold and white Rococo walls. She lingered, wanting to look, but Charlie pulled her out onto a stone loggia and down to a terrace below. There, a woman was sprawled artfully on a deckchair, the careful angle of her arm and the golden spread of her hair suggesting to Juliet that she had lain there a while, waiting to be discovered.

'Mummy,' said Charlie, leaning over the deckchair and obediently placing a kiss on the proffered cheek.

Juliet was aware of him gesturing at her to come over but she remained at the edge of the terrace, staring out over a low limestone balustrade framing the garden, a paradise materialising in the middle of a hidden coomb. Close-cropped lawn gave way to meadow grass speckled with ox-eye daisies, camomile and flowering clover, which sloped down to formal gardens nestled at the bottom of a sleepy valley; a perfect marriage of English country garden and Italianate splendour. Naiads peeked out from behind clumps of buttery primula, while fingers of creeping ivy and twists of forget-me-nots softened the geometric topiary cut from dark green box hedge. An old wall in the same rosy brick as the house ran along the side farthest from Juliet, clematis, honeysuckle and wisteria clambering over it in a pruned tumble. Presiding over the top of the garden was an orang-ery reached by a sandstone staircase made wild and roman-tic by violets sprouting between its treads. From the terrace, she marvelled at the lower gardens. These revealed a series of rectangular pools lined with a parade of yew hedges clipped into perfect spheres. In the centre rested a round green pool, a surprisingly virile faun bathing in the waters, the fountain trickling from an urn in his arms. The air was thick with the smell of cut grass and roses unfurling in the sun.

'Why haven't you painted this?' asked Juliet, turning to Charlie. 'You grew up here. You've seen this, but you've never shown me a single picture of it.'

Anger fluttered at her throat, making her voice stick. Monet dreamed of a garden such as this, planting flowers so he could repaint them in oils.

Charlie was saved from answering by his mother rising like Aphrodite from her deckchair. She sailed across the terrace in her silk robe, her feet bare, toes perfectly varnished in red, like little wild strawberries.

'Hello, darling, you must be Juliet. I'm Valerie. Charles's mother. Don't say anything. I know. I was married frightfully young.'

Juliet hadn't been about to say anything. She thought Valerie looked exactly the right sort of age to be Charlie's mother. She guessed her to be a few years younger than her own mother and a good few bagels lighter.

'It's so kind of you to have me to stay.'

As Valerie offered up a cheek to be kissed, Juliet observed the slight lines around her eyes and mouth, covered with a thick layer of face powder. The scarlet band sweeping back Valerie's blonde hair tightened the skin on her forehead. Valerie pawed it with a thin hand.

'We've been dying to meet you. Juliet this and Juliet that. If I wasn't his mother, I'd be desperately jealous.'

Juliet understood that Valerie lived in a world of superlatives where one felt things frightfully, desperately and people were always dying for things.

'Darling, do you have a cigarette? And, tell Stevie to send down lunch, I'm simply famished.'

The three of them huddled at one end of the big terrace table, picking at an elaborate salad made from exotic leaves Juliet did not recognise. Valerie curled up in the only scrap of shade, while Juliet and Charlie sat in the sun, Juliet feeling her neck beginning to burn. Valerie did not appear to eat; if this was all she ate when famished, Juliet wondered what she managed when she was merely hungry. She smoked continually over the other two, something that Juliet thought to be the height of bad manners, but she rather suspected that, at a certain social elevation, manners were deemed bourgeois.

'I must say, you have the most beautiful skin. Luminous. What cream do you use? Please don't tell me that you're one of those dreadful soap and a splash of water people because it's fine when you're young and you are still young-ish. You're only—?'

'I'm thirty-one.'

'Thirty-one! Well, then, there is no excuse. You must have a proper regimen.'

Valerie drew breath by pulling on her cigarette. Neither Juliet nor Charlie filled the pause in conversation.

'And this—' apparently searching for words, Valerie swirled her cigarette, 'this fabulous *scheme*. Have you done anything like it before?'

As Juliet started to describe her years at Greene & Son, she realised that this pleasant luncheon in the garden was in fact an interview, and Valerie's apparently vacuous patter a way of prising information from her.

'But you never worked five days a week for your father, surely? Daddies don't like their daughters to work too hard.' Valerie gave a girlish giggle, but Juliet was no longer fooled. She knew that the guileless blue eyes behind the large sunglasses scrutinised her with the focus of a predatory fox.

'My father is very kind and understanding. After all, he's allowed me a day off every week to concentrate on our plans for the gallery. But I have to work. I have two children.'

Either Charlie hadn't told her, or Valerie took pleasure in her ability as an actress. Her mouth quivered in shock, and she pushed her sunglasses up her head, in order to better display her astonishment.

'Oh! Charles is such a naughty thing. If he'd told me, I would have asked your husband down too. I suppose he's having a dreary weekend with the little ones.'

Juliet found herself forced to confess her situation, which she was almost certain Valerie already knew.

'The children's father and I are no longer together.'

Valerie clapped her hands in delight. 'Divorced? Or were you never married at all? I know you artistic types. How thoroughly modern.'

'I was married. I am not divorced.'

'Mummy,' said Charlie, his tone sharp.

'What?' Valerie simpered. 'I'm just getting to know your friend. Are you going to get divorced?'

Juliet's pulse fluttered like a cornered butterfly.

'Stop it,' said Charlie, tossing down his napkin like a gauntlet. 'For God's sake, leave her alone.'

'Sit down, Charles. You know I can't bear a scene.'

'Be nice,' said Charlie, sitting. 'Or else we shall go, and that will entirely ruin your seating plan for dinner.'

'See how cruel he is to his poor old mother?' said Valerie, appealing to Juliet. 'I didn't mean to upset you, my dear. It was much easier for me; Charles's father simply died. Oh don't put on that awful face, darling. I know you liked him. But really, the man was a dreadful bore. He liked his garden more than he liked me.'

'Let's talk about the gallery,' said Charlie. 'We've all agreed Juliet must run it. It has to be her.'

'No one talks business over lunch.'

'Then I'll ring for coffee,' said Charlie.

'A pleasant weekend?' said Juliet, turning to him once they were finally released. She looked as if she was about to swat him, but then suddenly she laughed.

Charlie crumpled in relief, so grateful that he wanted nothing more than to hold her as she laughed, but he didn't dare. He'd never touched Juliet beyond the oddly formal handshake when they said hello. Once or twice he'd tried to rest a casual hand on her shoulder, but she'd looked at him in surprise and he'd drawn back, hurt and faintly embarrassed, a schoolboy caught in his first crush. She came up to the studio every weekend when they worked on plans together for the new gallery but he still felt as though she lived at a distance from him. The only time he was ever allowed to touch her was when she modelled for him. If she agreed to let him sketch her while she studied the accounts or sipped her tea, then she did not object when he altered the shape of her arm, or with shaking fingers – how he hoped she could not tell – smoothed away her hair so he could see her face. He found that he asked to draw her when he knew her position was wrong, and he would be compelled to move her.

'Oh. I think perhaps you'd best never marry,' she said between hiccups of laughter. 'It really wouldn't be fair.'

Charlie, who had begun to laugh with her, stopped.

'Don't look so fierce, Charlie. I've met your mother, God help me. Now I'd like to meet your father.'

Mr Fussell's portrait hung in a bright drawing-room cum study overlooking the garden. The walls were painted butterscotch yellow, the plasterwork icing white. Even the sofas and armchairs were covered in a pale caramel candy stripe reminiscent of sweetshop paper bags. Juliet felt like Gretel grown up, although rather than a gingerbread house this room was an Antonin Carême confection. There were matching white bookcases with carved roses that looked as if they were made of sugar rather than wood. When Juliet read the titles of the books, she realised every one was a gardening manual.

'My father's lair. See, it has the best view of the garden.'

The bay windows framed the ponds and lawns in such perfect proportions that outside looked more like a work by Fragonard than real life.

'My mother doesn't come in here much. That's why the painting's here. She was always telling Daddy to bugger off to his study and stay there.'

Juliet blinked. She still wasn't used to the way Charlie swore, casually using 'bugger', 'damnation' and 'bollocks' as condiments to sprinkle over his conversation. She was not offended, simply aware that he lacked her middle-class aversion to bad language. In thirty-odd years she had never heard her father swear and her mother only once – on the day she finally accepted that George was not coming back.

Juliet studied the portrait in the trim gilt frame. It was of a balding, middle-aged man, thin-lipped and with pouches beneath his eyes. He looked neither happy nor sad, kind nor cruel. She backed away and regarded him again from a distance. The man remained flat and cold; his face empty.

'It's nothing like him,' said Charlie.

'Why didn't you paint him?'

'I was going to. But then he died. And I was only fifteen. I'm not sure that mine would have been much better.'

'You should take it down. One day you'll forget exactly what he looked like so you'll look at this to remember and then eventually you'll see this blank man instead of him.'

Juliet perched on an overstuffed sofa, pretending to be at ease, and glanced around the room again.

'The light's good. I think we should hang the paintings in here.'

'Mummy won't like it. Yes. We absolutely should.'

Juliet wished she drank. Then she might feel less nervous. After tea she and Charlie had arranged all the pictures they'd brought and all in the right order, poised on easels around the room. Juliet had written out neat labels for each one. The light was perfect – late afternoon sun drifting across the lawns and turning the walls the colour of *crème caramel*. The evening wasn't simply about the pictures though: it was about her. She fidgeted inside her special-occasion frock, a sleeveless blue dress cut just below the knee. Charlie had told her to bring a 'cocktail dress' but Juliet had never had a cocktail and was unaware that drinking them required a particular outfit. She'd gone to Minnie's on the high street and the girl there assured her that this dress was just the thing; now, standing here, Juliet had her doubts.

'You look the business, love. Not as good as me. But you know, you did what you could.'

Juliet turned, smiling, to face a man of about twenty-five with hair conker-brown and as tightly curled as wood shavings. He preened in a dinner jacket slightly too large for his pickpocket build.

'I feel like a Teddy Boy. But a fucking handsome one. Let's blow this place and go somewhere good, Fidget, my love.'

As he spoke, Jim slipped an arm about her shoulders and walked her around the pictures.

'You done good.'

'You like the new frames? I know you didn't want to . . .'

'No. You was right and all. I just didn't see it before. Jesus. It does something to them blues.'

'I like the light in here. It should be good for another couple of hours. Is everyone here? Do you have the other pictures?'

'Course. Me and Phil brought the lot. Max did two new ones special. Well. Probably not special. But he did two new ones anyways. Here.'

Jim heaved up a pair of canvases wrapped in brown paper that he'd stacked against the wall and placed them onto the large desk. Juliet prickled with excitement as she fumbled in the desk for scissors. The other artists – Charlie, Jim, and Philip – she knew. They shared the Fitzrovia studio and one by one Juliet had been allowed to meet them, Jim confiding that Charlie had wanted to keep her to himself for as long as he could. But Max she had never met. He'd been a friend of Charlie's father, lending a voice to Charlie's cause when he'd rejected Cambridge for the Royal College. It was Max who'd persuaded Valerie to pay for the rent on the studio and allow her son a generous allowance. So perhaps it was gratitude that had made Charlie bring a selection of Max's paintings to the studio for Juliet to consider for the gallery. Max didn't like strangers and he never came to London, not any more. She wondered what he looked like. Despite having seen so many of his paintings, somehow she could never picture him.

'What is it about that fellow? Always his stuff you get gooey over. Enough to make a chap jealous.'

'Come on, Jim. You know I'll always be your girl.'

Juliet blew him a stage kiss, at ease with him in a way she never was with Charlie.

'Always. You and me, we got to stick together, doll.' He surveyed Juliet's display for a second time, nodding his approval. 'Give me a tick and I'll get the last pictures from the car.'

He went out whistling; if he felt overawed by his surroundings, he wasn't going to show it. Juliet wished she were as relaxed or as accomplished an actor. She sliced through the layers of string and paper swaddling Max's pictures, relieved Jim had left her alone to open them. She lifted out the larger canvas and leaned it against the bookcase, taking a few steps back before turning to look.

A flock of greylag geese swept across an empty moor, but the colours were all inverted. The geese were pink so that at first glance they looked almost like flamingos; the dark moor wasn't brown but red and purple, while black stars fastened onto a grassy sky. The paint was so thick in places that Juliet wondered if Max had given up on using brushes altogether and used his fingers to ply the canvas. Despite its oddness, the painting did not seem abstract or showy; instead she wanted to smile and say, 'Ah yes, of course geese look like this. How silly of me to think they could be any other way.'

She unpacked the second, smaller, painting and set it down beside the geese. A robin. This time the colours were true to life but the robin's eye wasn't the black bead of a bird but the eye of a girl, big and blue with tremulous lashes. And again, Juliet knew that he had captured something about the bird, something true that she had not known until then. She thought of the little garden robin that Leonard and Frieda sometimes fed, and how it beseeched the children with its sad eyes. Was it a painting of a feathered girl trapped like Papagena or just a greedy garden bird?

Jim and Charlie returned and came to stand beside Juliet.

'Right, what's our boy done this time? Always with the birds,' said Jim, shaking his head. 'I like it. But Jesus, why not a cat or a fox or a bloody hippopotamus, just for a bit of variety?'

'He used to paint other things,' said Charlie. 'It was only after the war that he started with the birds. In fact I've got a couple of early ones around here somewhere.'

'Show me,' said Juliet.

'Now? Do we really have time?'

'Please. I want to see.'

Juliet's fingers tingled and she ignored the pictures waiting to be propped onto easels. Charlie shrugged and stooped to rummage through a large cupboard. In a minute he straightened and pulled out a large portfolio, placing it on the floor.

'A few of the things in here are Max's. He left them when he stayed here during the war. Apparently I trailed about after him while he got drunk and flirted with my nanny. According to my father he was very good at playing the *artiste* back then, especially when there were girls around. Ah – here we go.'

He drew out a sheet of watercolour paper and handed Juliet a pastel of a young, bosomy girl with a trace of a smile, mischievous and tender.

'That was Hazel. She was the nanny. She actually was very pretty, but Max was not above flattering a girl if he thought it might help get her into bed. Not that they usually needed a whole lot of encouragement from what my father told me.'

Juliet took it to the window, a spotlight of sunshine striping the paper. The unfinished girl stared back, her eyes creased against a bright afternoon long ago. Juliet studied her, trying to glimpse the artist beyond the edge of the page.

'Max had the ideal portrait painter's gift – he always drew the sitter how she wanted to be seen.'

Juliet wondered what it would be like to have Max paint her.

'Did you ask him again to come tonight? And did you give him my note?' she asked.

'We shoved it through the door,' said Jim. 'He weren't there. Didn't come to the door anyways. Them pictures was just left in the porch for us. Well, we assumed they was for us.'

Charlie frowned. 'Juliet, I told you he wouldn't. He doesn't go anywhere. He won't see anyone he doesn't know. He gets up. He stalks his birds. He paints them. He gets drunk. He goes to bed.'

Charlie bent to gather up the papers and stuff them back into the portfolio case. Juliet's fascination with Max Langford irritated him. Charlie liked – no, that wasn't true – admired

Max's work. As a boy he'd adored him – the young and glamorous friend of his father, the former war artist, a pencil behind his ear and an inappropriate story to confide. Max had appeared indifferent as to whether anyone liked him or not – appreciative but baffled by the affection others inevitably bestowed on him. Back then Charlie had marvelled at the effortlessness with which Max painted and sketched, presuming it to be an effect of age and that when he too grew up, pictures would fall off the end of his brush with no more effort on his part than flicking paint. For Charlie it was never easy. Painting was often a great pleasure, he could imagine doing nothing else, but it remained an act of will. He found himself resenting both the continued ease with which Max seemed to work, and the fervour of Juliet's admiration. When she had first visited the studio to consider work of his various friends and colleagues for the new gallery, she'd spent hours and often days or weeks looking through their portfolios, deciding who they should include and which pieces. Max, once again, had been a different case. She had glanced at a series of watercolours of mallards and other dabblers. 'I want these. All of them,' she'd said, without a second look.

In the hall a clock chimed the half hour with an elegant tinkling of bells.

'We need to finish up,' said Charlie. 'Everyone will be here soon. Help me with these.'

Under Juliet's direction, Jim and Charlie set out the final pieces. As they stood back admiring the display, Phil entered with a pretty girl on his arm. Her fine blonde hair was the exact colour of Charlie's, her wide mouth a copy of his, and Juliet guessed her to be his older sister.

'Goodness, you've been busy,' said Sylvia, lifting her cheek to be kissed by Charlie with precisely the same movement as her mother.

'This must be the famous Juliet.'

She offered her perfectly manicured hand to Juliet who shook it, conscious of her own bare nails.

'I see that I picked the right moment to make my entrance,' said Philip. He rubbed his hands together and turned to Charlie. 'Have you rung for drinks?'

Juliet watched as Charlie pressed a small brass button beside the light switch and, with Sylvia's hand tucked under his arm, drifted among the pictures, pointing out something here and there with a wave of his cigarette. Unlike Jim's hired suit, Charlie's fitted him perfectly. Like an egg into an eggcup, she thought. It was odd to see Charlie dressed so smartly. She was used to him in his carefully faded jeans and meticulously battered shoes and at first she was puzzled: he looked wrong somehow, but then she realised that he looked right. The other Charlie, the familiar one, was the one playing dress-up. Unlike Charlie and her, Philip and Jim were always at ease. Neither of them pretended or aspired to be anything other than what they were. Philip was part of the smart set – he'd paint the odd racehorse or hunter if he needed cash – and never felt the need to conceal it. Jim was equally proud of his background. His parents managed the pier arcade at Clacton-on-Sea as well as the town's 'oldest and best' chip shop. It was Jim whom Juliet envied most. He succeeded in combining ambition (no stinking of cod and grease for him) and loyalty to his roots. Juliet liked his Clacton paintings best – fat women with an ice cream dripping in one hand and a fag smouldering in the other, the sea thrashing with wagging dogs and children and pale grandparents and pregnant girls bursting forth from their swimsuits, and the pier at the end of season, unlit and deserted except for a boy having a pee beside a seagull.

Juliet fidgeted inside her new dress. It was a nasty man-made fibre and she was too hot and the fabric clung to her legs like wet leaves. Sylvia's lemon silk dress flared at her hip, making her already slender waist impossibly small. Juliet wondered whether such a dress would suit her – it didn't much matter, she could never afford such a thing.

She felt a hand on her shoulder.

'Are you ready?' asked Charlie. 'Everyone's here.'

Juliet tried to remember when she had last stood before such a crowd. Probably on her wedding day, she decided. At least then she didn't have to speak. The boys lingered among the pictures at the back of the room. Jim winked at her but Charlie looked decidedly nervous. Only Valerie appeared perfectly calm, lolling against the Rococo pillar beside the door, her lilac gown sculpted into perfect Grecian folds. Valerie's friends, or rather *'Charlie's father's pals – all perfect bores, but rich bores, which I believe is what's required'*, lined the room clutching glasses of rapidly warming champagne. It was much too hot and Juliet considered whether she ought to have placed the paintings in the hall but no, the light here was perfect. The pictures looked right and that was what mattered. She cleared her throat, feeling sweat patches bloom beneath her arms and stain the nasty fabric. The expensive crowd waited, stared. But these weren't the looks she was used to at home – those were a blend of pity and curiosity with a dash of condemnation. These were merely stares of frank interest – Juliet was from a species they weren't used to and they inspected her with the same attention they would a new breed of hybrid rose. She glanced at Sylvia who looked like she'd just stepped out of a *Vogue* sketch, each blonde lock slicked into immaculate disarray, and then took in the perfectly brushed dinner suits of the assembled men. The only other time she'd seen grown men dressed identically were on her rare trips to *shul* where she watched the parade of black Homburg hats and long black coats make their way along the street – only the variations in beards told the men apart. Juliet waited as Sylvia allowed her cheek to be kissed by another lily-scented society girl, lips never quite brushing skin. Juliet sighed. There was no point pretending to be anything like them. They'd scent an impostor quick as a foxhound. She moved uneasily from foot to foot, unaware that she'd tucked one leg behind the other, heron like, as she began to talk.

'I've not been to art college, or learned about Rembrandt and Van Dyck at the Courtauld. I have no qualifications at all, and I'm not quite sure why Charlie has asked me to do this . . .' she paused and glanced over at Charlie who had gone rather pale, as though he too was suddenly not quite sure. 'But when I look at a painting or a sculpture or sketch, I get a feeling in my . . .' again Juliet hesitated, the word she wanted was *kishkies*, Yiddish for guts, but she decided that might be a trifle foreign for this resolutely English crowd '. . . a feeling in my belly that tells me, "Yes, this is the real thing." I don't care about fashion or fads in art because, frankly, I don't know what's current or what's not. I choose work by whether it gives me that tingle deep inside. All these pictures do, and I hope when you look at them you feel it too, that deep down pulse of something turning over and wriggling in your soul.'

The audience listened, polite and well mannered. Souls weren't really appropriate pre-dinner chat, but they understood Juliet wasn't one of them and gave her the benefit of the doubt.

Across the room, Max's birds caught her eye like a lover, the pink geese glowing in the swell of evening light and she smiled, suddenly calmed and ready to confess to this room full of strangers.

'When I was a little girl and struggling to love God, my mother took me to the National Gallery. She showed me Rousseau's *Tiger*, and Monet's *Waterloo Bridge at Dawn*, and told me that God was in the pictures. I looked and looked and never mind how closely I studied them, I couldn't see God lurking among the trees or peeking out from behind a pillar. I loved the pictures for themselves. The truth is, I don't need God any more, but I do need art.'

Juliet's cheeks flushed, realising as she spoke that it was true. If her parents were here they would be dismayed, her father fretful of the consequences of his daughter displeasing an angry God, her mother more concerned about the tittle-tattle of the neighbours. But now she'd started, she found she could not stop.

'The Bible would have us believe that God breathes into us giving us life. When we die, that breath is exhaled and we return to dust and clay. But these paintings have the breath of life in them. Those rosy birds fly across that sky and those bathers cavort in the sea so cold, so sweet. That isn't God, that's Charlie and Jim and Max and Philip puffing them with life.'

The audience watched Juliet, frowning a little at her mentioning not only the soul but now God. Yet there was something in her tone and in the space between her words that made them forgive her for such a violation of social niceties.

'We're told that everything must have a function. This is a sentiment my father applauds. He is a practical man who has no use for knick-knacks or *chatchkies*. He values useful objects like a walking stick or a pair of spectacles. But art does have a use. It helps us see the world more clearly. Like my father's beloved spectacles, art sharpens our perception. We see Max's birds or Jim's bathers and when we look at the sea again, we understand it better.'

Juliet sighed and chewed her lip, worried she'd said too much and not enough. Next was the part she loathed. She possessed that middle-class aversion to asking for money – it felt too close to charity to be comfortable – but it must be done.

'We're starting a gallery but we need enough money to keep us going for a year,' she said, forcing herself to look around the room. 'I'm not going to tell you that you'll make your money back in two years or that you'll double it in five. The figures say that you should, but this isn't about money. I'm going to dowse for talent, to seek out artists who bring their work Golem-like to life, so that we are transformed as we look at it and return to the humdrum world refreshed and full of colour.'

As Charlie listened, he glanced across his parents' friends and knew with some relief that he had been right. He hadn't been fooled by some misplaced infatuation. He knew that she'd tickled them; she wasn't the sort they were used to – she was a girl not a gal. They were particularly intrigued at the idea of a woman running a gallery. The room rustled with the sound of chequebooks being opened. Charlie smiled to himself, knowing that more than one gentleman would wake the following morning and survey the stub of his chequebook with considerable surprise at his generosity.

Later that night, Charlie gripped Juliet's hand and pulled her down the steps at a run and out into the darkness of the garden, the others close on their heels, a pack of joyous hounds dizzy with the exhilaration of a successful hunt. Charlie whooped with happiness, the others taking up the cry. Juliet allowed him to draw her on, faster and faster through the damp grass, the lights from the house leaking onto the lawn in yellow streaks. She remained silent. The amount of money frightened her, even though she knew it to be what they needed – it was she who had sat up in the kitchen long after the children were in bed, poring over papers and reaching back for her classroom arithmetic. Now she had a raffle ticket for change. For everything to be different so that she never had to return to Greene & Son where she could no longer tell the days apart. The boys would have other chances. They were all so young. She had a year to make the gallery a success. She stumbled on a loose pebble. 'Wait, I've lost my shoe.'

'Leave it. Come on.'

'Come on where?' she asked, kicking off the other shoe and running barefoot, the stones of the pathways cool and flat beneath her toes.

'The pool! Let's swim.'

Juliet slowed, dropping Charlie's hand.

'Isn't it a bit late?'

'Midnight is the only time to swim.'

'Absolutely!' called Philip, catching them and thrusting a bottle of champagne at Charlie, who finally stopped in order to swig.

'I don't have a bathing suit,' said Juliet.

'We don't mind,' said Charlie, alcohol making him brave.

'You can borrow mine,' said Sylvia, with a look at her brother. 'I brought a spare.'

Juliet tried to appear grateful. From the terrace, the sound of the party drifted down like curls of cigar smoke. A trio of moths fluttered before her, their wings white against the dark. She smelled lilac and the fragrance of mimosa, an echo of her grandmother's perfume. Somewhere an owl cried out and somewhere another answered. They reached the line of rectangular ponds, and the men started to unbutton bow ties and unfasten starched collars. Juliet leaned back against a pyramid hedge. She hadn't realised that the largest pond was a swimming pool but now she could see the cold metal of the steps leading down into black water. It looked just as dark and deep as the ponds beyond and she wondered if fish lurked at the bottom.

'Here, have a sip. Scotch courage.'

Jim slipped her his hipflask. In the darkness, she saw the gleam of Jim's very white, not very straight teeth. She sniffed at the flask and then took a nip. Coughing, she thrust it back at him.

'Keep that to clean your brushes.'

Jim chuckled, 'All right. All right.'

'Jim, please don't tell anyone, but I can't swim.'

Juliet rubbed at the prickles of gooseflesh creeping along her arms. Girls like her didn't go swimming. Her mother hadn't approved of public baths. Nasty places with verruca-encrusted floors and men who ogled. A swim in the sea was acceptable but even on the rare trips to the seaside at Bournemouth or Margate, Juliet had never learned. The deepest water she'd ever encountered was at the *mikvah*. The first time was before her wedding – starting with the ritual clipping of her nails, scraping out the last thought of dirt, even inside her ears and nose. Her body was a mass of nooks and creases and holes that must be clean, clean, clean. Naked and intrigued, Juliet had descended the steps into the cool waters of the *mikvah* itself. All the way under, water over her head. An indoor Ophelia, hair drifting like riverweed. If she drowned in the *mikvah* perhaps she'd go straight to heaven – but did she even believe in heaven? She'd opened her eyes, as she knew she must. Even eyes must be clean – husbands must not be tainted by a speck of menstrual blood. She didn't say the prayers, instead reciting a few choice lines from 'Dover Beach' (*'The sea is calm tonight, The tide is full . . .'*) until she'd finally emerged clean and holy and interested that the next time she visited she'd no longer be a virgin. Juliet tried the *mikvah* once or twice more in the early years of her marriage – wishing that the waters really could wash away all the problems and effect a transformation. Of course it had not worked, and it was George she wanted to send to the waters, to scrub all the secrets from his skin. He remained as far away as ever, an underwater man swimming in mysteries and hidden things. The ritual became nothing more than an occasional habit, a comfortless superstition in which she no longer believed.

Now she looked at the pool, the water dark and deep.

'You honestly can't swim?' asked Jim.

Juliet shook her head.

'Don't get in then, Fidget. You can't drown just now. It'd ruin all our plans.'

Juliet tried to smile. Jim unclipped his bow tie and shoved it into his pocket, discarding his jacket and starting to unbutton his cummerbund. Juliet turned away only to see Charlie and Philip stripping out of their trousers and peeling off socks. Everywhere she looked, it seemed that there were men undressing. The triangles of topiary were festooned with items of clothing, looking strangely festive. Until then she had never seen any man undress except her husband. She felt terribly provincial.

'Here. This should fit you.' Sylvia thrust a bundled bathing suit into her hands. 'Let's change behind that hedge.'

Juliet followed Sylvia behind a block of yew and with a swiftness remembered from frigid school changing rooms, wriggled out of her dress and into a rather daring blue bathing suit.

'There. It fits,' said Sylvia, satisfied.

Sylvia was dressed, or rather undressed, in an even more daring two-piece. The kind that Juliet had only ever glimpsed in second-hand fashion magazines perused at the dentist's.

'When you're back in town, you should come and see my pictures,' said Sylvia.

'Oh? How funny, Charlie never said you painted. I'd love to see. It would be nice to have a woman among all those boys.'

Sylvia laughed and adjusted her bosom. 'I paint a little but mostly I restore pictures. I'm at the Courtauld. You should visit. You've not lived until you've seen Rembrandt in the all-together.'

Shivering, they padded back to the pool, skin mottled with cold. Juliet stood on the edge, toes dangling over the cool stone, and suppressed a shudder. The water churned with pounding limbs and cries and splashes raining upwards, misting her bare legs. She tried to count the number of bodies, but they were diving and rushing underwater, shouting and falling and coming up only for air and to grab bottles of champagne. Seeing the two women, a head emerged, seal-like, and bobbed to the edge.

'Well? Are you coming in or not?' demanded Charlie.

Sylvia turned to Juliet. 'It'll be warmer in than out. You coming?'

'In a mo. You go on.'

Sylvia arched and dived into the black, swallow-like. Arms encircled her and yanked her under, as she shrieked in terror and delight. Juliet crouched and trailed her fingers across the surface, scooping up handfuls of reflected light, watching it pour from her hand.

'Come on,' said Charlie, floating on his back a few feet from Juliet. She saw that he was naked and willed herself not to look away, not to expose her dreary, middle-class discomfiture.

'Come in!'

'I'm fine here.'

'Leave it, Charlie.'

Jim heaved himself out of the pool, and sat beside Juliet on the edge. He reached for a cigarette, swearing softly when he instantly made it too wet to light, and disappeared to find another, returning a minute later.

'You can relax,' he said. 'I've put my trousers back on.'

Juliet winced. 'I prefer my friends with clothes on. Does that make me a prude?'

Jim laughed, scratching at the squat muscles on the base of his neck.

'You're a divorcée. You're supposed to be unshockable.'

Juliet smiled and looked away. In the water a man lifted Sylvia above his head and let her fall with a terrific splash. From over the garden wall floated the huffs and sighs of unseen cattle.

'Can you please try to stay still, just for a minute, Fidget my love?'

Juliet glanced back at Jim and realised he was poised with his sketchpad, a wedge of pencil tucked behind his ear.

'All right.'

It was very cold and she clenched her teeth to stop them chattering, but this was much better than the prospect of swimming. She watched her pale legs swinging under the surface, toes twitching like fishes. There was something restful about the shouts and slap of skin on water and beside her the scratch-scratch of Jim's pencil. Unlike Charlie, Jim did not ask her to talk as he worked and they sat in easy silence, Juliet watching those playing in the pool, Jim watching her.

'You're still shifting about. Stay still.'

'I'm trying. It's cold.'

'What are you doing?' Charlie hoisted himself half out of the water, cramming his shoulders between them, making a puddle so that Jim was forced to squirm away to avoid soaking his trousers.

'What the hell, Charlie? I'm trying to draw.'

'Well, don't. It's a fucking party.'

Jim shoved him and Charlie ducked under, re-emerging a second later.

Ignoring him, Jim flicked his pencil across the page with silken ease. Charlie reached out, snatching at the paper, but Jim was too fast and twisted away, swatting at him with the back of his hand. Juliet leaned back, trying to avoid the spray. Then, with a shout, Charlie grabbed her ankles and pulled her in.

She fell without a sound, swallowed up by the dark water.

Juliet felt herself sink, saw her limbs claw at the water. It was so quiet. The water flooded her eyes and nose, choking her. My lungs are clean, she thought. It's the seas and streams and rock pools that change us. A gentile steps into the *mikvah* waters but a Jew emerges. Pain burst in her chest as she tried to breathe and swallowed only water, burning water, scalding her insides. She kicked and grabbed at the water oozing between her fingers and toes, wrestling it for breath. Her fist thumped something, a fish, a foot. She was nothing, just a writhing mass of fear and fighting. Arms, strong, warm, folded around her and pulled her up, up and into the air, coughing and squalling, words surrendered to grunts and cries. Hands pummelled her back and she spat out water, then lay back on the cold paving, spent.

'What the hell, Fidget? I'll never get the deposit back on these bloody trousers now,' said Jim, swaddling her in a towel.

He crouched beside her, forehead tight with worry. Charlie lingered, hands folded across his chest, face white. 'I'm so sorry. I'm so sorry. I didn't know you couldn't swim.'

Juliet lay still, too exhausted to speak. The others in the pool had stopped their carnival, still drunk but pretending sobriety, suddenly aware of the cold.

'I'm all right,' she said. 'I'm sorry about the trousers.'

She closed her eyes, breathing deep, unencumbered breaths. After a few minutes, she reached for her dress and pulled it on over the bathing suit, and stood, unsteady as a lush. Wet patches splotched the fabric and Juliet was glad the horrid dress was ruined. She reached out her hand to Charlie to show he was forgiven.

'I'll be all right.'

Charlie continued to stare, a waxwork of himself. With great effort, he blinked. 'Shall I take you back to the house?'

Juliet listened to the festivities resuming in the pool. The slap and splash of laughter. On a pinnacle of hedge a barn owl perched like an umpire, his plumage tennis white. The bird made her think of Max.

'No thanks. I'm quite happy,' and realised as she said it that it was true.

When she woke the next morning, it was to find Jim's sketch pinned to the mirror in her room. Instead of her reflection, she saw Juliet from yesterday in her bathing suit, sitting on the edge of the pool. 'There I am,' she thought. 'Always about to fall; never falling.'

Mrs Greene couldn't understand it. She clutched Mr Greene's hand and ignored the plate of cherry macaroons set out on the table. She scrutinised Juliet, wondering if she already looked different. Did ambition show on the face like a mole or a glint in the eye?

'So, you're leaving the factory for good?'

Juliet nodded. 'If the gallery does well enough.'

'But you've always worked for your father.'

'And now I want to try something new.'

'You can't carry on as you are? A few days doing that art business, and the rest of the week with your father?'

'No, Ma,' said Juliet quietly. 'I must do this properly or not at all.'

Mrs Greene had never really understood her daughter. All she'd wanted was for Juliet to marry one of the nice boys who went to their *shul*. The nice boys had nice mothers (Mrs Greene knew them all). No one had known anything about George's mother – that ought to have been their first warning. Once upon a time she had asked her name and George had replied 'Evà' and that had been an end to it. All these years later, Mrs Greene was able to concede that it was pleasant not having to share the grandchildren with another woman. She could not have borne it if they'd loved their other grandmother best. Mrs Greene was a woman destined to be a grandmother – it was her greatest role. When Frieda was born, she'd hiccuped with happiness on seeing the small, red creature lying in a crib at the foot of the hospital bed where Juliet slept, immobilised by tucked linen. Frieda had opened a bruised, blue eye and Mrs Greene, quite unable to help it, had snatched her up, folding her into her bosom saying, 'Hello. I'm Mrs Greene. Edith. I'm your grandmother.'

But Juliet had always pleased herself. She listened patiently and pleasantly to advice that she never took. And she sat there now, hands folded demurely on her lap, half-nibbled macaroon abandoned on a doily (why her daughter could never learn to use a plate, was another mystery to Mrs Greene).

Mr Greene cleared his throat. 'We could find you more things to do at the factory. Different things.'

'But Dad, there aren't different things. The factory is just fine as it is. You don't need me.'

'We'll have to hire another secretary.'

'And she'll do the job just as well as me. The boys, the gallery. They need me. It'll be exciting.'

Mrs Greene harrumphed, bewildered by the appeal of excitement. The pleasure of life was in its consistency, the careful placing of one day in front of another with no unnecessary surprises. In her view the Jewish calendar was rigged specifically to avoid them – she always looked forward to lighting the candles on Friday night, waiting for the children to come round and eat their chicken and spit out the chopped liver while Juliet informed them that it was a delicacy they'd enjoy when they were older. The year had its rhythm: first *sukkout* and meals out of doors, then falling leaves and apples and honey and New Year. If she wanted, she could look up in the large calendar on Mr Greene's desk the Torah reading for any Saturday in say, 1965, and she'd know what story she'd be listening to on that morning in the future. The calendar kept life tidy, but Juliet had always been messy. As a girl with pigtails skew-whiff she'd left her puzzles out on the floor so the pieces always vanished up the Hoover, and while as an adult her hair was combed and her house clean, she wilfully refused to keep her life neat.

'Everyone works at your father's factory. *Everyone*.'

'I always knew Juliet was different,' said Mr Greene. 'She never needed spectacles. The only one in the family.'

When Juliet had gone, leaving a small heap of crumbs on the table and tumult in her parents' hearts, Mrs Greene brewed another pot of tea. The ritual of filling the kettle and listening to the familiar bubbling of the water was more soothing than any prayer. If Juliet had taken one of those nice boys, maybe that handsome John Nature who was always so keen on her, her life would be as neatly ordered as Mrs Greene's immaculate hall cupboards; but even as she thought it, she knew it would never have happened. Even without a George, Juliet

76

would find every morsel of trouble. Fancy allowing a strange man she'd met on the street to paint her picture! It was a relief she hadn't posed naked. Already the rabbis watched her with fretful eyes, afraid that she would bring the good name of the community into disrepute. Rabbis Plotkin and Shlonsky told Mrs Greene that they could not explain what worried them about the behaviour of Juliet – she was polite and mildly spoken, her children neat and well behaved. It was just a tingle in the beard, they said, the sense that in a room full of girls in white dresses, Juliet had always worn red ribbons in her hair.

Mrs Greene sighed. Now, starting an art gallery with that fast young man and his friends. None of them Jewish. None of them from round here. She certainly didn't know their mothers and she suspected that even if she did, they wouldn't get along. If Juliet hadn't been her daughter, Mrs Greene might have considered her not quite respectable. The thought made her dizzy and she scalded herself on the tea-kettle. She dropped it in the sink with a crash, breaking a porcelain plate that had been her mother's. What would her mother say about this business? Grandma Lipshitz who had crossed the sea because of a mistake with an apple and left her true love because Laws Cannot Be Broken. Grandma Lipshitz who despite her illness willed herself to live long enough to meet baby Leonard. Before she realised it, she was crying. Hearty, messy sobs that made her shoulders shake and her nose drip. She reached into her pocket for a handkerchief and couldn't find one, which made her cry harder still.

Mr Greene hurried in from the living room to find his wife running water from the tap over her burned hand, tears sliding down her cheeks, fat as raindrops.

'Edith. Edith. It will be all right.'

'No. It won't. We have to find George or we're going to lose her.'

Mr Greene gave her his handkerchief and she dabbed at her eyes. 'Did you keep that telephone number?'

'What number, Edith?'

'You know. *That* number.'

'Oh. Yes. I did. Just in case.'

Mr Greene retreated to his study, returning with a small business card which proclaimed in cursive 8-point script: '*Gerald Jones: Private Detective*.'

Mrs Greene folded her arms across her floral bosom, and declared, 'I don't care where George Montague has got to. We're going to find him.'

CATALOGUE ITEM 100
Juliet 'Fidget' Greene Aged Nine and a Quarter,
John MacLauchlan Milne, Oil on Canvas, 1937

JULIET GRIPPED HER father's hand through her mitten, and performed a double hop-skip every other step in order to keep up with his stride. The leaves crumpled most satisfactorily beneath her polished shoes and her breath mingled with the morning fog, making her wonder if the fog wasn't coal smut after all but the breath of a million Londoners. The sun, like an elderly gentleman, made a half-hearted effort to rise and then abandoning the attempt, slipped back between smooth sheets of haze. Juliet didn't mind. Neither pea-soup fog nor pea soup for lunch could spoil her mood because today she was going to work with her pa. It was the Christmas holidays and her mother was in bed with a cold. Juliet felt bad about the cold and tried to subdue her delight at the prospect of an entire week of going to work with her father.

Mr Greene hurried her along, pausing only to purchase his newspaper from the stand at the corner, adding to his *Financial Times* a copy of *Girl's Own*, which, after observing her father, Juliet tucked solemnly beneath her arm. He halted outside a furrier's window and Juliet gazed up at the mannequins sporting leopard coats and mink hats and the fox-fur stoles with dangling paws treading the air. Mr Greene lifted the latch on a hefty wooden door and the two slipped into a communal hall. A meaty stink drifted out from the furrier's and Juliet peered with fascination at the firmly closed door leading to Fox &

Bromley Furriers, curious as to whether Mr Fox had two legs or four. At the end of the dim hall a lift cage rattled and clanked, and a minute later the doors heaved open and an ancient man ushered them inside. His back was so crooked that he looked to Juliet like a jack-in-the-box stuck at the bottom of his spring.

'Lucky you, Mr Greene. Got your assistant in today, I see,' he said, slamming the cage doors. When the lift shuddered to a stop, a woman hovered outside the doors, poised to take their coats. She wore a pair of slender-stemmed (Greene's) spectacles on a fine metal chain around her neck, her grey-blonde curls neatly cupped by a hairnet.

'Good morning, Mr Greene. Miss Greene.'

'And to you, Mrs Harris,' nodded Mr Greene, allowing her to retrieve his hat.

Mrs Harris skilfully drew Juliet away to a back office filled with another five Mrs Harrises, all smiling ladies of middle years whose English-rose complexions had faded to potpourri.

'We've set aside a desk for you, Miss Greene.'

Juliet attempted to affect nonchalance, and tried not to run in her eagerness to reach the desk where pencil, paper and an old typewriter had been set out for her use.

'May I be part of the typing pool?'

Aged nine, Juliet could think of few things more exciting or glamorous than the prospect of joining the ranks of the typing pool.

Mrs Harris presented her with a short dictation to type and Juliet fed the first sheet of watermarked paper into the type-writer, wishing the week could last for ever.

Juliet was bored. She'd read *Girl's Own*, which was full of silly stories about little girls being terribly helpful to their mothers. The typewriter ribbon kept sticking, the letters they gave her to type were frightfully dull and although she did her best to improve them, to her disgust she discovered that Mrs Harris was re-typing all her work without the enhancements she'd made. Despite her disappointment in Mrs Harris, Juliet condescended to join her for lunch at one o'clock with the other girls. As they reached the stairwell (Mrs Harris didn't like to use the lift, complaining it gave her the willies) Juliet heard a loud male voice talking in a foreign accent. She was tremendously excited, having never met a foreigner before. Abandoning Mrs Harris, she followed the voice.

Outside her father's office a tall rather elderly man in a tweed jacket and sporting a suitably foreign hat was talking to her father, who stood with hands behind his back, rocking slightly on his brogues. Mr Greene adjusted the spotted hand-kerchief in his breast pocket, a symptom of mild disquiet.

'I can't pay full price at the minute, but I could give you a painting for the specs,' said the foreigner.

'Well. I don't know. We do offer the odd exchange but—'

'Oh yes,' interrupted Juliet, sliding into the hall. 'All the rabbis come here for their glasses. And nuns. Even though we're heathens and not Catholics. None of the men and women of God pay anything at all. Are you a man of God? I don't think it matters much which one.'

The two men turned to face Juliet; Mr Greene looked a trifle pale.

'The wee girl is your daughter?' asked the foreigner.

Mr Greene managed to sigh and smile at once. 'Yes, indeed.'

The foreigner brightened. 'A picture of your daughter then. A portrait. I can paint her this week while I'm waiting for my new specs.'

Mr Greene was about to object – what would he do with a painting? – but then he considered the advantages. First, a portrait might make Mrs Greene happy and second, he didn't really know how to keep Juliet out from under everyone's feet for an entire week. He'd already sensed a weariness emanating from poor Mrs Harris, and a couple of the letters from the typing pool brought to him to sign had been mighty peculiar before they'd been hastily removed and re-done. A painting that kept Juliet out of everyone's hair suddenly seemed a splendid bargain for a mere pair of spectacles.

Juliet loved having her portrait painted. She loved the little studio Mrs Harris set up for them in an empty office. It had no curtains or blinds on the windows and the whitewashed walls had escaped the wallpaper outbreak that had spread in a brown paisley scourge throughout the rest of the office. She loved the smell of oil paints and sat tight-lipped in the bath each night as Mrs Greene tutted and sniffed and washed and rewashed her hair, wishing she wouldn't and that she could go to bed stinking so deliciously. Most of all she loved Mr John MacLauchlan Milne even though it transpired he was not really foreign, only Scottish. After an hour in his company she decided that was nearly as good. Mr Milne was as old as her grandfather but he had once been a cowboy in Canada. He knew rope tricks and he'd been to France and painted lobsters and Paris cafes and sailing boats in warm harbours. He even showed her on his palette the exact colour of the Mediterranean on an August night.

Juliet perched on a tower of cushions placed on a chair and tried to keep still.

'Can you stop talking for a few minutes while I paint your mouth?'

Juliet considered this for a moment. 'I can try. But it's doubtful.'

Milne laughed, a deep smoker's chuckle emanating from his chest, and started to blend coral and white on his palette.

'I suppose that's why you paint mostly landscapes, because they keep still and don't talk.'

'Landscapes don't keep still. Not for a second. The light is always changing and the shadows moving. There's wind in the trees and a shiver in the grass. Now shush.'

Juliet held her breath. She tried to imagine she was one of the brown-red squirrels in the park sitting quietly poised over a nut. She didn't even dare blink. She was so still, so silent, she might even have been dead and then her mother would be oh so sad and this picture would be of poor, tragic Juliet who died much too young and her uncles and aunts and cousins would traipse round to the house during the *shiva* and drop off beef brisket and gaze on her portrait and weep. Juliet let go of her breath like letting the air out of a balloon and toppled off her cushions.

'Sorry, Mr Milne.'

The painter set down his brush and pulled out a cigarette. He blew smoke out from between his teeth. 'You're not a child at all. You're a fidget.'

Juliet and Mr Greene eased past the snake of women queuing in front of the grocer's. She considered that a few miles away Mrs Greene would be standing in a similar line, waiting for meat, sugar, bread, maybe a little bit of fish. This was post-war marriage: men worked and women queued.

After the blitz the warehouse containing Greene & Son was the only building remaining on the street. It perched alone like the last ship in harbour moored in a dock of rubble. Everywhere people picked their way across the wreckage, carrying shopping baskets, briefcases and satchels. A flurry of schoolboys paused to play tag around an old bomb crater. Juliet thought it had once been a Woolworth's but she couldn't quite remember.

By the time she was seventeen, the novelty of going to work with her father had waned. Juliet and Mr Greene were the last to arrive at the factory and the din of the grinding machines echoed down the stairs. Juliet sighed, rubbing her forehead, the familiar headache starting early. Mr Greene turned to her, his face full of concern.

'I want you to have your eyes tested. Go and see Harry Zeigler beside Boots. Just tell—'

'—him who I am. Yes, Dad, all right; I'll go.'

Juliet was sure that there was nothing wrong with her eyes but agreed in order to escape for an hour. It was the noise of the factory and the boredom of it all that made her head hurt. She knew her father would be thankful if she could develop a mild short-sightedness. He would have loved nothing more than to fit her with a nice pair of spectacles – such a blessing, such a talisman against harm. Even though he never voiced it, she understood that her father believed it was the presence of the blessed spectacles that kept his factory safe during all the air raids on Penge.

'I'll pop down during my lunch,' said Juliet, kissing him.

Comforted, Mr Greene disappeared to find his brothers while Juliet joined the ladies in the back office where Mrs Harris still reigned. The hair tidied into the hairnet at her nape was now entirely grey, but she seemed as timeless as a schoolmistress. If she stayed on at the factory, Juliet supposed this would be her own fate. Not to age but to fade like a picture left too long in direct sunlight. Juliet was determined that was never going to happen to her. She shook her melancholy away with a flick of her head, and listened to the ladies as they imagined their ideal lunch.

84

'I want cream buns. None of that artificial rubbish but a proper old-fashioned cream bun with icing on the top and a red cherry. Oh, and I want six of them.'

'You'd be sick, Ellen.'

'I wouldn't.'

'I want roast beef with roast potatoes cooked in goose fat so that they're good 'n' crunchy and peas and carrots and sprouts – fresh not tinned.'

'I want an orange. I used to love an orange.'

'You can keep your oranges and your roast potatoes. What I want is a proper drink. I'd like a gin and ginger and enough of 'em to topple a lush.'

Mrs Harris turned to Juliet. 'What about you, dear? What do you miss?'

Juliet chewed on her shorthand pencil, but the truth was she didn't remember food ever having been like this. She was young when the war started and it seemed to her that she'd lived her entire life on rations. Each year had been measured out in stamps.

'I'll be missing lunch anyhow. I'm going to Zeigler's to get my eyes checked.'

'Ooh, you lucky thing. He's got a new assistant.'

'Yes, didn't you see him, Juliet? He was in last week seeing about Mr Zeigler's order.'

'Lovely-looking young man, he was.'

Juliet shook her head. 'I must have missed him.'

Instantly the others offered up eager recollections.

'I remember him. German.'

'No. He was French.'

'Definitely Hungarian.'

'Definitely a dish. He looked like Clark Gable with a *schnoz*. Such a pity you missed him.'

Juliet felt that indeed it was a pity. Nothing much happened at Greene & Son and now it had she'd missed it. She was quite determined that old Harry Z wouldn't be the one to test her eyes.

At half past twelve, Juliet slipped on her coat and hat and hurried along the high street to Harry Zeigler's Penge Opticians thinking about the optician's assistant. The young men she knew were all the same. The kind her mother referred to collectively as 'nice boys'. She glimpsed them each Saturday at the *shul* as she sat at the front of the women's gallery with her mother and aunts and their collected friends. Bored and hot, Juliet would lean over the rail, studying the men in the hall below. The rabbis sang and the men bobbed and itched, adjusting yarmulkes, muttering prayers and swallowing yawns. The women gossiped above, their chatter falling like rain, the men hissing when it grew too loud. Juliet stared down at the young men, supposing that someday she would marry one of them. It didn't seem to matter much which one. Their families were all like hers: second- and third-generation immigrants from Lublin, Gombine and Boleslaw. They'd swapped *shtetl* life for bus timetables and pinstriped suits and games of bridge. Their grandparents had stepped off boats in London or Glasgow to the echo of fiddle music, wailing song and stamping feet, nothing like the sophisticated refugees who now arrived with their doctorates and certification from the Bar, their violas and Danube waltzes. The nice boys at the *shul* traced their roots back to the bagel makers of Gombine, not to psycho-analysts from Vienna. Juliet tried to picture the German / French / Hungarian optician's assistant. He was tall. Much taller than the nice boys. And he had brown eyes. Very dark, and sad from all he had seen. He'd play the piano with long, delicate fingers and he'd be able to dance – a regular Fred Astaire with a Jimmy Stewart smile.

She halted outside Harry Zeigler's shop but did not enter, slipping into the alley at the side. Reaching into her handbag she pulled out a packet of cigarettes, struggling to light one in the breeze. After a few minutes the door to the shop opened and out stepped old Mr Zeigler. Once he had toddled off along the high street to the deli for his sandwich, she slid out of the alley and round to the front door of the shop. Workman had fixed a sprauncy new sign declaring Harry's Specs. The sign caught in the wind and creaked like a gallows.

'Is this your first eye test, Miss?'

'No, no. It's just, I've been getting these headaches—'

'Best to be safe.'

'And my father . . . Mr Greene . . . from Greene & Son . . .'

'No charge of course, Miss Greene.'

'Thank you. That's very kind.'

'Come this way. I wish Mr Zeigler was here himself to see to you, but he's just stepped out this minute. Such a pity. Never mind, Mr Montague will take excellent care of you, I'm sure.'

The woman behind the counter directed these last words at the young man emerging from the darkness of the optician's studio. His back was to Juliet but as he turned, she realised that she was holding her breath. She felt almost dizzy. She smiled and almost had to clap her glove in front of her mouth to stop herself from laughing out loud with happiness. It was true what the girls had said. He was handsome. And tall. And she liked his *schnoz*; it wasn't too big at all, it gave him character. Realising she was staring at him, she flushed.

George Montague reached out to shake her hand.

'Miss Greene. A very great pleasure.'

They shook. His fingers were long and cool and his eyes were indeed brown, the rich colour of polished wood. He beckoned her into the darkness of the examination room and closed the door. It was small and windowless, hastily partitioned or else promoted from a store cupboard, but the gloom separated it from the rest of the shop so entirely that Juliet felt the two of them had entered another tiny suburb, distinct from daytime London. She had never been alone with a young man before and certainly not in a darkened room. Going to the pictures was different. Even if a particular young man took you there for a date, you shared the darkness with another hundred courting couples. The air buzzed with kisses but you were not alone. She wished for a little more light, longing to look at him again. The last time she'd wanted to see a man this much was when she'd waited for three hours in the pouring rain hoping for a glimpse of Clark Gable.

'If you would please be sitting.'

She sat.

'I am placing this in front of first the right eye.'

With gentle hands he wrapped a blindfold across Juliet's eye, using her fingers to hold it in place while he fastened it. Her hair caught in the knot and he brushed it away from her neck. Juliet felt a shudder of gooseflesh and hoped he had not noticed. All the boys were the same. This man was not.

'Are you from Germany, Mr Montague?'

'Hungary. The blindfold is comfortable all right?'

'Yes, perfectly, thank you.'

Juliet found herself speaking when she had willed herself to be silent. 'How do you find England, Mr Montague?'

'Damp. Safe. Empty.'

'Empty?'

'I leave behind big family. Now England is empty. You read the letters on chart, please.'

Juliet read aloud, forcing herself not to glance at him. When she finished he retied the blindfold over her left eye. She said nothing, sitting quite still as his fingers once again smoothed her hair away from the knot. He had to prompt her to read the letters. Once she reached the end he made a satis-fied click with his tongue and, pulling his chair close, removed the blindfold, tucking it away in a drawer.

'You have headaches?'

'Yes.'

Yes my head hurts with boredom because nothing ever changes and one day I shall be so bored that I shall marry a nice boy.

He turned on the light. It was warm inside the room and Juliet felt a tickle of sweat in the small of her back. She noticed the cheapness of his suit, the cut too loose and fabric shiny, and yet he looked elegant, as if it was a costume he'd been forced to wear for a play and any moment he'd shrug into his dinner-jacket. Most people were thin nowadays but he was thinner than most. He brought out a little torch and leaned so close his knees bumped hers. He took her face in his hand. His fingers were cool on her cheek. She wanted to ask if he played the piano.

'Please to open your eyes.'

Juliet did not realise that she had closed them. She looked up into the torch, seeing nothing but white light. She blinked and he was looking back at her, looking into her.

Mrs Greene would have preferred Juliet to pick one of the pleasant boys from *shul*, but no one could deny that George was a very handsome young man with the most delightful manners. Mrs Ezekiel had muttered that very little was known about his family but Mrs Greene had objected that one really couldn't ask *under the circumstances* and it was very tactless of Mrs Ezekiel to bring it up at all, at which Mrs Ezekiel had scowled and said, 'No offence intended, I'm sure,' and the two women had ignored one another until Passover. Mrs Greene tried to believe Juliet when she said that George's lack of history was romantic and made him enigmatic. Mrs Greene wasn't sure that enigma was the most important quality in a husband, but she didn't like to upset Juliet, and the girl was drunk on happiness.

The first time Juliet brought him to the house was the day after he'd proposed. He had not asked Mr Greene's permission beforehand, which Mrs Greene tried very hard not to consider as a slight. Juliet, however, viewed it as dashing and romantic. George went down on both knees (he was not a man to do things by halves) and declared, 'We do not need the blessing of the old people, we are young and passionate and we shall elope if we musts.' Juliet did not think that her parents would appreciate being called 'the old people' but she applauded the general sentiment.

The four of them sat in the good front room, teacups poised on saucers as Albert Lipsey laid out a selection of diamonds on the doily in the middle of the coffee table. Juliet – in this, at least, a good Jewish girl – chose the largest and the shiniest. Before George could blanch, his father-in-law-to-be led him quietly aside and suggested a congenial payment plan that would see his daughter with the ring she desired and his son-in-law able to afford it without penury. There was only a minor kerfuffle when Albert became convinced he'd dropped a diamond, and they all had to hunt about for it under the couch and down the back of the cushion covers – George searching most diligently of all. Poor Albert left convinced that he'd either lost a diamond or his marbles. Putting this unpleasantness aside, Juliet gave George a tour of the house as Mrs Greene put on an extra-fat chicken to roast for supper. Her cooking combined the heartiness of traditional Jewish cuisine with traditional English fare and the house began to whiff of boiling semolina and cabbage. Juliet led George into the gloomy dining-room to show him her portrait. Drawing back the curtains as far as they would go and switching on the light, she stood aside.

'It is you, yes?'

Juliet nodded. 'Yes. I was nine or ten. It was painted by an old Scotsman in exchange for a pair of specs. I think my father got rather a good deal in the end.'

George kissed Juliet with glee. 'Such a beautiful picture. We must have it in our house! One day we will have a baby girl and she will be as beautiful.'

Juliet flushed, quite breathless from the romance and the talk of babies and the illicit thought that making them with George might be fun, and if a child didn't appear for a year or two or three that would be perfectly all right.

Mr and Mrs Greene were delighted to give them the picture as a wedding present. Though, to be on the safe side, Mr Greene also gave them the deposit for the house to put it in. After the wedding, the portrait took pride of place in the Montagues' small living room, the girl's orange sweater a note of colour amid the heavy reproduction furniture.

Juliet tried not to mind and to tell herself that George couldn't help it. At first she had been amazed. On their honeymoon in a damp hotel in Margate, he'd beaten her at chess in half a dozen moves though not long before she'd been in the school chess team. The next day it had poured with rain so, unable to stroll along the front, they'd sat in their room playing rounds of cards – George didn't seem to mind what the game was as long as there was a game. When she'd run out of pins to pay him, he'd stripped her of her scarf then her amber brooch, next her slippers and skirt and at last, as Juliet willed him to win more quickly, her stockings, brassiere and lace honeymoon knickers.

The disappointment started the following night when, tired of playing a poor opponent for pins, he slipped out to find a game with higher stakes. Juliet sat on the bed in her new silk nightie, shivering in the dark and wondering when he'd come back. He woke her with kisses and soothed away her hurt with whispers in Hungarian and clever fingers.

Her earrings disappeared first. They were sapphires, a Hanukkah present from Mr and Mrs Greene. George was so solicitous. He made her cups of hot tea and helped to dry her eyes and crawled on his hands and knees under the bed to try to find them and later, when hope was lost, he filled in the insurance claim form. Somehow it was George who cashed the cheque and he never quite remembered to take Juliet to the shop in Hatton Garden to choose a replacement pair. Juliet rarely found as much in the housekeeping tin as she'd thought was there, and on opening her purse at the grocer or the butcher often discovered that it was perfectly empty when she'd been sure there had been a pound in it.

And yet, George could be generous. When he was on a lucky streak, he'd arrive home with bouquets of crimson roses and perfumed freesias, until Juliet ran out of vases and every room was brimful with flowers stuffed into milk bottles and teapots and tooth mugs. After a lucrative fortnight he had the entire house fitted with top of the range Rosenblum carpet; smart burgundy for the stairs and hall, a rich mustard for the lounge. He won her a gold charm bracelet which she made him return – she couldn't bear to think of some other wife sobbing over her lost things. He appeared one afternoon with a fabulous mink coat, showing Juliet the receipt so that she knew it was new and not the fruit of another's misery. He wrapped her in it, naked, and for a precious afternoon she believed that all would be well. She wore it to *shul* and gloried in the admiring and envious glances. The following month it disappeared from her wardrobe. She told everyone that it had been much too hot and she'd decided to get rid of it.

At least George wasn't dull. Her friends measured their troubles by the number of cigarettes it took to smoke while they recited them. They grumbled how Bernie had got fat and Maurice picked his ears at supper and Edgar never climbed into Betty's bed any more at night – not that she wanted him to, mind, but to be denied the opportunity of denying him like that was awful, just awful. Juliet stayed quiet. George continued to slip into her bed and she found that she was usually willing when he did so.

When Frieda was born he was wonderful. For the first months of her pregnancy Juliet said nothing, smiling to herself in the queue at the greengrocer as she remembered the little fish inside her. When at last she confessed, George cried. Not a few sentimental tears but inelegant sneezing sobs where the tears mingled with snot on his chin. For nearly a year nothing disappeared. He changed nappies, never saying that it was a mother's job, and slid out of bed during the night to give the baby her bottle. In the dark, Juliet could hear him singing to Frieda in Hungarian, soothing her with words Juliet did not understand. And yet, there was something else she did not confide to her friends. She told George lies.

'The housekeeping money is all in the custard tin.'

'No, my father didn't give me anything this week.'

'No, darling, the picture is worth nothing. It was painted by a nobody when I was very small. My father didn't even want to pay him a pair of spectacles for it.'

The artist had found a modest degree of success at last and wanted to borrow his painting of Juliet Greene for an exhibition in Edinburgh, but Juliet Montague had politely and regretfully declined. She spent an entire afternoon and half a packet of cigarettes puzzling over what excuse to send to her old friend John Milne, but she knew with cool certainty that if the picture went off to Edinburgh it would not return to the living room for long. When Milne died a year or two later, she hid the obituary and interrupted her mother when she started to tell them all about it over the Friday night dinner table. She chattered loudly over Mrs Greene, telling her about how Betty's Edgar had run off with a flame-haired dancer from a London show until Mr Greene had waved his napkin for quiet and reminded them both of *lashon hora* and Juliet blushed for shame while hoping that the light in her husband's eye was inspired only by the thought of the red-headed dancer.

But the picture did not vanish and Juliet relaxed. George had been so good since Frieda was born. He must have changed. Still, she kept valuables hidden, partly out of habit and partly to keep George out of the path of temptation. When she was pregnant with Leonard, Mr Greene presented her with some premium bond certificates for both children which, after casting about for a suitable hiding place, she stashed behind the picture frame. Her marriage *ketubah*, a ten pound note and the deeds to the house – she slipped them all into a large envelope and taped it to the back of the painting.

The arrival of his son triggered another spate of disappearances. George was overwhelmed with love for this small, red creature who would bear his name all his life, and in time pass it on to sons of his own. George went out to celebrate with some friends and returned three days later without his coat or his shoes or the watch with his name engraved on the back Juliet had given him for his birthday. She said nothing but understood that the housekeeping money must once again be stashed in different pots around the house, a little always for show in the custard tin to put him off hunting further but more in craftier places – under the floorboard in the hall, inside the Hoover bag, and taped behind the picture frame.

The day George vanished was ordinary. Juliet could trace his morning in the puddles of mess he left around the house. At half past seven he made tea, dribbling milk along the counter and leaving the used leaves congealing inside the pot for Juliet to clear away. He walked Frieda to school on his way to work and kissed his daughter goodbye without tears or sentimental speeches. He spent the day writing prescriptions and running eye tests for white-haired, rose-water steeped ladies, popping on his hat and coat and leaving at the usual hour of a quarter to six (later Mrs Greene insisted that Juliet telephone Mr Ziegler to check, even though Juliet knew by then it was hopeless). George did not seem preoccupied or worried and remembered to enquire after the delicate health of Mr Ziegler's wife. The only difference between this day and any other was that George never came home. When Juliet returned from her mother's at half past six George was not there. She didn't pay much attention, busy with Leonard who had eaten too many of his grandmother's potato *latkes* and was grizzling, and with Frieda who had eaten too few and was now hungry. At seven o'clock she bathed the children and put them to bed. It was not until she came downstairs again at half past that she noticed the picture was gone.

For an hour she sat and stared at the empty space on the wall. The frame remained, only the canvas had been neatly prised away and the gilt now encircled the wallpaper roses. Spying one of Frieda's crayons, she traced inside the picture-shaped hole in blue and then again in purple and green. Once she had finished, she sat back down and wondered what she ought to do. She supposed she ought to cry. It was expected. She had better cry before she stepped out to telephone her mother but Juliet did not feel like crying. She looked up again at the empty wall. The picture had vanished and so had George. Juliet knew he was never coming back. The missing picture told her. It was the only object she valued and he knew, *he knew*.

'I thought you said that George had gone. Not that daft picture.'

Mrs Greene arrived in a flurry of anxiety and sufficient tears for both of them, and fixed onto what Juliet considered trivialities.

'He wouldn't leave on your birthday.'

'If he's leaving, one day's as good as another.'

'But there's no note.'

'He took my picture. He didn't need to write a note. There's nothing more to say.'

'Maybe someone broke in and stole it. I'm sure George will be along shortly.'

Juliet found herself in the odd position of having to persuade her mother that her husband had really left her. Mrs Greene remained inconsolable that he had not left a note – although at first she insisted that this meant he couldn't intend to be gone for long, as though he had merely popped out for a pound of cod or a packet of humbugs and been unavoidably delayed. Eventually it was the matter of the missing bond certificates and a ten pound note that convinced her.

'Well then! He's a thief. My son-in-law, the thief.' Mrs Greene paced and sighed. 'I never liked him. Never trusted him, not one grotty little inch.'

She burrowed in her cavernous handbag for a clean hand-kerchief. 'He had a look I never cared for. I wish you'd married one of those nice boys.'

Juliet recalled her mother dancing round and round the small living room polkaing in George's arms, face sweaty and red as she accepted a snifter of schnapps. Even now, at this awful minute, Juliet couldn't bring herself to wish that she'd settled for a nice boy.

That night she lay alone in the bedroom staring at the empty bed beside hers, the sheets unruffled, pillow undented. The house was quiet in the dark. She strained for some miracle of sound. A key in the lock. The shuffle of footsteps in the hall. There was nothing. Only the tick of the radiator downstairs, the scratch of apple leaves on glass where the branches leaned in close to the house. She glanced again at the empty bed and realised she was very cold, so cold that if it was any other night she would slip out of her bed and into George's and he would turn to her without waking, opening his arms for her to wriggle inside them.

It would have been easier if Leonard could remember that his father had left, but he kept forgetting and Juliet was forced to tell him again and again that Daddy had gone away.

'On a holiday?'

'A very long holiday.'

'When will he be back? For Hanukkah? For my birthday?'

'No, darling, I don't think so.'

'He's at the seaside.'

In Leonard's eyes people only ever went on holiday to the seaside. Juliet wondered if Leonard pictured his father walking up and down the sand in striped trunks, bucket in one hand, lolly in another, buying picture postcards that he wrote and never sent.

Unlike her brother, Frieda never said a word. She perched on the edge of the couch, her short legs dangling, feet not quite touching the brown rug and watched Juliet with greenish eyes.

'You understand, my love, that Daddy's gone.'

Frieda sat very still and then nodded once. Juliet shifted on her seat, uneasy at the girl's silence. She felt the space where

97

the picture used to hang empty behind her. Frieda watched her without blinking and Juliet toyed with the fabric of her skirt, reading accusation in her daughter's gaze.

'I don't know why he went. But I'm here, my darling. I'll never go anywhere.'

Still Frieda said nothing, she only sat with hands folded primly in her lap and stared.

Juliet knew other women whose husbands had left them, but none whose husbands had disappeared. George simply walked out of Harry's Specs that day and vanished. Mr Ziegler said he would hold the position open for a month but after that he would be forced to advertise. Juliet wanted to tell him to advertise right away. She knew even if the others didn't. After a week, her father insisted she telephone the police.

'He's not been murdered, Pa.'

'No, but we must prepare for the worst.'

Two policemen came and sat in the living room, setting down their helmets on the coffee table like huge boiled eggs. They scribbled details down in spiral notebooks and drank cups of tea and Juliet realised that for the first time in her life she was being pitied. The older policeman, a large man whose buttons strained to contain his belly, asked the questions and his boyish companion shot Juliet sympathetic glances and wrote down her answers. As they stood up to leave, Juliet caught the older man's arm.

'Don't feel sorry for me. I'm not daft. I know he's not lying in a ditch somewhere. I know he isn't coming back.'

'They do sometimes, madam.'

Juliet smiled. 'Not George.'

After the police came the two rabbis. They traipsed into Juliet's house with their long beards and sweeping black hats and perched side by side on the patterned sofa with the

98

grimness of a pair of crows heralding bad news. Sandwiched between her parents she struggled against an impossible urge to giggle.

'Won't you have some poppy-seed cake?' asked Mrs Greene, appealing to the rabbis who exchanged uneasy glances. 'It's from Rose's Deli,' she reassured them, in case they'd heard the rumours that Juliet did not keep a kosher kitchen.

'In that case, how could we refuse,' said Rabbi Plotkin as Rabbi Shlonsky beamed his agreement. 'And perhaps some hot water and lemon?'

They all waited, poised on the stiff upright chairs carried in from the kitchen while the rabbis ate in silence, spraying crumbs over their beards where they lodged like tiny shrivelled sloes in a hoar frost.

'How long has he been gone, my dear?' asked Rabbi Plotkin.

Rabbi Shlonsky smiled, showing the seeds trapped between his teeth.

'Nearly a fortnight,' said Juliet.

'And any word? A letter? A telephone call?'

'No.'

'The most important thing is that if do you hear from him, you must not be angry and you must not scold him.' He peered sternly at Juliet like a headmaster over the top of a pair of imaginary spectacles. 'I know it's hard for you ladies,' he smiled at Mrs Greene, 'but you must hold it inside. The only thing that matters is that he comes back and you don't put him off.'

'And what if he doesn't come back?' asked Mr Greene, his voice thin.

The rabbis exchanged a look.

'Let us not worry about that just now. Let us hope he does return.'

Juliet sat up straight. 'If he doesn't come back, I intend to divorce him.'

99

The rabbis leaned forward together and once again Juliet recognised that look of pity. 'You may divorce him in the civil courts, my dear Mrs Montague, but . . .' Rabbi Plotkin hesitated.

'But what?'

Rabbi Plotkin sighed and Rabbi Shlonsky settled back on the couch looking grey and unhappy. 'Unless Mr Montague sends you a bill of divorce, you are still married in the eyes of God.'

The elderly Rabbi Shlonsky cleared his throat and spoke for the first time since he had entered the house. 'In Jewish law only men can divorce women. Until your husband returns or dies or divorces you, then you are stuck. You are married and not married.' He stared at her with watery blue eyes and said the word for the first time. 'You become an *aguna*.'

Juliet felt a shiver of unease, like a child on hearing a sexual word for the first time – something at once intriguing and sinister. She wanted to know; she didn't want to know. The conversation continued around her. She felt, rather than heard, her mother begin to sob beside her, wobbling like a pudding set with gelatine.

'But one day, she'll want to marry again.'

'That's why we must find him. But don't cry, Mrs Greene, he may well yet come back. Husbands often do, you know.'

Juliet realised that only Rabbi Plotkin spoke. The white-bearded Rabbi Shlonsky merely looked at her with those pale eyes.

'I know he's not coming back. I *know*.'

Mrs Greene coughed in annoyance and, tugging the hand-kerchief from Juliet's fingers, noisily blew her nose.

'You don't know anything of the sort.' She turned to the rabbis. 'It's because he took that silly portrait of Juliet with him. She's got it into her head it means he's gone for good.'

Rabbi Shlonsky frowned. 'He took your picture?'

'He stole it.'

Rabbi Shlonsky shifted on the couch, fanning out his black coat. 'Portraits often make trouble. Especially those of women.'

The others smiled politely, uncertain of the correct response, but Rabbi Shlonsky had found his subject and his flow could not be staunched. 'My grandfather was a very famous rabbi in Gombine and like many of the true mystics he wouldn't have his likeness captured. His *shul* wanted him to have his portrait painted but Grandfather refused. He wouldn't even allow a single photograph to be taken in case he left a piece of his soul behind. But the people of his *shul* were very devoted. They loved the great rabbi of Gombine and he was very old and they wanted something to remember him by, so they had a local artist paint his picture, spying through the window while he slept.'

Here Rabbi Shlonsky paused and the others all leaned forward, curious.

'Well?' asked Juliet. 'Did he die? Did he leave the village, abandoning his congregation because of their betrayal and go into the mountains never to be seen again?'

Rabbi Shlonsky looked puzzled. 'No. He never found out about the picture. No one ever told – he would have been upset. I told you, everyone loved him. He was a wonderful rabbi. Now I have the portrait in my study. I like it very much.'

Even Rabbi Plotkin looked rather taken aback and said nothing for a minute. Then, shaking himself, he turned back to Juliet.

'The important thing is not to worry. We pray that Mr Montague does come back. If not, we pray that we find him. If not, well . . . we worry about it then.'

'When precisely do we worry?' asked Mrs Greene, who liked to be organised about these things.

'If there's anything to worry about, we worry now,' said Juliet. 'I told you, he's not coming back.'

Mr Greene rubbed his temples where a headache was starting to pulse.

'In the meantime the synagogue will help, Mrs Montague.'

It took Juliet a moment to realise that Rabbi Plotkin was offering charity. Mr Greene understood instantly and was already shaking his head. 'No, no, we don't take handouts. It's for us to help her. We're her family.'

Juliet squeezed Mr Greene's hand. 'I'll be quite all right, Rabbi. I'll work.' She turned to her father. 'I'll go back to work at Greene & Son, if you'll have me.'

For the first time that afternoon Mr Greene smiled a weak and watery smile. Juliet tried, but found that she could not return it. She'd married George at the age of eighteen in part to escape Greene & Son. Now, at the venerable age of twenty-four, she found herself going back to the factory and this time with no prospect of escape or reprieve.

Early on Monday morning, Mr Greene called for Juliet and together they walked the children to school before taking the bus to the factory. Perched on the top deck beside his daughter, Mr Greene had to stop himself from humming. The whole business was most unfortunate, but he couldn't help feeling satisfied that at last his Juliet was coming back to work at Greene & Son. For months after she'd left, he experienced a dull pang every time he peered into the back office and realised she wasn't there. The bus took the next corner rather too fast and Juliet thumped into his side. He reached out and patted her hand.

'Well, here we are again, like old times.'

'Yes,' agreed Juliet. 'Like old times.'

She glanced out of the window and saw that it was starting to rain, fat beads drenching the pavement. For the hundredth time she wondered why George had taken the portrait. The cash and the bond certificates she understood. Had he been in such a hurry that he couldn't wait to remove the money taped to the back of the picture? She imagined the portrait lying discarded in some gutter or thrust into a rubbish bin, the rain seeping into the canvas, the paint starting to crack and flake.

CATALOGUE ITEM 3
Look, Look She Flies!
Max Langford, Watercolour on Paper, 12 x 15in, 1959

Mrs greene didn't like it one bit. Mr Greene remained silent on the matter, preferring not to be trapped like a thief between his wife and daughter but succeeding only in irritating both. Philip and Jim thought it was a daft idea but that Juliet should be left to get on with it. Charlie was silently furious, brooding with unhappiness. Only Frieda and Leonard were delighted.

'A holiday? A whole two weeks? Is it by the sea? Just us?'

Leonard continually questioned his mother for the pleasure of hearing her confirmation. He'd never been on holiday before. There had been day trips but Leonard had never once stayed in a hotel, let alone a cottage. The word conjured all kinds of romance. Straw roofs. Walls made of mud. Cows in the kitchen.

While Juliet was pleased by the idea of a holiday and gratified by the fervour of the children's enthusiasm, there was another reason for the trip and this was the source of Charlie and Mrs Greene's disquiet. She'd rented the cottage in order to be close to Max Langford. His pictures were so familiar to her, like a favourite place – Mulberry Avenue in May when the cherry trees formed a procession of frothy bridesmaids, the Bayswater Road on a Sunday afternoon – and yet she had still not met him. Excitement made her almost as dizzy as Leonard, who had packed for his holiday a full fortnight in advance without being asked. Charlie's insistence that Max was a recluse and all species of peculiar only increased her determination. She attempted to mollify him. 'Perhaps I'll persuade Max to come to our first exhibition at the gallery. It'll be funny if he's not there.' Charlie had not replied. They both knew that somehow, without intending it, Max had caught her in the hairs of his brush, and she was stuck as firmly as a fly in a bead of drying paint.

Charlie insisted on driving them. He'd announced that Juliet's trip to Dorset coincided with a visit to his mother, a visit he had apparently long intended but forgotten to mention. He could drop them on his way. Leonard was almost as thrilled by the prospect of a drive in Charlie's car, a brand new scarlet Morris Mini-Minor, as he was by the holiday itself. They left London on a hot August evening, the dusty city grey as old laundry, and arrived in Fippenny Hollow as the moon rose above the hills like a polished silver pocket watch. Juliet was glad that Charlie knew where he was going. To her every lane and hedge looked the same, a Minotaur's maze speckled with daisies and lady's bedstraw. They passed stone gates labelled with National Trust opening times.

'The Langford Estate. Or it was before Max gave it to the Trust.'

'Why did he give it away?'

'Money. And running a place like that is a vocation. Or it needs to be. Max isn't like that. All he cares about are his pictures and his stupid birds.'

His anger exasperated Juliet, and she looked out of the window into the green darkness. Sometimes just the mention of Max's name was enough to send Charlie into a fit of petulance. He hurled the car around the bend, forcing her to grip the seat. She glanced back to check that both children were still asleep, suddenly wishing they'd taken the train.

They drew up beside a stone cottage and Juliet climbed out, inhaling the sickly scent of honeysuckle. Charlie roused Leonard, helping him onto the verge, where he stood blinking and unsteady beside Frieda, who clutched her cherry-red rucksack.

'I'll give you a hand with the bags,' said Charlie.

'No. Thank you. We'll be all right,' said Juliet, wanting him gone.

Charlie studied her for a second and then with a shrug climbed back into the car and roared away between the funnel of hedges, leaving them on the lane, the unlit cottage gazing at them with empty eyes.

The three of them stood among the clutter of suitcases and fishing rods and buckets, and stared. It had been a hot day, clear and cloudless, but now the August night was cool and full of stars. The sky was packed with them, clear and white and so many that it was impossible to fix on just one light without feeling giddy.

When the children were at last asleep in bed, Juliet slipped out of the house, the key tucked into her pocket. The cottage was half a mile from Max's. She just wanted to see where he lived. She wouldn't knock on the door; not tonight. Wrapping her cardigan around her shoulders she walked up the lane into the mouth of the trees. The country gloom unnerved her. Every bush and stretch of grass put forth bodiless noise: rattles and whispers and the hurry of feather or fur. The thick summer canopy swallowed the stars and the ground echoed with her footsteps. She heard something – not the scuffle of creatures in the undergrowth or the wind ruffling leaves, but music through a window. A track branched off from the lane and into the wood and it was from here that the music drifted out of the darkness. Juliet followed like Gretel tracing her breadcrumbs.

In the green heart of the wood squatted a brick house, small and ugly. The trees and scrub had crept closer and closer, as though playing a game of grandmother's footsteps that the red house was losing inch by inch, year by year. The strange music filtered through the trees. She leaned against the papery trunk of a birch and listened. There was a light upstairs and she waited, hoping for a glimpse of him. She was determined to persuade him to paint portraits once again. The bird paintings were magical and lucid and odd, but Juliet wanted to see that eye turn its gaze onto people. She remembered the sketch of the girl he'd drawn before the war – the mischief and flirtation held in a few pencil strokes.

'Max Langford. I'm Juliet Montague and you're going to paint me,' she called into the night.

After four days, Juliet began to wonder whether she would ever meet Max at all. She knocked on the door of the house in the woods twice each day and peered among the trees in case he was sliding fox-like through the shadows. He was not. She slipped notes through the letter box asking him to call round for tea, writing that unless she heard to the contrary she would expect him. There was no reply. Juliet, Leonard and Frieda sat round the scrubbed kitchen table in the cottage, poised over boiled eggs and scones and some kind of elderly veined cheese, Juliet telling the children that their visitor surely must appear. Any minute. Any minute. The minutes came and went. He did not.

Charlie called at the cottage every morning. He didn't ask Juliet whether she had seen Max, for which she was grateful. He offered no advice but neither did he gloat. Leonard scrambled to the door the moment he heard Charlie's car. He had recovered from his disappointment that Charlie was neither his father nor a spy, and accompanied him on various fishing and painting trips around the countryside. This was how, on their fifth day at Fippenny Hollow, Juliet discovered the way into the house in the wood. Charlie and Leonard returned home in time for supper, Leonard rosy-cheeked and happy, a trout in one hand and a watercolour of its slippery corpse flapping in the other. He held out both for approval.

'We were painting by the Piddle. Did you know that the river is called the Piddle, so it's not rude. And a man came by. He was walking with his dog. I wanted to paint the dog but it wouldn't keep still. And he looked at my fish picture. The man not the dog. The dog just sniffed it. And the man said that it was really good.' Leonard paused, waiting for Juliet to agree.

'It's a wonderful painting, darling.'

Satisfied, Leonard continued. 'And he said that there is a painter in the wood. A famous war artist. And he teaches people at his house on Fridays. And that I'm good enough to go. When is Friday?'

Juliet looked at Charlie, who kept very still and would not catch her eye.

'Tomorrow is Friday, darling. But I don't think you need another teacher. Not when you've got Charlie.'

Charlie stood over the stone sink with a bucket, gutting the fish with a knife, so that their scarlet and grey flecked innards slithered into the pail. Frieda sat at the table painting her fingernails pink. The exact shade of the trout gizzards, noted Leonard, wondering whether he should swipe the varnish for his next picture.

'Come with me on Friday,' said Juliet to Charlie. 'You know I must go. But you should come too.'

'I'll think about it,' said Charlie.

'Come on. You were friends. You *are* friends. It was you who showed me his pictures in the first place.'

She smiled, taking a fish from him. She wiped her cheek, and smeared blood across it, noticing it on her fingertips like harlot's rouge.

Charlie frowned. 'What you have to appreciate, Juliet, is that he isn't like he used to be.' He paused as though reaching for the right words. 'Max Langford is a war artist without a war.'

On Friday night Juliet crossed back into the wood. The children were asleep, or else pretending to be. She waited until eight for Charlie to appear and when he did not she set out alone up the lane before striking along the track into the trees, unable to decide whether she was relieved or disappointed that he had not come. The day had been damp and the floor of the wood smelled of loam and leaf mould, sweet and rich like a very good and complex wine – the kind Charlie's mother served at dinner and Juliet sniffed and did not drink. This time the woods were not empty. Voices floated through the gloom; snatches of chatter and laughter. Juliet felt a pang of regret – she knew it was quite ridiculous but she'd hoped to have Max to herself. In a shopping bag she carried Leonard's watercolours, carefully wrapped up in a tea towel. While she felt slightly ridiculous taking a child's set of paints (complete with Tom 'n' Jerry stickers on the tin) she couldn't quite bring herself to ask Charlie if she could borrow his.

Yellow lights shone through the bands of tree trunks and from a hundred yards away she could see figures gathering around the front door, silhouetted like paper dolls against the light. After a moment's hesitation, she stepped forward to join them, feeling a prickle of triumph as she finally crossed the threshold into a narrow hall, where she was instantly caught in a crush of bosoms.

The painters were almost all women, matrons of middle age corseted in thick country tweed – the kind termed 'sensible' – and stout walking shoes. The ladies clasped paint sets and a hodgepodge of gifts: jars of piccalilli, a wheel of cheese, a milking stool, a jam jar filled with meadowsweet and willow herb. The ladies set these offerings on a plain wooden table. In the glow of an oil-lamp, the heaped table looked to Juliet like a kind of pagan altar, though to whom she was not sure.

The house was set too deep in the woods to have mains electricity and the sills and surfaces were dotted with paraffin lamps and candles so that the air reeked softly of kerosene and wood smoke. Juliet stayed quiet, listening to the hurry of strangers' hellos. From the outside the house was unattractive – a Victorian cottage built quickly and out of sight of the Langford mansion, the red brick pockmarked with soot, the tiled roof low and hunched – so she was unprepared for the interior to be beautiful. Charlie insisted on Max's oddness, his disregard for convention, and she'd come to expect a hovel with curls of mouldering wallpaper, skittering insects and rotting floors. Instead the paper in the hall was hand-printed – a repeating motif of red-stencilled woodpeckers thrumming their beaks against black books for woodworm. The floors were covered with rugs, mostly skins or fleece, and where they were not hidden they gleamed with beeswax. Woodcuts and lithographs of the surrounding countryside adorned the walls – standing stones under a buttered moon, a trio of moths, an owl in the afternoon – and she longed for the other women to move aside so she could study them. The colours of the skirting boards, banister and doors were ochre, rust and dusty green – the muted colours of Max's palette, so that Juliet felt as if she had slipped inside one of his pictures. Even the curtains had been painted by hand; she realised that the polka dots had been dabbed on with a brush and that Max had signed the bottom corner of the fabric. Through an open door she glimpsed a small, clean kitchen, the table lined with blood-ied newspaper and rabbits stripped of their fur, flesh raw and red.

The women began to shuffle forward like passengers at a bus stop and Juliet joined the end of the queue, filing through a low doorway into a sitting room. She heard a man's voice, cool and clear as an announcer for the BBC.

'Find a place to sit, ladies. We're very full tonight.'

The room was packed. The women perched on foldout chairs, stools and patterned sofas. Two elderly men crammed beside one other on the window seat, tight as books on an over-stuffed shelf. Every surface had been decorated – the round feet of the sofa were festooned with painted yellow claws, camels trekked along the ceiling cornicing, the round plaster mouldings forming dunes and humps. The cupboards were washed with blue, the ridges of the wood panels picked out in creamy lines. The chimney breast was formed from the ridged back of a dragon, green and gold, the fearsome toothed jaws opening into a fireplace where flames stuttered. The effect should have been overwhelming – it was a carnival of detail and colour and decorative styles, as though, unable to pick just one, Max had chosen them all – and yet the overall effect was quite beautiful. Juliet observed with interest the wry humour of the room; a giant moth flattened itself against the windowpane, and as one of the gentleman tried to brush it away she saw that it was painted onto the glass. She smiled, deciding that only an artist could foresee how it could all work together.

She found a perch on the arm of a sofa and peered over the grey heads, impatient for a glimpse of Max. She wondered now whether she should be excited or afraid. From Charlie's description of him, she half expected a blinking madman with wild eyes and unbrushed hair.

'Hello, Juliet Montague.'

Max stood at her elbow. She knew it was him even though he did not look remotely like a madman and his sandy-brown hair was almost tidy.

'You can't possibly work like that.' He gestured to her precarious seat on the arm of the settee. 'Either you want to paint properly or you don't and you can go home.'

Juliet was about to object to his rudeness when she realised he was laughing at her. He turned and walked away. The two rather large ladies sharing the sofa shuffled along to make space for her, and she unpacked Leonard's easel from her bag, wishing that it wasn't also covered with cartoon transfers. Standing beside the fireplace, arm resting on the scaled jaw of the dragon, Max cleared his throat.

'I mightn't do portraits any more but that shouldn't stop any of you from having a go. Watercolours, oils, pencil, pastel, I don't care. I don't care whether it's a likeness or not. That's not what a portrait is. You want a perfect likeness take a damn photo.'

A tentative voice called from the back. 'Who shall we paint?'

'Me,' replied Max.

Juliet's portrait was not going well. Knowing how poor an artist she was herself, she disliked painting and had avoided it since school. It was a relief that Max had said the likeness was not important since hers looked nothing like him, in fact it didn't look much like anyone. She was, however, grateful for the opportunity it gave her of studying him without embarrassment. He looked to be in his late thirties and was rather too thin, his hair was light brown, here and there fading to grey and yet he seemed oddly boyish, his movements impulsive and restless. He sat in an armchair beside the fire reading a newspaper and sipping whisky and soda, ignoring the strangers filling his sitting room. He certainly wasn't allowing the class to inconvenience his evening. Juliet wondered why he'd invited them here since he guarded his privacy so tenaciously. Perhaps the whole thing was a joke to him – an artist who found it amusing to allow in his curious neighbours and then dupe them into painting him. The room was growing hot with all the bodies and Max roused himself from his paper, ambling to the windows and throwing them wide. The sound of the woods trickled into the room. The creak and crack of the trees. The scream of a fox.

'I don't think you have much of a future as an artist,' said Max, pausing beside Juliet and examining her picture.

'No,' she agreed.

'It really doesn't look like me in the slightest.'

'You said that likeness wasn't important.'

'So I did.'

The matrons squeezed beside her on the sofa scrutinised their own pictures, wondering if the great man was about to pass judgement on them too. From around the room there were audible sighs and huffs that their model had wandered away but no one dared to complain. Without glancing at another picture he left the room. Juliet looked about, wondering if that was the end of the lesson, but none of the other students appeared perturbed and continued to dab away. Sure enough, in a few minutes he returned with a pipe and a refreshed glass and settled back into his chair. He'd removed his jacket and the ladies beside Juliet began to mutter in exasperation. Sensing mutiny, Max spat out his pipe.

'Not all subjects are easy. They fidget. Lose the clothes you've been painting them in. It's a useful lesson.'

Max proceeded to ignore them again, devoting himself to his paper and his pipe. The other students picked up brushes, some starting with fresh sheets of paper, others resolutely continuing their portraits. Juliet abandoned hers, aware that Leonard could have done much better. At the end of an hour Max rose, drained his glass and moved around the room steady as a minute hand, stopping at each easel to offer in confidential tones thoughts and criticism. He was patient and kind, finding something to like in even the rudest attempt. He crouched by Juliet's sofa again, suggesting to her neighbour a different technique to achieve a rougher texture. The woman was buttoned parson-like into a high-collared blouse and she thanked him, eyes watery with gratitude. Juliet was intrigued by the women's apparent adoration – he was generous without stooping to flattery but she couldn't see what merited such devotion. He reached her side again.

'You're much nicer to them,' she said.

'They want to learn. You don't.'

Juliet shrugged. 'I don't see the point of aspiring to mediocrity. I'll never be any good.'

'Then why try at all?'

Max tore Juliet's picture from the front of her watercolour pad and, screwing it up into a ball, lobbed it onto the fire where it blazed for a minute before crumbling into flakes of ash.

'There. Now it's doing some good.'

The class watched Juliet in silence. She felt the warmth of their looks, suddenly self-conscious, a child singled out by the teacher for poor behaviour. Through the open windows the sound of church bells tolling ten drifted in amid the whisper of leaves. Max clapped his hands.

'Thank you all for coming. We'll meet again in a fortnight.'

As the others rose, packing away brushes and easels and stuffing papers into shopping bags and satchels, Juliet didn't move. The two lone gentlemen shuffled past, nodding thanks to Max, raising their hats to Juliet in unison. In five minutes the room was empty. The only sign that it had been busy with people were the dents in the sofa cushions, the abandoned chairs. Max showed no surprise that Juliet remained and for a moment she wondered if he hadn't noticed. He prodded the fire with a toasting fork and spoke with his back turned.

'Would you like a drink?'

'All right.'

He wandered into the kitchen, returning a moment later with a bottle of sloe gin and another glass. Even though she did not drink spirits, she accepted the glass, and padded around the room in bare feet, free at last to inspect the assorted pictures. 'I've not seen these before.'

Max laughed. 'Charlie hates them. He stomachs the oils but these – the woodcuts and such. These he can't stand.'

'Why? I like them.'

'Too nostalgic. Too English. I'm a tremendous disappointment to Charlie. I survived the war only to retreat into the cowardice of nostalgia.'

He folded himself into an armchair. 'But I'm afraid that's what happens. One gets sick of England. The dampness. The littleness of everything. And then one goes away and pines for it. I sat and sweated in Luxor, painting planes and temples and dreaming of drizzle and strawberries.'

Juliet glanced around the room; the oil-lamps had stuttered into darkness and it was now lit by a handful of candles, the walls flushed from the embers' glow. In the half-light the caravan of stencilled camels commenced their slow march around the desert mouldings. The framed woodcuts and linocuts were mainly glimpses of the landscape, standing stones crouched on the back of a hill, the humped ridge of a fort, but Juliet sensed that in all these pictures something watched from the dark.

'They're not nostalgic. They're uncanny.'

'The thing is you long for home but once you get here all you can think of is where you've been. The coombs and rivers aren't quite as real as they used to be. Or they're not when I paint them.'

She studied them again. 'It's always autumn or winter. In fact, I don't think I've ever seen a single picture of yours where it's summer.'

Max smiled. 'Spring and summer bore me. All that endless green. I like the colours of autumn and the texture of winter. When the leaves are gone you can get into the heart of the wood.'

At the thought of the walk back to the cottage through the midnight trees, Juliet shivered. Silently she cajoled herself for her silliness – she was a modern woman who told her children not to be frightened by stories. It didn't work; Max's pictures unnerved her. The printed ash tree peeped at her between thin fingers, far too human. She took a small sip of sloe gin, sweet and strong.

'May I see some more?' She hesitated. 'The pictures from when you were a war artist?'

'I'm afraid you can't.'

'I'm so sorry. I shouldn't have asked.'

'It's all right. The War Office owns everything. They took the lot at the end of the war. I expect it's mouldering in some archive somewhere. Otherwise I'd gladly show you.'

Juliet settled back onto the settee, drawing up her bare feet like a roosting bird. She wanted to hurl questions at him. He sat facing her, suppressing the twitch of a smile, perhaps sensing the onslaught.

'How long have you lived in this house?'

'Since the war.' He glanced at her over the top of his glass. 'Paintings and painters go in and out of style. If all else fails I shall become a woodsman.'

'Don't you get lonely?'

'No.'

She supposed that the house itself with its painted butter-flies and dragons and camels was company. He waited, unblinking as one of his pictures.

'It's getting late. Won't your husband wonder where you've got to?'

Juliet shifted in her seat, unsure what Charlie had told him. 'No. He won't wonder at all.'

'But you are married?'

'Yes. In a way. But if you don't mind, I'd rather not talk about it.'

'All right. But you do realise by putting it like that, you've roused my curiosity.'

Juliet made no reply and, after waiting for a moment, Max continued. 'I remember now, quite clearly, Charlie saying "She's *married*." Trying to warn me off, I suppose.'

He refilled his glass and proffered the bottle to Juliet. She shook her head and he continued to drink and talk on, half to himself. She wondered whether if she left he would simply continue the conversation without her.

'I wanted to know a bit about you,' he said. 'This person who was suddenly frightfully keen on selling my paintings. Dealers from London call round from time to time and unless I'm really short of cash, I slip out and ignore them.'

'You ignored me—'

'But you didn't sound like one of them,' he continued, pretending not to hear. 'And you didn't seem a likely sort to go along with Charlie and his cronies in some scheme.'

'It isn't some scheme.'

'No. I suppose it isn't and you're the engine, I see. I did wonder. Charlie collects people like old socks collect holes. But they're not usually the type who do much of anything.'

As he set his glass down on a patterned table and rose to his feet, Juliet saw him wobble for a second before steadying himself on the mantelpiece and she realised he was smashed. It was the only symptom; he spoke with absolute clarity, rolling his words around behind his teeth like ice cubes. Knowing he was drunk, she felt bold. She looked up at him as he leaned against the fireplace. He was tall. As tall as George had been. She supposed she was being terribly irresponsible. She envisaged the disapproval of the rabbis, a communal shaking of beards, the wounded sighs of her mother but found she didn't care. Closing her eyes, she took a breath and, opening them again, looked directly at Max.

'I want you to paint me.'

'Paint you?'

'Yes.'

'That's not some modern euphemism?'

'It is not.'

'I've not done a portrait since the war.'

'I know. But I thought—'

'You thought I'd make an exception.'

Juliet felt her cheeks grow hot. She met his eye, resolute. 'I hoped.'

Max drained his glass and set it on the hearth with enough violence that the edge chipped.

'No paintings of people. Not even for you.'

The following morning Juliet was busy burning toast when there was a heavy rap on the cottage door. Leonard scrambled to answer it, voice sagging in disappointment when he realised it wasn't Charlie.

'Oh. I suppose you want my mother.'

Max followed Leonard into the kitchen and settled down at

the table, perfectly unselfconscious, picking at a bowl of slightly mouldy raspberries.

'Well, what's the fee?' he asked.

'The fee?'

'Since you sell me, you must know what I'm worth. What would a portrait by me cost?'

Juliet sat down opposite him and reached for her toast. 'I don't have enough. Not for one of your paintings.'

Now he turned and looked at her with that painter's stare, greedy and curious, as if she was a sum to be solved.

'I spent the night thinking about your picture. And perhaps there is a way it could be done. I have to be careful with portraits. Fate must be tricked.'

Juliet frowned, wondering what on earth he could mean.

He paused and licked his lips, then nodded once, resolved. 'Yes. All right. I'll paint you. But it's bad business to work for free. It will cost you something. Ah, I know the price. It'll cost you a secret, Juliet Montague.'

When Max had gone, Juliet walked over to where Leonard was sitting cross-legged on the kitchen floor. She crouched down beside him on the not too clean linoleum.

Leonard studied her in the murk of the kitchen. Her cheeks were rosy and she smiled at him. It was very quiet, the tick-tick of the wall clock, the merest rustle of roses outside, their scent seeping in through the open window. She brushed his cheek with her fingertips.

'Isn't it exciting that I'm going to have my portrait painted again?'

Leonard frowned and scrutinised his toes, unsure why he felt a pang in his belly, like when Mrs Stanton selected Kenneth Ibbotson to help her make the props for the school play when Leonard had wanted to so very, very much.

'Charlie did your picture already. I like his. I don't want you to get another one.'

Juliet laughed, hauling him up with her as she stood, pressing kisses into his hair.

'You'll like Max's too. That's the thing about pictures – you don't have to have just one.'

'This is our holiday. Just us. You promised.'

'Oh darling, it is. But Max used to live in the big house we drove past. He's promised to show us. Wouldn't you like to see that? A house as big as a castle?'

Leonard nodded but he wasn't listening any more. He was learning that paintings were the best way of attracting Juliet's notice. She sent him to school with mismatched socks and leftovers instead of sandwiches, permission slips for class trips were always late (unless it was for the National Gallery) and he had to tell her when his uniform was outgrown – she never noticed those things as other mothers did. But when he presented her with a picture he had done at school or a drawing doodled on a Saturday afternoon, Leonard knew he had her full attention. She examined his composition with genuine interest and the same seriousness she gave to the young men whom Charlie brought to the house on Sundays, sweaty from the train, leather portfolios clasped under their arms, eager to hear Juliet's verdict. On those occasions everyone except Leonard was banished from the kitchen as she spread the pictures across the kitchen table. They examined the work together in silence, while Leonard heard the prowl of anxious footsteps from the hall outside and smelled drifting smoke from a nerve-steeling cigarette.

For his mother there existed two kinds of people: not painters and painters. And, Leonard realised, she always liked the painters best.

Max took all of them to see the house. Even Charlie came and, to Juliet's surprise, he appeared in good spirits. He might have resisted her making Max's acquaintance but now that it had happened he seemed resigned and the two men were soon lost in happy disagreement and Juliet felt a lightness she had not experienced since her arrival in Dorset. Unable to all squash into Charlie's car, they ambled along the lane. Early morning clouds peeled away to expose a flawless summer's sky and the grass verge was adorned with wavering pink flowers like a jewelled Renaissance panel. A bus deposited other visitors outside the gates to the estate and Juliet found that they were just one group among herds of August sightseers. Max led the party up a driveway studded with roses, whose blooms had fallen and been crushed underfoot. Leonard dangled a camera around his neck – a loan from Charlie – and snapped at everything: an oak tree with a broken swing, a stump-tailed squirrel, Frieda. At a booth they joined a queue for tickets, which Max insisted on paying for. Juliet waited for the bespectacled National Trust lady to recognise him but she did not. Meticulously he passed tickets around the group.

'You must choose a husband. Who would you like – Charlie or me?' he asked, turning to Juliet.

Seeing her expression, he laughed and gave a ticket to Charlie.

'I'll choose for you then. Family entrance discount.'

He ushered them around to the front of a great Elizabethan manor built of honeyed stone. A gravel path led between two squares of rolled lawns and up to a vast oak door. Leaded windows faced over the countryside, but even in the morning sunshine the glass appeared clouded and dark. Figures carved in stone clung to niches on the top storey; weathered and ancient they peered down at the visitors below. The house was vast, three storeys high with more windows lurking under the eaves. Several black cedars shadowed the lawns but even these monstrous trees did not reach the level of the roof. Two wings, east and west, jutted at each end of the main house. Juliet felt as if she was staring at a city.

'Look, a monkey!' cried Leonard, pointing to the façade.

Juliet looked and saw a carved monkey clinging to a gable leering at her with sandstone eyes.

'Shall we go in?' she asked.

Max snorted. 'You don't like it, do you?'

'It's very grand.'

'It's a perfect Elizabethan mansion – if one cares about such things. It's even built in the shape of an E. My mother was an Elizabeth. I think that's why my father fancied her. Thought she'd fit in.'

Max fumbled in his pocket for cigarettes. Lighting his own, he offered one to Charlie who shook his head.

'I can't believe that you don't miss it,' said Charlie.

'These places aren't half so much fun without the cash to heat them or fix the roof,' replied Max.

'Don't you get depressed going around it?'

Max smiled. 'I don't go very often. But it is rather like visiting a grave.'

They trailed into a great hall panelled with ancient oak, Renaissance stone reliefs running along one side.

'Sir, your cigarette,' said a National Trust matron pointing at Max.

'What?'

'No smoking. I'll have to ask you to wait outside until you're done.'

Max went very still, his skin terribly white in the gloom, and for a moment Juliet was not sure what he would do. Then, he gave a snort.

'They asked me why the panelling has such a glorious patina. I told them the answer – generations of fag smoke.' He held up his hands towards the advancing guide who was sailing towards him across the marble floor, wielding a clipboard. 'It's all right. I'll put it out.'

He stubbed it out on the stonework beside the door – Juliet guessed out of habit – and ambled back inside.

'Shall we?'

Later, as they picked their way back through the woods, Juliet realised that what Max said was true – she did not like the house. She much preferred the brick cottage. Despite the army of guides and the tourists, the mansion smelled of damp disuse. It was a husk of a place and walking around was more like visiting a museum full of relics. She struggled to picture anyone living there, let alone Max.

The men walked in front, Max finding his way with ease, threading among what seemed to Juliet identical trees and criss-crossing paths. Frieda paused beside a cluster of purple flowers with tiny wax stamens like a doll's candles but as she reached to pick one, Max shook his head. 'Don't touch. Bittersweet nightshade. It's pretty but it'll give you a nasty rash.'

The brick cottage emerged like an apparition among the tree trunks, and the children rushed forward, as delighted as if it had been made from gingerbread. The bright afternoon did not reach this part of the wood. The trees grew too thickly and the light that did filter through the leaves was mottled and green. Max ushered them inside the house, and the children flitted through it like butterflies, alighting first on the staircase with its coloured treads and then spying the dragon chimney-breast before rushing to inspect the hummingbird stencilled on the window in the hall.

Leonard turned to Juliet. 'Why isn't our house like this?' he asked, his voice accusatory.

Juliet hesitated. Having seen Max's home, she too wasn't entirely sure why houses were any other way.

'Well, it's a lot of work to make a house like this,' said Charlie. 'You have to decorate it all yourself.'

'Yes, but I'd rather you didn't,' added Juliet, unnerved by the gleam in Leonard's eye. 'Poor Granny would have a heart attack if she came round for tea.'

Leonard said nothing but his face showed quite clearly that he thought this a very poor argument. Max produced a pot of thick black tea and a packet of biscuits, and filled glasses of water for the children from the tap, the water running peaty red. Leonard surveyed Max thoughtfully.

'Are you going to paint my mother? Charlie did a picture of her too. We've got it in our house instead of a fridge.'

Charlie looked up sharply. He placed his cup on the table, before turning to Max with forced nonchalance.

'Really? I thought you'd stopped doing portraits?'

Max shrugged. 'I had. Juliet agreed to pay my exorbitant fee.'

'You did?'

Juliet felt her cheeks grow hot. 'A secret. He said it would cost a secret. It was a joke.'

She appealed to Max, but he leaned towards Leonard and Frieda.

'A secret. A big juicy one for a portrait, don't you think?'

The children nodded, delighted to be included in the game while Juliet watched Leonard with unease, wondering what he would say, but it wasn't Leonard who spoke but Frieda.

'I know a secret,' she said.

'Darling, it's all right. It's a joke. You don't need to tell Max anything.'

Max smiled. 'No. You don't have to. But you can if you like.'

Charlie glared at Max, who gazed back at him with serene indifference.

'For God's sake leave them alone. Do the picture. Don't do the picture. Don't make such a song and dance out of it.'

Juliet took Frieda's hand and tried to persuade her to sit back down but Frieda shook her off, dancing around to the other side of the table.

'My dad isn't really dead. Even though Granny told me and Leonard to tell everyone that he is. He isn't. He disappeared when I was five and Leonard was two. And because he's only pretend dead, Mum isn't allowed to have another husband. Or a boyfriend,' she added, looking between the two men.

Nobody spoke. They all stared at Juliet and she wished they wouldn't. She felt tears gather in the corner of her eyes. The silence grew elastic.

Then Max threw his head back and laughed; a great raucous laugh that came from his chest and sounded like a fist hammering on wood. The children joined in first. Frieda grinned and then giggled, and seeing his sister laugh Leonard had to follow. Then Charlie caught it and finally Juliet. She wasn't sure what was funny, if anything at all, but the laughter was pleasurable, pulsing from her belly to her throat, and her eyes watered, and because it was laughing now and not crying she didn't need to blink away the tears. Max stopped first, wiping his mouth with his sleeve and pushing back his chair.

'Well then, Mrs Montague, it would seem I owe you a portrait.'

'Can we watch?' asked Leonard.

Usually Juliet believed portrait painting to be an intimate thing between artist and sitter, and yet on that afternoon in the warm kitchen circled by the yellow wood, the laughter joined them all.

'I don't mind,' she said. 'It's up to Max.'

Max disappeared to fetch his paints. He returned with a small easel and a set of watercolours.

'The only rule is no looking till it's finished. Agreed?'

The children nodded.

Max sat very still. He scrutinised Juliet without moving to pick up either a pencil or a brush. Dark eyes. Strong brows, feathered like down on a blackbird chick. He had heard her knock for him twice each day, and he'd listened to the sound of her on the other side of the door. Later from the window he'd seen her winding through the wood in her blue shorts and sandals. The shorts were nice. There weren't many women passing through his woods in nice short shorts showing a pair of healthy well-walked legs. The girl looked just like her. It was rather unnerving – mother and daughter were like Russian dolls, a big one and a littler one. He observed the slope of Juliet's forehead, the creep of hair. He didn't do portraits any more. Too dangerous. Then he was angry with himself. He wouldn't do it and they should all leave and then the light from the window caught her cheek and the highlight at her throat and he realised that to capture that might be something.

He worked quickly, stirring the peaty water with paint in a porcelain dish. It was nearly fifteen years since he'd last painted a person. That had been in France right at the end of the war. The countryside around the Bocage looked so like Dorset it was cruel, but there were guns amid the hedgerows. The combed wheat fields and huffing cattle had made it seem as if it was England herself being gutted. Afterwards it had been a relief to arrive back home and find her only partly broken. There had still been fields of corn and millponds and sticklebacks and apple orchards. The newer forests had been cut and burned but his snatch of woodland remained. The smell had not changed. The delicious rot of the forest floor.

And so he painted England again and again, a beetle, an elm, a mallard, the brave and wild pink-footed geese, oh the geese, but not people. Never people. Now he has promised to paint Juliet, but he will have to trick fate so she won't be taken.

They'd been sitting in the kitchen for hours. Charlie had disappeared for a walk and a cigarette while the children sneaked off to play caravans and nomads under the camel frieze, but now they had all come back, wondering if the picture was finished. Max's brush moved more slowly, no longer sweeping the page but dabbing it, then he set down his brush and scrubbed at the still-wet paper with a sponge, making a shuffling noise like bedroom slippers on carpet. He stopped, leaned back in his chair and stretched.

'Can we see?'

Leonard and Frieda crowded Max. He shooed them away.

'Go. Sit.'

They went. They sat. Charlie lolled against the kitchen counter. Max turned around the paper so that they could all look at once. And there she was. Juliet as a bird. A woman with the outstretched wings of a greylag goose, her feathers spread like fingers, wings and belly the exact shade of Juliet's brown hair, her eyes the same freckled green. Her mouth open in a cry and her neck long and slender, part woman, part goose.

Max looked at Juliet and smiled, his eyes bright.

'It's all right. I painted you, but I've kept you safe.'

CATALOGUE ITEM 4
Juliet in Motion,
Philip Murray, Acrylic on Canvas, 30 x 25in, 1960

EACH MORNING NOW, after Juliet had walked the children to school, instead of turning left to take the bus to Greene & Son, she turned right and hurried to the station to catch her London train. Everything, it seemed, was summed up in that turn – right instead of left. She found herself playing games – compulsively touching for luck the mulberry trees that lined the road, whispering *'Please let the gallery be a success, please.'* The thought of returning to the spectacle factory made her belly turn over like a tombola. Over Friday night chicken, she did her best to ignore her parents' looks of wounded puzzlement and smile at her father's attempts at reassurance; 'Never mind, my love, if it doesn't work out, there'll always be a place for you at the factory.' Opening the door to the gallery each morning was the closest Juliet had come in years to offering up a prayer in gratitude. She'd presumed she would be living out the rest of her life in a black and white illustration, only to discover that she'd stepped into a version hand-tinted with colour.

Wednesday's Gallery was situated along a rubbish-strewn mews off the Bayswater Road, and named for the day Juliet discovered Charlie on that April afternoon more than two years earlier. The building itself had once been a coach house and Juliet liked to think that it still stank softly of horses (which was pleasanter than acknowledging the smell probably came from the dozens of dead and fermenting pigeons they discovered on moving in.) The gallery's conversion was entirely overseen by Juliet. The front part of the building was dedicated to the exhibition space while the room beyond was a studio, although no wall separated the two spaces. Deciding to experiment with something new to the London scene, Juliet insisted that they leave it open so that visitors to the gallery could glimpse the painters and their pictures-in-progress. In truth it wasn't for visitors' benefit but for Juliet's – she loved to watch the boys paint or even just to hear the clatter of paint tubes as she busied about mundane things. She liked knowing that beside her the pictures were growing, pushing up through the boys' imaginations and emerging onto the canvas like spring shoots. It meant she was there to share in the excitement when Jim's package arrived. Rushing from the train as usual, she hurried into the gallery to find Charlie, Jim and Philip crowding around a small wooden packing crate, its lid prised open and sawdust innards spilling across the floor. Inside were a dozen white tins, snug as new-laid eggs. The three men gazed at them happily, none moving to pick one up.

'Acrylics,' said Jim.

Seeing Juliet didn't understand, he opened a few of the tins, laying them out along the bench. He dabbed a brush into a blue pot and smeared it across an empty canvas. Then yellow. Then red. The colours were so bright that the lines seemed to hum.

'Where are they from?' asked Juliet.

'America.'

They all stared at the stripes, thinking that this brave new paint must be like the country itself: the colours in the new world bolder and brighter than those of the old. That afternoon Jim started his painting of Juliet beside the swimming pool. He asked to borrow from her the sketch he'd drawn that night and pinned it above the canvas. Jim liked to work to music, Charlie did not, but this time Jim won and the afternoon filled with the growl of Ray Charles on the record player. Jim worked quickly and while Juliet watched around the edges of phone calls and press releases and discussions with the new framer, water seeped across the canvas, wet and blue. When she went home that evening he was still working and she didn't want to leave the studio, feeling as if she was quitting the cinema at the most exciting part of the film.

The following day was a Saturday and Frieda and Leonard came with her to the gallery. At first Juliet had been unable to convince her mother that it would be best for the children to break the Sabbath and come up to town with her, and Mrs Greene remained resolute that Saturdays were holy days set aside for God, boredom and chicken. But when she realised her protests were futile, Mrs Greene had eventually given up both scolding and sighs and devoted herself instead to making decent sandwiches so that her daughter did not resort to purchasing non-kosher snacks for the children from the stall at Charing Cross. Mrs Greene suffered collywobbles at the prospect of such a lack of religious hygiene.

Juliet was relieved that the trip up to town had not yet ceased to be an adventure for Leonard and Frieda. They arrived at Wednesday's in cheerful spirits, sandwiches and homework churned together in leather satchels. The doors were thrown open to catch the cool breakfast sunlight, and the melancholy tones of James Brown drifted out into the alley. All three men were already in the studio, Charlie and Philip standing quietly beside Jim who worked on with precise movements, layering more and more American paint onto the canvas. He'd clearly been busy all night and the debris of thirty hours of continuous labour lay scattered about him: discarded brushes, tins of acrylic, a jar of muddied water. A pile of fish and chip papers reeked in the corner. Jim himself stood brush in hand, unshaven and red eyed, surrounded by a constellation of empty coffee cups. Juliet and the children joined the others and waited together in silence, watching Jim work. The girl had appeared in the picture overnight, the dark fabric of her bathing suit skimming the pale skin of her bottom.

Juliet was used to watching Charlie work with oils, marking up the canvas and then adding slow layers of paint that took weeks to dry. The oil paintings were works in constant motion – a mistake could be corrected days later and the image emerged slowly onto the canvas, like the way the sun bleached the yellow wallpaper in the living-room at home, until only the bright disc behind the mantelpiece clock was left untouched. The acrylics were different. It wasn't just the vibrancy of the colours but the speed with which they dried. The picture grew before their eyes, pushing across the vast canvas in shades of blue and grey and egg yolk yellow.

'Who is she?' Frieda asked, pointing to the girl in the bathing suit who was becoming more solid with every brush stroke.

Jim started to answer, but just as he did so he caught Juliet's eye. She gave a tiny shake of her head. He corrected himself.

'Just an imaginary girl. A picture person.'

'Oh,' said Frieda. Losing interest, she withdrew to a paint-splashed armchair with the latest issue of *Jackie*. The others remained a few moments, sensing that this vast canvas was something special – the Marilyn Monroe in a room full of ordinary blondes.

'I'm going to rearrange the hanging order,' said Juliet. 'It needs space around it.'

For once Charlie and Philip made no objection. Forcing herself to break away, Juliet retreated to her desk and started to shuffle through some sketches, all of which looked thin and dull alongside the rush of American blue on the other side of the studio. She smiled as Leonard took up his usual spot beside Charlie at the small easel Charlie had knocked together as a birthday present. Leonard liked to paint on Saturday afternoons, flicking globs of paint at large sheets of white paper, so that spots of colour sprayed the concrete floor around him and made her think of a short and bespectacled Jackson Pollock. Leonard insisted on doing his homework at the easel, explaining to Juliet that fractions were much more satisfactory when propped sideways.

She tried to concentrate on finishing the exhibition catalogue and not look at Jim's picture, but she could feel it on the other side of the room, already filling the gallery with its presence. As she typed, she realised that Jim's picture titles were twice as long as the other artists', necessitating twice as much space on the page so that her eye was always drawn to his name. She suspected this was deliberate – Jim was almost as good a self-promoter as he was a painter. Philip set a cup of coffee in front of her and she looked up, murmuring her thanks.

'It is you in the painting, isn't it?' he asked, his voice low so that the children wouldn't overhear.

Juliet nodded, glancing towards Frieda and Leonard. 'I don't want them to know. They might tell their grandmother and she'd be terribly upset about the bathing suit.'

Philip suppressed a smile. 'Well, I shan't breathe a word.'

Juliet turned back to her typewriter but Philip lingered beside the desk. He examined his grimy fingernails with studied nonchalance and cleared his throat. 'Since Charlie, Max and Jim have all painted you, I thought perhaps I should too.'

Juliet glanced up at him. Of the three painters, he was the one she knew the least. If she was honest, even though he was nearly ten years younger than her, Juliet was a little afraid of him. He sauntered through life with that boarding-school swagger, born of therapeutic beatings and cold baths. While he dressed in the young artist's uniform of jeans and shirts, the denim was imported from America and the silk shirts purchased from Italian menswear emporiums with names Juliet could not pronounce. He was a modern dandy who smoked exclusive Jermyn Street cigarettes and spoke in an upper-class drawl without ever seeming to move his lips. Juliet was forced to lean forward to make him out, and consequently felt like a schoolgirl hanging on her teacher's every word. His paintings were accomplished and witty, though sometimes she wondered whether she was quite in on the joke. He was an excellent portraitist, specialising in both the horsy wives of his parents' wealthy friends as well as the horses themselves. Juliet excluded both types of horsy portraits from the exhibition on grounds of taste but Philip took it with characteristic good humour, wafting a cigarette and saying out of the side of mouth, 'Quite understandable, my dear. I only paint 'em for the cash. I quite agree they're total nonsense.'

Juliet studied him now, unsure if he was teasing but he stared back at her with pale blue eyes.

'Yes, all right,' she said. 'But I don't have time to pose. If you want it in the exhibition, you'll have to manage while I'm working.'

Juliet was uncertain whether she wanted to be subjected to Philip's scrutiny. She was curious to find out how he saw her. She suspected that in his eyes she was dowdy and suburban, but she liked the idea that Max and all the boys would have painted her. She couldn't help thinking of Max separately from the others. While Charlie's portrait hung in the living-room of the Chislehurst house, she'd placed Max's in her own room beside her bed so that it was the first thing she saw on waking in the morning. It uplifted her – Juliet with wings soaring into the sky. She hadn't shown the picture to her parents and somehow by silent accord the children had not mentioned it either. Her life was so different now and yet the small terraced house remained exactly the same. The chipped paint on the front door. The unkempt garden, the reproduction wedding-present furniture in gloomy wood. Everything about the house was the same except for the three portraits.

Juliet returned to the catalogue and tried to ignore the grey flicker of Philip's stub of charcoal across the page and the sensation of being watched. Her nose tickled but she wouldn't scratch it and, distracted, she mistyped a word. It was odd knowing that in this room two men were working on her portrait. She wondered briefly if this qualified her as a muse, but concluded with regret that she was merely a familiar object, like a vase of flowers or the umbrella stand in the corner. All three of the boys had painted that too.

Frieda padded across the room and removed James Brown, replacing him with the latest Cliff Richard LP. Frieda now apportioned her pocket money scrupulously between music and sweets.

'Turn that drivel off,' called Philip, and Frieda giggled.

'I won't,' she answered.

Philip put down his sketchpad and stalked across to the record player, rifling through a stash of vinyl propped against the wall.

'I bought this last week. Thought you'd like it,' he said removing Cliff and dumping it unceremoniously on Frieda's lap.

He pulled another record from its sleeve. 'Eddie Cochrane. Girls your age are going wild for him in America.'

Frieda grinned. That was the magic word. *America*. Every Saturday Frieda would try and put some Cliff on the turntable and Philip would produce something else that she must listen to instead. He knew more about music than anyone she had ever met. At nearly thirteen, Frieda decided it was high time that she developed a crush on somebody but her circle was sorely lacking in candidates. At school there were only girls. The Yiddishy boys from her street either had acne on their necks, nasty little wispy moustaches that made her think of spiders' legs or else they were too short and too concerned about getting into trouble . When Leonard's illegal Frisbee ended up on the synagogue roof on Yom Kippur it was Frieda and not one of the boys who clambered up to retrieve it, and it was she who'd received 'sermon number twelve: on disappointment' from Rabbi Plotkin. All her school friends were in love with somebody – pals of their older brothers and boys with slick hair who they'd 'just got chatting to' on the bus or else they mooned over posters of Tony Curtis on their bedroom walls. Frieda chewed on a stalk of liquorice and studied Philip. He had nice hair (golden blond with just the right amount of wave – not too girlish, not too flat) and his clothes always looked good. No one else's looked like that, not even Charlie's. At the thought of Charlie, Frieda grimaced. Charlie was no use – she'd never have a crush on him, not in a million years. He belonged to Leonard. And to her mother.

Philip stood beside her, lounging against the wall, eyes half closed as he listened to Eddie Cochrane croon 'Summertime Blues'.

'He died in April. He was only twenty-one. Younger than me.'

'That's so sad,' said Frieda, who wasn't really listening, but thinking that if she reached out with her fingertips she could brush the smooth skin on the back of Philip's hand. There was a black smudge of charcoal on his thumb.

'Will you take me to a concert?' she asked, as she did every Saturday.

'When you're sixteen. If your mother agrees,' replied Philip as he did every Saturday.

Frieda rolled her eyes. *If your mother agrees.* It always came back to her. Frieda slid down the wall to the floor, crossing her legs school-assembly style, and pretended to study the album cover and ignore Philip. She tried not to notice as he pulled his chair closer to Juliet and picked up his sketchbook again. Eddie Cochrane stopped singing and she could hear the rustle and scuffle of Philip's charcoal flicking across the paper over the static hiss of the record player.

'Can I be in it too?' asked Frieda.

Philip shrugged and turned to Juliet. Frieda screwed her hands into tight fists, nails making angry half-moons on the fleshy bit of her palm.

'Mum, can I?'

'I don't think so, darling.'

'Why?'

Juliet frowned. 'He doesn't have much time. And it's to go along with Max's picture and Charlie's. You're not in those ones so it wouldn't be tidy.'

Frieda studied Juliet. She offered too many reasons. That, Frieda decided, meant none of them was true.

'I want Philip to paint my picture.'

'People pay him lots of money for their portrait, Frieda.'

'He's painting you for free.'

Philip set down his charcoal and twisted round in his chair, cowboy style. 'I'll do your picture,' he said to Frieda, 'soon as I've finished Juliet's.'

He reached into his pocket and drew out a silver cigarette case, placing a cigarette in his own lips and passing another to Juliet. Frieda watched as he leaned forward to light it for her, tender and solicitous. She looked from her mother to Philip and decided that she hated them both.

The moment she saw it, Juliet adored Philip's portrait of Frieda. Unlike Charlie or Jim, Philip was private while he was painting and wouldn't allow them to see the picture until it was finished, refusing even to leave it unchaperoned in the gallery if he left before Juliet. She was glad he did not trust her, knowing that she was quite incapable of resisting an early peek. So when it was finally complete and he unveiled the picture for the first time, it was like a perfect birthday surprise and as she looked and looked, Juliet was filled with a warm happiness as if she'd stepped out into a sunny morning after weeks of rain. She was pleased that she'd insisted on individual portraits. She disliked family groups in pictures, they always seemed false – everyone frozen in a single, symbolic relationship with one another; they reminded her of rigid seventeenth-century portraits commissioned by pompous husbands to display the wealth of a plump new bride. Frieda needed her own space on the canvas – neither mother nor daughter liked to share. Philip had captured exactly that adolescent sulkiness, a girl caught between childhood and the promise of womanhood, still uneasy about the whole thing. She sat in the lone studio armchair and glowered at the viewer with her greenish eyes, skinny legs curled up beneath her, hand draped over the armrest as she dangled a drooping stick of liquorice between her fingers.

'I don't care what you want for it, you can't sell it,' said Juliet. 'Well, only to me.'

Philip laughed, evidently pleased by such enthusiasm. Juliet's response to her own portrait had been muted. She professed admiration, she was grateful, she agreed it was very clever but they both understood that she did not like it. On the one hand she'd been quite wrong: it was clear that Philip did not perceive her as suburban or dull but, she realised when he'd finished, he didn't know her at all. Juliet had been quite used to this. The rabbis and the neighbours and Mrs Greene's gossips all watched Juliet without seeing her, waiting for a mistake or evidence of some flaw until she felt herself to be nothing more than an assortment of bad decisions and habits. When she first saw Charlie's portrait and Max's watercolour and Jim's fledgling piece, she was relieved to recognise herself. It was like waking up after a dream where one is falling into nothingness and discovering with a flush of gratitude that you're still here after all – the glass of water is still on the nightstand. Philip's painting of Juliet was accomplished, the brush work skilful and the light on the brow very pretty, but it remained a picture of a stranger. This stranger looked very like Juliet and she had several sets of arms engaged in making phone calls, typing letters and mopping the brows of harried painters. Perhaps it was the efficiency with which the stranger went about these tasks that made her so unfamiliar – Juliet felt she lived at the edge of chaos, unable to finish anything how she would like – but the truth was simply that Philip didn't know her. It was not the fault of either painter or model and any lingering disappointment was dispelled by the brilliance of Frieda's portrait.

Frieda's own reaction to the picture was more ambivalent, although it changed over time. When Philip made her stand in front of the canvas, and uncovered his hands from her eyes, her first impulse was to cry. It was quite clear from the painting that Philip did not fancy her. He'd painted a little girl. She was pretty enough but it was a childish, pink-cheeked prettiness, not the bosomy languor that Frieda imagined she was conveying as she draped herself across the armchair. She also considered the failure of the picture to be entirely her mother's fault. Frieda had wanted to model in a miniskirt and had borrowed one from Margaret Taylor's older sister especially, but Juliet had vetoed it. If only Frieda had been allowed to wear the skirt then Philip would have fancied her and then he wouldn't have painted this silly picture of a rosy Renoir girl. What made it worse was that Philip never even asked her what she thought of it. She watched as he laughed, thrilled by Juliet's delight. Neither of them asked her opinion. Charlie did, but when she told him it was 'yuck' he only chuckled and ruffled her hair.

Max declined the invitation to the opening party. The others told Juliet he would not come but she refused to believe them until a small yellow card arrived inscribed in skinny letters: *Max Langford regrets that he is unable to attend.* On the back he'd added, *If you happen to be passing, you must pop in for tea.* At first Charlie tried to mollify her, insisting that a reply in itself was a kind of victory, but Juliet remained hurt and more than slightly irritated. She wasn't likely to be just passing through rural Dorset. It wasn't an invitation but a polite maintaining of distance. She read and re-read the card, searching for some additional meaning in the wording, but there was nothing except blank formality.

'What did you expect?' objected Charlie, openly exasperated by her disappointment. 'He can't drive, or rather he won't. He dislikes the train. His sphere is limited to where he can walk or bicycle.'

Juliet said nothing more about it but she felt sorry for Max as well as herself. Her world had expanded beyond the half dozen familiar suburban streets, unfurling like an Ordnance Survey map on a windy afternoon, while Max's remained limited to a few acres of woodland and a stretch of muddy river. Even though she knew that he saw universes contained within his little patch and could spend days quite transfixed as he painted a shining beetle posed on a leaf or a curl of fox turd, Juliet was not comforted.

While Jim's *Night Swimmer* was the critical star of the show and acclaimed in all the papers, *Frieda* was the picture most loved by ordinary visitors. Juliet could have sold the portrait fifty times over and before opening night was done, she replaced the discreet red spot with a handwritten notice declaring 'This work is NOT for sale.' Through the crowd, Juliet sought her out – smiling when she spied her on the wall, as though she'd caught the eye of a friend. The real Frieda was not so engaging. She petitioned Juliet for weeks to be allowed to attend the party and then refused to put on the party frock purchased by her grandmother ('It's so hideous, I wouldn't even be buried in it!') and skulked at the back of the gallery, licking the salt off peanuts and filching all the tinned pineapple squares from the spears of cheese cubes.

The gallery was packed with bodies. Juliet had no idea that so many people could be crammed into the space. Hardly anyone had troubled to RSVP (except for her parents, who'd posted a prompt and formal reply rather than simply mentioning it over the *kneidlach* soup on Friday night) and she'd mistakenly presumed no reply to mean non-attendance. Until then Juliet had lived in a community where invitations were punctually accepted – one never declined. Parties and suppers were carefully scheduled so as not to clash since the same people were inevitably asked each time and catering could be accurately calculated down to the last matzo ball. She wasn't to know that the London crowd never replied, that invitations existed to be balanced on mantelpieces, bookcases or bedsit fridges, and options must be kept open until the last moment.

That night everyone had apparently decided to drop by the party just to make sure they weren't missing out on anything. The day had been humid and the gallery was as tight and airless as a sealed biscuit tin. The atmosphere was grey with cigarette smoke and everyone was forced to study the pictures through a fog. At last the weather broke and it started to pour, sudden summer rain battering against the windows. The rattle on the flat roof was tremendous and the guests' polite cocktail chatter swelled into shouts. Feeling dizzy from the heat and the noise, Juliet propped open the doors and little puddles formed on the floor inside. She wasn't sure who anyone was – she'd studied photographs of the few who had replied but since most had not, she tried to distinguish between the various species of guests. The boys' pals and fellow artists were easy to spot in skin-tight jeans and T-shirts; the art critics and the friends of Charlie's mother steamed gently in linen jackets (the critics distinguished by their black-rimmed spectacles and their ability to drink). Beside the tables of sherry she recognised several of the local lushes, drinking with focus and without pause. She knew she ought to ask them to leave, but she hadn't the heart. Her parents huddled together near the door, too shy to talk to anyone, trying to be proud. She knew she ought to speak to the critics, but she felt a little sick at the thought.

Jim and Charlie stood before *Night Swimmer* with a friend Juliet did not recognise. He wore rather thick spectacles and bleached blond hair tickled his collar – something she had only ever seen on girls before. He scrutinised Jim's painting with a connoisseur's thirst. Charlie caught Juliet looking at them and beckoned her over.

'This is our friend, David. We were at the Royal College together.'

Juliet smiled and shook the boy's hand.

'Where did you get the acrylic?' he asked, turning to Jim. He spoke in a soft northern accent Juliet could not place. He grinned. 'Not from round here, I reckon. Only stuff I've found here is dull, dull, dull.'

Jim chuckled. 'From America. All the thrills are over there. Bars—'

'Sunshine. Sex!'

'—with the prettiest boys.'

At this both Jim and David laughed. Juliet glanced at the floor, feeling terribly unsophisticated. Until Jim she'd never met a gay man before. It was something she associated with Oscar Wilde and Sodom and Gomorrah, picturing top-hatted Victorian dandies in velvet smoking jackets and ivory-tipped canes sauntering along blazing biblical streets, thunderbolts going off like firecrackers. She hadn't even known about Jim until one Saturday morning when she'd arrived with the children to discover Jim and a cherubic boy of eighteen or nineteen fast asleep on the couch, wrapped in each other's arms. Juliet had roused them, making everyone coffee and embarking on excruciating chitchat with the exotic boy who, it turned out, was only from Bromley. Politely, she'd asked him to leave and blushing a furious scarlet told Jim not to invite guests to the gallery for 'late-night visits' when the children were coming. Jim had chuckled at her unease but refrained nonetheless.

She was saved from being further drawn into Jim and David's conversation by finding herself engulfed by a mink coat. Fur tickled her nose and she spat gently to remove it from her mouth.

'I see you've found my boys,' said the coat.

Juliet disentangled herself from the mink and discovered that she was face-to-face with an elegant woman of about forty-five, smothered in fur and draped in a velvet dress at once old-fashioned and beyond fashion. Despite the fur she was apparently untroubled by the heat or the crowd, which was beginning to remind Juliet of Waterloo station at rush hour. The woman shot Juliet a warm smile, but waggled a gloved finger in warning.

'You must remember that I discovered these boys first. I went to the college and I dowsed for talent and I found them.'

She paused at the end of this, removing a glove and waving its empty fingers with a flourish. Her voice held a slight *Mitteleuropa* accent and automatically Juliet was reminded of George.

'Juliet Montague, meet Bluma Zonderman,' said Charlie. 'Bluma, I'm so pleased you came.' He leaned forward and kissed her on the cheek with cheerful familiarity. Jim and David only gave small, polite smiles.

'Bluma's Jewish too,' added Charlie, as though this must be a fact of great interest to both women and that neither could have discerned it without him.

The two women met one another's eye with suppressed amusement. Juliet bit her lip, unable to explain to Charlie that while this elegant woman was Jewish, she was part of the set of glamorous refugees from Vienna or Berlin and as unlike Juliet as Charlie's smart friends. In the corner of the room she noticed her parents standing together hand-in-hand, speaking to no one, her mother surveying the party with frightened eyes.

'Well, gentlemen?' demanded Bluma. 'What do you think? I've made each of you my best offer.'

As the boys exchanged glances, Bluma turned to beam at Juliet. 'I'm creating a collection of artists' self-portraits. I'm going to be a Medici.'

Unsure how to respond to this, Juliet said nothing but Bluma seemed unperturbed by silence.

'It's a gamble. Everything is a gamble but I think you have it. Yes. The three of you have it.'

The boys stood in a row gazing at Bluma, taken aback by the force of her enthusiasm. Charlie was the first to speak.

'Yes. I'll do it.'

Bluma took his hand, grasping it warmly, a smile of frank happiness spreading over her face.

'Wonderful. Wonderful. And how about you, Mr Brownwick? I'll pay you twenty guineas.'

Jim nodded. 'Yeah, okay. Twenty guineas is all right, I reckon.'

Bluma clapped her hands in delight. 'And, Mr Hockney? Have you had time to think?'

There was a slight hiss as she said 'think'. Juliet tried to put George out of her mind.

David shrugged and plunged his hands deep into his pockets. 'I'm sorry, Mrs Zonderman,' he said. 'I like what you're doing and everything. But I can't. Not for twenty guineas. At my last exhibition they were selling my work for a hundred pound.'

Juliet's eyes widened. A student selling pieces for a hundred pounds? She'd priced Max's bird pictures at seventy but it had made her feel a little sick. She'd wanted to ask a hundred for Jim's *Night Swimmer* but in the end Jim had decided he didn't want to sell.

'Then I wish you luck, Mr Hockney,' said Bluma with a shrug. 'This is the fee. Nobody, no matter how famous, is paid more than twenty guineas. I would have loved a picture of you. I am sure I'll regret it.'

The boys disappeared in search of more cigarettes, leaving Juliet alone with Bluma.

'You can find talent. Trust that stir you get inside the belly that feels like joy or indigestion, when you stand in front of something truly marvellous. Sometimes you will get it right and sometimes not, but the truth is you're not ever really right or wrong. It's only luck. She'll be with you and then she won't.'

Bluma pointed to Max's painting of high-flying geese.

'He's the best painter but you'll have the least success with his work. He's too old. The public doesn't want middle-aged painters having a second spring. The pictures seem old-fashioned even though they're not. They want the young and modern.' She nodded towards Jim's *Night Swimmer*. 'He's your star. The brush work is ordinary and the light's a little flat but that's not important. It feels new. It isn't but that doesn't matter. And, best of all, it will reproduce beautifully. Those expanses of colour will print nicely and you won't notice the flatness.'

Juliet took a sip of wine to avoid making a reply. She didn't care what Bluma said, she was determined to make Max a success. It was his pictures that she loved the best and she'd make everyone understand. She started to excuse herself but Bluma took her arm.

'I won't tire you with any more advice except this: only sleep with one of them at a time,' she glanced towards the makeshift bar where Charlie and Philip were opening bottles of wine. 'Men are more fragile than you think.'

Juliet reddened in embarrassment and irritation. 'I'm not. I wouldn't—'

Bluma cut her off with a laugh. 'Well, when you do, remember my suggestion. It's as useful as anything I've said about painting. Now take me to some champagne.'

Grateful that the conversation was at a close, Juliet led Bluma to the bar. She wished that she could slip outside for a minute. In the cubby that passed for a kitchen she saw Frieda and Philip washing up glasses and laughing. Juliet sighed. She never seemed able to make Frieda laugh any more. Sometimes she felt that her daughter had joined the ranks of the disapprovers of Chislehurst. She watched Charlie's mother Valerie glide among the partygoers, sleek in a hot cerise dress that skimmed her knees, eyes perfectly stencilled into Elizabeth Taylor sultriness – her hand must be as steady as a draughtsman's. Juliet wondered for the first time if Charlie had inherited his skill with a pencil from Valerie. She was everything that Juliet was not. Perfectly at ease, Valerie understood whose jokes to giggle at, who needed to be flattered and with whom to flirt. Juliet watched in admiration and anxiety. This was supposed to be her party but she felt like a beech tree in the middle of a pine forest. She had tried to make herself look more like one of them. She no longer frequented Minnie's Boutique on the high street and her new skirts were cut a fraction shorter and a trifle tighter. She wore lipstick every day but she still couldn't sense, as Sylvia or Valerie could, when to reach out and brush a man's arm.

A slim hand slid into hers.

'You look like a wallflower, darling. This is your party,' said Sylvia. 'Come. I'll introduce you. Half of them came because they'd heard a popsie was running a gallery but now they're here, they're really rather impressed.'

Sylvia was the only woman artist included in the exhibition. Juliet was determined to discover more for the next, but it had taken some persuasion for Sylvia to agree to show. It was true that her style was enigmatic. She spent so much time restoring paintings by other artists that she absorbed a little of their style. Juliet supposed it was like listening to Beethoven on a loop and then being unable to get a chord sequence or a melody out of one's head.

Juliet allowed herself to be paraded before the collectors and critics, smiling until her lips were sore. With a smile and a laugh from Sylvia they sold one of Max's paintings, which turned out to be the only one to sell during the entire run. Whenever she started to feel nervous, Sylvia thrust another glass of wine into her hand, hissing like the rabbit from *Alice*, 'Drink, drink!' For once, Juliet did as she was told – finding talent wasn't enough: unless she wanted to return to typing letters at Greene & Son, she must learn to sell, sell, sell.

'Darling, it's going terribly well.'

Juliet looked round to see her parents hovering beside her. She kissed them both, feeling the sheen of sweat beneath the layers of powder on her mother's cheek.

'Are the uncles coming too?'

Mrs Greene started to rummage in her cavernous handbag.

'It's just us, I'm afraid, sweetheart.'

'Not even Uncle Ed?' asked Juliet, with a frown. Ed, the factory's salesman, had always been her favourite.

Mr Greene scrutinised a drawing over Juliet's left shoulder and Mrs Greene dabbed the shine from her nose with a starched handkerchief.

'He's selling specs in Bournemouth. He couldn't get back in time.'

At once Juliet understood. Her parents had never passed on the invitations to the rest of the family. They might be trying to tolerate this change in their daughter but they would not advertise it to the others.

'We'd like to buy a painting.'

Their flushed, good-natured faces displayed all the unease she felt and she tried to ignore a tingle of irritation.

'There's no need.'

Mr Greene frowned and clutched his wife's hand a little tighter.

'But we'd like to.'

Juliet wanted to be grateful but she felt like Leonard at his school craft fair when she'd been the only one to buy one of his toilet-roll telescopes. She knew her parents didn't like the pictures. Mr Greene valued objects with a purpose like spectacles or table lamps and while her mother was more flexible, Juliet knew her taste (Renoir, Monet, perhaps a little bit of Gainsborough for the splendid hats) and the paintings at Wednesday's did not fit. Mr and Mrs Greene were both simultaneously generous and careful with money. They'd give Juliet a handsome birthday cheque and pay her properly for her work at Greene & Son, but on lending her seven pence to buy some milk when Juliet was short of change, Mrs Greene expected the loan repaid. She took scrupulous pleasure in saving Green Shield stamps and the grocer's penny-off vouchers at the back of the paper, but thought nothing of lavishing gifts on her grandchildren. Money must be spent on good quality chicken ('You get what you pay for!') but meals out were a wanton extravagance ('It's a sin when there's food at home'). So Juliet knew that the decision to purchase a painting was not born out of a newly discovered passion for art but the desire to demonstrate their support, if not approval, of their only daughter.

'Which picture do you like?' she asked.

'We thought that one might be best,' said Mrs Greene pointing to one of Jim's pictures of the Clacton seaside. Fat ladies in flounced swimming costumes swarmed among seagulls and ice creams dripped onto dimpled thighs.

'Why do you like that one?' asked Juliet.

'Well,' Mrs Greene paused for a moment to consider. 'Well, I suppose, it's very small.'

Juliet sighed in exasperation. 'Do you even like it?'

Mrs Greene prickled. 'I thought that those large women in their silly frills would remind me not to have that second slice of cake.'

Mr Greene chuckled, glad that painting could have a useful purpose after all. Juliet wanted to tell them to stop being kind, that she didn't need their help and that this wasn't a school craft fair and she wasn't twelve and that paintings should be bought because they fill you with delight, not to provide encouragement for a diet, but a weariness overtook her.

'I'll go and mark it as sold,' she said.

A perm drove Juliet to leave London for the Christmas holidays. It seemed that everyone was getting one. The party had been full of bouffant hairstyles, all as perfectly leavened as a tray of golden *challah* loaves. When Juliet reflected on her unease among the guests, she concluded that much of it could be put down to the lack of a perm. If only her hair had more volume then she too might possess the smiling confidence of a Valerie or a Sylvia. She booked herself into the salon on the high street one Saturday morning and looked forward to a transformation both physical and existential. The *mikvah* had disappointed her but she had faith in this secular ritual. Mrs Greene wished that the appointment had not been made on the Sabbath, but – now resigned to her daughter's multitude of blasphemies – she requested only that Leonard be left with her. She recognised that in a battle between sermon and salon Frieda would not hesitate in her choice, but Mrs Greene still held out hope for the boy's soul.

While Juliet crouched with her head dangling over the sink, soap suds stinging her eyes, Frieda complained at the unfairness of a world that denied her having a perm as well. The girl maintained her stream of complaints while a thin-lipped woman with nicotine-stained fingers tugged Juliet's hair into rollers, then sat her under a dryer that singed her scalp. Frieda only stopped complaining when the rollers were finally removed, the combing out of the hair was finished and Juliet was enthroned before a mirror, with another angled behind so she could inspect the mysteries of the back. Then Frieda took one long look at her mother and announced, 'Thank God I didn't get one of those.' The perm transformed lucky women into chic sophisticates but Juliet was not one of them. Like the *mikvah*, the perm had failed to achieve metamorphosis.

There was nothing to be done. She couldn't stay at home until it subsided as there was too much work at the gallery preparing for the next show and, she decided, the distraction would be a good thing – it would prevent her from sitting on the loo in front of the bathroom mirror and succumbing to tears. She did her best to hide it under a hat but the hat wouldn't fit over the wobbling tower of hair. Trying to convince herself that it wasn't all that bad, she took Frieda to her mother's. Mrs Greene opened the door, looked Juliet up and down and declared, 'You broke the holy laws for this unholy mess?'

Hurrying through Bayswater to Wednesday's in the darkness of the December afternoon, Juliet avoided eye contact with passers-by, silently telling herself that heads were not turning owl-like to stare. She hesitated outside the gallery, key poised in the lock. The boys would be kind. They would make her tea and reassure her that the hair was perfectly fine and it just seemed out of place in Chislehurst. This was a London hairstyle, part of a new life, and no wonder it didn't fit in the old. She pushed open the door and found to her surprise that the boys were not alone – it took her a moment to find them in the rows of strangers filling the gallery. The electric lights had been left off and the room was lit instead by the glow from dozens of candles. No one noticed her come in and she leaned against the door examining the clusters of people sitting on the floor and perched on foldout chairs, all clutching an array of sketchbooks and notepads. Some scratched away with pencils or charcoal; here and there she noticed the flicker of a watercolour brush. A makeshift platform had been set up at the back of the studio and enthroned there, on the fat and ancient armchair, were a young man and woman both perfectly naked, the candlelight spilling shadows on their bare skin. The woman looked little more than a teenager, she had pale blonde hair (though not everywhere, Juliet couldn't help but notice) and an adolescent thinness. She leaned against the man, her cheek flattened against his shoulder.

Juliet must have made some noise as all at once the heads swivelled to stare at her, and the girl on the platform shrieked and started to shout for a dressing gown. Juliet pinked with irritation. The girl had been naked before the crowd without displaying any sign of unease so Juliet couldn't see what difference her presence made. The atmosphere created by the candles vanished in an instant as someone switched on the too-bright overhead lights. As the shrieking girl jammed her arms into the wrong sleeves of a dressing gown, Juliet grimaced. She felt like a boarding-school matron who'd stumbled into a dorm-room feast. The boy, however, made no attempt to conceal his nakedness and stood, hand on angular hip, gazing down at her.

'Jim, Charlie, who's that?' he demanded, his voice shrill and imperious.

Charlie emerged from the crowd, having the grace to look sheepish. He turned to Juliet. 'We didn't think you were coming in this afternoon – my God, what on earth happened to your hair?'

Juliet raised a hand to stroke the unfamiliar volume on top of her head. It felt strange, not really part of her at all.

'It's a perm. Everyone is getting them,' she said stiffly, daring him to say anything else. 'And my hair is hardly the point. Who are all these people?'

Jim and Philip slipped out from among the strangers and hustled Juliet into the cramped kitchenette at the back of the studio. The boys fussed, boiling the kettle for instant coffee and looking by turns defiant and embarrassed.

'It's a life-drawing class,' said Charlie.

'I gathered that,' said Juliet. 'Why didn't you tell me?'

It was Jim's turn to look uneasy. 'We thought you wouldn't like it. The naked people strolling about.'

Juliet clutched her teacup, feeling more like a maiden aunt than ever.

'Charlie and I started it,' said Philip, not meeting her eye. 'We found that most pretty girls we chatted up in bars would suddenly agree to take their clothes off when we told them we were artists. Well, that and half a crown.'

'It's how we found Marjorie,' added Charlie, nodding towards the blonde in the dressing gown. 'Though she's not terribly good. Can't hold a pose for more than thirty seconds.'

'I got bored drawing girls,' said Jim. 'Thought it was about time we had some blokes, young good-looking ones. I'd had enough of drawing old fat men at college. And then the kids at the Royal found out about our class and asked if they could come. Then the ones from the Slade. And now, it seems everyone is here.'

'So I see,' said Juliet. 'Do you charge?'

'A shilling a pop,' said Charlie, producing from under the sink a tin rattling with change. 'We were going to tell you. Eventually.'

'Yes,' agreed Philip. 'All the dosh is in there. We hardly spent any of it on fags.'

Looking at the three abashed faces, Juliet felt more tired than cross. She supposed they all thought she was square because she didn't talk about sex, sex, sex. Maybe she was frigid – it had been so long since George that perhaps she'd caught it through enforced celibacy. Celibate. Such an ugly smug word. Everyone else was busy doing it. The boys declared that they did it all the time, with girls, with boys, with themselves and had absolutely no qualms in discussing sex endlessly in her presence. And now the studio was chock-full of young people eyeing each other up, wondering who to pick to do it with later. Even the Chislehurst crowd did it from time to time. They might not talk about it, but she suspected that Mr and Mrs Nature found time between lokshen puddings to do it. After all everyone did it. Except her.

Marjorie couldn't be persuaded out of her clothes a second time, not even for another half a crown, and the class finished early. Later that evening as Juliet sat on the train returning her to the suburbs, she studied the pale face in the glass staring back at her. *I don't fit in anywhere any more.* She might spend her days in the gallery with Charlie and Philip and Jim but she wasn't like them. The boys couldn't understand that the few years separating them from her held a century of difference. Juliet had begun her life in the tradition of her grandparents and been taken to the temple to be named at eight days old, an event which marked the beginning of a life of feasting and fasting among the same few dozen faces. Her existence had been as regular as the hole in a Brick Lane bagel. Grandma Lipshitz would have recognised the impulse that made a girl of seventeen marry the first slightly interesting man to come into her village (despite the village being Chislehurst rather than a Russian *shtetl*). Even George vanishing was nothing new and there had been thousands of *aguna* drifting through the centuries before Juliet. The trouble was that Juliet had

153

been an *aguna* for so long it was now difficult to accept that she could become something else.

Outwardly her life was quite changed. She met Sylvia for lunch at cafes in Bayswater, and haggled with framers and printers and sent an invitation for a private view to the man at *The Times*, but each afternoon she declined the offer of drinks or a party and took the train back to the quiet of the suburbs. Each night she kissed the children and went to bed alone. Sometimes she wondered if loneliness had a smell to it like damp. Sylvia offered to set her up on blind dates with wealthy chums, which Juliet declined, knowing she'd never fit in with the county set. Mrs Greene sighed and tutted, as she pored over the marriage notices in the newspaper, muttering to Juliet, 'One day we'll get you in here again, with a nice chap, a decent sort,' convinced despite everything that what Juliet needed was a new and improved husband. Juliet said nothing, clattering plates in the sink to block out her mother's chatter. Taking a lover was appealing, but she did not want a husband, old or new.

A week later the school Christmas holidays began. Ignoring her parents' protests and not informing Charlie or the boys at all, Juliet packed bags for herself and the children and they boarded a train out of London. She sat in the corner of the carriage, pleasantly warm under a pile of coats, paying no attention to Frieda's complaints and only half listening to Leonard's enthusings. After an hour both children fell asleep, lulled by the steady motion. As the grey city gave way to open green, Juliet smiled and allowed herself to close her eyes. Waking at the right stop by sheer good luck, she bundled children and luggage onto an unlit and silent station platform. They climbed into a lone taxi, an ancient and rickety Singer saloon, which at half past eight deposited them at the end of a tree-lined track. The gloom was so thick it pressed against them and stuck in their eyes so that when they blinked they still couldn't see anything but black. Undaunted, Juliet led both children into the darkness, through the bare trees pointing the way with bony fingers and up to the cottage. A yellow light glowed from an upstairs window. Leonard leaned into Juliet, shivering in the cold as she knocked on the door, first rapping politely with gloved knuckles and then hammering with her fist. For several minutes there was no reply. Frieda started to complain. 'No one's even here. We're all going to die.'

Then the door opened and Max stood in the hallway.

'Hello,' said Juliet. 'We were passing. We've come for tea.'

Max asked no questions. He didn't ask why they'd come, merely remarking it was rather late for tea and that they might prefer supper. As he boiled eggs and cut thick slices of bread he did not enquire how long they were intending to stay or wonder what had brought them to his cottage on a winter's night. Juliet was unsure whether he refrained out of politeness or lack of interest. Either way she was glad, as she was not quite sure what to tell him. He did, however, comment on the perm. Almost as soon as they were settled around the kitchen table eating bread and honey, he took a wooden spoon and poked it into the basket of her hair. She squirmed away.

'What are you doing?'

'I wanted to know if it's a wig. It's very strange.'

Frieda grinned. 'It was supposed to be a perm. It doesn't look like that on most women. I bet it would have been okay on me, if I'd been allowed.'

Max nodded and turned to Juliet. 'You can't keep it. Not here. It'll frighten the birds.'

He pointed to the kitchen ceiling where a newly frescoed flock of swifts flitted under the eaves and along the walls. Juliet bristled, irritated that her hair was such a source of general amusement.

'There's nothing I can do. I just have to wait until it grows out. If I fiddle with it, it gets worse.'

Max produced a bottle of sloe gin and slid it across the table to her.

'Have a drink of that. Then dunk your hair in the sink and I'll cut it all off.'

Juliet was about to object but then she shrugged, pouring herself a measure of purple gin. 'I suppose it can only be an improvement.'

'Yes,' agreed both children, perfectly delighted. It was nearly ten but since Juliet hadn't noticed, they said nothing to draw her attention to the fact.

Knocking back the gin, Juliet retreated to the sink and, leaning over the basin, sloshed water over her head. It smelled softly of peat and ran rusty red through her fingers. As she straightened, Max wrapped a faded and ancient tea towel around her shoulders and steered her into one of the kitchen chairs.

'Sit.'

He produced a comb and started to draw it through her hair, warm fingers tickling at the base of her neck. She closed her eyes, soothed by the steady snip-snip of his scissors. His hands smelled faintly of turpentine. The boys had all now switched over to acrylic but there was something familiar and comforting about the scent of oil paint and turps on Max's skin. She fidgeted in her seat, unable to sit easily while he touched her. Wanting a distraction, she fumbled for her handbag and pulled out a pile of postcards from the summer's Picasso exhibition at the Tate, fanning them across the kitchen table.

'I thought you might like these. Since you couldn't see the actual paintings.'

Max paused mid snip to glance at the postcards. 'I did see them.'

'Oh,' said Juliet recoiling, hurt that he'd come up to town for Picasso but not for her.

'Not in London. In Paris during the war.'

'We went to see it eight times,' said Leonard happily.

'Ten,' said Frieda less happily.

'Charlie and the boys couldn't talk about anything else,' said Juliet.

Max smiled. 'Picasso will do that to you. He haunted me for years.'

'Not any more?'

'No. Now there are other ghosts, in different colours.' He stood back from Juliet and peered down at the postcards. 'I think something like that would suit you,' he pointed the scissors at a nude portrait of Picasso's teenage mistress, Marie-Thérèse, her bare breasts round as teacakes and her pale hair cropped into a fetching, asymmetric bob.

Juliet laughed. 'Most salons use pages ripped from magazines.'

Max shrugged and turned her to face him, cocking his head to one side like a sparrow. 'You're like her. Full of sunshine.'

'But wearing more clothes.'

Max shot her a smile and Juliet was suddenly aware of the children. Allowing her eyes to close, she relaxed into the warm drowsiness of the kitchen, listening to the metal rhythm of the scissors. The table was soon scattered with chunks of hair, drifting across the postcards like dandelion docks. At last Max paused, scissors held aloft. 'Well, what do you think, Frieda, Leonard?'

The children turned to stare at Juliet. Leonard grinned and even Frieda smiled.

They'd been staying with Max for a week, although they only saw him at suppertime. The children slept in the sitting-room on a sofa each, tucked up with itchy horse blankets around their ears, watching the camel frieze plod around the cornicing. Juliet slept in Max's bedroom. At first she refused but Max made it clear that he would not be in it, so she need not worry either about propriety (trying not to laugh as he said the word) or displacing him – he rarely slept at night and especially not now.

'Who can sleep when the pink-footed geese and the wild fowl are busy on the marshes?'

Juliet found that she could, perfectly well. His bedroom was sparsely furnished and unlike the rest of the house there were little or no decorative features, only a stylised portrait of a woman in yellowish tones with a long face and heavy-lidded brown eyes. It was an ugly picture and out of place but Max explained that it had been a present from his mother so he'd kept it. The floorboards were plain unvarnished wood, and there was no rug on the floor, just a simple beech bed, large enough for one, and a single chest of drawers in the same style. The room held Max's smell – linseed oil, paint and the leafy scent of the wood. On her first morning casting around, Juliet realised there was no mirror and she was forced to use the tiny one in her face compact to comb her newly bobbed hair and powder her nose. On the second morning she simply didn't bother. She spent the days quite alone, the children vanishing after breakfast to hunt wild things in the woods, reappearing breathless and mud-stained for further meals. Frieda, who in London ignored her brother and seemed to be grouching inexorably towards adolescence, reverted to childishness with relief. When she returned from a morning hunting with her cheeks pancaked in mud ('For camouflage,' explained Leonard) she met Juliet's eye, daring her to say something. Juliet did not, relieved to have a reprieve – however temporary – from snarling adolescence. The children neither wanted nor needed her company and Max she hardly saw at all. Sometimes he crept back mid-morning, slipping upstairs to the bedroom where he would sleep in Juliet's sheets until supper. Other days he didn't return to the house until dark, his clothes coated in leaf litter and snatches of hedge.

One morning Juliet woke to find the house silent. Max had not returned from his nocturnal ramblings while the children had already disappeared into the heart of the wood. She came downstairs in Max's dressing gown, her fingers not reaching the end of his long sleeves. After making tea, she sat in the quiet of the kitchen for an hour, listening to the rustle and knock of the trees. A little later she heard the sudden scuffle of a car engine, followed by silence and footsteps. She waited for the knock at the door but after a few minutes there was nothing. Intrigued, she padded to the hall and opened the front door to find a tall, rather thin man leaving a pair of canvases propped against the wall.

'Hello,' she said and the man jumped, clearly startled to see a woman appear on the porch. 'I'm Juliet. A friend of Max's.'

'Tom. Hopkins. Also a friend of Max,' said the man. He studied her for a moment before reaching out and shaking her hand.

'Is Max here? I've something for him.'

'No, I'm sorry. He's on one of his walks. I'm not sure when he'll be back. Come inside and have some tea. I've made a pot.'

Tom studied her with interest. 'All right. Help me with these.'

Together they carried the canvases into the kitchen. Not waiting for an invitation, Juliet began to unwrap them and laid them on the table. Each painting was a portrait of a young man, one lying in a buttercup field, the other sunbathing on an upturned boat. Both were naked. The brown paper wrapping lay half unfastened around them, and Juliet felt as if she had undressed them a little hastily and publicly, and resisted the urge to the draw the paper back across. She glanced over at Tom.

'These are wonderful. I should probably know you, shouldn't I. Are you terribly famous?'

Tom smiled at the barrage of her enthusiasm. 'No. I am not famous. My stuff's rather fallen out of vogue, I'm afraid.'

'People can be very stupid. We'll have to show them that they're wrong. Do you have a dealer? Can I sell you at my gallery? Well, it's not exactly *my* gallery but I do choose all the artists.'

Tom laughed. 'Don't hang about, do you?'

Juliet shifted from foot to foot, a little embarrassed to remember that she was still in her pyjamas, but also quite determined to have Tom's pictures at Wednesday's if she could. Jim and Charlie might sketch nudes and hold life classes but these portraits were no posed impressions of pink and white Marjories. There was a boldness in Tom's paintings of the boys, and a sadness too, as though the middle-aged painter studied youth and beauty with a wistful eye – his own youth lost and the boys themselves indifferent to his interest. There was a loneliness in them that she understood.

'I'd love to show your paintings at the gallery. Please say yes.'

Tom scratched his nose, and then grinned. 'All right. Why not?' he said. 'I was only going to give these to Max and he probably wouldn't even remember to put them up. There's a bunch of my canvases stashed in his shed.'

Juliet smiled, delighted. 'We should have that tea to celebrate. I think Max has some scones somewhere.'

They sat at the kitchen table eating slightly stale scones and raspberry jam with the two naked boys propped up on the counter, watching.

'How do you know Max?' asked Tom.

'Charlie Fussell introduced us and now I sell his paintings.'

'He's never mentioned you,' said Tom.

'Oh.' Juliet tried not to be hurt. 'And what about you? How long have you known him?'

'Years and years,' said Tom. 'Before the war. And during. We were both war artists. I suggested it to him. He was all set to go to prison as a conscientious objector but I knew his heart wasn't in the thing. He just wanted to paint people not shoot them. I thought that should be encouraged.'

He paused, reaching for another scone, to which he added a wodge of butter as thick as cheese. 'It might have been a mistake though. Perhaps the army or prison would have been better for him. It's worse in a way, to sit and watch and have to paint it all and not be able to do anything. Inertia and watching without looking away do funny things to a man.'

'Yes, I suppose they do,' said Juliet slowly.

She nursed her tea as Tom ate, flicking crumbs from his lap with elegant fingers. Most of the artists she knew had paint under their nails, fingers cracked and yellow from white spirit. Not Tom. His skin was smooth and clean. He smelled of expensive aftershave.

'I'm sure you like Max now,' he said, 'but you should have known him before. This version of him is like a black and white reproduction – only gives you an idea of the original.'

'Don't say that. It's too sad.' But Juliet wondered whether this was the reason she liked Max. There were still days when she felt that George had stolen the original Juliet and left behind a pallid copy.

Tom continued, half to himself. 'Max was quite something then. We were all a little in love with him.'

Juliet flushed and studied her cup, embarrassed that Tom admitted so openly his feelings for Max and that he evidently assumed she and Max were lovers. But then she was wearing his dressing gown.

When Max arrived back at the house a little later, she felt Tom observing them like a twitcher in a hide studying a pair of chiffchaffs, glancing from one to the other trying to determine their relationship. Max showed no embarrassment, tossing down his bundle of coats and paintbox and embracing his friend. 'Stay for supper,' he said.

Tom smiled. 'It's only twelve thirty.'

'Well then, you'll be staying a while. I'm off to nap. Tell Juliet all my bad habits. My murky past.'

'How do you know I haven't already?' asked Tom.

Max slapped Tom's thin shoulders, threw his head back and laughed. He left them alone again in the kitchen, and Juliet felt as if the light had suddenly been turned off. Glancing over at Tom, she caught a tiny sigh and understood that he felt it too.

While Max slept, Juliet spent the rest of the afternoon accompanying Tom through the wood with his sketchpad. He reeled off the names of the trees and even the types of moss and the fat insects scuttling busily up and down the bark. 'It was either become a naturalist or an artist. All the kids are busy with Pop Art. I'm just a simple figurative painter. I suppose that makes me obsolete.'

That evening they all shared a meal of bread and honey with a bit of duck liver and goose fat dripping.

The children were thrilled with the addition to the party, especially when Tom produced a bottle of wine from his car and gave the children a half glass watered down with water from the jug. The two men became loquacious as they reminisced.

The children stayed quiet, hoping that their mother wouldn't object to the wine or remind the men to curb their language. It was always the stories that made Juliet look down at the kitchen table and tuck her hair behind her ear that were the most interesting.

For her part, Juliet decided that in Tom's company Max seemed more like other men, losing the stillness that sometimes unnerved her. After supper, when the children vanished to play, Tom pulled a letter out of his pocket.

'I've something for you. Doubtless you'll say no because you're a fool, but maybe she'll talk some sense into you.'

'Well, let's have it,' said Max, not in the least offended.

'Cunard Lines are refurbishing the *Queen Mary*. It's an attempt to lure passengers away from the shiny new jets and back to the romance of the ocean liner. They want you to create new murals for the First-Class Dining-Room – something whimsical and English to tickle the American traveller's palate. I've spoken to them and they'll give you a pretty free rein and the money's not half bad.'

He handed the envelope to Juliet who opened it, raising an eyebrow at the generous terms.

'Oh, Max, you really should do it,' she said.

To her dismay Bluma Zonderman had been quite correct in her predictions – everyone clamoured for pictures by Jim and Charlie (YOUNG! MODERN! HIP! SEXY!) but no one wanted Max's bird paintings. They might be the most interesting and accomplished in the gallery, but neither critics nor buyers cared.

'If they like the murals, they'll commission you to design patterns for new china, curtains, motifs for carpets, menu cards, napkins – the works,' said Tom.

Max frowned. 'What nonsense.'

Tom turned to Juliet in exasperation. 'I said he's a fool. You talk to him. You know he needs the cash.'

'It might be fun,' said Juliet, leaning towards Max. 'It'll be like adorning the house, only on a grand scale.' She could see that he remained unconvinced and tried another tack. 'The cottage needs a new roof. You said so yourself. It leaks whenever it rains. What's going to happen next winter? You need to look at each stencil for a cocktail menu, every sketch for a mural as a tile for the new roof.'

'And they've promised you a pair of first-class return tickets to New York as well,' added Tom. 'You could take Juliet.'

Max laughed. 'I'm not taking any boats, but Juliet does make a good point about the roof. I'll think about it.'

Unwilling to press him further, Juliet and Tom watched as he pulled on his coat and thick woollen hat. He paused beside the door, ready to disappear for another night spent wild fowling on the marshes and heath. He turned first to Tom.

'Are you coming?'

Tom shook his head. 'No. Time for me to head back to town. Long drive.'

Max nodded and faced Juliet. 'Will you come?' he said softly, looking at her.

Juliet squirmed, not wanting to disappoint Max, not wanting to venture out. There were no curtains on the kitchen windows and outside it was pitch dark and the wind made the trees tap on the glass with thin fingers. She thought of the black wood stretching away to the bare marshes and of walking through the cold and damp and the bang of guns and of

164

getting lost and not finding her way back to the brick cottage. She shook her head.

'No thank you. Not tonight. Perhaps, tomorrow.'

'Tomorrow then,' said Max, disappearing into the darkness and closing the door.

After the men had gone, Juliet, Frieda and Leonard sat beside the hearth playing snap and endless rounds of rummy, all cheating amiably. The smell of the kerosene lamps gave Juliet a headache, so they played by firelight. The wind shrieked down the chimney flue, making it seem as if the fearsome dragon carved into the mantle was roaring, his mouth full of upside-down flames. The three of them wondered separately and silently where Max was on such a night.

Leonard pictured him swinging in a hammock slung from the branches of a great oak tree, a squadron of geese pink as flamingos perching beside him as he drew their portraits one by one.

He watched his mother, wondering why she hadn't gone too. He'd begged repeatedly. *Wild fowling*. It sounded even better than building *sukkah* dens with his grandfather, but Max had informed him that the night marshes were no place for children.

'You'd talk too much. Frighten away the birds.'

'I wouldn't.'

'You're a chatterbox. Couldn't help it.'

'I could. I could so, couldsocouldsocouldso.'

'See? A windbag of noise. Wait till you're twelve.'

Leonard had retired defeated, mystified by his mother and sister.

For her part, Frieda was glad that Max was far away. He wasn't like Philip or Charlie, or anyone. He was the wrong kind of weird.

Juliet fretted that he'd slip down a ravine in the gale (she was almost sure Dorset had ravines) and never be seen again. Distracted from their card game, they went to bed early, Juliet giving the children a medicinal spoon of cherry brandy as she tucked them in. That was Max's only stipulation. He wouldn't have children wandering around at night, 'poking into things', so they must be given brandy to help them sleep. Neither Frieda nor Leonard objected, considering it an infinite improvement on their grandmother's doses of cod-liver oil.

Max did return. But now every night before going out into the dark, he'd ask Juliet the same question, 'Will you come?' and every time Juliet shook her head, saying, 'Maybe tomorrow.' The gallery wouldn't reopen until the New Year and in the meantime she lost count of the days. In the mornings as she meandered among the trees, she felt like the inverse of Samson, her old strength returning with the cutting of her hair. Loneliness ripened into solitude and she stopped waiting for the hours to pass until suppertime with the others. Gradually she realised that she was well on the way to being in love with Max. He didn't rattle away like Charlie or Jim but what he said was measured and interesting. He confided stories about the war and his childhood in the big house and even, if she asked, about the other women he'd painted years ago. Oddly she found she wasn't jealous. She liked the way he listened when she talked, sipping at his whisky and leaning forward in his chair. For the first time in many years she'd spoken about George and the children and how it had been when he had gone, and Max had sat and let her talk without interrupting. When she'd finished, he hadn't said that he was sorry or offered any words of condolence or pity. He'd only poured her a drink, pressing it into her hands, which to her surprise had been shaking. He'd tossed another log onto the fire, then sat back down beside her without speaking. *There is space for me, in your silence*, she'd realised.

On Saturday morning she found an old pair of army boots and, padding them with several pairs of socks, walked for miles. Leaving the now familiar confines of Fippenny Hollow she found her way to the wildness of the heath, where the gorse was studded with yellow flowers and cooled by an icing of frost. In the distance she glimpsed the glister of the sea, cold and black under the low winter sun. The chatter of the boys and their drone of sex, sex, sex seemed far away. Although she couldn't help observing that even out here on the heath the rabbits were busy rutting under the bushes – she suspected for warmth rather than any urgent desire. Returning to the edge of the wood, where the golden scrub of heath gave way to trees, she met Max on his way back and they set out for home together. He hadn't shaved for a few days and the greying stubble lining his chin matched the silver tones of the wood. There was no need for small talk between them and they fell into step in easy silence, the only sound the crackle of frozen fern beneath their boots. The mild dampness had turned to winter cold, and as they reached Fippenny Hollow the morning fog froze in the trees creating a tinsel of hoarfrost throughout the wood. The midday sun struggled to rise above the tops of the beeches and, giving up, slithered back behind the hill. The ropes of rime had lingered into the afternoon without melting, strung across the branches like fine lacework scarves. Juliet felt she had fallen into one of the winter scenes at the National Gallery, a Bruegel perhaps, but when she told Max he shook his head.

'No, it has to be an English painter. Only an Englishman can understand the muted light. This is a quiet beauty all about texture and shadows and clouds. Constable was quite obsessed with clouds, you know. He kept journals talking about nothing at all but the day's clouds.'

'It can't have made for terribly exciting reading,' said Juliet. 'I thought the purpose of journals was to boast about love affairs or to say rude things about your friends.'

'Is that what you write in yours? Lists of your lovers?'

'No,' said Juliet, thinking it would be a disappointingly short list. 'I don't keep one at all. But if I did, I should be awful about everyone just in case, as it would serve them right if they read it.'

Max laughed. 'I had no idea you were so cruel. Listen.'

Juliet could hear no noise except for the birds and the creak of the trees. Daylight was fading into twittering dark and the air cracked with cold. Max glanced up at the sky.

'It's going to snow. Any meteorologist or landscape painter could tell you that from those clouds. You can hear it.'

Juliet looked up at the darkening sky, the belly of the clouds brushed with purple from the sinking sun.

'Will you stay inside tonight then?'

Max laughed. 'No, no. Tonight will be best of all.'

But that night after supper, Max did not turn to Juliet and ask, 'Will you come?'

At first, she thought he had. The question was as familiar as the wolf's line in a fairy story. But he had not asked. He merely stood, drew on his coat and left.

After he had gone she glanced at the window where the ledge was coated with snow, flakes clinging to the glass. Later as she played cards with the children by the fire, Juliet could not concentrate and Leonard and Frieda delighted in cheating even more than usual.

A bluebird popped out of a remade cuckoo clock whistling midnight and she hustled the children into bed, giving them their nightly dose of cherry brandy. Before going upstairs, she slipped into the kitchen for a glass of water. A sketch book rested on the table beside a bundle of spare watercolour brushes. It might have been something to go out into the dark and watch him paint with snow. She lingered beside the window, her reflection in the glass catching her eye, and then she realised it wasn't her face. It was Max.

She grabbed her coat and a bundle of scarves and laced her boots with trembling fingers, worried that by the time she went out he would have disappeared. She closed the door softly, trying not to disturb the children, trying not to think of them waking in the night and finding her gone. Max stood in the shadow of a hulking oak, both of them dusted with frost. He smiled when he saw her.

'You waited for me,' said Juliet.

He shrugged. 'I knew you'd come tonight.' He kicked snow from his boots. 'We'll meet the others on the marshes.'

'What others?'

'The guns. I don't shoot. I paint.' He shrugged out of a second coat, slung round his shoulders. 'I brought you this. That flimsy thing's no good.'

He passed her an ancient RAF flying jacket, the leather worn and cracked but the sheepskin lining warm from his body. He set off at a march through the wood, Juliet trotting beside him to keep up. It had stopped snowing and only a thin layer coated the woodland floor, but as the trees gave way to open heath, the land stretched away white under the sky. The brightness of the snow gave the night a weird daylight glow. The ground was frozen and rang out under the nails of Juliet's boots. Shivering, she wished she'd thought to grab a hat, but seeing her discomfort, Max placed his own worn deerstalker on her head. It smelled gently of sweat and damp wool.

'Keep up. We've a way to go.'

They walked for hours, or so it seemed to Juliet. The heath sloped down and they edged closer to the black expanse of sea, silent at a distance. As they clambered lower, the earth thawed in patches and became softer underfoot. Coarse blades of marram grass poked through the snow, black on white. Growing tired, Juliet started to slide, Max reaching out to steady her elbow.

'We're nearly there. See that stream? In the curve of the bend there are four guns.'

Juliet peered into the darkness and, as they came closer, saw the metallic shine of a gun barrel against the snow. Four men swaddled in overcoats and hats huddled in the bow of the stream, their backs concealed by a thick sprouting of grass. One of them raised a hand in greeting as Max and Juliet moved in to crouch beside them.

'Anything?'

'Not yet. We've heard them out on the marshes.'

Taking Juliet's hand, Max drew her down to lie in the hide alongside the others. 'Try not to get shot,' he muttered.

Four faces peered at her and four hats were lifted. Juliet wriggled uncomfortably, the mud frozen hard and cold beneath her. Within her boots her toes were numb and when she tried to wiggle them, she couldn't tell whether they moved or not. It was so cold and bright that the light itself seemed frozen solid, but inside her flying jacket she was snug. Squeezed between the men were three Labradors, squashed together like brown sausages in a pan, steam rising from panting mouths. There was no wind and the stillness solidified and lengthened. Beside her, she felt the others listening, listening. The dogs sniffed at the air, tails thumping in ragged time. Time passed; how much Juliet did not know. She wasn't wearing her watch and couldn't read the drift of the stars. She was awake but her thoughts followed the roaming of the clouds, smooth and dark. Licking her lips, she tasted pine and salt.

'The geese like the calm,' whispered Max. 'Soon. Soon.'

Then the night is full of wings. The hills echo with cries, and above the shrill of the curlews and the hard shriek of the mallards comes the melancholy call of the barnacle geese. The men raise their guns in a single movement, and Juliet slaps her hand to her mouth to stop from screaming out. Why shoot? Why shoot? In the ditch beside her, Max pulls his pad and brush from his pocket and dipping it in the stream he starts to paint. The cries go on and on, calling. Calling. Strange and unearthly they raise the hackles along the back of Juliet's neck. They sound more like the baying of hounds than birds. It's hours still until dawn but the light reflected from the snow catches the white of their bellies and for a moment Juliet wonders if they are geese at all but ice with wings. They rush closer, away from the distant tide edge, seeming to graze the gorse and scrub as they swoop low. Then they are here. The sky overhead is a hurry of wings and Juliet reaches up with cool fingertips. The bang and crack of guns. Pellets fly heavenwards and rain back to earth, dimpling the snow. A goose falls, broken, her throat pierced and silent. Then another. Goose after goose falls from the sky and Juliet stops trying not to shout out but it is too late or else the geese have no need of her. The pack turns for the shore, flying back to the sea and the safety of the wash, leaving their fallen littering the snow. The guns clamber to their feet and, whistling low for the dogs, start to gather up the carcasses. Max and Juliet remain, Max's brush flashes across the paper, dipped here in the stream and here in snow. She's never seen anyone paint so fast and realises that she's watching a war painter recording the aftermath of cold siege and battle. His

*cheeks are ruddy and his forehead slick with sweat and he
looks sloppy with joy.*

Leonard was not asleep. He heard Juliet leave, heard the whisper of voices in the wood. The house creaked in the dark. All houses did this. Grandma and Grandpa's house was particularly loud and it used to frighten him when he was small and woke in the night, but Granny had soothed him, saying that the house had old bones like her and deserved sympathy. But no house made as much noise as this one. It groaned and cracked like Kenneth Ibbotson snapping his knuckles in maths lessons. On windy nights Leonard didn't mind as much, as it made sense, but in the stillness the snaps and creaks seemed louder. It's because of all the wood, he told himself. He'd done that in science. Something to do with heat and expansion and contraction but he wondered in the dark if that was just something we told ourselves. He looked to Frieda who was fast asleep and considered waking her, but decided that Frieda rudely awoken was more terrifying than the wakeful house. He slid out of bed and padded towards the kitchen. That's what I'll do, he decided. I'll have another sleeping draught. Standing up on a chair, he reached down the bottle of cherry brandy and measured himself out a good-sized spoonful. Afterwards he still wasn't sleepy enough so he climbed the stairs, taking the brandy bottle just in case. He and Frieda hadn't been allowed into Max's room and a thrill buzzed through Leonard, though it might have been the brandy starting to take effect. The room was perfectly ordinary. It smelled odd. There was his mother's Yardley perfume mingling with something less familiar, but overall the room was like any other and Leonard couldn't think why he and Frieda had been barred from exploring. On the wall was a painting of an ugly woman with dark eyes. Leonard felt a little dizzy from the brandy and decided he hated the portrait. He hated all portraits. They were nothing but trouble. He grinned – he had the perfect solution, he'd slosh brandy on it and light a match and set fire to it like the flaming Christmas puddings that the regular kids had been drawing in art class. Unscrewing the cap, he chucked liquid up at the picture. Some hit; most dribbled down the wall. He had another go but there wasn't much left in the bottle. He knocked the painting off the wall and dropped it in the grate. There was a box of matches on the dresser and Leonard lit one and watched it trickle blue brandy flames across the surface of the picture. He waited for a moment and then chucked in the rest of the box for good measure and the flames turned from blue to orange. He settled on the floor to watch and realised his head felt very woozy. The woman in the grate stared back at him, her face aglow from the matches, her hair starting to burn red.

Juliet and Max returned to the cottage shortly before dawn. Juliet eased open the kitchen door and snuck through the house in stockinged feet to check on the children. They were fast asleep, Leonard snoring softly, and Juliet smiled, relieved she hadn't been caught. It filled her with exhilaration. Perhaps she was wrong; perhaps she could do anything and no one was looking. She was so tired she was drunk with it. Max caught her arm and pulled her back into the hallway, gently closing the sitting-room door. He didn't say a word but led her up the stairs to the bedroom they'd been sharing, though until now not at the same time. He started to undress, quickly and unselfconsciously, then climbed naked into the narrow bed.

'Get in.'

Juliet stood in the middle of the floor, fully dressed, unable to move.

'Isn't it why you came?'

Still she hesitated. Then she laughed.

'I suppose I did.'

She'd been trying not to think about what made her run away, and now she understood. Max propped himself up onto a thin arm. Dawn was firing through the window and he looked tired in the light. She could make out the bones beneath his skin and could imagine how he'd look when he was an old man.

'Why did you come here?' he asked again.

'To sleep with you.'

She started to slide out of her jersey and unbutton her blouse; her fingers were cold and she struggled with the buttons. 'It's been a long time since,' she reached for a euphemism and then decided that they were all quite ridiculous. It was time she said his name aloud. 'It's been a long time since George.'

'How long?'

'Eight years.'

She searched his face for shock or amusement but found none.

'Come on. You've waited long enough. Though, that's quite a pressure to put on a chap.'

Juliet tried to smile but it contorted on her face. 'I'm worried. I'm worried that I've grown frigid. It can happen, you know. After years and years.'

Still Max didn't laugh. 'Well, let's find out. Then at least you'll know.'

She stepped out of her trousers and then her knickers until she was standing quite naked on the wooden floor. It was chilly and prickles of gooseflesh rippled up and down her limbs. Max was looking at her with that painter's look, head to one side, studying the lines of her flesh and then she realised he wasn't any more. His expression was no longer scientific; instead he had the impatient look of a man who wanted to sleep with her.

He threw back the eiderdown and she climbed in beside him. She tried to say, 'I'm afraid I'm rather out of practice,' but found that he was kissing her and she couldn't. She tried not to think. Tried not to think that this act took her further away than ever from that other, former life. Tried only to feel the warmth of his hands on her skin, the roughness of those painter's fingers. She hadn't been to the *mikvah,* not for years, and she supposed one didn't purify one's body for an illicit lover, but Max's insistent kisses were moving down her belly and she was finding it hard to think of anything else. I must not cry out, she said, I must not.

Afterwards Max turned to her and grinned, a frank boyish grin.

'So not frigid,' he said.

'No. Not,' agreed Juliet.

They lay side by side not touching and Juliet decided that this intimacy was what she had missed most of all. She was relieved that the anxiety of the first time together was over and now they could fall into the happy discovery of regular lovers. Her thighs were damp and she could feel him leaking out of her – something else she'd forgotten – and she supposed she was being very stupid and taking a terrible risk. But at that moment she was fat with contentment and couldn't bring herself to worry. If it happened they could come and live in the woods. She laughed at the ridiculousness of the idea. Already as the sweat on her body cooled she was wondering about returning to the city.

'Look,' said Max, pointing to the fireplace.

A painting was lodged in the grate, the frame singed and twisted. Juliet slipped out of bed and padded across, shaking it loose. She pulled it free and saw that the woman's face was burned, her features smeared and blackened, obliterated by smoke.

'How the devil did it get there?' asked Max.

They sat around the kitchen table eating breakfast at lunchtime.

'Did one of you set fire to the picture in Max's room?' asked Juliet, her voice low and serious.

Leonard looked up stricken, suddenly unable to eat his boiled egg.

Frieda stared at her brother. 'Well, I didn't do anything,' she snapped.

'It was me,' said Leonard, miserably. He'd known since he'd woken up that morning that confession was inevitable.

'Why, darling?' asked Juliet. 'I can't understand it.'

Leonard screwed up his face and prodded his egg. He didn't know how to explain; wasn't sure if he wanted to. His hatred for the picture had made sense in the dark.

'It was ugly,' he said.

'That's no excuse,' said Max, drawing his chair close. 'If you don't like a picture, you should paint something better. You don't destroy art, Leonard. Especially portraits. The mystics believed that portraits and photographs contain a piece of the sitter's soul. They're dangerous things, portraits, and poorly painted or not, you must be careful with them.'

'Am I going to be punished?' asked Leonard, gloomily, looking at his mother.

'Are you sorry?' she asked.

'Yes.'

'Will you ever do it again?' asked Max.

Leonard shook his head.

'Then, no. No punishment,' said Max with a glance at Juliet.

Leonard sat at the table feeling guilt like a little fish nibble at his guts, but he was confident of two things. First, that a portrait that badly painted did not contain even the merest sliver of soul, and second, that one day he was going to paint much, much better pictures.

They took the train back to London three days later. Juliet did not sleep but smiled from Dorchester to Waterloo. Max waved them off on the platform, kissing Juliet an awkward goodbye in front of the children. Frieda watched them critically, considering that they looked much less dashing than the couples at the pictures. Juliet didn't even kick up her heels – although Frieda conceded that that might be because Juliet was holding a heavy suitcase and Max wasn't a terribly good kisser. He didn't look like the kind of man who'd be any good. Too old.

'Is Max your boyfriend?' asked Frieda, later on the train.

'I suppose so,' said Juliet and smiled again. Boyfriend. The word was so much simpler than husband.

'And you don't want us to tell Grandma,' said Leonard.

'No,' agreed Juliet, avoiding his eye. 'Don't tell Grandma.'

Juliet was relieved when her period arrived, punctual as the 227 bus, but deciding that it was silly to take more risks she visited the doctor. She intended to sleep with Max again, preferably soon. If only she could persuade him to come up to town. Dorset was a long way to go for – Juliet smiled – for sex. The doctor's surgery was filled with fretting babies and tired, grey-looking mothers. She'd tried to get an evening appointment but was told by the practice secretary that these were reserved exclusively for 'the chaps, since they have to go work during the day, poor things'. Juliet attempted to explain that she too had to work but she could hear the indulgent smile through the receiver, 'Oh, I'm sure your boss will give you time off, tell him it's a lady problem.' Sitting in the waiting room among the rows of nursing mothers, Juliet sensed them staring at her. She didn't care. Let them look. She could hear their silent chatter and understood what they'd murmur to one another the moment she left, '*Much too old for a career girl and look at that lipstick! No wonder she's not wearing a wedding ring.*' For the first time in fourteen years, Juliet had taken the ring off, sliding it to the back of her sock drawer.

'Mrs Montague.'

Juliet stalked across the lino and along the corridor, smelling of antiseptic and bleach and head-lice shampoo where she'd been countless times with both children for fevers and sprains and jabs and a confetti of childhood rashes. She couldn't remember the last time she'd been for herself. She stood outside Dr Ruben's office, poised to knock, more anxious than she liked to admit.

As she opened the door Dr Ruben smiled, his face glowing with genuine pleasure at seeing her.

'Hello, hello, my dear. It's been too long. Though, of course, we never wish to see patients. I missed you at our Hanukkah party. And you missed quite a piece of brisket.'

Dr Ruben had been the family physician since before the days of the NHS, the Greene family migrating with him from private practice to the new health service. Now, faced with his benevolent smile and those familiar half-moon spectacles, Juliet was aware that her palms were beginning to sweat. She wished that she'd made the appointment with some stranger at the practice but it was too late now. She'd taken the morning off work and Juliet Montague was no coward.

'I'd like to go on the pill.'

Dr Ruben's face lit up like a menorah.

'Mr Montague is back! *Mazel tov!* I had not heard. Mrs Ruben tells me nothing or perhaps she is sworn to secrecy and I'm doing her great disservice.'

Juliet said nothing for a minute, bewildered that this good doctor, this kind man, could be so delighted at a profligate husband's return. This was the same Dr Ruben who'd coaxed Juliet to rest and ignore the silly whispers and sly smiles and who'd called by on his way home every night for a week when Leonard developed a fear of going to sleep because of nasty dreams. '*No prescription needed but a bedtime story. Just needs to hear a man's voice.*' Juliet saw that his fingers itched to pick up the telephone and call his wife and talk over the splendid news.

'My husband has not returned.'

Dr Ruben frowned and pushed his spectacles further up his nose. The joy ebbed away from his face.

'But you wish to go on the new pill?'

'Yes.'

'But it is for married women only.'

'I am married.'

'But your husband has not returned.'

'No.'

Juliet sighed, sensing that this conversation could continue in circles for some time to come.

'Dr Ruben, I wish to take the pill. I am a married woman so I understand that you can prescribe it for me.'

'Well, yes, but . . .'

'The man I am sleeping with is not my husband. I've waited eight years. I think that's quite long enough. But I would very much like not to get pregnant.'

Dr Ruben stared at her, his happiness quite extinguished. Juliet remained silent. She would not beg and she worried that if she said very much more, he might refuse. Defeated, he reached for a pen.

She hesitated, hand poised on the door handle. 'Dr Ruben?'

He looked up, alarmed at the prospect of further unsavoury revelations.

'You won't mention my coming here to anyone – not to Mrs Ruben, not to my mother?'

He bristled. 'I took an oath.'

Juliet nodded, relieved just the same that she'd asked.

Juliet and Mr Greene washed up together after dinner. It was hot in the small kitchen, the windows fogged with condensation. As Juliet plunged a grease-slicked pan into scalding water, Mr Greene cleared his throat.

'Mrs Levi made some rather unnecessary remarks to your mother while she was queuing for chicken livers.' He wiped steam from his lenses. 'And she wasn't asked to bake her famous cinnamon *rugelach* for *kiddish* at Rosh Hashanah this year. She was very upset.'

Juliet said nothing and scrubbed the pan a little harder.

'She brought them anyway, mind, but I couldn't help noticing that in the end most of them were left, though last year Mr and Mrs Nature were forced to split the last one.'

Juliet sighed and reached for the pile of plates. She knew her parents' telephone didn't ring quite as often, and somehow her mother's friends found they were often busy when Mrs Greene suggested they bring their grandchildren round to play with Frieda and Leonard. Mr Greene rhythmically stacked the clean dishes. He did not utter an accusation but they both knew without it being said that Juliet's behaviour was responsible for the slow withdrawing of the neighbours. When George vanished, the good people of Mulberry Avenue had wondered how much of it had been Juliet's fault but they were not without sympathy. For years they had noted how she'd put a brave face on things and as they nibbled on *latkes* and salt-beef sandwiches, they had told one another it was marvellous how she struggled on. Now something had changed. Mrs Harris and her friends had noticed Juliet wasn't getting along quietly any more. There were rumours that she'd taken a boyfriend ('At her age, quite ridiculous!') and that the children went with her on her sordid liaisons in Dorset ('Who knew the West Country was such a bed of licentiousness and vice?'). It was common knowledge that she cavorted with artists up in town and she never went to *shul* any more, even on high holy days.

Juliet glanced at her father. He hadn't shaved with his customary precision and his heavy-rimmed spectacles couldn't hide the purple shadows beneath his eyes. He looked old. The guilt wriggled inside her.

'Dad, would it be better for you and Mum if the children and I moved away?'

Mr Greene lowered his tea towel in horror, his face pale. 'Don't take my grandchildren. We can manage a few queer looks but we can't manage without the three of you. I shouldn't have said anything.'

Juliet let the guilt lodge inside, stick in her chest. She thought that was the end of the conversation but when they came through to the lounge Mrs Greene sent the children upstairs to play, though she was usually very particular about them all sitting together in the living room making polite conversation. When Mr Greene poured Juliet a sherry, she knew it was very bad. Her first thought was that Dr Ruben had broken his promise, and her second was that her parents were going to try to persuade her to give up the gallery.

'Tell her, Davey, she's gone quite white,' said Mrs Greene.

Mr Greene cleared his throat. 'It's about George. Your husband George,' he added, as though Juliet might think he was discussing some other George.

Juliet felt dizzy. It was very hot in the front room. Mrs Greene liked to turn up the gas heater to a rage and the smell and heat made Juliet feel a little sick.

'Can I open a window?' she asked, getting to her feet.

'You'll let out all that nice, expensive heat,' objected Mrs Greene.

Juliet wanted to say that that was the general idea, but weakening she sat back down. She licked her dry lips.

'So, George?' she asked as casually as she could.

'Yes,' Mr Greene cleared his throat and glanced at his wife, reaching for her plump, floral-patterned knee. 'The thing is, we've found him.'

CATALOGUE ITEM 9
Sun-seeker on Venice Beach,
Tibor Jankay, Oil on Canvas, 30 x 45in, 1961

'TRAVEL TO AMERICA with a man, not your husband?'
whispered Mrs Greene, as though alarmed she might be
overheard even in the privacy of her own front room.

'Well, travelling to America with my husband would be
tricky,' said Juliet, frustration making her irritable.

'What will people say?' asked Mrs Greene, dabbing her
eyes.

'Nothing, if you don't tell them.'

Mr Greene cleared his throat and held up his hand for
peace. 'I thought we could send a letter. You shouldn't go
yourself and your mother's right, it's not—' he cleared his
throat, hunting for the right word, 'it's not *decent* to go with
your man-friend. We can send one of your uncles. Ed's always
wanted to visit America. I'll pay for his ticket.'

Juliet shook her head. 'No, Dad. I have to go. George would
never answer any letter. And if he is there, it has to be me who
finds him.'

Mrs Greene clucked in indignation, not ready to concede
defeat so easily.

'But what about the children? You can't have them with
you, living in sin on board a boat like that.'

Juliet bit her lip, unsure if her mother was more indignant
about the sin part or the fact it was on a boat. Before Juliet's
wedding, Mrs Greene had given her a cryptic warning about

the dangers of married love in unusual places. Juliet supposed the warning held for unmarried love too.

'We'll all have different cabins. The children like Max. It'll be an adventure.'

She did not confide to her mother that they stayed with Max when they visited him, allowing Mrs Greene to assume that they borrowed a cottage as they had on their first trip. Mr Greene frowned and removed his spectacles to clean them on his trousers with exactly the same gesture as Leonard. He didn't look angry, only sad, and this disturbed Juliet more than her mother's pink-ruffled fury. She picked at a mark on her skirt. There was no other choice. The morning after she found out about George, she'd taken a train to Dorset and arrived on Max's doorstep with two British Rail sandwiches and a flask of coffee and informed him that he must take the Cunard Lines job. She marched him to the village and waited inside the booth while he made the telephone call to accept the position and request that the pair of first-class tickets to New York be exchanged for four berths in tourist class. To her surprise and relief, Max had not objected. As soon as she had explained about George, he'd only nodded once and said, 'Of course you must go to America.'

The journey was arranged for the summer holidays. Juliet would close the gallery for August and reopen in September. Juliet, Max and the children would spend a whole month in America. But Mr and Mrs Greene had remained so appalled that they refused to come to Southampton to wave them off. Juliet suspected that her mother was afraid of coming face to face with Max. Knowing her daughter had a *goyishe* lover was one thing, meeting him quite another.

Nonetheless, when the day of their departure arrived, Juliet stood on the deck of the ship with Leonard and Frieda, all three studying the shore just in case Grandma and Grandpa appeared at the last minute. When they didn't, Juliet was forced to shrug and say lightly, 'It's a long way for them to come. They'll miss you all the same.'

Three days later they were already more than halfway to New York. Juliet, alone on the upper deck of tourist class, watched the sea green and grey under the clouds, the sun sneaking up from behind the curve of the earth. At this hour only the crew were up. Above, on the first-class deck, waiters in white scuttled to and fro, shaking out parasols and placing cushions on deckchairs – she shivered at the thought, it was much too cold for sunbathing. It was nearly six, or was it only five? The clocks altered every day and she was already starting to lose track of time. She drew her cardigan around her shoulders and leaned out over the rail.

Reaching into her skirt pocket, she retrieved the scrap of newspaper. The flimsy paper stock was starting to disintegrate along the creases where she had folded and re-folded it. It was written entirely in Yiddish save for the words *THE JEWISH DAILY FORWARD* printed in fat capital letters at the top of the page. Mr Greene had translated the relevant parts into English, inscribing them in neat pencil between the lines of newsprint. On the facing page there was a rogue's line-up containing grainy photographs of twenty men. Several had splendid moustaches caterpillaring across their top lips and there were one or two bushy orthodox beards. Some of the men smiled at the camera, others frowned, but none looked guilty or sheepish – these were all photographs taken before the crime. Above the faces Mr Greene had translated the headline: '*A Gallery of Vanished Husbands*'.

The picture of George Montague was halfway down the page. He beamed out at Juliet, as though delighted to have his picture in the paper. She couldn't remember when it had been taken or what had provoked that smile. It was odd to think of all the small things that she must have forgotten. A missing husband was a lot like a dead one, but without the guilt when one started to forget him. Beneath the picture of George was a puzzle of Yiddish, but Mr Greene had provided an English translation.

On 8 April 1952 George Montague deserted his wife and their two infant children, Leonard and Frieda. His wife has not heard from him since. Mr Montague is believed to have come to America. He was thirty-one years old when he vanished. His wife asks that either he come home or issue a divorce through the nearest rabbi for the sake of his fatherless children. Anyone who knows of Mr Montague's address should contact Mr G. Jones via box no. 8674 Brooklyn, NY.

Juliet always felt peculiar reading this. Her family had been reduced to its merest facts like an over-boiled stock, and her own voice replaced with the words of the mysterious Mr G. Jones (private detective). She had no name, only 'his wife', and she asked questions in print that she had never asked in life. She supposed that Leonard and Frieda were 'fatherless children' but somehow that made her think of orphans out of Dickens and it didn't seem to have much to do with the scowling Frieda cooped up in her bedroom with the record player filched from the front room or Leonard dropping Meccano around the house. They certainly weren't infants. But when pressed, her father explained that it was a description aimed at stirring the heart, since there was always a hope George himself might read the advertisement. And when it came to cultivating guilt, Juliet had to concede that her parents were maestros.

It was odd to see George surrounded by so many strangers, but by now he was a stranger too. She hadn't looked at a picture of him for years. Soon after he'd gone she'd scissored him out of all of their photographs, unable to bear him smiling at her as though nothing had happened. She knew that Leonard had hunted through her closet and trinket boxes searching for him. Perhaps Frieda had too, but was better at tidying up properly afterwards.

Juliet glanced down at the newspaper. Beside the photograph of George someone – not her father – had written in fat red felt pen: *George Molnár. Gorgeous George's Glasses, Culver City, CA.* There was nothing else. No clue as to the identity of the writer. All Mr Greene could tell Juliet was that an envelope had arrived at Gerald Jones's Brooklyn mailbox with the torn-out page inside, this new information scribbled across it. There was no accompanying note, no request for a cash reward or offer of further details.

She slid the torn page back into her skirt pocket. It was time to find him. She wondered what it would be like to finally be free. No longer an *aguna* but a divorcée. It sounded glamorous – the word was swaddled in fur coats and diamonds. Juliet smiled. There mightn't be any diamonds for her but there might be her portrait, although she expected that George had sold it years ago. She felt a pang of anger and sadness – she longed to recover that piece of herself.

Sometimes at night lying in the dark beside Max she could feel the tug of the invisible chain tying her to George. He made her not quite respectable. While Juliet no longer had any interest in respectability, she wanted to select the method of her own notoriety. She knew that once she was divorced, every Friday night she would have to put up with her mother inviting round a sausage string of possible suitors – all equally nice and equally dull. Mrs Greene wouldn't relax until she was safely married again. Juliet smiled to herself, wondering if it had ever crossed Mrs Greene's mind that once she was divorced she might marry Max. Not that she was planning on marrying anyone; not even him. She was tired of being someone's wife. The ship slapped against the tide, the water cracking along the hull. Light brushed the horizon, the ocean rushing endlessly past on every side.

'George Montague, I'm coming to find you,' she called out into the dawn. From the bow of the ship a tern slipped into the air, skimming above the surface of the waves for a moment before soaring into the morning air on vast white wings.

That afternoon the sea turned rough, white-topped waves rushing the side of the ship which tipped to and fro like a gin-addled grandmother in her rocking chair. The queasiness grew in Juliet's stomach and finding Max stretched out in their cabin and the small room reeking of cheap whisky, she sought refuge on one of the children's bunks. It was quiet in their tiny cabin – Leonard and Frieda, blissfully untroubled by seasickness, had ventured out to search for entertainment in the tourist-class lounge. Lying on Leonard's bunk, Juliet drew the curtain across the porthole, blocking out the tossing horizon. She fell asleep for several hours and when she finally woke it was dark and the sea was calm.

'We tried not to wake you up,' said Leonard.

'And you've been asleep for ages,' said Frieda.

'I won a dollar at bingo. Look,' said Leonard, holding up a green note. 'I'm going to spend it all on a hamburger dinner.'

'Still think you cheated.'

'Did not.'

Juliet sat up, forgetting she was lying on the lower bunk bed, and cracked her head. As she rubbed a burgeoning lump on her forehead, she saw that both children were sitting cross-legged on the tiny patch of floor beside the sink. She looked at their faces pale in the gloom, pupils fat with watching. Mr and Mrs Greene had been adamant that the reason for the trip be kept hidden. *Whatever you do, you mustn't tell the children why it is you are really going, Juliet. Tell them anything you please. That it's the holiday of a lifetime. But they don't need to know anything more about the whole nasty business. They've forgotten him and they don't need it all stirred about again.*

Her head throbbed.

'Pass me a glass of water, love,' she said to Frieda.

Frieda emptied out a tooth mug and carried it to Juliet who sipped the cool water with relief. It tasted faintly of peppermint. She sighed. She was so tired of keeping secrets. Reaching into her pocket, she felt the familiar rustle of the newspaper.

'Come on, let's freshen up and go up for dinner.'

Retreating to her cabin, Juliet combed her hair and splashed water on her face, before perching on the edge of Max's bed. She did not ask whether he was joining them – he had not ventured into the dining-room since their first night on board. He smiled at her through half-closed eyes.

'I'm sorry. I'm not very good at this.'

'No,' agreed Juliet.

'I'd forgotten how much I hate being at sea.'

Juliet shrugged. She was hungry and she could tell from the stink and the slurring that Max was already drunk. None of the men in her family drank very much – a glass of kosher wine on Friday, a drop of schnapps to mark a holiday – and she found Max's sporadic bouts of drinking discomforting. While a bout lasted, it kept her at a distance, and she understood that even if there hadn't been a George, an ordinary life of easy companionship would never have been possible with Max. She tried not to mind.

Sprawled on the leaf-stencilled eiderdown, he made her think of Antaeus, the demon-god whose strength was tied to the flesh of the earth. Held aloft by Hercules and separated from the soil, he lost his strength. Max's soul was in the woods of Fippenny Hollow and unable to smell the leaf litter or the summer rot of the woodland floor, he pined and withered. The sea air thinned him. Yesterday she'd rummaged in his spongebag looking for some more toothpaste, but instead of toiletries she'd found a rustle of drying leaves – oak, ash, beech and a clump of larch needles instead of the more conventional sewing kit.

In the newly redecorated tourist-class dining-room, Juliet and the children sat at communal tables beneath one of Max's murals. Only if she looked very closely could she see that the cricketers in their whites had the faces of British birds – owls batted against chaffinches and a blue tit bowled. The designs were a riot of whimsy, a folklore collection of a rural England that never quite was. She thought it slightly strange to be away at sea on a floating celebration of earthiness – beneath the dining-room banister March hares cavorted under harvest moons and sly Jack-in-the-Greens peered out from oak trees as orchards dropped fruit onto village greens and thatched cottages.

Waiters swept to and fro serving jellied ham in aspic. The tinned peas suspended in the translucent gelatine glistened like algae in ice. Only Leonard looked thrilled, declaring he'd never had a more disgusting meal. Juliet yearned for dry land and a soft-boiled egg. Two days left until they reached New York. Max would be better once he was ashore. She tried not to think about the fact that he couldn't bear London. America would be different, she was sure of it.

After dinner, when the children were in bed, Juliet put on her coat and went up on deck. It was cold, the wind humming in chords through the ship's wires, and most of the passengers had disappeared below to smoke in the warmth of the lounge.

Juliet shivered and huddled on a deckchair, watching the black water foam in the dark. She checked her watch – nearly eleven. She smelled Max's pipe before she saw him.

'Hello. I'm over here,' she called.

He came towards her staggering slightly into the rails, then pausing and forcing himself to walk straight with the exaggerated step of a drunkard.

'Damn choppy sea.'

'It's nothing to do with the sea. It's perfectly calm tonight.'

He wasn't wearing a jacket, alcohol making him oblivious to the cold. He sat down beside her on the deckchair with a thump, knocking tobacco out of his pipe and onto the floor where it glowed red.

'Did I tell you about my last trip to sea?'

'No. I don't think so.'

Max took out his pouch of tobacco and started to re-pack his pipe with clumsy fingers, spraying half the leaves over his trousers.

'It ended in a shipwreck. Did I tell you that?'

Juliet shook her head and turned to look at him, his face white in the dark.

'It was during the war. From Cairo I'd been sent to Cape Town and then ordered back to England. I was pleased to be going home. I'd stashed in my cabin some twenty sketchbooks and countless watercolours – soldiers sleeping in the desert, field captains, mules outside the citadel, drawings of veiled women – you know the sort of thing.'

Juliet nodded even though she'd never glimpsed any such pictures by Max.

'And I'd been doing a neat line in portraits of soldiers – dozens of them asked me to whip up a quick picture for their wife or sweetheart. Some of these chaps had been away for years and they were getting jittery – suppose their wives forgot all about them? We all heard stories about the Yanks. A nice heroic picture would jolt the missus into a bit of fondness, or make her kick out her Yank for a night or two, or so they hoped.'

He finished stuffing his pipe and produced a box of matches but his hands were shaking too much to light it. Juliet took them from him, feeling the ice cold of his skin, and struck a match. He sucked on the pipe stem in silence for a minute, the smoke mingling with steam from their breath.

'What was the name of the ship?' asked Juliet.

'The *Laconia*.'

'I think I've heard of it.'

'Very possibly. It was one of the more famous disasters. We were somewhere in the South Atlantic when the torpedo got us. It was early on one evening and I was just having a drink before dinner. The ship shuddered, groaning the way a man does when he's been shot, and then all the glass along the bar shattered, broken bottles hailing down on us. I don't remember being frightened but I do remember worrying about the pictures in my cabin. I'd promised to post those portraits on to the chaps' wives when I reached Blighty. And,' he paused, a little embarrassed, 'I'd bought myself a rather expensive watch in Cape Town. Seemed a pity for it to go down with the ship. Here, give me a bit of that coat will you?'

Juliet sighed and took off her coat, wrapping it across both their legs, blanket style. Max shuffled in closer.

'In my cabin I stuffed my jacket with the portraits. Watercolours mostly. The odd pencil drawing. Anyway, when I got back up on deck ropes were dangling down the sides and the crew was trying to get the few women and children into lifeboats, but the ship was tilting at a god-awful angle. More than one soul was tipped straight into the drink. I didn't linger long enough to see if they were fished out again. If you ever wondered whether I was a hero, the answer is quite simple – I'm not.'

'I can't say that your heroism is really something I've thought about,' said Juliet, keeping her voice light.

Max shrugged. 'No, perhaps not. But most women like to believe their boyfriend has heroic potential, even if it is rather deeply buried. I was only keen to remain alive. It didn't seem likely but I was pretty determined to give it my best shot. I didn't much fancy climbing down a rope into a boat myself, I can tell you, but there wasn't much alternative. I burned my hands until they bled but I landed feet first into a lifeboat. When it was full, the seamen did their best to cover the boat with a scrap of tarpaulin. Underneath it stank worse than a rotting deer carcass because some green member of the crew soiled himself.'

From the first-class deck drifted the sounds of the band cranking out last decade's hits – Dean Martin drifted into a rendition of Bing Crosby. The ship rocked to and fro, cradled in the waves. The sea was calm, only the regular tilt of the tide slapped against the sides. Juliet tried to picture the *Laconia* in the distance, hull blazing.

'We sat in that little boat for four days. Grovelling under the tarpaulin for shelter. Now and then we saw the submarine. After two days we ran out of food and after three we ran out of water. All I had was my watch and the portraits stuffed into my jacket.'

'But you survived.'

'On the fifth day a boat appeared on the horizon and sailed right for us. The crew prayed it was an Allied ship. It wasn't.'

'What happened? Did they leave you?'

'No. The boat was Vichy French and the crew none too friendly, but at least they pulled us out of the water. I was the last to get out of the lifeboat. Nothing to do with gallantry – I was too tired to move. It was hot and we all had terrible sunburn. I lay under my jacket, trying to shield my hands and face – not that it worked. Look, you can still see scars from the blisters.'

Max leaned forward for Juliet to inspect a shiny mark above his lip.

'But when I was safely aboard the Vichy ship, I realised that I'd left my wretched jacket in the lifeboat – all the portraits of the men stuffed in the pockets. I tried to climb back down but they wouldn't let me. I'd like to say that I put up a fight, gave some officious shit a fat lip, but I didn't. I was so tired. All my fight was gone. I sat on deck as the lifeboats were cut loose and watched for as long as I could, watching all those men drift away.'

He sat quite still for a minute, staring out over the water.

'Some of the men came back home at the end of it all, but most of them didn't. Lost during overseas campaigns. Missing Presumed Dead. I kept a log of the men I painted – needed the addresses to send the pictures to their wives, and when I looked through it, I realised the attrition rate was awful. Catastrophic. Never mind a chap hoping he wasn't sent to Africa or some other bloodbath, he needed to pray he wasn't painted by me. I realised my damn sketchbook was a doomsday book. If I painted you, then the odds were you wouldn't make it.'

'Darling, I'm sure that isn't true.'

'It might be true, it might not, but frankly I can't take the risk. I made a promise that after the war I wouldn't paint anyone else.'

Juliet laid her head on his shoulder and reached for his hand, stroking the coarse nub on his forefinger callused from hours spent holding a brush. Sometimes she almost forgot that Max wasn't quite like other men. But, then that was why she loved him, each of them had a piece missing. Neither made any attempt to fill the void in the other but they were good companions, easing one another's loneliness when they were together.

'I can't come with you, Juliet,' he said softly.

'What do you mean? You are here.'

'I'm not coming to New York.'

'Don't be ridiculous. We're nearly there.'

'Yes but I'm not going ashore. I've arranged it all with the purser. I'm going to stay on board and go straight home. Your ticket and the children's are all valid. The three of you might have to share a cabin on the way back—'

'How can you just abandon us in New York? I've never even been to France before.'

'You'll be just fine. You'll be better off without me.'

Juliet released his hand and wriggled away.

'I can understand that you don't like being on the boat – it must be awful for you. I didn't know about the *Laconia* and I'm more sorry than I can say. But New York's on bloody dry land – it doesn't make sense.'

Max shrugged and looked away, avoiding her eye. 'I have to go home. I can't do this. It was stupid of me to come.'

He reached out and patted her knee as if she were a dog. 'You can all come and visit and tell me all about it when you're back. I've wired Tom. He's going to pick me up from the docks and take me home. '

Angry, she pulled away from him so that the overcoat fell onto the ground.

'You'll be all right, old girl.'

'Oh do shut up.'

Max stood, steady and more sober now. He scooped up the fallen coat and tucked it around her shoulders, before kissing the crown of her head.

'I'm sorry, Juliet.'

He ambled away into the darkness and she watched him go, the glow from his pipe turning into a red pinprick. She licked her lips, salty from the sea air. From an upper deck came the strains of the second-rate band and she pictured pastel-rinsed ladies shuffling in the arms of their husbands. Lights strung along the ship's stays wobbled in time to the current. Automatically, she dipped her fingers into her pocket and brushed the scrap of newspaper.

The children did not seem upset that Max wasn't coming with them. Frieda said nothing at all and unsure if she was even listening Juliet repeated it.

'I heard you the first time.' Frieda shrugged. 'Charlie wouldn't have abandoned us.'

'No,' agreed Leonard with a look at his mother.

In a fit of remorse, Max had given Leonard his camera. As they disembarked Leonard squinted up and snapped a picture of the small figure waving at them from the upper deck, pipe held aloft in one hand, paisley scarf flapping. He and Frieda waved back with helicopter arms and great enthusiasm. Juliet did not.

That night they couldn't sleep. They huddled in their dingy downtown hotel room, too tired and too excited. Somewhere beyond the brown and fluttering curtains lay New York City. *New York*. Leonard poked his finger into the cigarette burn on the counterpane. Something danced in his belly.

'Are you awake?' he called in a stage whisper.

'Yes,' answered Frieda.

'Yes,' added Juliet.

Both children giggled, delighted that their mother was joining in the game. Perhaps such topsy-turvy things were simply part of life in America.

'What time is it? I'm not at all sleepy,' said Leonard.

Juliet groped on the nightstand for her watch. 'Four.'

'Can we get up?'

Juliet shrugged under the covers. 'I suppose so.'

'I want a hamburger dinner. I've got my dollar from bingo,' said Leonard.

'All right,' said Juliet. 'If anything's open.'

Both children were out of bed, pulling on yesterday's clothes before she could say anything else and break the spell. In a few minutes they stood in the hotel corridor, the yellow electric light pulsing as though batted by invisible moth wings. The three of them held hands automatically; for once Frieda didn't complain. Outside the hotel the sidewalk was quiet. The background thrum of the city was like a static whir. The streetlights throbbed pale white and a taxi dawdled past, half-heartedly searching for a fare. Across the street a diner's neon sign blinked, the restaurant shining into the dark street like an illuminated liner out at sea. Tugging the children's hands, Juliet hurried them over the road and inside. Leonard's face was pale with excitement.

'They have booths. With red benches.' His voice was hushed with awe.

'Come on.' Juliet started to draw him in but Leonard stood stock-still.

'No. We have to "Please wait to be seated".'

He pointed to a plastic sign. There was a tiled counter along one wall, and behind it a tired fry cook in whitish over-alls scraped at a hotplate. On his head he wore a folded linen hat that to Leonard's eye looked just like a paper boat, the sort Kenneth made in maths class and they sailed on the pond during break. He sighed in happiness. America truly was a magic land where restaurants stayed open all night and people wore boats on their heads. A waitress ambled over, lips smudged with scarlet even at this hour. She smiled at the children, revealing a tiny fleck of lipstick on her teeth.

'How are you doing this morning? Sit wherever you like.'

Leonard gazed around at the sea of empty booths and the tempting expanse of counter, quite unable to make up his mind. Juliet ushered them into the nearest booth, suddenly feeling very tired. The waitress hovered, waiting to take their order.

'What can I get you?'

'A hamburger,' said Leonard, resolute. Cornflake Jones's father had once gone to America on business and tried the hamburger and said it was the tastiest thing he'd ever eaten.

'One hamburger. Anything to drink? A milkshake? A malt?'

The children gazed at her blankly.

'I'll bring you two chocolate malts. You'll love 'em,' she grinned.

Juliet felt more tired than ever, exhausted by the woman's cheerfulness. She listened in a daze as the children chattered about the trip, '*on holiday all the way from England . . . Los Angeles . . . a bus that takes four days and Frieda gets carsick . . . it's going to be so awful, I can't wait.*' She watched their reflections in the glass. It was still dark outside and they were framed like a painting – the polished counter, the cook in his whites, the waitress with her slash of lipstick, and in the distance the lights pinging on halfway up the sky as the first of the morning risers started to think about a new day.

❧

The journey passed in a blur of truck stops and picture-book mountains and greasy coffee and teeth-brushing by the side of the road. They sat on the bus sweating into the coarse fabric seats and watched America out of the window. Juliet felt so small. Smaller than one of the garden ants scuttling from their garden nest under the pear tree to the kitchen table. She felt as if she'd sipped from the 'Drink Me' vial like Alice in Wonderland and had shrunk into a doll-size Juliet. As the bus travelled further west, the plains stretched empty into a blank horizon, punctured only by the odd farm and the endless straight grey road. In England the lanes curved around hedges and hills and trees – even after a tree had vanished the curl in the road remained to tell you that once an oak or an ash had been rooted there. Here no trees grew beside the road and the ground was level, ironed flatter than even Mr Greene's best Saturday trousers. Sometimes Juliet and the children fell asleep, lulled away for hours only to wake in what looked like the same place, unable to tell from the endless sky and flat grey grass whether they had moved on at all. Days fell into night. From early evening the sky began to kindle along the horizon, slowly at first, no more than a match flicker, until it caught and fired the drifting clouds. It blazed in a too rich vermilion. If Max used such a red in a painting, Juliet would have complained that it was too much – a sickly, child's red – but the colours here looked different. Juliet's tweed jacket lost its texture under the bright midday sun, but her purple Liberty scarf shone, the flecks of yellow buzzing gold.

Each evening they stopped at a restaurant beside the road. They were all the same, dusty and tired. The creased travellers filed out of the bus on stiff and unsteady limbs in order to eat and pee and climb aboard again, ready to rattle away into the darkness, heads knocking against the bus windows, sweater-pillows slipping.

Leonard lost count of how many days they'd been on the bus – was it two or three or a hundred? – or the number of times

Frieda had been sick. She looked skinnier and crosser than ever and in the diners sucked Coke through a straw and scowled at him as he drank milkshake after milkshake, never worrying about it coming back up again. Sometimes he sat next to Juliet, sometimes Frieda (except when she was going to throw up) and every now and again he sat next to strangers, real-life Amer-i-cans. Leonard liked this the best. Between Louisville and Fort Smith he sat beside a travelling salesman with a briefcase full of imitation watches (that kept real time just the same) and as they shared meatloaf sandwiches with tomato ketchup Leonard listened to his history of troubles with drink and the troublesome ma-in-law who'd driven him to it, and looked at the pictures of 'my boy Huck Junior'. Leonard wondered if his father was sitting on a bus some-where sharing sandwiches with another kid and showing him pictures of 'my boy Leonard'. He expected so.

They reached downtown Los Angeles in the middle of the afternoon on the fifth day, stumbling off the bus into fierce Californian sunshine. It was hot and airless between the build-ings, the fronds of the grimy palms perfectly still. Unable to bear another bus, Juliet herded the children into a taxi that deposited them half an hour later outside a gloomy apart-ment building in Venice. Juliet looked over the children – Leonard in dirty trousers and wild, unbrushed hair, and Frieda her skin grey, eyes ringed with purple as she blinked in the light. Trying to ignore a gathering headache, Juliet hammered on the front door. It was answered after a few minutes by a thin man with a perfectly bald head and a fulsome, furry beard – making him look, according to Leonard, like an upside-down egg in an egg cosy. The bald man led them up several flights of stairs, the children dragging their suitcases, thump-thumping on every step. He ushered them into a small apartment on the top floor and, on handing Juliet a key, disappeared back down the stairs.

When he had gone, Leonard and Frieda were filled with a sudden rush of energy and started rootling around the room, opening cupboards and poking at the shower and toilet partly hidden behind a mouldy plastic curtain. Leonard flung open a door and gave a cry.

'This isn't a cupboard! It's a – garden,' he concluded, reaching for the right word.

Frieda and Juliet followed him outside and onto a concrete roof. A lone shrivelled pot plant balanced on the roof ledge was the closest thing to a garden, but beyond the tangle of telephone cables and the nests of electricity wires was the ocean. And it was an ocean, not a sea like at Margate or Swanage. It was huge and blue and the sand stretched away hot and white, edged in the far north by a ridge of mountains half-concealed by a bandage of mist. Juliet narrowed her eyes, searching the shore. *Are you here, George? Will you let us find you?*

'Can we swim?' asked Leonard, transfixed by the glittering expanse, drawn like a magpie to silver.

'Tomorrow.'

'We need to hire bicycles,' Juliet called through the manager's door. She rapped again, and he eventually emerged in a pair of orange pyjamas, a hand-rolled cigarette drooping between his fingers.

'Bicycles?'

'Yes.'

Mickey the bald and bearded manager gaped at Juliet, ash from his cigarette littering the already filthy carpet.

'What in God's name do you want a bike for?'

Juliet swallowed a sigh. 'To get around.'

Mickey threw his head back and laughed, revealing two rows of neat yellow teeth like kernels of sweetcorn. He wiped spittle from his mouth with the back of his hand.

'I'm sorry. It's just that no one – *no one* – rides a bike to get places in LA.'

He paused, waiting for Juliet to get the joke but she merely stood quite still and waited. 'You need a car,' he added at last.

'I can't drive.'

Mickey looked at Juliet for a minute and then stepped out into the corridor, wafting with him a stale smell emanating from his room. 'You have cash?'

'Some,' said Juliet, picturing the dwindling stash in the icebox upstairs.

'My brother's out of town for a few weeks and I could give you a loan of his car at a very reasonable rate.'

'I think you missed the part where I said I can't drive.'

Mickey wafted away her objections with his cigarette. 'It's easy as pie. I'll teach you a bit and then afterwards you can drive around and practise.'

An hour later Juliet sat behind the wheel of a huge tan Plymouth, Mickey beside her and Leonard and Frieda in the back, thrilled at their mother's audacity. This was something else not to tell Grandma.

'I think you got it,' said Mickey towards the end of the afternoon.

Juliet made no answer, concentrating heart and soul on steering the enormous car along the road. It wallowed out into the middle like a boat caught in the tide and streets that had seemed so wide now appeared alarmingly narrow. Mickey was a surprisingly good teacher. He was patient – grinning his yellow smile as he dangled his cigarette out of the window – and he also appeared to have no concerns over the wellbeing of the car, not wincing even when Juliet grazed a row of parked cars or thudded into the kerb as she took the corner of Wilshire Boulevard. He made her practise parking and then drive them all the way up to Sunset in the traffic that at rush hour was thickening like porridge.

'Here we are,' he announced, suddenly.

'Here we are?' repeated Juliet, unaware that they were driving somewhere in particular.

'Told you there isn't nothing to driving. You can drop me here.'

He waved at a bar with a green neon sign. Juliet pulled over without a signal, a chorus of car horns berating her. Mickey leaped out with sudden dexterity.

'How will I get home?' called Juliet.

Mickey stared at her. 'You got a car.'

'Yes, but I don't know how to get back to Venice.'

Mickey scratched his nose. 'Ask the kid. He probably knows.'

With that he was gone. Juliet turned to look at Leonard on the back seat.

'Do you know?'

Both children shook their heads. The car horns rising to a crescendo, Juliet accelerated away. She tried to guess the direction of the sea, failing to distinguish the sun through the scarf of fog. In the back of the car, the children held hands. Caught in a surge of traffic, Juliet found herself propelled onto the freeway. Unaware of how to escape, she sailed along in the middle lane watching a flotsam and jetsam of cars float by her on both sides. The afternoon wore into dusk and, as the cars thinned she found herself stepping on the accelerator with an electric buzz of exhilaration. Then suddenly the city was left behind. Scrub gave way to desert and the hot dirt from the open windows battered Juliet's skin. She smiled with pleasure. *I could go anywhere. I'm not lost, I'm free.* The little house in Chislehurst felt very far away. A sign loomed at the edge of the road: '*Las Vegas 200 miles*'. After the endless bus ride, that didn't seem so very far. Everything that mattered most to her was in the car. *I could vanish too*, she thought. *Drive and drive and drive and never come back and move here and become someone new.* A great black bird watched her from the side of the road, hunched on a scrap of twisted metal, hostile and indifferent. The road rushed on, grey and endless and the first of the stars appeared in the sky beside a lemon slice of moon.

She glanced in the mirror and saw that both children were asleep, coiled awkwardly on one another. Love pricked at her. She remembered coming home from the hospital clutching baby Frieda, terrified she'd shatter like the china babies in her dreams. George had prised her out of her hands and laid her down on their bed, and they'd both sat staring at this immaculate creature with the angry red face, at once awed and terrified. Frieda could still make her uneasy. When Frieda was six, Juliet had collected her from school and they'd sat on the bus in silence, Juliet searching for things to say, trying topic after topic, sensing her small disapproval. Leonard was different. She'd known the moment the midwife handed him to her that they'd be friends. He'd first grinned up at her at only two weeks old, even though everyone told her it was impossible. Smiling, she pulled off the freeway and parked. Opening the glove compartment she discovered a bottle of bourbon. She slid out of the car and took a swig, conscious that she drank not for pleasure but because this was a moment that needed to be marked. Alcohol seals occasions as varnish does garden benches. Even the most austere of rabbis drank at weddings. It brought them closer to God, or so they said. She tipped a circle of liquid on the ground, watching it seep into the dust and thought of Max in his green wood. And then of George.

Cars swarmed past, throwing up grit and noise and then the road was still again. She could climb back in the car and drive on for ever, but she chose not to. She chose to go back.

The following day Juliet began her hunt for George. They traipsed along the walk path beside Venice Beach, past a couple of painters who had set up easels on the edge of the sand and a handful of ageing surfers struggling in the shallows, their white beards the same colour as the choppy water. While the children attempted to build a sandcastle, observed by a couple of drunks who offered them some beer-bottle tops for battlement decoration, Juliet looked up 'Gorgeous George's Glasses, Culver City' in the telephone directory. Armed with an address, she wondered how to explain the visit to the children. Leonard laid his spectacles on the towel beside her and then rushed over to Frieda, knocking her into the sea. Juliet lay back on the sand listening to their shrieks. She picked up Leonard's specs, wiping away a smear on the lens with her shirt. She hesitated, wondering if she dared. Could she be so wicked? Then, before she could talk herself out of it, she wrenched the spectacles, snapping them in two. She stared at the broken pieces, heart beating, feeling a little sick at what she had done. The children emerged from the sea and flopped back on the towel next to her, panting. Leonard groped for his specs. His eyes welled up as he found them. 'Oh,' he said. 'Oh.' He crouched in the sand and peered through them like two monocles. 'I can't see,' he said, his voice breaking. 'I'll have to go home.'

'Oh darling, we can get them mended here,' said Juliet. 'It was an accident, I sat on them and they snapped. I am so sorry.' She leaned over and kissed his cheek, salty with tears and seawater. 'I know a place that's not too far.'

Gorgeous George's shop was at one end of an ordinary suburban street lined with low houses and dusty palm trees and
lawns mouthwash green. She opened the car door, clipping it
against the kerb, and led the children towards the shop, steering the half-blind Leonard around a fire hydrant.

Paint peeled off the doorframe and the display of spectacles in the window needed a good dust. A fly thudded against
the glass. Juliet felt dizzy with nerves. She wiped moist palms
down her dress and paused outside the shop, suddenly not
ready to go inside. It was almost sixteen years since she'd
marched into Harry's Specs on Penge High Street determined
to meet the dishy new assistant, George Montague; fourteen
years since she'd married him under the *chuppah* and eight
years since he'd kissed her goodbye on her birthday and gone
to work and hadn't come home. She glanced at the children
and anxiety kindled into anger. Juliet took a breath and
stepped inside ready to face George. It seemed right that they
should meet again in an optician's store.

'Hi, my name is Vera. How may I help you?'

A woman in a smart yellow summer dress shot Juliet a
perfect shop assistant smile. She looked about forty with
bottle-black hair and Pacific-blue eyes edged with thick lashes.
She wore open-toed sandals, toes painted red like little pieces
of candy. Juliet delved into her handbag and produced
Leonard's broken spectacles.

'I'm afraid we had an accident. I hoped you might be able
to fix them.'

Vera took them from Juliet, placing them on the counter.

'Let's take a look.' Her voice was low and beneath the
Californian accent sounded a note of something European.
Juliet frowned, trying to place it. 'Sure we'll be able to do
something for you but I'm sorry to say the optician isn't in
today.'

'Oh.'

The fluttering in Juliet's chest subsided; she wasn't sure whether in relief or disappointment. At the edge of the store, Frieda and Leonard played dress-up with fat plastic sun-specs. Juliet swallowed, forcing her voice to remain casual.

'Is this George's store? George Montague. Sorry. George Molnár?'

Vera looked up sharply, saying nothing for a moment, and then retrieved her shiny service smile.

'Yes, the store belongs to George. Do you know him?'

Juliet frowned. 'I'm not sure. I think maybe, a long time ago.'

Vera bent over the counter. 'Are you here on vacation?'

Juliet nodded. 'Yes, from England.'

'And the name, please? For the ticket.'

'Leonard Montague.'

There was a giggle from the corner of the shop and the display stand wobbled ominously. Frieda caught it before it fell.

'Stop playing with that and come over here,' snapped Juliet. 'Stand here quietly until we're finished.'

The children slid over, Frieda leaning against the counter, still wearing a giant pair of sun-specs with orange polka-dot frames.

'Can I have these?'

Juliet glanced at the price and winced. 'No. They're far too expensive.'

Vera said nothing, only stared at Frieda, her head cocked to one side, then with what appeared to be a great effort roused herself into a fresh round of sales patter.

'They're all the rage. All the movie stars are wearing them.' She paused. 'I can give you a discount. Two dollars off.'

'Please, Mum, please. They're the most beautiful sunglasses in the world.'

Juliet had to laugh at her fervour. Frieda wiggled the glasses down her nose. They were enormous.

'Fabulous,' said Vera. 'Pass them to me. I'll adjust them.'

Frieda surrendered the specs and Juliet sighed, realising she'd been outmanoeuvred.

'There'll be no more presents for the rest of the trip,' she said, but Frieda was twirling around in ecstasy.

'I'll never want anything again, *ever*.'

'Can I have sun-specs too?' asked Leonard.

'We do a marvellous prescription-only range,' cooed the assistant, still eyeing Frieda as she spun nearer and nearer the rack of spectacles.

'No,' said Juliet.

'Come back tomorrow afternoon and I'll make sure the young man's glasses are fixed.'

Juliet licked dry lips. 'Do you think George might be here?'

'No,' said Vera. She did not smile.

Juliet ushered the children out of the shop. She paused in the doorway and looked back at Vera. Suddenly she could place the accent lurking beneath those bright American vowels – it was Hungarian, the same as George. It sounded different on the woman, in a cocktail mixed with New World sounds instead of the familiar London blend, but Juliet recognised it all the same.

That night when the children were tucked up on the foldout sofa bed, Juliet did not sleep. She stepped through the door that was not a cupboard and out onto the rooftop. The sea glittered in the dark. From somewhere down below a vagrant or a dog rifled through the garbage cans. She tapped her pocket, listening to the rustle of newspaper. Was her George now running an optical store in Culver City? Or was it an entirely different George? She tried to picture the grand reunion. She was nine years older than when he'd vanished and the children were nothing like the babies George had left behind. Then, Leonard had been a doughnut-cheeked toddler, toppling around the living room with his milk-sop smile. Juliet felt a pulse of the old anger. She forced herself to uncurl her fists. And George himself. What would he be like? Try as she could, in her mind he remained as unchanged as a photograph. She tried to age him – thin his hair, plant a bald patch on his scalp, give him a blossoming paunch and a pair of horn-rimmed specs – but he always looked like an actor playing dress-up. She sighed and there was the old George again: black hair, suit hanging loose however many potato *latkes* Mrs Greene pressed on him. She saw the once loved lopsided smile and the restless tap-tapping foot as he crooned Hungarian ballads to Frieda.

In the morning she forced the children to shower and put on clean clothes, despite their objections. She winced when Leonard knocked her coffee all over Frieda's white trousers, aware that his temporary blindness was entirely her fault. After rinsing the trousers through, she dangled them over the telephone wire she used as a laundry line and lit a cigarette. Frieda sat beside her in her knickers and shivered.

'There's an optician here in Venice,' she said.

'Oh.' Juliet tried to sound uninterested.

'We didn't need to get in the car and drive all the way to Culver City.'

'But then you wouldn't have got your beautiful sun-specs,' said Juliet.

'No, I suppose not,' agreed Frieda slowly. She took a bite of peanut butter toast and eyed Juliet with her grandmother's stare.

The car was warm to braising, and the children wriggled, damp thighs squealing against hot plastic seats. They got lost twice – pulled along in the gush of LA traffic, the children managing not to snigger even as Juliet uttered two bad words. Vera had said to come back in the afternoon, but Juliet was determined to be early – perhaps then she'd catch George. Unawares would be better. She'd present Leonard and Frieda to him. '*These are your abandoned children. This is your son.*' A giggle burst from her lips like an unexpected burp. She never said things like that. Those weren't her words – they sounded like the stupid advertisement her father had penned for '*The Gallery of Vanished Husbands*'. Maybe George wouldn't recognise the children and she'd leave without saying anything to him at all.

They arrived shortly before ten o'clock. The hazy morning was ripening into apricot sunshine and men in identical open-necked shirts were mowing identical handkerchief lawns all along the street so that the air was filled with the cut-grass scent of a British summer. Juliet shuddered, unexpectedly homesick. The shop door was open and they entered, Juliet glancing about for George or Vera. It was perfectly empty. The children darted back to the rack of sunglasses, bickering happily, and Juliet stood quietly in the middle of the shop. The hand on the dusty wall clock crawled round and round and outside the lawnmowers whirred. Several minutes slid by and still no one appeared. Juliet looked about her and then slipped behind the counter. She hesitated, heart ticking in her ears, unsure what she was looking for. A stack of order forms lay on a spike beside the cash register and customers' specta-cles roosted inside a rack of cubbyholes. There was nothing personal. No photographs of grinning kiddies or oddly famil-iar golden '*G.M.*' cufflinks. At the back of the shop stood two painted doors. Juliet opened one and peered inside. It was an empty optician's studio: the high-backed leather chair, the eye chart, the wooden box stuffed with lenses like a selection box of chocolates. She closed the door and stepped towards the other. It was marked in small black letters 'Private'. Beyond here waited George – she was sure of it. Her hand fluttered to her throat and she smoothed her hair. Closing her eyes, she pictured a blue-papered sitting-room with a sofa and a starfish lamp and inside George sipping coffee and reading the paper with a dab of toothpaste on his chin.

'Mrs Montague?'

Juliet opened her eyes and found herself face to face with the woman from yesterday.

'I'm sorry, I was—'

Having no explanation Juliet faltered, but Vera just smiled her white smile and shrugged.

'I came early. Just in case,' said Juliet.

There was a clatter as Leonard collided with the display stand and expensive sunglasses began to hail to the floor.

'It's all okay. Nothing broken,' said Vera hurrying over and scooping up the stand.

'Is Mr Molnár here?' asked Juliet, her voice casual.

'Not today, ma'am. He doesn't work much any more,' added Vera. 'He *is* nearly eighty.'

'Oh,' said Juliet, shoulders sagging with disappointment. She studied Vera, who smiled back at her, face empty as a mannequin. 'The George I knew would be much younger.'

Vera shrugged and went to retrieve Leonard's spectacles from one of the cubbyholes. 'It'll be a dollar for the repair and five for the sunglasses.'

Wordlessly Juliet counted out the bills. Disappointment flickered around her in waves until she felt quite dizzy.

'Do you have a loo – a restroom?'

Vera shook her head. 'I'm sorry,' she answered too quickly. 'Use the one in the drugstore across the street. Leave the kids here. I'll watch 'em.'

Juliet mumbled her thanks and hurried out into the sunshine, the cacophony of buzzing lawnmowers making her head ache. She rushed across the road, automatically looking the wrong way so that a fat blue truck had to swerve to avoid her, the driver honking his horn and shaking his fist. She fled into the drugstore, the door clattering behind her. Inside it was neon bright, the fluorescent tubes blinking even in the middle of the day. Rows and rows of red and blue and yellow cartons of soap powder screamed 'THE BEST', 'THE BRIGHTEST', 'DAZZLING WHITES' at her on both sides so that she felt she was walking through a tunnel of Pop Art.

The restroom smelled of bleach and cheap vanilla perfume. Even in here the light was too bright, the bulb pulsing. She thought of Max and his hatred of electric light. Teasing him one night in bed, she'd called him a Luddite and an old grump but he'd smiled that sly smile and puffed out a lungful of pipe smoke and declared with a shrug, 'What is it with Charlie and the rest of you? All of you want to shine neon lights into the dark places. Why do all mysteries need to be solved? There is a pleasure in uncertainty.'

Juliet stooped over the sink, splashing cool water on her face and wrists. Was this her fault – was she guilty of wanting to shine light into the dark? She thought of Vera and her small watchful eyes. She reminded Juliet of some of the curtain-twitchers back home. There was something about her that Juliet didn't trust. It would all be so much easier if whoever had scribbled '*Try George Molnár*' on the scrap of newspaper had given their name. But whoever that stranger was, he or she had believed that George Molnár of Gorgeous George's Glasses was her George and not an eighty-year-old man. Over the years she'd persuaded herself that she was reconciled to not finding George – in the way that one accepts a limp or a headache that never quite fades – but that wretched piece of newspaper with its scrawled note had given her hope, and all those years of careful resolve had been bulldozed in an instant. They'd travelled so far and unless she found George there would be no divorce. She'd never be free of him. And she'd never find her painting. Juliet straightened and reached into her bag for a comb. She thought of the little house in Chislehurst with its walls slowly filling up with pictures. Charlie's portrait of her in the front room, Philip's on the stairs, Jim's sketches pinned to her mirror and Max's bird-Juliet beside her bed so that it was the first thing she saw every morning. Over the years there would be more paintings, a lifetime of them, but there would always be one missing. That piece of her would remain lost, chained to George. She bent over the sink, noticed a grey crack in the porcelain and ran a thumbnail along it. She felt sure of only two things – that Vera was from Hungary and that she was lying.

In the optician's store, Leonard and Frieda fidgeted, bored with waiting. Vera stood behind the counter, filing her nails and glancing at the door again and again.

Leonard's confidence had been restored with his sight and he was busy transforming a glossy flyer into a paper aeroplane. It waddled into the air, staggered a few feet and then landed ignominiously on its back like a dead fly. He sighed and gathered it up for a fresh attempt.

'Your technique's all wrong.'

Leonard glanced up to see a freckle-faced boy of seventeen or eighteen grinning down at him.

'I said you didn't need to come in today, Jerry,' said Vera, emerging from behind the counter.

Jerry shrugged and gave a great yawn. 'Yeah. I was bored.' He turned back to Leonard. 'You wanna know how to make a real paper airplane?'

Leonard nodded, awed by the stranger. Jerry squatted beside him, grabbed another flyer and started a series of elaborate folds as the boy watched, trying to memorise each sequence with more concentration than he'd ever given anything before in his life. Jerry stood up and presented a perfect paper aeroplane to Leonard on the palm of his hand.

'Try her out.'

Leonard launched it with a hearty snap of his wrist and the plane glided the length of the shop before landing elegantly on the counter.

'Wow.'

'You got how to do it?'

'I think so.'

'Good job, champ.'

Frieda eyed Vera, wishing that she could have such long crimson nails – she was even more elegant than the girls in the shiny magazines at the dentist. She wondered if her mother had painted her nails that colour before her father left. Men liked vermilion fingernails – all the magazines said so. She turned her attention to the new arrival, watching him from behind her sunglasses. He was very tall with reddish hair and strong freckled arms and he hadn't even noticed her. She attempted to drape herself around the back of a chair. Jerry looked up and winked. She tried not to smile.

'Hey, I know you,' he said.

Vera looked up quickly.

'Yeah, take off those specs,' said Jerry.

Obediently, Frieda propped them on her forehead.

'Yeah, for sure. It's Elizabeth Taylor.'

Frieda smiled and went bright pink, clashing beautifully with her orange sunglasses. Vera, who had stopped filing her nails and had been staring at the children, let out a sigh that might have been relief and retreated behind the counter.

Juliet returned from the drugstore and held open the door for the children.

'Come on now. Thank you for watching them,' she called to Vera.

She did not notice the paper aeroplane clutched in Leonard's hand or the tall teenage boy with black eyes who watched them through the glass as they hurried away.

Vera Molnár waited until Juliet Montague was safely down the street, not moving until a full five minutes after the car had disappeared past the window, the children's faces a pale blur. Then she crossed to the door and silently turned the 'Open' sign to 'Closed' and clicked the lock. She leaned against it for a second.

'Are you all right, Mom?' asked Jerry.

She smiled. 'You're a good boy, my little *aidesh*. I thought we'd take an early lunch.' She reached into the till for a hand-ful of change. 'How about some of those hotdogs from the deli? Will you go get them?'

Jerry shrugged. 'Sure.'

She waited until he'd gone and then disappeared through the door marked 'Private' into the house at the back of the shop. She measured out several spoons of thick ground coffee, slid the pot onto the stove and then, as she waited for it to boil, stepped into a small blue-patterned living-room. The curtains fluttered in the morning breeze and a bee landed on the television set in the corner. Vera perched on the worn sofa and looked at the wall where she'd pinned up a poster of some Van Gogh sunflowers. The print wasn't very good, the petals more brown than sunshine, and it wasn't straight. It also failed to conceal the unbleached rectangle on the wallpaper around it, where a larger picture used to hang. Vera remembered it well – that picture had been the one good thing they owned. It was a portrait of a young girl with brown hair and greenish eyes, her skinny legs folded beneath her as though she couldn't stop fidgeting. If Vera hadn't known otherwise, she would have believed it to be a portrait of the kid who'd come into the shop – what was her name, Frieda? But Vera knew it wasn't Frieda. She knew the painting was of George's other wife. Mrs Juliet Montague.

For the next week, Juliet prowled the walk path beside Venice Beach, pacing up and down as though George was lurking between the cracks in the cement. She wrote to the private detective in Brooklyn, asking him for the envelope the newspaper scrap had arrived in, but he'd replied on a postcard of the Empire State building to say that he'd already trashed it and couldn't recall the postmark. He wasn't a detective of the first rank. Meanwhile the children swam and squabbled and ate too much ice cream and surreptitiously watched their mother.

Leonard began to wonder whether he'd got it all wrong and that it wasn't his father who was the spy on a secret mission but his mother. He kept a close eye on her, waking up in the night to check that she was still in bed and hadn't sneaked off to go on a stakeout, but she was always there – he could hear her sighing in the dark or smell the burning cigarettes that she lit and did not smoke. Leonard, however, had read sufficient detective novels to know that covert means must be employed to catch her and so checked her pockets while she was in the shower. He discovered the frayed piece of newspaper and studied the gallery of photographs. So she was on a mission. A mission so secret that he and Frieda weren't supposed to know about it. He sat on the kitchen linoleum and studied the photos of the assorted men, trying to insert the circled picture of 'George Molnár' into vague memories of his father. He screwed up his eyes in concentration and pictured the snap of his parents on their wedding day – Juliet in a white dress beside a man in a suit with a gouged-out hole instead of a head. Leonard replaced the hole with the face of George Molnár – like when Leonard had stuck his head through a cardboard cut-out of a cowboy at the fairground and Grandpa took his picture. He scanned the rows of men. If he could pick, who would be the father he'd choose? He was glad George didn't have a beard because they tickled and stuff got lost in them – bits of lunch and keys and things. From the bathroom the sound of trickling water stopped, and Leonard heard the soft thud of his mother stepping out of the shower. Silently, he slipped the newspaper back into her pocket and considered whether to tell Frieda about his discovery. The door to the roof was ajar and he could see her perched on the edge of the wall (where they'd been told never ever to sit) dangling her legs, blowing fleshy bubbles the size of beach balls and then popping them with a grubby finger. Since they'd arrived in California Frieda was rarely without a sticky pack of Bazooka Joe.

'Frieda, can I have a piece of gum?' he asked, padding out to join her.

'Bog off,' she replied.

Leonard turned around and went back inside. No, he decided, he wouldn't tell her anything at all.

On Tuesday as Juliet hurried along the walk path to collect bagels for breakfast, she passed a few artists at work, easels sunk into the edge of the strand. Instinctively she slowed to look at the pictures. The first couple were unremarkable pastels of the sea by cheerful hobbyists – the colours flat, the water much too still – but the last caught her eye. She lingered behind the painter's chair, not speaking as she watched him work. A girl with brown-red hair flew above a star-filled sky, the night sand drifting white below her. As Juliet waited, the sea turned choppier and blacker under his brush.

'So, you like it, or no?' asked the painter, not turning around.

'Yes,' said Juliet.

She stood for a while, watching the white horses rise out of the painted sea and night-time gulls encircle the flying girl, until the man pointed with his brush to a bench.

'Sit. You're making my legs ache.'

'But I won't be able to see.'

'Then I shall break and sit with you.'

The painter stood and turned to face Juliet. He grinned, raising his sunhat, a herringbone trilby, in salutation. He was in his sixties, hair thinning and grey, eyes the same blue as the sea in his picture.

'Tibor Jankay,' he said, offering a smudged hand.

'Juliet Montague.'

They shook hands, smiling, pleased with one another, and settled side by side on the bench.

'Who's the girl in the picture?' asked Juliet.

'You,' said Tibor.

Juliet laughed.

He pulled a large sketchbook out of a bag, passing it to her.

'You can look, if you're interested.'

He lit a cigarette and pulled his hat low to shade his eyes, dozing contentedly in the sunshine, humming to himself. Juliet thumbed through a series of sketches, most of them in charcoal, most of them of the same girl drawn in bold, simple lines, her hair tumbling like rushing water and her profile displaying a good strong Jewish nose. Every now and then she was drawn in colour – her hair was usually red-brown, but here and there it was crimson or yellow, but it didn't matter, it was always the same girl. Juliet sighed.

'You don't like?' said Tibor, opening an eye.

'I do, I do. I'm on holiday and I hadn't realised how much I missed looking at pictures,' she said.

'Ah well,' he said. 'I like pictures too. Pictures and sunshine. This is the best quality sunshine in all the world, fifty-three per cent better than every other kind, did you know that?'

Juliet shook her head, unsure if he was kidding. Tibor produced a fat Hershey bar from his pocket.

'You want some chocolate? It's not like the good stuff from Europe, but it was either good quality chocolate or good quality sunshine.'

He spoke with the same *Mitteleuropa* accent as Vera, only the notes from the old country were stronger, closer to the surface. Not wishing to be rude, Juliet accepted a soggy square. Apart from this elderly man, the only person she knew who wanted chocolate for breakfast was Leonard. She supposed she ought to get back to the apartment and rouse the children, but it was pleasant sitting on the bench with Tibor, basking in the warmth of the Californian morning. As he passed her another square of chocolate, Juliet realised with a jolt like a hunger pang that she was lonely.

'You're the first grown-up I've really talked to since we got to America,' she observed.

Tibor smiled. 'I'm not so sure I'm a grown-up.'

Juliet laughed. Most people would have asked why her husband didn't keep her company, or else commented on the fact that she was a woman travelling alone.

219

'Come back tomorrow, same time, same place and I'll paint you.'

Juliet started. She'd never even considered that she might have her portrait painted over here. She closed her eyes, filled with warmth at the thought. The city was so busy, everyone zooming from place to place in their cars, the Montagues had slid unnoticed into its slipstream and no one would notice when they left. But a portrait painted here on Venice Beach would connect her to this place. It would last even after they'd sailed for home.

'It would be nice. I'll try to come tomorrow,' she said, regretting a vague promise to take the children to see the Hollywood sign.

'You'll come.'

Juliet licked the chocolate off her fingers. Yes, of course she would come.

The next morning Tibor was waiting for Juliet as she traipsed along the walk path, a huge string beach-bag clutched in her hand and the children at her side. Leonard was curious and Frieda snarled in a temper. Why did everyone want to paint Juliet? But then she caught sight of Tibor and her mood improved. She'd assumed that most painters were like Philip or Charlie or Jim but this man was more like Grandpa. He was welcome to paint her mother – Frieda wouldn't pose for him, even if he asked.

The wind was up and the beach busy with tropical flocks of kites, while a handful of surfers dabbled in the waves – most of them flopping about in the shallows pummelled by the tide, but one or two galloped across the cresting surface like bareback circus riders.

'I'm going for a swim,' announced Frieda, wriggling out of her jeans and strutting off across the sand towards the surfers.

'Stay where I can see you, and keep an eye on your brother,' called Juliet.

'I'm right here,' said Leonard. 'I'd rather stay and see the picture.'

'Very good,' said Tibor. 'You may assist.'

'Are you using oils or acrylics?' asked Leonard.

Tibor chuckled. 'You are a painter too?'

'Yes,' said Leonard, preening a little. 'But I don't mind just being an assistant today.'

Juliet spread out a towel and lay across the bench, watching the kites flap against the sky, and listened to the patter of the men.

'You've got a foreign accent,' remarked Leonard.

'So do you,' replied Tibor.

Leonard paused, considering. 'I suppose for you I do. But your accent isn't American foreign or English foreign, it's *foreign* foreign.'

'Hungarian.'

Juliet glanced at Leonard, wondering if this meant something to him, whether he remembered that his father was Hungarian.

'Did you always like doing paintings?' Leonard asked.

'All my life. And that is a long time,' said Tibor stretching out his arms. 'It would have been a short time, but a picture saved my life.'

Leonard stopped rinsing brushes and looked up at Tibor. Juliet wriggled round on the bench.

'You,' he said pointing with a palette knife at Juliet, 'don't keep fidgeting. Stay still and I'll tell you.'

His brush moves across the canvas, quickly in bold red strokes – he has the confidence of an artist of many years who doesn't much care whether anyone else likes his picture or not. He's never sold a picture, not in sixty years. He likes to joke that he'd sooner sell his kids but he doesn't have any kids, only a house full of pictures. Pictures all the way up the stairs, on the landing, in the bedroom, piles of them stacked against the wall in the spare room and leaning against crates in the garage. He doesn't care that there isn't any room left – they're not for sale. Not now. Not ever.

Her hair appears first, flying in the wind like the tail feathers of the kites. Next comes the hot disc of sun, bouncing on the horizon like a yellow beach ball. He talks. They listen.

'I was on a train, a terrible train headed for somewhere unspeakable. One of those places that steal men's souls. We were packed in so tightly that even when someone fainted or died, they kept standing up, rooted in place by the others. But in my pocket I had my chisel and I chipped away at one of the wooden panels until it was just wide enough for a skinny man to fit through and I was skinnier even than you.'

He wiggled a brush at Leonard, who sat watching, not wanting to interrupt.

'My neighbours screamed at me, yelling curses that I'd brought trouble on them all and everyone would be punished for what I had done. I argued and begged for them to come with me. But do you know how many did?'

Leonard shook his head and Tibor continued.

'None. Not one. So, I went alone. I spied through my peep-hole, watching the white landscape rush past. Sometimes there was a farmhouse and sometimes a few of them together, little wooden houses huddled to make a village, but I waited until the train was far, far from anywhere, and then as the women screamed at me and the men rained fists down on my head, I slid out through the broken panel and onto the snowy tracks. I lay still as a mouse when he knows a housewife with a rolled-up newspaper is waiting to clobber him. The train roared over my head and I thought that probably I should die but I choose that I die like this than shot in the back of my head or—'

He paused, catching sight of Juliet who shook her head, ever such a little. He shrugged and continued.

'Your mother is quite right. You don't need to know all these things just now. So the train goes on for ever, cars and cars of it rattling above my head and then suddenly it is quiet and I'm alone. It's dusk and the cold is getting colder. You are from England?'

Leonard nodded, blinked.

'Then you don't know what real cold is. Your country is a little damp but you are a summer boy. In the East, the cold freezes your bones so they shatter into dust and make more snow. I knew that I must find somewhere to spend the night or I would die anyway. But I was nowhere. A big empty nowhere with nothing but white snow and black trees and here and there the hungry yowl of a wolf, skinny as me. My coat was thin and I had no scarf and I walked until the moon was up in the sky, until at last I saw a light. A lonely farmhouse on the edge of the waste.'

'Did they let you in?' asked Leonard. 'Did you get supper?'

Tibor smiled. 'I was much too frightened to knock on the door. Instead I crept into the farmyard where there was a huge haystack made of straw and chicken shit and I crawled inside, stuffing handfuls of the stuff inside my clothes to keep warm.'

'Wasn't it scratchy?' asked Leonard.

'Terribly itchy. There were wriggly creatures inside the straw too.'

Tibor glanced up and caught Juliet's eye so that she understood this bit was for Leonard's benefit.

'So, I fall asleep. So fast asleep that I fall through the world and then the sky, past the moon and yellow stars.'

As he said this, Juliet saw that in the corner of the picture he was painting a bright starfish in the sand. He leaned back, examining it, and with a tiny shake of his head smeared yellow beach across the starfish and it vanished into the canvas, hidden in the layers of paint like a fossil.

'And in the morning, I wake up to a fierce pain in my leg and then my backside – something is biting me. I burrow out of the haystack and the farmer stands over me with his pitch-fork, ready to jab it into me again. "Thief! Jew!" cries the farmer and he grabs at me and I know that he's going to fetch the police. He's got me by the collar and I am choking but I cry out, "I'm not a thief. I'm going to pay for my night's accommodation!" The farmer stops jabbing at me with his wretched pitchfork in order to laugh. It's a nasty thin sound like the rattling of an empty tin can. "What will you pay me?" he says. "Your coat? Your shoes?" I look at my broken boots and my coat and I think, "If I give these to you, I'm already dead. I'll die tonight of cold." And then I remember that in my pocket, I have a pencil and a sketchbook. "Your portrait!" I say. "I'm an artist and I shall draw your picture, if you don't like it, then, you can turn me in or take my shoes, whatever you like."

'He grunts something, and I think it is a yes as he takes me into the farmhouse kitchen so he can sit in the warm. I'm grateful as I don't think I can draw outside with shivering fingers. It is a bare room with a single table and a dirt floor and a tiny stove that is not too clean and two chairs. He sits on one and I take the other and I begin to sketch knowing that my life depends on it. My fingers are swollen with chilblains and they don't move the way they should – I'm like a piano player trying to perform Beethoven in gloves – but I force them to do my work. I draw him as he wants to be seen – a heroic figure, strong and fierce, but I make awful sure that it is still him. He

224

won't want his friends to laugh and deny the likeness – I keep in the piggy eyes and the vodka nose. I show him.'

Leonard leaned forward. 'And? What then? You didn't finish the story.'

Tibor was silent for a moment, then he stood, squinting against the sun. Juliet gazed at him, eyes big with sadness, understanding he'd softened his story into an adventure for Leonard. She wanted to say something, didn't know what it should be. Tibor acknowledged this and nodded at both Juliets – the flesh and the painted. He adjusted his hat and turned to Leonard with a shrug.

'And what then? I live. I spend the rest of the war as a pedlar-painter going from house to house, drawing farmers and their wives and their pretty daughters and their ugly ones and I live.'

Juliet watched as Tibor turned back to his easel. A painting saved me too, she decided. Charlie's portrait rescued me from quiet despair and brought me into a world of colour.

The next morning Tibor continued his painting of Juliet. Leonard stuck beside them, at first watching Tibor and then asking for a piece of paper for his own picture.

'What are you going to draw? The sea? A portrait?' asked Tibor. 'An artist needs the correct tools for the job.'

Leonard cast his eye across the beach to where Frieda sprawled a few yards away sunning herself.

'Portrait.'

Tibor reached into his bag for a set of pencils. 'Start with these.'

Frieda glanced round and glared at Leonard. 'Who says you can draw me?'

'Be quiet or you'll ruin my concentration.'

Frieda grumbled and closed her eyes but the trickle of a smile revealed she was pleased. After half an hour Tibor set his own brush down and leaned over Leonard's drawing, studying it with solemn concentration. He gave a single nod.

'Yes. The kid has got her. The mouth is a little big, and her chin is not so sharp but the eyes. Yes. There she is.'

Juliet looked at the picture and kissed the top of Leonard's head. Frieda wriggled round to see.

'It's not terrible.' She almost smiled. 'Come for a swim, squirt.'

Squabbling happily, the children raced across the sand.

Tibor stretched and gave a great yawn. 'So, Juliet Montague, why are you here in beautiful California? Just a simple holiday? I think France or Norfolk might be easier. Norfolk is England, right?'

'I'm here because of a painting. A painting and a gallery.' She reached into the pocket of her sundress and brought out the scrap of newspaper. He scrutinised it, his lips moving as he read the Yiddish.

'*The Gallery of Vanished Husbands*,' he said, translating. 'This man with the circle round him, he is your husband?'

'Yes.'

'And you think he is here in Los Angeles?'

'Yes. But I haven't found him yet.'

'You should try this Gorgeous George's Glasses. It says—'

'I've tried already. He wasn't there. Do you know where I might ask about him? Someone must know him.'

Tibor stared at her blankly.

'He's Hungarian,' said Juliet. 'His name was Molnár.'

Tibor shook his head and went back to his painting. 'I don't know any Molnár. I don't know any Hungarians any more. They all go to a cafe.'

Juliet sat up, knocking over a vase of brushes so that a

river of green water trickled along the cement. 'Will you take me?'

Tibor shook his head. 'No. I never go. I tell you where it is.'

Juliet toyed with asking Mickey to keep an eye on the kids but decided on reflection that they'd be safer alone. She waited until they were in bed, listening to the rhythmic patter of their breath to signal they were asleep, and then crept out of the apartment, shoes clutched in her hand.

Leonard, who was only pretending to drift off and was a little concerned he might have overdone it with the snoring, sat up in bed and listened to the click of the door. He knew she was plotting something from the minute he saw her put on lipstick instead of brushing her teeth. He crept down the stairs in the dark behind her, trying not to trip over his pyjamas, which were embarrassing hand-me-downs from Frieda, listening as the front door to the building opened and closed. He rushed down to the porch, watching through the glass as his mother climbed into the Plymouth and drove off. He watched the tail-lights of the car vanish around the corner. Perhaps tonight she'd find him. Perhaps tonight his father would come home.

The steering wheel slid through Juliet's damp palms, the tyres squealing against the kerb as she parked. The lights from the cafe dribbled out onto the pavement, nicotine yellow. She wound down the window and listened for a moment to the grunts of laughter and drifting music. Years ago, she'd been to plenty of these places with George. In the first days of their marriage he'd taken her with him – and she'd even enjoyed sitting at his elbow watching as he played chess, pinking with pride when he trounced the old men who lost with Slavic melodrama, slumping back against their wooden chairs and grabbing at her arm, '*Ach, your husband, he kills me! He robs the blood from my veins. Show a little pity and fetch a fellow another schnapps. And a little poppy seed cake.*'

A fiddle cried out into the night and boots stamped a long-remembered rhythm – a *shtetl* lurking in Culver City. She wished Tibor was with her but he'd been immovable in his refusal. 'I won't go back there. Hungary is much too cold. I told you it's this quality sunshine that keeps me kicking.'

Juliet hoped that the noise and the packed bodies would mean that she could slip in to the cafe unnoticed, but the fiddler lowered his bow and twenty pairs of eyes turned to stare. Looking straight ahead, she walked to the bar.

'A coffee, please.'

A balding middle-aged man bent with some difficulty, his shirt buttons straining to contain his spreading stomach. He filled her a small glass with clear, pungent liquid. She sniffed at it dubiously.

'What's that?' she asked.

'Coffee,' said the man with a snort.

Behind the bar a stout woman in a flowered pinafore dried glasses with a dirty tea towel and yelled at unseen children. From somewhere echoed the sound of a TV show and canned hilarity. The patrons stopped staring at Juliet and returned to their games of chess and cards and recreational bickering. In a corner someone read the *Jewish Daily Forward* and Juliet wondered about the husbands featured in this month's gallery. The faces around the cafe were familiar – there was her father's bald head, Uncle Jacob's smirk and Uncle Ed's filthy laugh. She relaxed a little. The fiddler began to play again, a leisurely polka – slow enough for even the very old or very drunk to dance to.

'I'm looking for this man,' she said, pulling out the newspaper clipping of George and passing it to the man behind the bar.

He studied it, scowling. 'You police?'

Juliet laughed. 'No. I'm his wife.'

'Even worse.'

Juliet tried to take back the scrap of paper but the barman kept his fingers over it. The woman with the dishcloth held out her hand for the picture. Meekly, he surrendered it to her and slunk off to rearrange the glasses.

'You are looking for this man?' asked the woman jabbing at George with a chipped scarlet nail.

Juliet nodded.

The woman studied her from top to bottom and seemed to approve. She banged on the bar for silence and held the picture up above her head, showing it round the cafe.

'Any of you know this man? George Molnár. His wife is here looking for him.'

There was muttering and laughter in a mix of English, Hungarian and Yiddish.

'Who sent you here?' called an elderly man in a white T-shirt and open sandals that revealed thin, hairy toes.

'Tibor. Tibor Jankay.'

'Tibor? *Mein Gott.* When you see him, tell him he still owes Edgar twenty bucks.'

'Sure,' said Juliet. 'When you tell me if you've seen George Molnár.'

'Don't trust him,' muttered the woman to Juliet. 'He knows nothing. Just likes a little attention from a woman. His wife has ignored him for years.'

'Where you from?' asked another man, younger than the rest and handsome underneath the loosening of his jaw line.

'England.'

'All that way to find this George? I hope he's worth it.' He winked.

'My wife wouldn't go to Beverly Hills to find me,' added

the first man. 'Not if I was having a heart attack and a stroke and the screaming heebie-jeebies all at once.'

'I know a George Molnár.'

Juliet looked round at a round man with a shining, sweating face, sitting behind a chess set. He licked his fat lips with a darting tongue.

'He had an optical store, Gorgeous George's or something.'

Juliet stepped forward. 'Yes, yes, that's the place.'

The man glowed with dampness, moisture beading on his head. He wore little pebble spectacles, and had round blue marble eyes and three half-moon chins, so that to Juliet he looked as if he was made entirely of circles. With a saveloy finger he pushed his specs up his nose.

'He had a wife. A pretty little thing. Sharp tongue. Sharper elbows. Only met her once or twice, but it wasn't you.'

Juliet shook her head. 'No, it wasn't me,' she agreed. 'Are you quite sure the man was this George?'

She retrieved the paper from the woman behind the counter and presented it to the round man. He gave a single nod.

'It's the same. I liked him. Good card player. Too good. If you weren't careful with George you'd lose your shirt.'

With that she knew it was her George. Her legs turned to cotton wool and she leaned back against the wall. The round man watched her, absently picking up a chess piece to scratch his ear.

'Yeah, I remember his wife. She was Valerie or Veronica or something.'

'Vera?' asked Juliet softly.

'That was it,' said the man, slapping the chess piece back down on the table. 'Vera.'

Juliet didn't bother trying to sleep. She needed to think. The pale city night melted into a half-hearted dawn, a lacklustre sun

230

slinking up over the buildings. She hadn't experienced proper darkness since the bus ride from New York. In Los Angeles daylight gave way to the neon dark of late-night drugstores and streetlights and the acid glow of the office buildings. She longed for the deep night of Fippenny Wood – Max insisted that one needed darkness to purify the soul. At dusk he'd pour them both a drink, sighing with pleasure at nightfall. She'd thought it was funny – a man's love of the dark – until now, faced with this ruthless, light-filled city. It drove away her thoughts. Tibor's sunshine was suddenly too bright. No wonder his Venice paintings were all livid reds and yellow sand – there was no room for brown and grey and the eyelash soft green of woodland moss. It was a place of colour but no texture.

When the children woke they found Juliet's bed empty and the secret door to the roof ajar. Leonard burst outside, half expecting to find his father sipping a cup of coffee on the terrace beside his mother, in the same way he used to fling open the cupboard door under the stairs at home ready to find a burglar. But his mother was quite alone, sitting on the wall, lighting cigarette after cigarette. She sent Frieda down to the beach to tell Tibor that she was ill and couldn't pose for him. Leonard stayed behind, perched on the wall, wishing he could ask what had happened, but his mother's unusual stillness made him nervous – like the jumpy feeling in his belly before a spelling test. She sat and stared at the sea without seeming to notice it at all.

Frieda ate bubblegum for breakfast and Leonard finished the chocolate in the icebox in full view of Juliet but she said nothing, not even when he declared, 'Well, I hope this doesn't give me a tummy-ache or upset the old *kishkies*.' By three o'clock they were starting to worry. Frieda wasn't sure whether in the list of telephone numbers their grandmother had provided there was one to call in the event of sudden craziness. But at half past four Juliet roused herself and insisted that they all shower and be ready to leave in less than an hour. Relieved at her mother's return to reality, Frieda was preparing to make a fuss when she noticed that Juliet's face was pale with anger. Not the kind of anger caused by Leonard leaving a library book outside in the rain or even the sort Frieda had ignited when she'd borrowed Juliet's expensive face powder and spilled the tub all over the bedroom carpet. This was a different shade of anger, quiet and adult. When Leonard reached for her hand, Frieda let him take it, even though she wasn't a kid any more and his fingers were candy sticky.

They climbed into the Plymouth, neither of the children daring to ask where they were going, and drove inland through streets of low-rise Lego houses. Juliet halted the car, turned off the engine and sat twisting her watchstrap. Leonard nudged Frieda, pointing out the shop front opposite: Gorgeous George's Glasses.

'Let's go,' said Juliet with sudden resolve.

She marched both children across the road and, avoiding the front door to the shop, led them up a narrow alley to the rear of the house and to a second door. The lights were on and through the open window drifted the smell of roasting chicken fat which mingled with the sound of urgent baseball commentary from a wireless set. Juliet reached for the bell. There was shuffling from within and then the wireless fell silent. Vera opened the door.

'Hello, Mrs Molnár,' said Juliet. 'Where's George?'

Vera held a cigarette in one hand and a glass of wine in the other. Her face showed no surprise, her eyebrows painted in a perfect immovable arch, but the hand holding the cigarette trembled so that ash spilled onto her bare feet.

'You'd better come in.'

Frieda and Leonard followed their mother, tripping into a

small, untidy kitchen, every surface littered with cookery books, chopping boards, bowls filled with coloured shells and glossy apples. Piles of grey laundry lay heaped on the counter – jockstraps and socks drying over a packet of matzo meal.

'Jerry!' yelled Vera.

There was the squeal of sneakers on lino and then the red-haired boy joined them in the kitchen. His mouth formed an 'O' of surprise when he saw the Montagues, and he glanced at his mother, who smiled serenely and poked in her purse with one hand, not surrendering her glass of wine or cigarette.

'Jerry, we've guests for dinner. Pop to the store and get some ice cream? And I'm not sure there's enough chicken. Pick up a pizza too.' She handed him a rolled-up bill. 'Take the children with you.'

Frieda scowled at the word 'children' but trailed outside after Jerry and Leonard nevertheless. They walked in silence for a few minutes, each sensing that something significant was happening back at the house, but none of them quite sure how to address it.

'How are those paper airplanes working out?' asked Jerry at last.

'Super,' said Leonard, perking up.

Jerry laughed and then lapsed into silence. 'You wanna see something cool?' he said after a pause.

Leonard and Frieda nodded – of course they did. Jerry led them along a side street. After ten minutes a red sign flashed before them, 'The Studio Drive-Thru Movie Theater'. He halted, hands in his pockets.

'We don't have any money,' confessed Frieda.

'Or a car,' added Leonard helpfully.

Jerry grinned. 'Don't need 'em. We're not going in the front.'

The houses gave way to a row of faded shop fronts – a pizza parlour, drugstore, nail salon and a large parking lot. Jerry marched to the back of the lot and, checking over his shoulder, scrambled up a bank. With a strong freckled arm he hauled up the others. There was a high fence, but with familiar confidence he kicked at a panel and squeezed through, Frieda and Leonard following close behind. Jerry leaned back against the wooden panels and gave a happy sigh.

'See,' he said, waving his hand like a prince showing off his kingdom.

The setting sun ignited the clouds a red as bright as their grandmother's electric fire. The glow spread across the cars parked nose to tail, the sun flashing off a hundred windshields. At the front was erected a vast movie screen. Jerry studied it for a second and then sniffed.

'Saw this last week. Was Okay. Kinda dull. Though she does take her top off at the end.'

He sprawled on a scrubby patch of grass, the others flopping down beside him.

'I can watch anything for free this way,' he said. 'Saw *West Side Story* and *The Guns of Navarone* and everything with John Wayne.'

Leonard nodded his approval but Frieda wrinkled her nose.

'What's the point of seeing *West Side Story* without the music?' she demanded.

Jerry grinned his milk-white grin. 'I got a portable radio. My dad gave it to me. I tune it in to the movie theatre and I sit up here and watch the movie and listen along and it costs me *bupkis*.'

Leonard stared at him, awed at his ingenuity with the portable radio, but most of all jealous that his father had given it to him.

Vera swept the laundry off the kitchen table and onto the floor and started laying places for dinner. Juliet counted five settings.

'When will George be back?' she asked.

Vera closed the cutlery drawer.

'Hell if I know.'

'No more silly lies,' snapped Juliet. 'Where is George Montague?'

Vera sank onto a chair. The oven clock ticked and the soup gurgled on the stove. She drained her wine glass and took a breath, her accent growing stronger under duress. 'I don't know any George Montague, but George *Molnár* is gone. Disappeared three years ago.'

Juliet closed her eyes and felt a weariness seep into her soul like damp. She'd come all this way to find him, only to discover he'd vanished again.

'Do you know where he went?'

Vera shook her head. 'He was here one day and then he wasn't. Took some money. Quite a lot of money. And a photo of Jerry and a painting of a little girl.'

Juliet's heart beat a little faster.

'A painting?'

'Yes. We used to have it in the living room. She had dark eyes and brown hair and a naughty look that made me think that she was often sent to bed without any dinner. George never told me who the picture was of. I never asked but I guessed. I liked the picture. I liked it very much.'

'So did I,' said Juliet. 'He stole it when he left us.'

Vera stretched her legs, a bare toe wiggling through a hole in her stocking. 'The picture was very valuable?'

'Quite valuable.'

'Then I suppose that's why he took it. But so long as he was here, he didn't sell it, which was strange. Expensive things didn't last long with George.'

'No,' agreed Juliet. She supposed she ought to tell Vera the unsavoury truth. 'I'm afraid when George came to California and married you, he was still married to me.'

She looked to see what effect this was having on the other woman, but Vera stared back at her, perfectly impassive.

'He never divorced me, Vera. We're both married to George,' said Juliet slowly, uncertain that she had understood.

Vera studied Juliet for a minute and then smiled, not unkindly. 'Yes, we are both married to George, but what you don't understand is that I am his first wife, not his second.'

Juliet felt suddenly very cold, even though the mist and grease from the roasting chicken was slicking the windows with steam.

Vera conjured with her cigarette. 'I mean that purely in a practical sense. I married Georgy Molnár on 1 August 1939 in the Rumbach Street synagogue in Budapest. I was already six months' pregnant with our daughter Ana. Tamas arrived the following year. Tamas had the same blue eyes as Leonard but he did not need spectacles.'

Juliet blinked and swallowed at the lump in her throat. In her mind she could hear her father's voice – spectacles were a blessing, a talisman against harm.

'We were happy enough for a while. Georgy and I always fight. But the babies kept us busy and we were as happy as most people.'

'And Jerry?'

'Is the youngest. He remembers nothing of before in Hungary. Thank God.

'In 1944 they took Georgy away with the other men. I guessed he was probably dead. The children and I stayed in the ghetto. We managed for a while and then we didn't.'

Juliet watched Vera like a painter, trying to decipher her face. Lines around her eyes, her teeth perfect white. Too white. Juliet realised that they were dentures. Vera noticed her staring and clicked her tongue under the teeth, lifted up the bottom set to reveal her gums, raw and pink as an earthworm.

'There was not enough to eat in the ghetto,' said Vera. 'I got sick and one morning I got out of bed and spat out my teeth one by one like orange pips into a bowl.'

Without her teeth, Vera looked suddenly old. Then she slid them back in place and was herself again, calm and rouged.

'What happened to Tamas and Ana?' asked Juliet.

'Typhus. Perhaps it was for the best. To die in their mother's arms, nursed and loved. What came later was worse.'

These unknown children were the brothers and sister of her own children. George had gone but the rest of them remained connected like a chain of paper dolls.

'I'm so sorry.' She swallowed tears, sensing that they would only irritate Vera.

'You ask, so I tell you,' said Vera, her voice flat. She sucked hard on her cigarette. 'I have Jerry. We have a nice house, enough to eat. Good friends. I listen when they complain about their husbands. This American life is not so bad.'

'But George found you again?'

'Yes. I thought he was dead. Then one day in 1952 he comes back. He was in England and heard we were in California and he comes and finds us.'

Juliet blinked. 'I always thought he disappeared because of some gambling debt. But it wasn't that at all. He left us for you.'

'Yes,' said Vera.

She offered no apology. Juliet supposed Vera did not consider it her fault that George abandoned Juliet and his other children. He chose Jerry over Leonard and Frieda.

'It's stupid really, but I thought he left us because of money, but he didn't. He left us for you.'

237

'Not for me. For the little ones. He wanted Ana and Tamas. But there was only Jerry and me.'

In the silence that followed, Juliet tried to imagine explaining Vera to her parents and laughed. She would tell them that George was not at the optician's in Culver City and insist they mustn't search any more. How could she tell them the truth? *George left me and went to America to return to his first wife. She wasn't dead. George and I were never really married at all. My children are bastards. Mamzerin.* Juliet sighed and her laughter subsided like the tide. She wasn't an *aguna* or a chained woman or a living widow, she was something worse – a bigamist and an adulteress.

Leonard and Frieda meandered back to the house. Jerry held the pizza box, doling out slices. At the end of the street, all three paused by silent consent and sat on the kerb.

'Why are you here?' asked Jerry.

The topic had been raised at last. To Leonard's surprise, it was Frieda who answered.

'Well, we came here looking for our dad. Our mum thinks we don't know. Do you want to know what I think?'

Jerry nodded.

'I think our mum thinks that your mum stole him or is having an affair with him or something'

Frieda spoke at great speed and with great confidence, pronouncing 'affair' with what she believed to be a French accent.

'My dad's gone too,' Jerry said, handed out the last slices of pizza.

'But the radio?' said Leonard.

'He gave it to me before he left. I think he would have taken it with him. It was real expensive but I was at the movies and I had it on me so he couldn't. I don't know if I miss him or I hate him.'

The words tumbled out of him, a confession of feelings that he only knew he possessed as he spoke them aloud. Leonard and Frieda carefully said nothing so as to spare him the humiliation of their sympathy.

The three children ate their pizza side by side in the growing darkness. Leonard studied Jerry. He looked very like the newspaper cutting of George Montague. Jerry chuckled at something Frieda had said, and Leonard watched him and felt something familiar and buried stirred inside. He remembered a man's laugh and a pair of dark eyes. He had the strangest feeling that Jerry was his brother. They sat in the gloom, the streetlights pinging on in a burst of pale light, with only Leonard guessing that they were all missing the same man. He wanted to tell Jerry but he wasn't quite sure how, and then Frieda and Jerry were arguing about who looked better on horseback, Gary Cooper or John Wayne, and so Leonard finished his pizza and wiped his fingers along his trousers and said nothing.

Tibor finished his portrait of Juliet the day the Montagues were due to catch the bus back to New York. He suggested they have a little goodbye party and official unveiling on the beach. Juliet and the children dressed up in the portrait's honour – even Frieda humming as she donned her favourite spotted sundress that showed off her tan. They wandered along the beach in the afternoon sunshine, watching pelicans scoop up fish in vast, prehistoric beaks. This was a magic holiday land and Leonard struggled to think of Venice existing along the same timeline as Mulberry Avenue, Chislehurst. It had been the best summer ever – full of intrigue, adventure and ice cream and to top it off, he was certain he'd grown almost an inch.

Frieda was equally content, though she'd have preferred to be taking back with her the story of some rosy summer romance. On the other hand, she decided that she could just make one up and no one at school would ever know. She resolved to fine-tune the details on the journey back to England.

Tibor waved as he saw them coming. He was in a cream linen suit and clutched a bag of goodies. The portrait sat on her easel, covered with a cloth.

'Here, have a little something,' he said, passing glasses of orange juice to the children. He gave another to Juliet, tipping in a snifter of something else.

'A cocktail,' he said, when she raised an eyebrow.

'To friendships and sunshine,' said Tibor, clinking his glass against Juliet's.

Leonard grinned. Grandma had always been very clear that it was common to clink.

Tibor nodded his approval. 'He's got it. And I have a something for you.' He delved into his bag and retrieved a brand-new set of pencils and a bound sketchpad of good, thick paper. 'You've the knack for drawing. Maybe it'll only be a hobby, maybe something more, but you might like to find out.'

'Thank you,' said Leonard, taking the presents reverently in both hands.

'That's terribly kind, Tibor.' Juliet smiled. 'Can I see my picture now?'

They huddled around the easel as, with a magician's flick, Tibor removed the cloth. A naked woman with cherry-bun breasts soared across the sky above Venice Beach, her hair rippling out behind her. The sky was August blue; the green sea thrashed below. The woman's eyes were closed, perhaps against the glare, but Juliet could tell that she looked happy. The portrait leaked happiness. And yet there was one disappointment. Juliet felt it rumble in her belly.

'Well?' demanded Tibor, for once wanting an opinion.

'The woman is me?'

'Of course.'

'She looks – sorry, I look just like all the other women you've painted. The same smile, the same flying hair and the same heart-shaped chin.'

Tibor shook his head. 'No. All the other women look like you. I'd been painting you for many years before I met you on the beach.'

Juliet met his gaze. He silently tipped his hat. She couldn't tell whether it was true or not. She wasn't sure whether it mattered.

'I love the picture,' she declared, realising as she said it that she really did. 'I can't wait to show it in London. How would you feel about me selling your work in my gallery?'

'I never sell.'

'But you'll sell me this one?' she asked.

'No. Of course not. I never sell a picture. I love them all. How can I give her away?' he asked, pointing at the portrait on the easel.

The afternoon was ruined. Of course she'd presumed that she'd take the picture home with her. Frowning, she tried to recall if it had ever been discussed and reluctantly concluded that it had not.

'Now it's time for cake,' said Tibor.

At eight o'clock Juliet walked the children back to the apartment to finish their packing, returning to have one final drink with Tibor and say goodbye before the taxi came. It was quiet on the beach apart from the rush of the tide. The sea swallowed the traffic and city noise in its roar. She searched the gloom for Tibor, but he wasn't there. The cocktail had gone to her head and the sound of the waves swirled in her ears. The painting sat on the easel, dusk turning the colours into silver and grey.

Her lips parted in a private half-smile. George had stolen her portrait and a piece of her remained lost. *I won't leave another part of myself behind. I won't have another man keep a little piece of me.* She looked around again, but Tibor was still nowhere to be seen. She tried to tell herself that he expected her to do this, that he'd disappeared to make it easy for her. She seized the painting and ran back along the path, her plimsolls slapping on the asphalt.

The children said nothing when they saw the rectangular package wrapped up in a beach towel in the luggage rack on the bus, but they seemed pleased and more pleased still when instead of hanging it in her bedroom, Juliet displayed the portrait at the top of the stairs – braving Mrs Greene's tongue-clicking and sighs.

Juliet guessed that Tibor never reported the theft, but imagined the story became one of his favourites. Over dinner or schnapps he'd declare to his fellow guests that he never sold a painting but would admit with great delight that once upon a time a woman stole one.

Juliet wasn't the only thief that night. When she reached inside her pocket and pulled out the scrap of newspaper, the photograph of George was gone. He'd been carefully cut free so that a square hole took the place of his face. Her husband had vanished even from this gallery. She suspected that Leonard had taken him, but somehow it was easier not to ask.

Leonard kept the photo carefully sandwiched in his new sketchpad. For the first weeks they were home he only looked at his father, scrutinising his face for any likeness with his own. Then, one rainy October afternoon about a month after their return from America, he took out his pencils, sat on his bed and started to draw him. The first attempt wasn't bad, he decided, but he thought it best to try another. He added in a dash of Jerry, then gave George his specs. Holding out the finished sketch, he gave a snort. This one wasn't right at all. He flicked over the page, took up his pencil and began another.

Lazing on a Sunny Afternoon,
Tom Hopkins, Photograph of Mural at Ashcombe House, 1964

IT WAS NEARLY half past six and Juliet was late. She knew that three streets away her mother was fretting over the fate of a roast chicken. Every Friday they were late for dinner, and every Friday Juliet promised Mrs Greene that the next week they would be on time and the chicken wouldn't be spoiled. There was always so much to finish at the gallery before the weekend, and she realised it would be easier to dispense with the ritual of *Shabbos* dinner and stay until eight or nine to work. She told Charlie that leaving early on Friday was something she did to placate her mother – but the truth was that Juliet valued the rhythm of those nights. However busy and harassed she had been during the week, no matter how frantic before an exhibition or frustrated when a rival poached one of her newly discovered artists, she knew that come the evening she would be sitting around the highly polished dining table set with the good placemats brought back from the Canaries by Uncle Ed in 1955. Frieda and Leonard made a token show of reluctance but Juliet understood that it was her job to stand firm so that they could *kvetch* in safety, knowing that Friday chicken was an immovable event. There was a pleasure in the ordinariness of it, as reassuring as a nursery lullaby.

Frieda stood beside the door in her coat, waiting for Juliet as she came downstairs. She wore thick woollen tights even though it was June and warm. Her dress came well below her knees and was a stiff, dull brown. Juliet had given up leaving her Chanel lipsticks in the bathroom since Frieda never touched them. It had started slowly, Juliet couldn't quite remember when she'd first noticed, but some time after their return from America Frieda started declining the Saturday trips up to the gallery with Juliet and Leonard, instead going to *shul* with her grandfather. Juliet wasn't worried; certainly not at first. Lots of teenagers turned to God for a year or two. As Juliet's hemlines grew more daring and the parties she was invited to a little louder, the cocktails stronger, Frieda proclaimed that she didn't approve of bare legs or ladies drinking champagne or schnitzel fried in butter. Or her mother. That, at least, was what Juliet concluded, but she said nothing and dismissed it as religious affectation and hoped she'd grow out of it. She suspected that Frieda's faith had bloomed to irritate her – the more Juliet withdrew from religion, declining even to fast on Yom Kippur, the more frequent Frieda's visits to the brick synagogue in Cedar Avenue became. Yet her bedroom was divided neatly into two halves: the bookshelves filled with sombre religious texts and tomes on morality, but the desk remained crowded with singles and LPs. The Kinks jostled beside *The Complete Kosher Kitchen* and 'Can't Buy me Love' sat on top of *A Girl's Guide to Jewish Ethics*. As long as Frieda still spent all her pocket money on tickets for The Shadows and hitched up her skirt at the end of the street when she believed her mother wasn't looking, Juliet decided not to worry.

The phone rang in the hall but Juliet made no move to answer it, perfectly confident that it would be Mrs Greene. She hadn't wanted to install the phone at all but as the gallery became busier and clients or artists wanted to talk on evenings and at weekends it had become impossible to resist. The phone continued to ring and Juliet continued to ignore it. Frieda picked up the receiver, her face falling when she realised it was for Juliet.

'I'm out,' mouthed Juliet, thinking of Mrs Greene's wrath and the soon-to-be-incinerated chicken.

'She's right here,' said Frieda. 'May I ask who's calling?'

Juliet shook her head and sighed.

'It's a Mr Gold for you,' said Frieda.

Juliet took the receiver and frowned. 'I'm sorry, Mr Gold, but I can't do it. Please stop calling. I don't wish to be rude, but you don't want art, you want wallpaper.'

There was a chuckle on the other end of the line. Then a voice with a soft northern accent spoke: 'At least come and see the house. How about next weekend? You have kids, right?'

'Yes.'

'Bring them along. I'm having a bit of a party. One of the lads might even come. It'll be fun.'

'It's very kind, Mr Gold. I really must go.'

Juliet replaced the receiver and started to call for Leonard but Frieda was eyeing her with an odd look.

'Who was that?'

Juliet frowned. 'An old school friend of Charlie's. He's made quite a success of himself and has bought a rather splendid country house. He wants me to find art for it.'

Frieda looked puzzled. 'Isn't that what you do?'

'Now you sound like Charlie. I find the right piece for the right person. Paintings should be loved, not fixed to a wall because someone thinks that they're hip this month. Mr Gold's never even been to the gallery. He doesn't know what he likes. He just believes that Wednesday's is the place to be seen buying art.'

Juliet noticed a box lying beside the front door, and bent to open it.

'Don't,' said Frieda.

246

'What on earth do you mean?'

Frieda lolled against the door, plunged her hands into her pockets and eyed her mother carefully.

'They're plates.'

'Plates? Whatever for?'

'I told Rabbi Plotsky that you don't keep kosher at home so Mrs Plotsky sent round some clean plates. I don't want to eat *treif* any more.'

Juliet recoiled. The rustling of disapproval from the neighbours she had grown quite used to, it was a back-ground buzz that one learned to ignore like a traffic hum, but Frieda's disdain was different. Juliet's cooking had never been splendid, but they always ate together – even if it was wieners from a jar and slightly stale toast. The sharing of a meal joined them, but now Frieda was insisting that she wanted to be set apart. Juliet looked at her daughter and felt the space between them open and settle, cool as snowfall. She wished that she could snatch Frieda away from all the well-meaning busybodies in Chislehurst, take her to London. But she knew with quiet unease that if she moved, Frieda would not come.

Juliet stopped buttoning her coat and glanced at her daughter. She had seen an opportunity to prise Frieda away from her religious fervour.

'Mr Gold might interest you. He manages that pop band. The Rigbys.'

Frieda started to laugh. 'Allan Gold wants you to find paintings for his house and you said no? You really are crazy. If he asked you to scrub his floors you should have said yes.'

'You want to meet him? Because he's invited us for a weekend.'

The change in Frieda was instant. The stiff and

disapproving girl softened like chocolate in the sun, and her eyes suddenly brightened as she grabbed her mother's arm.

'We have to go. We have to. Call him back this instant and say yes. Will the Rigbys be there? I'm going to marry Matt Rigby. Or Ringo Starr.'

Frieda squeezed her arm and Juliet realised that it had been a long time since her daughter had spontaneously touched her. She refrained from saying that she'd thought Frieda was planning to marry a rabbi rather than Ringo.

'We'd have to drive there on a Friday night. You couldn't go to *shul* with your grandfather.'

Frieda hesitated only for a moment. 'Please. Mum, please. I have to meet the Rigbys.'

For the first time in many years, she gazed at her mother with something close to awe.

'All right. I'll call Mr Gold in the morning,' said Juliet. She was quite willing to accept an invitation if it meant reminding Frieda that art and music were more tempting than God.

Sylvia and Charlie had been asked too, and they all arrived together jammed into Sylvia's ancient Land Rover, Frieda and Leonard squashed irritably onto a single seat. They spilled out onto the gravel driveway, rubbing cramped legs and gulping mouthfuls of warm sunshine. Sylvia was perfectly dressed as always, in a pale linen skirt and blouse, hiding a late night behind a pair of dark sunglasses. Leonard and Frieda lingered beside the car, Leonard clutching a bag with his homework and Frieda for once bare legged, having dispensed with her usual woollen tights. She kept fiddling with her hem, as though unsure whether to hike it up above her knees. Juliet glanced at her, hoping that this visit was a good idea.

She wished that Max could have come. No matter how

tempting the invitation, he hadn't left the solace of Fippenny Wood since the unfortunate voyage to New York. When she'd returned from America she'd intended not to see him again, or certainly not as a lover, and yet when she'd travelled to the cottage to inform him of this she'd found herself in bed with him. In the morning she'd examined her feelings with candour and concluded that since she was not in general weak-willed she must, in fact, still be in love with him. Over the last few years she'd come to accept that this was permanent and that Max's limitations as a partner, rather than distressing her, suited her very well. For the most part she enjoyed neither of them being dependent on the other and her life in London being completely her own. The weekends with him in Dorset she savoured. On this occasion, however, she felt a twinge of regret, wishing for once that she could have loved an easier man, one who viewed weekends at country manors as a treat rather than a terror.

The house was on the edge of Cranborne Chase, nestled snug in the crook of a huddle of low hills. Allan Gold had bought it that February and the driveway teemed with armies of builders, plumbers and electricians, all trying to haul the ancient and tumbledown mansion into the twentieth century. Juliet's first feeling was one of pity. Beneath the scaffolding and blue tarpaulins was a handsome Georgian house, but like an ageing beauty whose husband won't let her grow old in peace, carpenters had replaced her windows and roofers patched the broken slates and rebuilt the crumbling chimneys, tugging and pinching her into an approximation of her old charm. The work needed a season or two to soften, for now the paintwork was too bright, the varnish a little orange and the new tiles gleamed black, devoid of lichen. In order to re-point the stone, the wisteria had been stripped away from the front façade and all her creases and cracks were exposed in

249

the glare of the June sunshine. Only the gardens remained wild and as yet untamed. A riot of fierce roses bloomed in yellows, crimson and white – some in tangled shrubs, others climbing the trees and dangling down from the canopies, so that it looked at first glance like the ash and elm bloomed with multicoloured blossom. Half a dozen canvas chairs had been set out on a long and uncut lawn that was already starting to seed, the feathered grass wobbling in the breeze. A young woman snoozed in one of the chairs, sucking her thumb, her cotton skirt riding up to reveal a pair of pink knickers. A pitcher of something that probably wasn't lemonade sat on a low table in front of her.

Juliet turned to Charlie. 'I hope you brought your paints.'

Charlie smiled and shook his head. 'No, this is a weekend of pleasure.'

'I brought mine,' said Leonard, but Juliet had noticed a slight man sailing across the drive towards them and didn't hear him.

'This is my old pal Allan,' said Charlie. 'Allan, meet Juliet.'

'So pleased you decided to come,' declared Allan, kissing Juliet on the cheek and shaking Charlie's hand. 'And you brought the young people. Super.' He turned to Frieda. 'We'll do the tour in a bit and I'll show you Matt Rigby's first guitar.'

Frieda glowed.

'I really am pleased Charlie twisted your arm,' Allan was saying, smiling at Juliet.

'I haven't agreed to take the job yet,' she said.

'Oh, but you will,' said Allan. 'No one can resist my charms for long.'

Juliet laughed, wondering why Charlie had told her Allan was queer, but hadn't thought to mention he was Jewish.

Everything about Allan was neat. He was trim and

immaculately dressed in a beautifully cut suit and perfectly polished shoes. His wavy hair was combed smooth and the knot in his tie absolutely symmetrical. The small matted burrs that clung to Juliet's trousers and to everyone else's didn't dare touch Allan. A crowd of rabbits hopped untidily across the grass and Allan frowned.

'I haven't got to the garden yet,' he said, waving vaguely at the matted shrubs and crowded beds studded with ground elder and creeping ivy. 'I'll have to hire someone. I want to rebuild the orangery. I'd like to grow oranges. And maybe pineapples. And I'd like some peacocks. Do you know where I can get peacocks, Charlie?'

Charlie shrugged but Sylvia shook her head. 'I wouldn't. Peacocks make an awful racket. Quite horrid.'

'Oh, what a pity,' said Allan, sounding terribly disappointed. 'What about ornamental chickens?'

He jumped back to avoid a pair of workmen struggling under the weight of several enormous planks. He watched them intently, and Juliet suspected that despite his aura of frenzied charm, Allan knew precisely what was happening in every cranny of the house and garden. He turned back to his guests with a warm grin.

'You must be hot after your journey. Let's go and find you something to drink,' he said, leading them into the house.

Juliet noticed that nailed to the magnificent gothic doorway was a small wooden *mezuzah*. Allan kissed his fingers and brushed it as he passed. 'A year ago I was still living in my parents' house in Manchester,' he muttered, half to himself.

The house reeked of damp and half the huge floorboards in the great hall had been uprooted like some strange indoor forest. The wallpaper was mostly stripped, and the remaining ribbons were darkened by mould and the ceiling soot-stained, but the light that filtered through the large windows filled the

251

room with sunshine. Juliet sighed with happiness – despite the damage the hall had perfect Georgian proportions, the ideal balance of light and space.

'I'm going to paint it all white,' said Allan.

Juliet shook her head. 'Don't. Not if you are serious about paintings. The glare will affect the colours. You want a soft green. Or an earthy orange might do.'

'All right. You're the boss.'

Juliet raised an eyebrow, knowing she was being played, finding that she didn't really mind.

'Once it's been painted the right colour, what would you hang here, above the fireplace?' asked Allan.

Juliet took a moment to consider. 'This is a home, not a museum. You want something that people will notice as they walk in, but not such a statement that it detracts from the elegance of the room. And, you want a piece that you'll enjoy for many years – not something that makes you smile once at an exhibition but something you'll be happy to see when come downstairs in your dressing gown on a Sunday morning for a boiled egg.'

'I'm a fan of the boiled egg,' teased Allan.

Juliet was quiet for a moment, tilting her head from side to side as she considered.

'Not a Warhol. Not one of Jim Brownwick's swimming-pool paintings.'

She moved round and surveyed the space from another angle, and then nodded once. 'I think a mural would be right. You want something painted directly onto the plaster, a painting that will become part of the fabric of the house. Even after you're long gone it will stay like a Roman fresco. A symbol of house parties past.'

'Oh, I like the sound of that,' said Allan.

'I like Max Langford—'

'But no one else does,' interrupted Charlie.

'But he's too rural, too strange for here,' added Juliet, ignoring him and looking at Allan. 'You want someone elegant and a little bit romantic. Tom Hopkins.'

'Wonderful! Will you ask him?'

'Yes, all right,' sighed Juliet, realising that she would inevitably find the pictures for the rest of the house. She could rarely see a splendid wall without imagining the perfect picture to hang on it. And, some of her newer artists could really do with both the cache and the cash.

'Get Tom Hopkins round this weekend. Call him now,' said Allan, seeming to bounce on the spot.

Juliet laughed. 'There's no hurry.'

'Why wait?' said Allan. 'I'm going to ask him to do it, so why waste a minute?'

Juliet looked at him and saw that beneath the blue eyes and the smile was a man enjoying the novelty of getting his own way.

'Please,' he said, more softly this time. 'I'd like you to be here when he comes. Talk to him about the kind of thing he'll paint. If it was about music I'd know exactly what to say but pictures isn't really my thing.'

'Fine,' said Juliet, knowing when to surrender. 'Where's your telephone?'

The others waited in the hall for her to come back, listening to the rattling percussion of the builders removing the scaffolding outside. Juliet returned after a few minutes.

'You're in luck. He'll come. He's off to visit Max and you're on the way. He wants a hundred pounds. I told him I thought that would be all right.'

Allan beamed. 'Yes, yes. And we'll see if we can't persuade him to stay.'

Sylvia, quite accustomed to grand country houses, sneaked

back outside to sleep in the sunshine. Charlie was irritated that Juliet had not suggested him to paint the mural and retreated to the kitchen to hunt for a bottle of wine. So it was only the Montague family who accompanied Allan on the tour of the rest of the house. As Allan explained his plans to Juliet, Frieda stalked around in ecstasy, waiting for a Rigby or a Shadow or a Kink to spring through every doorway. She pored over each room in dreamy excitement, as thrilled by the muddy wellingtons in the boot room ('One of these might have touched the foot of Matt Rigby!') as the signed photos of Allan with the stars themselves.

'It's all a bit forlorn now,' said Allan, 'but give it six months and the place will be spiffy again. Had to do the outside first. Patch the roof. Mend the floors. All the boring bits. We're only getting to the fun stuff now.'

The reception rooms were mostly devoid of traditional furniture and were instead stuffed with beanbags, piles of blankets and the odd Lilo. However, every room did seem to have a fully stocked drinks trolley. Juliet noted that Allan was not letting the fact that his house was only half restored, undecorated and unfurnished get in the way of regular parties. In a pretty, sun-filled sitting-room there was a heap of patterned fabric lying in a crumpled heap, but on second glance Juliet realised it was a girl and a boy fast asleep in one another's arms. Allan appeared not even to notice them. Juliet glanced at her children, wondering whether she'd made a mistake in bringing them here. This wasn't really the sort of country house where they'd get cream teas and croquet on the lawn. Leonard studied the couple with some interest and nudged Frieda.

'Why don't you both go outside for a bit?' suggested Juliet.

'Or, you can go choose yourselves a room to sleep in,' said Allan. 'There's plenty of 'em. Go anywhere you like that isn't taken.' He gestured vaguely at the first floor and the children disappeared in a flash before Juliet could object. She listened to the clatter of footsteps on the staircase and turned back to Allan.

'They won't find any guests . . .' she reached for the right word. 'Any *busy* guests, will they?'

Allan frowned, puzzled. 'Shouldn't think so. People come here to relax.'

'Right,' said Juliet, not reassured.

'There'll be more people coming later. We're going to have a little housewarming.'

Juliet felt a nudge of apprehension and pondered whether she ought to marshal Leonard and Frieda into the car and demand that Sylvia drive them to the nearest station.

'The lads should be along in a bit,' said Allan with a touch of pride. 'They always enjoy a party.'

Juliet sighed. That was it. They had to stay. She couldn't possibly bring Frieda along on the promise of meeting the Rigbys and then whisk her away before they appeared.

Juliet followed Allan into a vast, modern kitchen. It was the only room in the house that had been finished. There was a large and gleaming range, a splendid refrigerator and a long table with a dozen chairs. French doors were flung open to the garden and filled the room with the warble of goldfinches and squabbling starlings. The countertops had been scrubbed spotless and hanging above one was a spice rack as well stocked as a county library. The room smelled gently of the sweet scent of proving dough. Beside the range lay racks of cooling pastries: *rugelach*, poppy-seed biscuits, honey cakes and miniature strudels, the pastry just the right shade of wheaten gold. A chocolate cake with treacle-black icing squatted on the table brooding over an array of fairy-cakes and brownies, all decorated with a constellation of Smarties.

Allan lifted a tea towel from over a large basin and peered underneath, sniffing at it with a proprietorial air.

'Brioche,' he announced.

'You made all of these?' asked Juliet waving at the cornucopia of cakes. The kitchen was better stocked than most patisserie windows.

'Of course,' said Allan. 'My dad's a baker by trade. I was supposed to follow him into the family business. In fact, I did for a year or two. The longest years of my life,' he added grimly, sitting down at the table.

He slid a cup of coffee and a plate of biscuits across the table to Juliet.

'Well, you have a gift,' she said nibbling at a *hamantaschen*. 'I can't cook at all. The family recipes all stop with me. I'm a tremendous disappointment to my mother.' Her tone was light, but somehow her voice faltered at the end. 'I was supposed to work in the family business too,' she added.

'I ran off to London and tried to become an actor just to escape it.'

'Were you any good?'

'No. Dreadful. And I got arrested for importuning men outside a public lavatory.'

Juliet stared at him for a moment – taken aback at the casual manner in which he confided his humiliation. Allan smiled at her surprise, and then gave a small sigh.

'It was pretty awful at the time. I slunk back home to the shop and baked currant buns in penance for a year.'

Juliet laughed. 'I think my mother would forgive all my transgressions if I could produce such elegant *hamantaschen*, even once.'

Charlie slid into the kitchen, unnoticed at first. He lingered in the doorway and watched the easy confidence between the other two. Sometimes he felt it was always like this. He introduced people to Juliet and she laughed with them in a way she never did with him. At first he told himself it was because she fancied him – one was never at ease with the object of one's desire, every schoolboy knows that. He had waited for her to leave Max, to realise he was a stunted man, spoiled by war, and turn to him. But she didn't – not even after Max abandoned her on the trip to America. And as the years ticked by, steady as a pocket watch, he realised hope had made him foolish. He watched her and wished, but that was all. She saved her share of the gallery's profits, choosing not to buy a larger house or luxuries, instead, year by year she'd paid back the investors in the gallery, buying them out one by one, but Charlie had resisted. He had only a little stake compared to hers, but he'd held onto it, hoping in this at least they were partners.

Allan spotted him in the corner and hailed him with great delight.

'Ah, there you are, sir. Come sit. We're comparing the ways in which we've disappointed our families. It's a great gag.'

Charlie glanced at Juliet and saw that she looked sad, sadder than he'd ever seen her, and at that moment he understood. She and Allan were different from him – perhaps that's why he hadn't told her that Allan was Jewish. He hadn't wanted her to know that they were in the least bit alike. Instead he'd made a thing out of Allan being queer – he knew it made Juliet uneasy in spite of herself. But it didn't matter in the end. Here they were colluding together across the kitchen table like a pair of old gossips. Charlie remembered Allan at school: the odd one out, the small, sickly Jewish boy. The queer and the Yid. He'd befriended him. He'd seen that he was funny and a little wild and allowed Allan to sniff around the edges of the smart set. The thing was, Charlie realised, the magic circle now belonged to Juliet and Allan and they could not admit him to it. You don't want me, he realised, looking at her. You never did.

Juliet caught his eye and smiled, pushing the plate of biscuits towards him.

'Here, try a *hamantaschen*. I used to adore them when I was small and Allan's are every bit as good as my grandmother's.'

Charlie took one and bit into it, the summer taste of apricot and sugar dissolving on his tongue. He swallowed, unhappiness and sweetness choking him.

In the afternoon everyone disappeared to rest before the party. The garden sweated in the sunshine, the flowers drooping like old men in the heat, and the various guests sought spots in the shade or retreated into the cool of the house. It had fifty rooms, but only a few of them were furnished. Frieda and Leonard had each selected a bedroom but neither contained an actual bed. Leonard's had a mattress with a clean sheet and he decided he was lucky after inspecting Frieda's larger room, which was entirely bare except for a pair of vast picture windows and a heap of bath towels.

Leonard padded over to the window and stared out at the view stretching cloudless and blue out across the hills of the chase, the banks tickled with buttercups and sprays of daisies. He wanted to paint it. It was a familiar urge that had been building in him like a pressure behind the eyes. Ever since America he'd been drawing. He'd filled several sketchpads with a catalogue of portraits of his father – it was a habit now – but he also tried to capture other things. The back of the hill looked to him like a lumbering bull, asleep on its side, the curl of woodland a pair of fierce horns. His fingers itched in his pocket. How would he mix that blue? He sighed, remembering the Latin test on Monday he ought to be swotting for. To his grandparents' delight he'd passed the exam for the prestigious grammar school at the end of the road, and since his entry there at the age of eleven Friday nights had consisted of discussions about where he might choose to go to university. Of course the only real choice was between Oxford and Cambridge. He would be the first member of the family to go to university and the day he went up would be the day the Greene / Montague family pride was restored. On this matter, at least, his mother and his grandparents were united.

'Do you think there's anything for tea?'

Leonard was constitutionally unable to work on an empty stomach. Frieda shrugged, less concerned than her brother about the strict punctuality of meals.

'I bet this is where Matt Rigby sleeps when he's here,' she said.

Leonard doubted it, expecting that even pop stars preferred to sleep in beds rather than on a pile of bath towels. He stared out of the window but the Latin test pricked at him. 'I should probably do some revision.'

Frieda shook her head in disgust. 'You're about to meet the most brilliant musician in the world, and all you can think about is homework. It's bizarre.'

Leonard said nothing. 'Bizarre' was one of Frieda's current words. It was used to describe everything and everyone she viewed with suspicion – from Mrs Kempton's geography lessons ('So bizarre!'), to Leonard's choice in trousers ('Just bizarre!') and most things to do with their mother ('Beyond bizarre!') In this instance it was also inaccurate. Leonard did not really want to think about homework. The thought of it rubbed him like a blister when all he wanted to do was paint.

At six o'clock the doorbell rang. It took everyone by surprise, most of all Allan who hadn't realised that he had a doorbell, let alone one that worked. The folk he invited usually just wandered into the house, not bothering with such niceties. Consequently no one answered it and the bell continued to ring. Leonard gave in first. He'd been meandering from room to room, searching guiltily and half-heartedly for a place to study, and seeing no sign of movement from anywhere else opened the door himself, anticipating one of the dishevelled musicians from one of Frieda's LPs to amble inside.

'Hello,' said Tom Hopkins. 'Your mother summoned me.'

Leonard grinned. 'Yes. She does that.'

He stood back to allow Tom into the hallway. Tom picked his way across the partially lifted floorboards and set down his small leather bag and glanced about with distaste.

'Seems more in need of a carpenter than a mural painter.'

Leonard shrugged.

'Ah, well,' said Tom. 'I suppose I should find your mother and receive my instructions. Do you know where she is?'

Leonard wandered over to one of the large picture windows overlooking the lawns, and saw on the grass a series of striped deckchairs like half a dozen sweetshop bags. The afternoon was ripening into a rosy evening and the light glowed on the figures in the chairs. Juliet lazed on the first, her feet bare and hair swept back beneath a red scarf that dangled down like the scarlet braids of a Lady Godiva. Charlie sprawled on another, scowling in his sleep. Allan sat perfectly upright on a blue-striped one, his trousers falling into immaculate creases, a copy of *The Times* in one hand, a small cigar in the other, the ash tumbling into an obedient pyramid. Above, darts of wagtails shot across the sky, high enough it seemed to pierce the scraps of cloud.

'Shall I go and wake her for you?' asked Leonard.

'No,' said Tom with a chuckle. 'I think we've found our subject.'

'Can I paint some of it?' asked Leonard.

'Are you any good?'

'Yes,' said Leonard.

Tom smiled at his youthful confidence. 'Let's see, shall we,' he said, handing him a brush.

Leonard took it, pushing away all thoughts of Latin verbs.

Tom hesitated, brush aloft. 'Ought we to go and check that your mother approves the plan?'

Leonard shook his head. 'I've only been here an afternoon and no one will mind. It's chaos. I say we just get on with it.'

Tom shrugged. 'And I suppose if Mr Gold doesn't like it, he can always paint over it.'

Tom and Leonard worked quickly, first preparing the surface with a warm wash of colour and then as it dried, each chose a wall and started to paint. Tom began with the figure of Juliet, her crimson scarf a flame in the afternoon sunlight. On the opposite wall Leonard sketched the broad back of the hill, feeling his shoulders relax and sink as he worked, as though he was soaking in a hot, hot bath. Slowly the grass appeared in a green shadow creeping across the ridgeway, then the darkness of the woods and the cleft of the chalk path, a rib of bone through the middle. The birds circled, eyes yellow.

'I like it,' said Charlie's voice from behind him.

Leonard grunted in thanks, but did not turn around.

'What are you dilly-dallying for?' said Tom. 'Pick up a brush.'

Charlie frowned. 'Oh no. I can't do that. Juliet wanted you to do it.'

'For Christ's sake, man. Stop whining,' snapped Tom. 'Take the wall behind the fireplace.'

Charlie obeyed.

The other guests and revellers arrived in trickles. They wandered through the front door – left open to air the paint fumes – and most of them ventured no further than the hallway. Eventually someone decided it would be useful if the remaining floorboards were replaced and the house was briefly filled with hammering. Next beanbags and blankets were spread across the floor and stairs, and everyone sat and watched and smoked. As evening slid into dusk, candles appeared and the painters worked on, their shadow brushes huge against the walls.

Juliet and Frieda sat together on the stairs. The house was filling with smoke from cigarettes and joints and the fizz of burning tea lights so that the three painters appeared to be working in a mist. Juliet watched the painting unfurl across the walls, the three friezes stretching out towards one another. The moment they met would be something, a joining of the world.

Frieda scrutinised the door, waiting for the moment when the Rigbys would appear. For a while her heart rushed and thudded – every new person who emerged through the gloom might be Matt Rigby – and then it slowed. Disappointment seemed inevitable. They would never come. She had nicked herself shaving her legs with Leonard's stupid Woolworth's razor for no reason. She ought to have worn her thick brown tights and frumpy dress to irritate her mother after all. Angrily she wiped the rosy lipstick from her mouth.

Joints slid from reveller to reveller but Juliet and Frieda passed them straight on, never venturing a puff. Vague disquiet tickled at Juliet – this wasn't a place for kids – but somehow she couldn't draw herself away from the paintings emerging on the walls. And besides, she told herself, the partygoers now arriving looked no older than Frieda. She swallowed the voice that wondered about the parents of those other kids.

Tom, Charlie and Leonard moved quickly now, their movements quite distinct, like three conductors of a Mozart concerto; same notes on the page, different sound. Tom remained in his shirt and tie, quiet, methodical – his brush gliding across the wall in confident, easy strokes. He was painting Juliet's face and to her amusement she looked boyish – an Orlando lost in Arden, snoozing in the forest, hand open in sleep, a lily in her palm. In contrast to Tom's calm precision, Charlie had stripped to the waist and he sweated as he painted, perspiration streaming down his back. On the wall above the fireplace he'd illustrated Ashcombe Manor itself, her seven chimneys smoking, the driveway filled with workmen, builders toppling across scaffolding, every window blazing but empty.

'Come on,' he called, turning to the crowd, brush in one hand, beer in the other. 'Who's going to be the first to choose a window and paint themselves in?'

Allan leaped to his feet, eyes bright and black. 'It has to be me,' he said. 'I am the pie-maker.'

He snatched a brush from Charlie and started to draw a man peering out from behind the front door. The figure was toppling forward, a mop of dark hair perched on his head, a tray of cakes floating above one hand, the other beckoning the viewer inside.

Charlie laughed. 'It's not half bad. Who's next?'

As people surged forward, eagerly grabbing brushes and daubing crude versions of themselves on the wall, Leonard drew a tiny figure in an attic window. No one realised that rather than a self-portrait he'd painted the face of George Montague. When he'd finished, he resumed working on his own mural on the far side of the hall. The crowd jostled around Charlie, baying with joy.

After a while Juliet slipped away from the bustle and crossed over to watch Leonard work. He'd rolled up his sleeves and his pale skin was freckled with paint. Juliet observed the scene expand across his wall – a stag with colossal branched antlers paused at the top of the hill, birds and leaves perched on them. The sun hovered above the ridge, still orange but holding the thought of dusk. His painting lacked the finish of the older artists, and here and there the perspective had gone askew, but it buzzed with energy. *Oh*, thought Juliet, oh, I hadn't noticed how good you've become. But worry tinged her pride. Leonard was gifted, she realised, but would it bring him happiness? She considered her artists at Wednesday's – success was as much down to luck as skill. She thought of Max hiding from the world in his dark wood. She closed her eyes. 'Please let Leonard go to university,' she murmured. 'Let him want something else – to be a doctor, a lawyer.' *My God*, she thought with a rueful smile, *I've turned into a Jewish mother in spite of myself*. She glanced back at Leonard's slight figure – I wish upon my son an ordinary life of fatness and fatherhood and simple joys.

Evening slid into night-time and the moon sailed high and full above the ridgeway, illuminating the chalk paths snaking up the hillside and casting a weird snow-light on the garden, the ash trees throwing thin moon shadows on the gravel. In the corner of the room, people began to dance to unheard music. Then trays of cakes and biscuits from the kitchen appeared and were passed around the gathering. Realising they were hungry, Juliet and Frieda helped themselves to poppy-seed *rugelach*. A group of girls lying on beanbags beside the door began to croon in wavering harmonies, and Juliet and Frieda found themselves swaying in time. Laughing, Juliet grabbed her daughter's hand and to her delight Frieda did not pull away. Instead she tugged Juliet to her feet and started to dance. They shuffled in a makeshift waggle on the stairs, toppling into one another. Someone produced a guitar and started to play, the music shifting and weaving amid the sound of another instrument – a zither perhaps or a harp, Juliet decided. Zither was a funny word. Zither. Zither. She tried it again and started to giggle. The word caught on her tongue, she tried to explain to Frieda what was funny but her mouth was fat and wouldn't make the words and that was funnier still. Frieda's cheeks were flushed and she looked so pretty and Juliet wanted to tell her but her mouth still wouldn't work and that made her terribly, terribly sad. And the music was louder now, the windows rattling, or maybe it was her teeth and then Frieda was letting go of her hand and running away up the stairs, her face no longer rosy but greenish as she retched in her hand, her long hair hanging in sweaty strings. Juliet wanted to rush after her but her legs were marshmallows and as she tried to follow, she found herself sitting back down on the stairs with a thud. A little too late, she wondered what had been in the *rugelach* besides poppy-seed.

'Hash,' said Allan. 'Just a touch.'

Juliet looked at him in surprise, not realising she'd spoken aloud, not realising he was even there.

'Oh,' said Juliet. 'Oh dear.' She tried to tell Allan that she wasn't interested in drugs, not at all, and he really ought to have warned her and she would like to find Frieda now and take the children home and she was actually very cross but all that came out was 'Bother.' She looked down and saw Leonard having an earnest conversation with a tall man with scruffy hair, who reminded Juliet a little of a chap on the cover of one of Frieda's LPs.

'Yes, that's Matt Rigby, all right,' said Allan.

Juliet frowned. Was she simply beaming her thoughts direct into Allan's mind? The hash must be very powerful indeed.

Leonard and Charlie and the man who was Matt Rigby were building a fire in the grate, chucking onto it the wormier of the floorboards and dousing it in booze so that flames shot up the chimney, the roar briefly heard over the music like a cry from the Serengeti.

Allan squeezed in beside Juliet on the stair, placing an arm loosely around her shoulders.

'You see, you had to come. There wouldn't have been a happening without you. Look at us. You and me. A couple of *Yidden*. But they all want to be here. They all want to be part of it.' He laughed, but his face was sad. 'A queer and a divorcée in the midst of it all.'

Juliet was sweating. She felt it trickle between her shoulder blades and coat her eyelids. Somewhere was the thud thud of a drum, vaguely she realised it was the beat of her own heart. She leaned forward, suddenly overcome with the need to tell Allan the truth.

'I'm not a divorcée. My husband never divorced me. But he never divorced his first wife either so I was never really married at all. I'm an adulteress. Well, I don't really know what I am.'

Allan leaned in, his pupils huge. 'You're wonderful. You're Juliet Montague and you're super.'

Juliet heard herself giggle without finding anything funny. The sound burst out of her with a pop.

'Juliet Montague,' she said the name slowly, tasting it. 'Am I her? I was never actually married to George Montague – it was all pretend, all a lie. Am I really Juliet Montague after all?'

Allan leaped to his feet, swaying on the stairs. His tie was skew-whiff and his hair had broken free of its Brylcreem and fell into untidy waves. There was a red stain of something dribbled down the front of his shirt.

'You have to start again. Burn the old Juliet. Throw her onto the fire!'

Through the fog, Juliet experienced a pang of concern. Physically the old Juliet was very much the same as the new, and she didn't fancy singeing either.

'That sounds sore,' she said.

'Burn something symbolic!' Allan roared with laughter.

'Oh,' said Juliet.

She glanced down into the hall where the flames swayed in the grate, revellers dancing in front of them, girls and boys stripped to the waist in the heat, the firelight turning their skin a warm orange. One of the boys was Leonard. He danced with his eyes half closed. Charlie dipped his paintbrush into the ash and started to scrawl a sketch on Leonard's bare back, signing his shoulder with a flourish. In turn, Leonard smeared charcoal on his brush and drew a huge swirling moustache on Charlie. One of the girls shrieked with laughter and waved at Leonard who obliged by drawing her a moustache too. Suddenly, everyone was daubing one another's bare skin with patterns, taking handfuls of ash from where it had spewed out of the fire and rubbing it on arms and wrists and cheeks and brows.

'Come on,' said Allan, tugging Juliet to her feet and drawing her into the throng. 'Burn the old!'

Still clutching her hand he hauled her through the crowd and to the hearth. He emptied out his pockets, tipping the contents onto the flames – briefly a pad of ten pound notes glowed red and then fluttered into dust.

'What on earth are you doing?' cried Juliet.

Allan only laughed. 'Your turn.'

Juliet reached into her pocket, drawing out a piece of hair elastic and her purse. Allan was right; she needed to burn all ties with George. She wouldn't be trapped any longer. She rummaged in the purse searching for something saying 'Juliet Montague'. Her fingers touched her library card. She pulled it out and tossed it straight into the flames, watching the cardboard glow briefly, the black letters MRS JULIET MONTAGUE ADULT MEMBER flutter and then vanish.

With a tinge of regret she remembered that she had three books due back next week and that she'd have to get another ticket.

Leonard took her hand. His fingers were slick with sweat, and the patterns on his back smudged. Juliet noticed he was clasping an exercise book. A second later, he tossed it onto the fire.

'What was that, darling?' she asked.

'My Latin homework,' said Leonard. 'And you should know, I'm probably going to fail the test on Monday. And the one after that. The thing is, Latin doesn't matter. Only painting does.'

Juliet sighed and squeezed his hand. 'We shouldn't have had those biscuits. *Rugelach* can be very dangerous.'

Leonard smiled. He didn't tell Juliet that he hadn't eaten any of the *rugelach* and his mind was perfectly clear. He suspected that she wouldn't remember anything he'd said, but at least he had tried to warn her.

They drove home in silence. No one wanted to speak. To their collective relief, Charlie turned up the radio and everyone stared out the windows watching the sunny afternoon drift by, the rushing hedgerows buttered with yellow cowslips and daubed with dog roses. The Rigbys came on the radio.

'Turn it off,' snapped Frieda.

'Why?' asked Charlie, nonetheless switching it off.

'All of that, and Matt Rigby didn't even come,' said Frieda.

Leonard turned awkwardly in his seat to look at his sister. 'Yes he did. All of them came.'

Frieda gawped at him. 'You're lying.'

'No, I'm not. I talked to him. He's okay. We chatted about music and art and then he drew a penguin on my neck. Look.'

He pulled down his collar to reveal a charcoal smear that once might have resembled a penguin. Frieda peered at it and then closed her eyes and sank back into silence. That was it. The final sign. Matt Rigby had come to the party and she had missed him because she had accidently eaten hash and was being sick in the loo. Her head pulsed with distant pain and she remembered the previous night. She'd lain on the ripped linoleum floor, her head wedged beside the toilet bowl, the porcelain cooling her forehead. The sound of music had wafted up between the floorboards, and she'd thought she could see it – the notes were waves of blue and green with speckles of gold and red. They'd caught in the light fitting on the ceiling, and banged against the window before seeping out of the cracks in the glass. She'd lain on the floor for hours, alternately vomiting and watching the music drift through her fingers. There had been an odd-shaped stain on the ceiling, a gathering of mould that looked like a drawing of Moses in the storybook her grandfather had read to her when she was very little. Moses had opened his mouth and swallowed the music notes that had swum up to the ceiling like multi-coloured tropical fishes. Never mind that the Rigbys hadn't showed up, she'd decided at the time. Watching Moses gulp fishes was much better. He had opened his mouth wider than the world and between his teeth she'd seen a galaxy of weaving fish.

As the lanes gave way to roads and traffic and the grey haze of the city, Frieda realised it had been a sign. She wasn't supposed to meet the band and she wasn't destined to marry Matt Rigby. All this time she'd been toying with the trappings of religion to annoy her mother but now for the first time she felt the tingle of faith. Somehow her pantomime had turned real. When she reached home, she'd put on her thick tights and on Friday she'd go to *shul* with her grandfather.

After they arrived home Juliet took a long shower. When she came downstairs in her dressing gown, to her dismay she found Frieda unpacking the crate containing Rabbi Plotkin's kosher plates. She stood in the kitchen doorway and watched as Frieda stacked them neatly into the cupboard. She waited in silence, a pain in her chest.

'You're not to touch these,' said Frieda without turning round.

CATALOGUE ITEM 42
The Last Time I Saw Her,
Max Langford, Oil on Wood, 20 x 35in, 1966

MRS GREENE WAS thrilled about the wedding. In her gloomier moments Juliet believed her mother was more excited than the bride to be. The only advantage of the short engagement was that Mrs Greene couldn't purchase any more prospective hats – the spare room had metamorphosed into a milliner's showroom lined with candy-coloured effusions. Frieda was only quietly delighted, flushing a perfect pink when teased about the handsomeness of the groom. Juliet didn't think he was handsome in the least, deciding that the best one could say of Dov was that he was unobtrusive, like a plain desk lamp or inoffensive curtain fabric. He blinked and gulped a lot as though trying to swallow his Adam's apple and keep it down. It never occurred to Juliet that she was the cause of his anxiety. Despite all the years, the stigma of her status pursued her like a shadow and Frieda never confided to her mother the anxious discussions between the rabbis and Dov's conservative family. The Cohens were very fond of Frieda and understood that the boy seemed to like her very much indeed (in fact, it almost amounted to passion, which was only just respectable) but since the arrival of the first Rabbi Cohen in Britain fifty years earlier they had enjoyed a seamless respectability and no one wanted the Montagues besmirching that beige, unblemished record. Everybody liked Mrs Greene and Mr Greene was a solid fellow, a real *mensch*. But George

Montague? No one really remembered him but they told one another that they did, and his weakness for cards bloomed into a seasoned wickedness. The only decent thing that could be said about George was that having taken it upon himself to vanish, he wasn't present to trouble the decent folk of Chislehurst. Juliet Montague, however, remained a problem. First there was the gallery and the indecent paintings – Mrs Cohen had ventured up to town for a private view, just to see what was what, mind, and discovered that the place was full of nudes – girls and even boys with everything on display like wieners in a hotdog stand. The next problem with Juliet was the boyfriend. Juliet was rumoured to have had a lover for many years, an older man, a lascivious painter ('Was there any other kind?' Mrs Cohen asked the good ladies on the luncheon committee) who wasn't even Jewish. But the last obstacle to decency was Juliet herself. It went beyond what she did (peddle obscene paintings) or that she had a (*goy*) lover. It was something about Juliet. She was always very polite and even baked the odd strudel for her mother's summer parties. Still, nearly everyone agreed that there was something about Juliet Montague that couldn't be trusted. She might make strudel, but Mr Harris had a sore stomach afterwards and she was suspected of using lard instead of margarine. She was polite but there was pertness in her gaze.

Juliet tried to ignore the whispers as best she could. She knew the tittle-tattle upset her parents and for that she was sorry, but she refused to believe that it wounded Frieda or it was she who brought out Dov's bullfrog gulping and glistening brow. Juliet found it impossible to imagine how this damp young man, who seemed to wilt like a heat-addled tulip in her presence, could be engaging when she wasn't there. She asked Leonard who, though not a fan of Dov, prevaricated out of loyalty to his sister, declaring that he could be 'rather funny now and again' – though the only instance he could think of was when once before dinner Dov had forgotten he'd put his hat on his chair and sat on it, squashing it quite flat. It *was* funny. It was also an accident. In truth there was nothing poor Dov could do to make Juliet like him or approve of the match – she simply thought that at nineteen Frieda was far too young to marry.

'Are you marrying him to punish me?' Juliet asked her, more than once.

Frieda rearranged the long material of her skirt and fixed Juliet with the disapproving look she couldn't bear.

'Mum, I know you find it hard to fathom but my marrying Dov isn't actually about you.'

Juliet licked her lips and wished she could find the right words. There had never been that ease between them that she enjoyed with Leonard. It wasn't that she loved him more, she just never fretted about what to say to him. She took a breath.

'Well, darling, if it's about sex, you don't have to get married. It's not like it was. We can go and get you some pills from the doctor and you can sleep with Dov, if that's what you want. Maybe even other men.'

'I don't want to sleep with other men. I only want to sleep with Dov.'

Two angry points of colour appeared on Frieda's cheeks, but for once Juliet ignored the warning sign and carried on.

'Take the pill then and only sleep with Dov. But go to university. Get a degree. If you still want him, marry him when you graduate.'

Frieda narrowed her eyes. 'I don't want to go university. I want to be a wife and a mother. That's the most important thing in the world.'

Juliet felt the full sting of her criticism and it stuck in her throat like a fishbone. She looked away so that Frieda wouldn't

273

see the tears that threatened. Try as she might, she couldn't face the thought of organising the wedding. All those religious types with their marauding happiness, pleased at the wedding, pleased that they'd saved another soul. She blinked and smiled. The best she could hope for was sufficient time for Frieda to change her mind.

'When were you thinking? Perhaps next January, I've always liked winter weddings. All that red.'

'June,' said Frieda, daring Juliet to contradict her.

'Oh, but darling, I can't organise it in time for June. There's the summer show at the gallery.'

Frieda sighed and pouted, giving an excellent impression of being hurt. 'That's all right. Granny will take care of everything.'

Juliet swallowed, understanding that this was what Frieda had really wanted. Juliet could not be trusted. She must be kept far away from delicate social arrangements and Jewish events. There was nothing more to be done. She retreated.

Granddaughter and grandmother delighted in colluding. A June wedding. The flowers would be marvellous and they'd have English strawberries for dessert. Mrs Greene was determined to arrange everything properly, as if the trouble with Juliet's marriage could be put down to an inadequate wedding with substandard floral arrangements. If every detail in Frieda's was correct then, like a shrub planted carefully in the right soil, everything else would follow just as it should.

Juliet tried to take an interest and study guest lists and seating plans but seeing how few of her friends Mrs Greene and Frieda had allowed, she only felt more miserable. She pleaded for the inclusion of the gallery boys – though they weren't boys any longer, but men over thirty with families of their own.

'Darling, it's nice that you've invited Philip, but really you must ask his wife. And what about Charlie and Marjorie? And Jim simply has to come. He'll be terribly hurt if he's not invited.'

Frieda scowled and bit her lip. Her crush on Philip had not receded even as his hairline started to thin, and she'd never quite forgiven him for marrying the gleaming Caroline five years before.

'Caroline won't come. We're not smart enough for her.'

'Of course she will. Philip's terribly fond of you.'

Begrudgingly, Caroline was added to the list.

'Must I have Charlie? He's Leonard's friend, not mine.'

'Yes,' said Juliet. 'And Marjorie too.'

'I don't like her,' said Frieda.

Juliet sighed. Few people did. Charlie had surprised everyone by marrying Marjorie, the nude model. She'd been an extremely pretty girl, but the roses had faded fast. She'd not lived up to the promise of youthful beauty, and instead of transforming into a lovely woman had become an ordinary and rather unhappy one. Whenever Juliet caught Charlie looking at his wife, he always seemed to wear an expression of surprise and disappointment. Juliet felt sorry for her. Charlie's family were not kind to Marjorie – the daughter of a painter-decorator was not their sort. The jokes that Marjorie's father liked to make about himself and his son-in-law being part of the same profession ('Paint's just paint in the end, however you slap it on!') were not appreciated. That wedding had been an absolute disaster, Juliet remembered. Valerie had got frightfully drunk before the ceremony and Juliet had had to take her for a lie down during the speeches. En route, Valerie had grabbed her arm and confided in a gin-scented whisper, 'I'd rather he'd married you – even a divorced *Jewess* would be better than this.' Unfortunately

Valerie turned out to be quite right – once Charlie lost interest in painting Marjorie, they had nothing left in common.
Marjorie liked being in pictures, not talking about them.
They'd not had any children and in disappointment Charlie
continued to pour his affection onto Leonard. Marjorie tried
to befriend him too and to Juliet's relief at least Leonard was
kind to her.

'Marjorie comes,' said Juliet. 'And Jim.'

Frieda huffed. 'But, suppose, you know.' She squirmed. 'He
might bring someone with him.'

Juliet laughed. 'He will not bring a gentleman friend to
your wedding, Frieda, and I'm quite certain that he won't flirt
with the rabbi. Jim isn't partial to beards.'

Frieda scowled, hating being teased. 'I don't think Dov's
family would like it. It *is* against the law.'

Juliet looked up sharply. 'Then I strongly suggest you don't
tell them things that are none of their business. Don't pick up
the Cohens' nastier habits, Frieda.'

Frieda said nothing and added his name to the list in tiny
writing, as though if she wrote it very small, no one would
notice him on the day itself.

'And you missed off Max. No need to post his invitation,
I'll give it to him when I see him at the weekend.'

Frieda studied her mother with steady green eyes for a
moment before declaring softly, 'I won't have that man at my
wedding.'

Frieda's childish dislike had hardened like old varnish into
hatred. Over the years Juliet had done her best to ignore it but
now she recoiled, jolted by the revulsion in her daughter's
voice.

'He's your friend,' Frieda continued. 'I won't have him. I
won't have Dov and his family look at that man and at you
and say *things*. He is not coming.'

At that, Frieda actually stamped her bare foot on the carpet and Juliet watched her open-mouthed, unsure whether to laugh or shake her.

Later in the week the boys offered little sympathy. When Juliet arrived at the gallery, Charlie was in a foul mood. He'd spent the last month labouring on an abstract triptych far from his usual style and, observing Juliet's indifferent shrug, concluded that it wasn't working, wasn't going to work. He started to paint over the canvas in thick, furious strokes of white, experiencing a masochistic delight as weeks of work vanished in a snowstorm.

'What did you expect? She's never liked Max.'

'It's Freudian. Girls never like the chap who's diddling their mother. Unless it's their father of course,' added Jim helpfully.

'I know she avoided him, but she seems to actually hate him,' said Juliet.

'I don't know why you're so upset. It's not like Max would even go with you to the wedding,' said Charlie. 'I mean can you see him coming to Chislehurst and staying in your little house and putting on a morning suit as you fasten a pair of pearlescent cufflinks and dab cologne behind his ears?'

Juliet ignored him and turned away to look through a selection of canvases Jim had brought by. While the studio still formed part of the gallery, Charlie was the only one to use it regularly. For the first years of his marriage he'd worked mainly at his and Marjorie's home in Dorset but slowly he'd crept back to London a night and then a week at a time. Sometimes she suspected that he slept at the gallery. Jim and Philip no longer worked in the studio, and while Juliet tried to encourage new painters to use the space if they needed it, Charlie usually frightened them away within a month or two

– accusing them of using his brushes or leaving doors unlocked or talking too much.

She studied the first of Jim's paintings, a silkscreen print of a Devon swimming pool, the water cool in the sunlight, ripples like fish scales, and smiled. Unhurried, she spread out the rest, already hanging them in her mind. As well as mounting the gallery shows, Juliet sold Charlie, Jim and a dozen others around the world. She didn't sell Philip's paintings. She'd never cared for his racehorse portraits and they had proved too lucrative for him to spend time on other work (Juliet suspected that Caroline, like most thoroughbreds, was expensive to keep). While Philip remained a friend, he had little need of her services.

Juliet's favourite part of the year was the summer exhibition where she displayed now-established artists like Jim alongside new discoveries.

'Who've you found for this year's show?' asked Jim, surveying the canvases stacked in piles against the studio walls.

She sighed. 'No one yet. But I'm going to take Leonard to the art school shows and dowse for talent there.'

'Leonard's getting pretty good himself,' said Charlie. 'Did you see the finished collage?'

Juliet shook her head, still transfixed by the blue ripples in Jim's pool and only half listening.

'You should think about including one of his pictures. Give the kid some confidence,' said Charlie.

'Perhaps,' said Juliet. 'Oh, I like this one.'

She pointed to one of Jim's canvases, a large screen-print of a snub-nose adolescent boy fast asleep beside green lido waters.

'We'll show this here, but I'm going to put on a frightfully high reserve. I think we should send it to New York and see what they could do.'

Jim shrugged, smiling at her frank enthusiasm. Charlie speeded up his whitewashing, irritated that Juliet hadn't shown any great zeal for his latest pieces, more irritated that he didn't like them either.

'Tom Hopkins has some great new work,' said Juliet. 'I'm going to include at least three. I'd like them all in the show but there simply isn't room.'

She fumbled through a series of unframed canvases stacked against a wall and then brought out a painting of a naked boy bathing beside a millpond, blue evening light shading him, above a purple sky scattered with dandelion-clock stars. It was a blend of English pastoral idyll and Picasso colour games. Jim and Charlie came closer to look. Charlie laughed.

'I like your bather, Jim, but the old boy's got there first.'

'Youth doesn't have the patent on innovation,' said Juliet. 'And besides, the two of you aren't so young any more. In a year or two you'll both be considered part of the establishment and you'll have to start smoking cigars and playing bridge.'

'Show me the others,' said Jim.

Juliet rooted through the stack of canvases, producing a series of Tom Hopkins' paintings, most of them portraits of young men sleeping, eating, daydreaming, swimming – never smiling, never looking at the viewer, always waiting to be watched.

'I like Tom,' said Jim, half to himself. 'Sometimes I think we're the only two figurative painters left in bloody England.'

'There's always Max,' said Juliet.

Jim and Charlie did not reply.

For the rest of the afternoon, Juliet laid out canvases around the gallery, experimenting with various possible hanging orders and then rejecting them with a huff. She barely noticed the light fading to yellow, and rain starting to rattle on the flat roof.

'Put out everything you're considering for the exhibition so far,' said Charlie. 'Put it all over the floor, against the walls, everywhere.'

'I'm getting on just fine,' said Juliet.

Charlie shook his head. 'Do it. I want to show you something.'

She didn't move.

'Please.'

Juliet sighed and with Charlie's help propped the remaining pictures all over the gallery. In an hour, everything was laid out and the floor entirely hidden. It looked like a garish, giant patchwork quilt.

'Now,' said Charlie. 'Do you see?'

Juliet looked at him and frowned, shook her head.

'All right. Stand on the chair and then look.'

She balanced on an old fretwork chair, and peered down at the sea of pictures. Some were abstract – sharp grey lines pierced blue expanses, here and there advertising slogans were daubed in sickly yellow, there were gouaches, collages, water-colours and reliefs. As always, Juliet found herself seeking out Max's pieces. They weren't recent works but paintings from several years before. When they hadn't sold the first year Juliet decided she'd exhibit them again and had done for the last few summers. It was her gallery after all and by now they seemed to her talismans of good fortune – no matter that Max's pictures didn't sell; she was sure they brought luck to all the others.

'You can see the problem then,' said Charlie following her gaze, his voice light with relief. 'I knew you would.'

'I have no idea what you're talking about,' said Juliet still standing on the chair and feeling quite ridiculous.

Charlie took a breath and spoke slowly, his tone measured and prepared.

'Max's paintings don't fit. Everything else is modern. You find painters with ambition who look to the future and try to imagine it in pencil and charcoal and oil and glass. Max has given up. Look, those pictures of his aren't even new. Or maybe they are but they're just the same as everything else he's done for the past twenty years and I can't tell the bloody difference any more.'

Juliet climbed off the chair and stared at Charlie and then at Jim who lurked in the corner refusing to catch her eye.

'I like Max's work,' she said. 'It's voiced. I like that it's different.'

'No. You like Max. His work is nothing but scraps of nostalgia. It's titbits of old England with flourishes of over-the-top ornamental design. He's like a pre-war Liberty catalogue.'

Charlie's voice shook as he spoke, whether from fervour or nerves Juliet couldn't tell. A warm clot of anger settled in her stomach like undigested matzo balls.

'He is a great painter.'

'He had the potential to be a great painter. You see only what he might have been, not what he is. Max Langford is a disappointment. A man who went off to paint the war and came back crippled. Now he works with one hand tied behind his back. He's surrendered to neo-Romantic shit and I won't,' Charlie paused, glancing at Jim, 'we won't, exhibit with him any more.'

Juliet surveyed them both, conscious that her hands were trembling. 'You're both as cruel as Frieda.'

Charlie shrugged, refusing to rise. 'You can either show his work or ours.'

Juliet turned to Jim. 'You agree?'

'Yes,' he said, studying paint spatters on the floor. 'It's a blind spot for you, my love. You just don't see his stuff any more, not really.'

'Supposing I choose Max?'

Charlie blinked and said nothing. The rain on the roof swelled into a gallop. They both knew she hadn't sold a single painting of Max's in more than a year. Juliet's mouth was dry and her tongue stuck like Velcro to the roof of her mouth. Even after all these years of friendship and working alongside one another, Charlie could still make her feel like the provincial girl from the *shtetl*. She'd never quite managed to shake off the littleness of her beginnings.

'Talk to him,' said Charlie. 'Soon.'

It was Tom's advice she sought before speaking to Max. They were both heading to Dorset for the weekend to see him and met on the train. Tom insisted on their sitting for the duration of the journey in the first-class buffet car, ordering champagne as soon as they sat down.

'Really, I wish you wouldn't,' said Juliet.

Tom re-folded his long legs. 'It's the done thing in first class, I believe. Anyway, don't all ladies like champagne?'

Juliet smiled. 'Actually, I'd much prefer a cup of tea.'

Tom threw his head back and laughed, a fulsome sound. 'That's why we're pals, you and me.'

Tom listened as Juliet spoke, head cocked to one side like a garden blackbird waiting for crumbs. She noticed that he looked tired. The once thick dark hair was combed with white, and his skin was yellow and translucent – like an old painting starting to crack. She broke off mid-sentence to ask, 'Are you quite all right, Tom? You're looking a little thin.'

He smiled. 'Working too much, eating too little. Nothing a touch of gin and a few hot dinners won't fix.'

Juliet shifted on her seat, not quite believing him, but deciding it was rude to ask more questions. Tom rubbed his eyes and gave a sigh of real weariness.

'I don't know what you do about this other business,' he said. 'I always thought that Charlie was fond of our Max.'

'He used to be.'

'It's a wonder they don't chuck me out too. I'm nothing but a mythmaker and landscape painter. I haven't changed subject in more than thirty years. The world flits by faster and faster but me and mine stay just the same.'

Juliet reached out and took his hand. 'Don't even think it, Tom. Everyone at the gallery loves your work. None of the boys wants you to go. It's Max they've got it in for.'

The train stuttered through the suburbs, the grey kitchen-sink-school cityscape giving way to green pastoral and hedges strewn with feathered lace. Tom said little and hunched in the corner of his seat, so quiet that Juliet wondered if he'd fallen asleep. Usually this part of the journey relaxed her – as the train carried her further from the city the knot in her stomach would ease, but today it remained, tight as heartburn. If she didn't include Max's pictures in the show, would he even notice? In the seven years she'd known him he'd never been to a single exhibition. No, she shook her head, she couldn't do that, it smelled of cowardice. Perhaps she could hold a solo exhibition of his work next year. Fidgeting on the hard seat, she realised with unease that she couldn't remember having seen a new painting of Max's for months – he'd never be able to fill a solo show with new work. The train eased into Salisbury and Tom interrupted her thoughts. He stood abruptly, knocking over her tea and, not pausing to apologise, rummaged in the luggage rack. He heaved down a painting swaddled in brown paper and thrust it into her arms.

'Take this. Give it to Max. I can't come this weekend.'

He turned and hurried to the doors, stepping out onto the platform. Juliet dropped the package onto the seat and rushed after him, calling from the doorway.

'Tom! What are you doing? Come back. Give it to him yourself.'

He was already halfway down the platform, a thin, stooped figure. It started to drizzle. He turned and called back to her. 'I'm sorry. I can't. Give him. Give him,' he paused, swallowed, 'my best.'

The guard slammed the door as the train pulled away from the platform. Juliet craned forward, leaning out of the window. 'Tom! Tom!'

He waved and vanished into the hurrying crowd.

Max didn't notice that Tom wasn't with Juliet. He was making supper when she arrived, and she suspected that he'd forgotten Tom should have been there too. She meant to give him Tom's parcel straight away, but somehow she propped it up against the banister in the hall and didn't remember it at all until the letter arrived a few days later. That evening was the first of spring, and they took their plates outside to perch on the front step and watch the first of the sleep-addled bees emerge from the trees. It was too early for the leaf canopy to be in full umbrella and so the late afternoon light slid through the trees, making green and yellow mosaics flit across their skin. Max was in good spirits, loquacious even, and just as Juliet began to wonder about the source, she noticed the tell-tale stain of paint on his fingers and beneath his nails. Leaning over to kiss him, she inhaled the once familiar smell of linseed. For months she hadn't smelled it on him. The scent used to be part of him and when it disappeared it had taken her a month or two to place what was different – like biting into a favourite cake and realising it was missing an essential ingredient. She breathed deeply and smiled. Max was painting again. As they ate rabbit stew and sipped badly fermented plum wine, Juliet couldn't bear to puncture the smooth perfection of the evening. She resolved to tell him about the gallery and the wedding in the morning.

When she woke, Max was already up and working in the lean-to shed at the side of the kitchen. Alone she made coffee and wandered around the house, savouring the busy stillness of the wood. Early sunshine rushed through the windows, warm and yellow, throwing buttery light on all the paintwork and under its glare Juliet noticed for the first time that some of the ornamentation was starting to look old and worn. The ochre dragon on the fireplace had lost his gleam, his scales chipped like an old tooth, his crimson flames no longer as fierce. The golden camels caravanning around the cornicing had faded into the desert behind, so that only the black beads of their eyes shone against the sand. Here and there Max had tried to patch them up – the butterflies fluttering across the windowpane had re-glossed wings, but although it could have been her imagination or the effect of the light, their fretwork patterning lacked the delicacy of before. Juliet sighed and decided that, much like herself, the house's inhabitants were simply starting to age.

In the middle of the afternoon Max came inside humming, his trousers spattered with paint. He insisted that they have a picnic lunch – the fact it was after three o'clock didn't concern him – and he marched her through the wood to the edge of the great house. They sat on a felled oak, eating egg sandwiches and strong cured sausage as they watched tourists meander through the gardens of Max's ancestral home.

'We don't usually come this way,' said Juliet.

'No,' agreed Max, through a mouthful of apple. 'But I fancied seeing the place again. Sudden attack of nostalgia. I suppose I avoid it in general. I don't mean to but it is quite odd watching strangers traipse through my mother's rose garden with their guidebooks in search of cream teas.'

'I wish I could have met your mother,' said Juliet.

Max laughed. 'I'm awfully glad you didn't. She wouldn't have liked you – a Jew with a missing husband and worst of all *ambition*. Definitely not her sort.'

Juliet frowned, wondering whether she ought to be hurt, until Max put his arm around her, pulling her close and kissing her.

'I like you. You're my sort,' he said.

Juliet smiled – coming from him this was a Shakespearean declaration of devotion. Above a kestrel circled, his cry echoing into the fading afternoon. She closed her eyes and listened. The conversation about the wedding and the gallery could wait another day.

The letter arrived the following morning, while Juliet was sleeping. When she traipsed downstairs Max was sitting at the table, the letter already in his hands. He held it out to her.

'Read it. It's from Tom.'

Something in his voice made her obey. She sat and started to read, '*Dearest Max—*'

'Aloud.'

She began again. '*Dearest Max, I'm an anachronism like that monstrous house you grew up in. All those painters, the big ones like Warhol, the tiddlers like Charlie Fussell and the ones in-between like Jim Brownwick, are all searching for something modern, something new. And the truth is: I Just Don't Get It. Their stuff babbles at me and I put on a jacket and I go to their wretched shows and I sip warm white wine and I look and I look at the pictures and prints and reliefs and try to see what they all see but I can't. Instead I look at them with their happier lives and see there is no room for me and my work. No one is interested. They don't think I have anything to say. And perhaps I don't. I've only ever had one idea – the human figure in a landscape. And it's been enough for me to paint for a lifetime. But I'm done. I'm tired of being an irrelevance. I'm sick again and this time I can't face it. The pills have been swallowed and now there's nothing to do but wait.'*

Juliet broke off with a cry. 'Is this real? We must do something.'

Max shook his head. 'What can we do? Look at the date – he wrote it two days ago. Finish it. Please.'

'I can't. I won't. You read it.'

She shoved the letter at him but Max gently placed it back in her hand.

'Please. I can't face it alone.'

He drew her onto his knee and he wrapped his arms around her middle. She took a breath.

'I don't feel anything yet. Dying feels much like living.'

She stopped and Max motioned for her to continue.

'There's nothing else.'

She showed him the paper. The words trembled and slanted like falling trees, tapering away into squiggles, then oblivion and the empty page. There was no signature or hurried sign off – there was nothing at all. Juliet pictured Tom's final morning. She saw him climbing out of bed, shaving and dressing properly in one of his aged but immaculate suits – he always looked as if he had just stepped out of a gentleman's outfitters from twenty years back. She pictured him brewing his cup of Fortnum's tea, setting out his fountain pen and watermarked stationery, looking out of the window at the pleasant spring morning swelling over Primrose Hill, before swallowing his pills and writing his letter while he waited to die. The letter would always be in the present tense. The moment before death preserved like a blow about to fall. She glanced round at Max and saw that he was crying too, round

287

tears streaming down his cheeks. She reached out to brush them away but he stayed her hand, kissing her fingers.

'No. We should cry. Who else does Tom have to weep for him but us?'

Tom's housekeeper had found the body, the letter beside it, envelope neatly addressed and stamped. Knowing him as she did, she ignored the proper protocol and posted the letter before telephoning the police. There was to be no funeral. He had no relatives. Max remembered that there had been a boyfriend some years before, but he couldn't recall his name, let alone his address. The afternoon after the letter's arrival, they took the parcel out into the wood and unwrapped it. Max was well on the way to being drunk. He'd not eaten since the morning and had worked his way through a grimy and ancient bottle of spirits he'd produced from the back of the shed. He pulled a knife from his pocket and slit the string from around the parcel. With something like tenderness he drew back the brown paper, unwrapping the painting like a baby from its bath towel. He shook it free and held it up under the trees.

The painting was of a beautiful sandy-haired boy lazing on a pinstriped lawn. In the background stood an ugly, sandstone manor, softened by a splash of rosebushes. The boy was naked. Every strand of hair was lovingly painted in gold or russet or blond, the bleached furze along his arm catching the light. His knees splayed to the side, penis curled against his leg. Unlike Tom's other paintings, in this one the boy looked directly at the viewer, his eyes blue and his smile arch.

'Oh,' said Juliet. 'Oh. It's you.'

She remembered that Tom had once told her that in his youth Max tempted girls and boys alike, and even now she

288

experienced an adolescent flutter in her belly. Here was Dorian Gray unmarked by age, his skin flushed with sunshine.

Max swallowed hard, unable to speak for a moment. 'Yes, this was me, aged eighteen, at art school. Before the war.'

He shoved the painting at Juliet and turned back to the house. She heard the door slam. Gathering up the discarded paper, she followed him, picture tucked under her arm. He waited for her in the kitchen, glowering over a mug of something foul-smelling and black.

'I'm leaving.'

Juliet sensed the world grow quiet, the birds' singing muffled and the creak of the trees silenced. Dizzy, she leaned back against the kitchen cabinet, managing not to drop the painting as she laid it on the table. She felt rather than heard Max speaking, and it took her a full minute to realise he was talking about leaving the gallery rather than her. She felt a brief pulse of relief and then sadness balled in a lump at the back of her throat.

'This is their fault,' Max was saying. 'Charlie Fussell and his stooges. They drove Tom to this.'

Juliet clenched the wood of the countertop, watching as he circled the table, oddly articulate through his alcohol-fuelled rage.

'They're not painters. They're unthinking mirrors, as reflective as bloody tinfoil. An artist must think and feel and respond. They believe that they paint the times, but they don't. It's nothing but surface art. Sometimes what they do is pretty for a poster and other times it's ugly for the sake of ugliness. They've confused monstrosity with profundity. Unless you're a thinking painter you're just a maker of knick-knacks. That's all they are – knick-knackers.'

He paused, leaning over the back of a chair and downing the rest of the liquid in his mug.

'And then there's Tom who was quiet and thoughtful and principled and melancholy and they killed him. I won't see or speak to any of them again. And I won't have my pictures shown with them. I'm sorry if that upsets you, but what is a man if he allows his principles to be painted over? I can't and I won't.'

Juliet nodded, his fury making her dumb.

'I've spoken to a dealer in Blandford, Kitty West. I like being shown by a woman,' he added. 'You can pass along any unsold pictures of mine to her.'

Juliet thought of all of his paintings stashed in the gallery, familiar to her as her own reflection – they were her friends, her talismans. Sometimes after a long day she opened the door to the cupboard just to glimpse that window into the sky – as long as she looked she wasn't in London any more but in Dorset, looking at greylag geese through Max's eyes.

'No,' said Juliet, voice firm. 'She can take the new work but those pictures are mine.'

'Yours to sell. Not yours.'

'I love those pictures. I won't give them up.'

'Is that why you haven't sold them then? Hoarding them to yourself.'

Juliet stared at the furious stranger, his eyes black with drink. She swallowed, retreating from his fury, blood buzzing in her veins.

'You know that isn't true. But if you want the old pieces back then you'll have to come to London and fetch them.'

Max stared at her but she met his eye, both of them knowing that he'd never come up to town and her beloved pictures were quite safe.

Juliet went upstairs, shoved her clothes into her suitcase and caught the next train back to London. Sitting in the carriage, she resented the impossible prettiness of the countryside. The perfect green of the water meadows and the blue haze beneath the trees of the bluebell woods flashing by only annoyed her. She wanted drizzle and grey skies. She drew her coat around her and allowed herself to cry, messy sobs that dribbled down her chin until an old lady in a tea-cosy hat leaned forward to offer her a tissue. She wondered whether it was she who'd left Max or if it was he who'd broken things off with her. It didn't much matter. She must do her best not to miss him. At least she wouldn't have to tell him that Frieda refused to invite him to the wedding. With another sob, she realised that Charlie was probably right and he wouldn't even care. Loneliness curled around her, thick as smoke. For the first time in many years she thought of George.

Mrs Greene yielded over the flowers. Frieda wanted to hire one of those fancy florists in the high street and, believing that a bride ought to be pandered to in almost all instances, Mrs Greene agreed. She supervised Mr Greene's writing of the cheque even though it pained her, knowing as she did that there were a dozen pretty plastic vases all nice and new in the synagogue cupboard and a multitude of flowers in the garden. But she drew the line at the cake. There she was immovable. Shop cake was worse than inadequate: it was slovenly and no daughter, granddaughter even, would eat it at her own wedding. She was willing to try to copy those nasty colours in the window displays that Frieda admired so much and bought bottles of green, blue and yellow food colouring from the Co-op and experimented in a variety of garish sponges.

Mr Greene soon tired of being forced to taste crimson cake glued onto a chocolate base with sickly yellow butter icing and on finding his comfortable front room vanished beneath a snowstorm of nylon white bridal magazines, he retreated to Juliet's house. There at least the wedding chatter was limited to meal times and the kitchen mercifully free of sticky bottles of food dye bleeding onto every surface. There was, however, another problem. He'd escaped the frantic joy of his wife and granddaughter but as he watched Juliet over the top of his *Daily Mail*, Mr Greene realised that she was unhappy. Fatherly tact prevented him from enquiring as to the cause, so he said nothing. Instead he allowed her to make him cups of tea but ensured that he washed up his cup himself in a tiny, and unnoticed, act of sympathy.

Lining the stairs of the small house was a series of Juliets. Charlie Fussell had started it, and now every artist with whom Juliet worked seemed to have painted her at some time or another. At first Mr Greene had found his daughter's penchant for having her portrait painted a very odd thing, something a little close to pride, and he worried that it might irk his jealous and cantankerous God, but Juliet remained un-smoted and, over the years, he'd decided it was a rather intriguing thing to do. Most people's daughters only provided them with grandchildren and *latkes* and *tsorros*, but Juliet wasn't like other daughters. There were no *latkes*, or only soggy burned ones, but there was something else. She was *interesting*. Mr Greene appreciated that most of his friends were a little dull. He liked them very much and understood he wasn't an exciting man himself, preferring ease and quiet over adventure, but he admired his daughter's spirit. Each of the portraits caught a little piece of her. None was the whole person, but walking swiftly up or down the stairs he passed through a crowd of Juliets. He liked some, was indifferent to others and detested one or two. It was a strange sensation to suddenly have so many daughters – it quite exhausted him. Surreptitiously he watched the flesh and blood Juliet *potchki* about in the kitchen, and he was overwhelmed with the need to tell her that she was the one he loved best. His hand shook and he wanted to tell her that whatever sadness was making her rub her swollen and sleepless lids, it too would pass and all would be well in the end. Sensing his gaze, she turned.

'Shall I make a pot of tea, Dad?'

'Yes. Thank you very much. I'll wash the cups.'

In order to escape Mrs Greene and Frieda's ecstatic wedding preparations, Juliet took Leonard to see the end of year show at the Royal College. Artists telephoned Wednesday's every day, trying to arrange a meeting in the hope Juliet would agree to represent them, or else they arrived at the gallery without an appointment and clutching portfolios. She examined everything with careful interest, new artists and established alike. What Juliet liked most was to find new talent among the students and then track them for a year or two – to ensure they had the necessary tenacity – and then try a few pieces in an exhibition. The only ones she politely and immediately rejected were the ones she took to calling the 'bottom-patters'. These were usually older and privileged chaps who, intrigued to find a woman running a gallery, were quite unable to resist the odd indulgent pat of her behind.

The brief spell of summer sunshine had retreated into English drizzle; the sky was a faded grey. The whole city reeked of damp, like socks that wouldn't dry out. Leonard was quiet on the train into town, scarcely speaking and barely responding to Juliet. She'd made no comment, hoping that this wasn't a sudden surge of adolescent irritability. Usually Leonard was so even tempered. She decided it was probably just the weather.

The students' private view had been the night before but Juliet always preferred the stillness the day after the opening. She liked to look around as the cleaners swept up the stray peanuts and paper napkins and debris of other trash. She paused for a moment in the hush of the hall, listening to the scratch and scuffle of the mops, and then with a practised eye glanced around the room before making her selection. She wondered which of the artists would be lucky and which ones would be nibbling *vol-au-vents* at drinks parties in twenty years' time saying, 'Actually I went to art school.' Then she thought of Tom and his letter and forced herself to look at a mediocre landscape. She mustn't think of it; she mustn't.

'Come and tell me what you make of this one,' she called to Leonard, poised before a self-portrait of a young woman emerging from the shower, face thin and pale in the steam of the bathroom mirror.

Leonard hunched in a corner, hands in his pockets, hardly looking at the pictures. He shuffled over, standing obediently in front of the painting.

'How do you feel?' asked Juliet. 'Do you get that tingle? Or nothing. You have to sense it in your *kishkies*.'

Leonard sighed, wondering why the only time his mother ever used her smattering of Yiddish was when talking about art. He didn't care about this picture or any of them. Charlie had promised him that she'd understand, or at the very least be sympathetic. Leonard wasn't so sure. But in the end the words toppled out.

'I'm leaving school. I'm not doing my A-levels, I'm going to art college.'

Juliet turned to face her son, exhibition quite forgotten.

'You can't.'

Leonard frowned, anger pinking his cheeks in two round dabs. 'What do you mean, "I can't"?'

Juliet swallowed, forced herself to smile. 'I mean you should wait. There's plenty of time for art school. But you need A-levels too. Things don't always work out quite as you hope.'

Leonard shook his head and moved away from her. Hurt prickled inside him.

'You don't believe I can do it. You don't think I'm any good. You'll *schlep* up here and spend hours gazing at these frankly ordinary pictures and no, I don't like this stupid portrait, the colours are far too blue and that brush work is careless and the skinny girl has nothing behind her eyes. It's self-indulgent trash. But you ask me to stand here and study it when you don't even notice my stuff.'

To his disgust, he realised he was crying. Juliet stepped forward, ready to comfort him, but he shook her away.

'No. Leave me alone. I want to paint. You understand that in other people but not in me.'

He wiped his tears on his sleeve but to his humiliation they would not stop, and the more they fell, the angrier he grew.

Juliet stared at this furious young man who was her son and knew he was lost. She'd always hoped that he'd learn to want something else, but it was no good. She wanted to tell him that she was frightened and that for every Hockney or Warhol or Jim Brownwick there was a Max Langford or a Tom Hopkins. In the end it was more luck than talent. Talent hadn't helped Max. Or Tom. She wanted to explain to Leonard that indifference and failure can drive a man to write a letter to his oldest friend as he sits in the sunshine and pops tablets and waits.

Leonard shook his head, eyes big with disappointment. 'You've really nothing to say?'

He gave a shrug and shoving his hands back into his pockets slouched towards the door. Juliet hurried after him, only now conscious that she had not spoken aloud.

'Please,' she said. 'Please.'

But Leonard turned to face her. 'What, Mum?'

Juliet swallowed. Found she had no words. Leonard sighed, turned and stepped out onto the street. She watched him go, a slim figure bent against the rain, soon lost among the colourful splurges of other people's umbrellas. Retreating into the hall, she glanced around the exhibition and saw that Leonard was right – the paintings were ordinary. The girl in the shower drab and blue.

Unable to face going home, Juliet found herself walking towards Wednesday's. In a few minutes she was wet through, the leather of her shoes squelching on the pavement. There is nobody left, she thought. She might not have lived with Max in the usual way, but while they were apart she stored up the things she wanted to say. A fight with Leonard could be picked through, the knots teased away with Max at the weekend. He'd listen quietly, hands folded beneath his chin, offering advice or solace only when she was quite finished. Even the prospect of talking to him had stopped her feeling alone. I could bear the business with Leonard, thought Juliet, when I still had Max.

Juliet realised it had stopped raining and her face was wet with tears. The sun slid out from behind the clouds as she reached the Bayswater Road. She hurried along beside the railings, glinting wet. A blackbird bathed in a puddle on the grass but in the park beyond an optimistic deckchair attendant was setting out chairs during the sudden spell of sunshine, brushing raindrops from the striped canvas. Juliet experienced a twist in her guts as she remembered Tom's portrait of her sleeping in the deckchair. At the end of that weekend she'd left a little piece of herself snoozing in the hallway at Ashcombe House. For her birthday last year, Tom had given her a framed photograph of it. The wind picked up and filled the canvas seats making them billow like sails. She thought of Tom. *You were so unhappy and we didn't know.*

She turned off the Bayswater Road and threaded her way to Wednesday's, letting herself inside the gallery. It was closed to the public while she prepared for the summer exhibition. A dozen of Tom's pictures were stacked against the wall. She couldn't decide whether to include them in the exhibition or save them for a proper retrospective the following year. Turning round one of the frames and seeing two small figures against the glow of a late autumn afternoon, she observed how much Tom's style had influenced Leonard. She was surprised that she'd never noticed before.

'Is that you, Juliet?' called Charlie from the studio.

Juliet sighed, wishing he wasn't there, and waited a moment before answering, 'Yes, it's me.'

'Oh, good. I've some things I want to show you.'

Juliet removed her coat and wandered into the studio. Charlie sat at an easel, tubes of discarded paints and snatches of fraying fabric littering the floor around him. He clearly hadn't been home for several days and was sporting an inadvertent beard, the stubble studded with grey. His eyes were red-rimmed and bloodshot. Amid the debris on the floor, Juliet spied several empty wine bottles.

'You're soaked,' said Charlie, gesturing to the trail of puddles and Juliet's wet hair.

'What do you want to show me?' asked Juliet.

Charlie pointed to an array of canvases on which thick swirls of paint were imbedded with pieces of floral fabric and scraps of newspaper. 'What do you think?' he said.

Juliet looked at the collages and felt nothing. There was only weariness. She reached for some placating remark, something muted and yet not unkind.

'I hate it. It's just awful.'

They both jumped, equally surprised at her remark. As Juliet heard herself, she realised it was true.

'It's decorative trash but worse than that it's ugly. It's ugly without an idea. It's mute.'

Now she'd started she couldn't stop.

'What Tom said was true. You've turned into a knick-knacker. You ran out of things to say years ago so you churn out echoes – sometimes of other better artists and sometimes of the painter you used to be. But the echo got too thin. I can barely even hear it any more. There's just,' she paused, reaching and then gave up with a shrug. 'There's nothing at all.'

Charlie stared at her, his face grey. But Juliet was angry now, her weariness driven away by pleasant fury, warming as a dose of whisky.

'You drove Max out. And for what? For these?' She gestured at the stack of collages. She swallowed, reeling her anger back in, then spoke slowly, her voice no more than a whisper. 'I want you out. I won't have you as part of Wednesday's any more. I've enough saved to buy you out.'

Charlie looked at her without saying a word. He picked up his coat and a half-full bottle of wine and left. After he had gone, Juliet sat down on the cold concrete floor and sobbed. When she had finished crying, she walked to the mirror and saw that her eyelids were bruised.

The day of the wedding was fine. The rain had continued all week and Frieda and Mrs Greene had been glued to the wireless listening to every forecast, long range, shipping, local. In the end, despite the universally gloomy prognosis, the sun slunk out on Sunday morning and, like a petulant teenager who'd finally given in and agreed to tidy up, shone out across the suburbs, drying all the puddles and wet grass. Juliet feigned cheerfulness, telling herself sternly that everything might work out for the best and perhaps Frieda would be happy. The house was sickly with the scent of lilies which Juliet had never liked; they made her think of funerals rather than weddings and the perfume was too strong, reeking like a great-aunt who'd dabbed too much *eau de toilette* behind her ears. Yet Frieda's excitement seeped from room to room, making even Juliet smile. Her wedding dress was cream with little nylon roses stitched around the high Victorian collar and the net veil was sturdy enough for catching fish, according to Leonard. He was also moving out after the wedding. Charlie had found him a place – an act of kindness Juliet could not forgive. She had to acknowledge that the prospect of independence agreed with Leonard; his spots were drying up, and he wore his powder-blue suit and shiny tie with renewed confidence. He spoke to her with civility and coolness, answering a request to lay the table or a question about the arrival of the carnation buttonholes with the formal politeness one would afford a stranger until, unable to bear it any longer, Juliet was forced to retreat upstairs to her bedroom.

She brushed her hair and put on her wedding outfit, a simple cream suit with navy trim. There were little buttons to fasten along the spine of the dress, which in the shop the assistant had helpfully secured. Now, standing alone in her bedroom with the back of the dress flapping open, Juliet sighed and wished she'd purchased an outfit intended for the husbandless and loverless. Perhaps she ought to design garments with no tricky inaccessible zips or buttons. She had bought a hat which she knew didn't go with the outfit and didn't suit her. It was an awful thing, all garish frills and flounces, but Mrs Greene had reminded her only the day before that married women must wear hats in *shul*, and it had been far too late to find anything else.

Nearly eleven and the wedding car would soon be here. Juliet wished she could summon a spoonful of excitement and feel like a real mother-of-the-bride instead of this dreadful unease. Padding across the landing past portraits of assorted

Juliets, she opened Frieda's door. She was sitting in front of the mirror, her hair pinned up in elaborate curls. Mrs Greene barked at a cowering hairdresser who wielded her tongs in fear, poking nervously at the billowing pile of hair. Juliet hovered in the doorway feeling like an intruder until Frieda glanced up and gave a worried smile.

'Do you think this do is a bit over the top?' she asked.

'No, darling, it's wonderful,' lied Juliet. She turned to her mother. 'Button me up?'

Mrs Greene abandoned her assault on the hairdresser and moved to Juliet. 'What is this? Such flimsy fabric. You should have gone to Minnie's in the high street and mentioned my name. She'd have given you a good thick skirt for the money. And you've got much too skinny. Did you even eat that strudel and the schnitzel I put in the fridge?'

Mrs Greene finished fastening the buttons and the tirade fizzled out. Juliet kissed her on the cheek.

'Thank you, Ma. You look very nice.'

Mr Greene's voice floated up the stairs, calling that the car was ready. The hiring of a white Rolls-Royce when Mr Greene had an appropriately serviced Ford Anglia in the garage was another quite unnecessary expense in Mrs Greene's view. She peered out of the window, lip curling as she realised the chauffeur's whites were grubby and he'd taken the opportunity to sneak a fag by the bins.

Frieda noticed none of this. She was Scarlett O'Hara and Elizabeth Taylor rolled into one. Soon she'd be Mrs Dov Cohen and have her own house. Leonard and her grandfather waited at the bottom of the stairs. Frieda, nervous and thrilled to at last be playing this role, swept down the narrow suburban stairs, meticulously ignoring the descending rows of Juliets. There must be half a dozen of the things on the stairs alone – and only that one stupid picture of Frieda done when she was a little girl. She'd like a portrait of herself now in her wedding dress. Now, that would have been a good present from her mother – not that collection of silver-plate spoons and the dreary picture of the house in the wood.

Mr Greene and Frieda were bundled into the waiting Rolls, Frieda whispering happily to her grandfather that the chauffeur had held open the door and lifted his hat. Mrs Greene, however, observing the spatters on the mudguard and the dent on the driver's door, retreated into the kitchen in disgust. This was when the mistake arose. Mrs Greene failed to notice that Juliet didn't get into the wedding car.

However, no one had told Juliet she should be in it, so she'd assumed that the taxi taking Mrs Greene and Leonard would also convey her to the wedding. Thus, when she emerged from the loo at a quarter past eleven it was to find the house empty and silent and that both wedding car and taxi had gone. For one blissful moment, Juliet wondered if she could just remain in the warm hush of the kitchen, but of course she couldn't, one had to watch as one's children made the wrong decisions as well as the right ones. Grabbing her purse, she ran out of the door, and managed by a miracle to catch the first bus going past, which by an even greater miracle happened to be travelling in exactly the direction of the synagogue. She sat on the back row in her finery, congratulating herself that she would not, in fact, be very late to her daughter's wedding. It was only when she hurried into the *shul*, ten minutes after the bride's arrival, past the assorted ushers and the sweating rabbi and into the hiss of the assembled congregation, that she realised she'd left the hideous green hat on the kitchen table. There was nothing she could do. The women leaned together in the gallery, the whispers gathering – *so Juliet Montague has taken the bus to her own daughter's wedding, arrived late and, worst of all, with her head quite bare. Is she declaring that divorce or no, she isn't going to behave like a married woman any more?* The scandal was thrilling and far more interesting than the prospect of the shop-bought flower arrangements that had supposedly cost Mr Greene forty pounds.

Juliet slipped through the door into the room at the back of the *shul* to witness the bedecking of the bride, knowing that Frieda would never believe it was an accident. But, as she listened to the joyful disapproval of the Cohens, Juliet wondered whether it was really a mistake. It was ridiculous after all these years to wear a hat to *shul* like a good Jewish wife. Better to be bareheaded and brazen. If there was a God, Juliet hoped he'd appreciate her honesty.

After the reception, Juliet walked home alone. The house was quite empty. She'd never lived by herself before. Until eighteen she'd lived with her parents in the neat detached house in Mulberry Avenue, moving out only on the day of her marriage. She remembered arriving here after the honeymoon in the fading afternoon, fumbling in her handbag for the shiny new key. It had felt terribly adult, to have keys to one's own home – she'd half expected everything to be in miniature like in a Wendy house but no, it was a real, grown-up-sized house and George had heaved her over the threshold, half dropping her on the kitchen floor. They'd gone to bed, though not to sleep, and tripped back downstairs in their dressing gowns to drink hot chocolate (Juliet) and bourbon (George) at half past two.

Juliet trod up the front path, her shoes nipping at her heels like a Jack Russell, and hoped that whatever happened next, Frieda was happy at this minute. Somehow, as the years passed, the troubles with George faded enough that, like wallpaper smeared with a layer of paint, the roses began to show through once again. As she turned the key in the lock and entered the kitchen, she shuddered. It had stayed exactly as it was left. The milk curdled on the table from the last family breakfast. The drip-drip of the tap she'd never had fixed. Leonard's muddy shoes discarded beside the door. At the sight of his shoes, Juliet felt a hiccup of sadness rise in her throat. Both children gone. It was too soon – they were both much too young. And now for the first time in her life at thirty-eight years and – she glanced at the calendar – two months, she was quite alone.

The following morning an invitation arrived embossed on yellow card:

The Hambledon Gallery Summer Party,
including new works by Dorset painter, Max Langford.

Kitty West requests the pleasure of your company
on the 31st July, 7.30 p.m. Salisbury Street.
Blandford Forum.
RSVP.

At the bottom, a looping female hand had added: 'Max and I do hope you'll come, KW.'

Juliet deposited the invitation straight into the kitchen bin. Half an hour later she retrieved it with a curl of mouldering apple peel stuck to the envelope. Irritation and hurt prickled her skin. She definitely would not go to the exhibition. No question at all.

The exhibition was held upstairs in a small brick building in the market town of Blandford. The summer was cleaner in Dorset than in London. Juliet was nervous and tugged at her skirt, unsure whether she was over- or underdressed. One could never tell at these country events. The gallery building had a bowed Georgian shop front in which were propped several canvases of hot Mediterranean landscapes – an odd contrast with the old-fashioned prettiness of the sloping houses and shops trundling down the hill outside. A rural county town was a strange place for an art gallery but perhaps that was why it appealed to Max. At the prospect of seeing him again, Juliet felt slightly dizzy, as she did after too much of Mr Greene's awful plum schnapps. It had been a mistake to come but somehow she'd couldn't turn and leave. It wasn't even eight, but as she entered the low shop door, the bell tinkling into the street, she supposed that she must be the last to arrive. The limewashed room heaved with people smelling sweetly of sweat seeping through country tweed. Juliet was swept up in the warm press of bodies and funnelled up the stairs and handed a glass of champagne – good stuff, not the yellow acidic wine passed out at most gatherings. Glancing around the paintings she realised she'd been guilty of prejudice – she'd been expecting dreary but competent watercolours of amiable country scenes with perhaps the odd awkward oil or portrait which held charm only for the sitter's pals. Instead, she took in modern and skilful paintings by some of the country's best artists. As she studied a gouache of Stonehenge, the vast stone slabs metamorphosed into Mondrian rectangles of grey and blue against the expanse of Salisbury Plain, she decided that there was nothing provincial about the pieces or the prices. There was no work here for under a hundred guineas. She felt a hand on her shoulder.

'I'm so glad you came.'

Juliet turned and found herself face to face with a woman of about fifty with curling grey hair, thin un-rouged lips and bluish eyes. Around her neck she wore a pair of large metal-framed specs. She took in Juliet for a minute without smiling, and Juliet felt herself shift under her scrutiny like a first-former caught by the head girl wearing non-regulation socks. At last the woman gave a tiny nod and stretched out her hand saying, 'I'm Katherine West. Everyone calls me Kitty.'

Her voice was clipped and smart, and Juliet decided at once that Kitty was the way lady gallery owners were supposed to be – she was the type who knew instinctively when to serve Pimm's, how to nibble a cucumber sandwich and whether fish forks were in vogue. She was quite certain that Kitty managed to send out invitations to exhibitions without resorting to *Debrett's* before addressing every other envelope.

'Max will be so pleased you came.'

Juliet glanced about, trying to glimpse Max amid the throng, wondering whether or not he was even here. He'd never made it to London and he might well have decided that even Blandford was too far away. Kitty was still speaking but Juliet hadn't taken in a word. Kitty frowned and repeated herself with the patient and exasperated air of someone speaking to the slow or foreign.

'I was saying that Max has told me all about your portrait collection. I think one day that I shall paint you. Do you have many portraits by women?'

Juliet tried to look grateful while privately deciding that being painted by Kitty was a frightful prospect – voluntarily laying herself open to such scrutiny and disapproval.

'I must admit I don't have many.'

Kitty slid her spectacles onto her nose and peered at Juliet, inspecting the angles of her face.

'Well, I think I ought to paint you. Next time you're visiting Max, I'll pop by.'

Juliet drained her champagne, wondering why Max hadn't told Kitty that things between them were finished. At least it meant she wouldn't have to pose under that gaze. As Kitty moved away to greet other guests, Juliet allowed herself to be topped up with more champagne. She considered whether she dreaded seeing Max more than not seeing him. Seeing would be worse, she decided. Definitely.

'Hello, you.'

She turned to face him and instantly felt a sob rise up in her throat which she battled to swallow like a piece of bread. He was so familiar and yet when he held out his hand she could not take it. She'd been away from him long enough to notice that he had aged, his hair was now more white than blond and his leanness stretched into thinness. He leaned in and kissed her, brushing her hairline with his lips. With a pang, she realised he no longer smelled of linseed. He'd stopped painting again.

'Come.'

He took her arm and steered her through the throng to the back of the gallery. It was hot and the air stale and Juliet felt a channel of perspiration tickle the length of her spine. Max seemed to collide with everyone, and Juliet issued a litany of mumbled apologies.

'Why'd she invite so many damned people?' complained Max, making no effort to keep his voice down.

'The more people there are the better chance that someone will buy one of your pictures.'

Max snorted. 'Well, that doesn't seem likely. If you couldn't sell them.'

Juliet faltered, taken aback by this change of heart. Max sighed, 'I know I was awful. Just awful.'

Juliet swallowed, unwilling to talk, inhaling the choking hotness of the room and aware of the strangers pressing against them on every side.

'And I am sorry.' Max stared at the floor, a school-boyish gesture in a middle-aged man. 'But I still can't come back to what is it? Tuesday's?'

Juliet tried not to mind that after nearly a decade he still didn't know the name of the gallery.

'There's just one picture. And you won't want me when you see it,' he said.

Juliet was about to argue when the crowd slid aside for a moment and she saw the painting, and found herself quite unable to speak. It was her portrait. Not as a bird or metamorphosed into any creature but as herself, Juliet Montague. He'd painted her in his bed at the moment of waking; she glanced up at him from the tumble of sheets, shoulders bare and freckled, green eyes fat with sleep, only half aware of the watcher. As she looked at the painting, Juliet understood for the first time that Max loved her.

He's painted me. Every piece of me. Here I am.

He'd never told her that he'd loved her and she couldn't bring herself to ask if he did in case she hadn't liked the answer. Sometimes she suspected that he thought of her as a habit – something he enjoyed but could always give up should it be required. Seeing the portrait she knew this was not true. She was necessary to Max. The awfulness of the wedding, the gossips who whispered her name, the good folk who hadn't seen her for years except as a cipher for bad luck and a warning to daughters – none of it mattered. Juliet Montague was invisible to them but not to him. She found that she was crying.

'Have you noticed the title?' asked Max gently.

Juliet wiped her eyes with the back of her hand and read, '*The Last Time I Saw Her.*'

'It's true, I'm afraid,' said Max in a low voice. 'I'm going blind. There's the shape of you,' he reached out and brushed the space around her cheek, 'but your mouth has gone, and your nose. I'm a figurative painter, and now I can only see in bloody abstract.'

'Oh, Max, I'm so sorry.'

'There. That's it. What I was afraid of. I don't want pity. Not from you.'

'It isn't pity. It's sympathy. I'm sad for you. I'm allowed to be sad.'

He frowned. 'Don't look at me like that.'

'You don't know how I'm looking at you. There's a big hole around my face,' said Juliet, doing her best to keep her voice light.

Max harrumphed. 'Let's go to the pub. I've had enough of here. Too many bloody people.'

'All right,' said Juliet, allowing herself to be led away but staring over her shoulder at her portrait, feeling it pull at her like a lover standing on a station platform. She noticed with dread a little red round 'sold' dot on the frame.

They sat in the garden of the Greyhound listening to the rustle of the River Stour at the edge of the water meadows beyond.

'Why didn't you tell me before?' she asked.

'I didn't know how,' said Max draining his first pint then clasping his second. 'I know that you love my paintings. I know that look you get when I show them to you. It's greedy. Ugly and most unfeminine. I didn't want that look to disappear. I'm a painter who can't paint. I was always a fairly useless creature – but now . . .'

He laughed. She reached out for his hand and then withdrew again before she had touched him, not wanting to be accused of pity. She supposed she was allowed the facts.

'When did it start?'

'A few years ago I first began to notice a weak spot in my left eye. A bit of blurred vision. It was always worse after painting in bright sunlight. I thought it was lack of sleep. Too much booze. The usual. For a while I thought it might have been caused by a nasty bout of malaria I had in Egypt back in the war. Then last year it got much worse.'

'Did you see a doctor?'

'Eventually.'

'What did he say?'

Max shrugged. 'Chronic and progressive eye disease. They did lots of tests and told me to go up to Harley Street and visit a specialist. But when I pressed, they all agreed that all he would tell me was that I wasn't blind yet, but I would be soon.'

Juliet was glad that he couldn't see her face, and held her breath so he couldn't tell that she was trying not to cry. 'And now? What can you see?'

Max finished the second pint. 'Now the weak spot has grown to an empty hole in the centre of my vision. Painting is a torment. I peer around the subject – if I try to focus on the thing itself I can't see it all. I can only see you now by not looking. I have to catch you at the edge of my vision.'

'How on earth did you paint that portrait of me?'

Max grinned. 'Months and months. I've never spent so long on any painting. Never will again. It's my last. So it had to be of you.'

He turned and looked at her with those too blue eyes and Juliet could almost not believe that he couldn't see her. They weren't bloodshot or yellowed but white and clear and useless.

They sat for the rest of the evening in the garden of the pub, listening to the twittering of the house martins as they zoomed low over the Stour and the sighs of the cattle drifting amid the long grass. The orange sun sank into a coal fire of clouds and transformed a pair of dawdling swans from white into gold but Juliet observed them in silence. She told Max instead about the wedding and he laughed over the hat incident, snorting beer from his nose. Then she confessed how she worried that she'd lost both children – Frieda to a dreary husband and a dull life of chores and the raising of children and baking of endless loaves of *challah*.

'And Leonard? Why is Leonard lost?' asked Max.

'He wants to paint.'

'Ahh,' said Max, understanding. 'That was always the case with him. There was nothing you could do. It's an affliction. Like alcoholism. Or good looks.'

Juliet smiled and realised he was flirting with her. She understood that Max assumed that she would return with him to the cottage in the woods and everything would be almost as before. She closed her eyes and thought of the portrait.

'It's yours, you know,' said Max. 'The painting. I gave it to Kitty to sell in a fit of pique and then I told her I wanted it back but she wouldn't give it to me. She said if I really wanted it, I'd have to buy it like anybody else. So I did. Fifty sodding guineas it cost me. She charged me every penny of her commission.'

Juliet leaned over and kissed him. He smelled of alcohol and the wood.

'The children will come back,' said Max. 'Give them time. Count it in portraits. In one, two, three, four or ten Juliets they will come back to you.'

CATALOGUE ITEM 75
Woman Bathing,
Max Langford, Clay and Wire Mesh, 1982

'PLEASE DON'T TELL your grandmother.'

Frieda looked at Juliet in surprise. 'That's all you have to say? Not "You must think of the children" or "I never liked him"?'

Juliet poured Frieda another cup of coffee, wondering if she ought to be offering her a glass of something stronger but the only liquor in the house was an ancient bottle of schnapps she'd won in a raffle. 'You always think about the children and you already know I don't like him. He's too dull for you.' Juliet sighed. 'I always hoped that if you stayed married that at least you'd find an exotic lover.'

Frieda laughed. In her thirties she'd discovered that having an eccentric mother wasn't quite the curse it had seemed when she was in her teens. 'I did sleep with a Frenchman when I went to Paris.'

Juliet smiled and helped herself to another chocolate biscuit. 'I'm glad. I hope he was handsome.'

Frieda sighed. 'Not really. He was a little fat and starting to go bald. But he was nice.'

Juliet rolled her eyes. 'Never mind nice for once. Your husband is nice. For now you need selfish and frivolous and fun – you remember the Gainsborough portraits of the Regency rakes I used to take you to visit at the National? You need the modern equivalent of one of those.'

'You want me to sleep with a man in red velvet trousers?'

'If that's what he happens to be wearing, then yes. I want you to have some fun. Go out with a man who's a bit of a dish and who'll break your heart. It'll do you good, you know. A dash of heartbreak.'

'And don't tell Grandma.'

'Exactly.'

The women lapsed into silence, both considering Mrs Greene, who like a sturdy apple tree had suddenly gone from being in her prime to being hollow and thin, frail against the wind. She still wore coral lipstick every day and brewed eight-hour chicken soup on a Friday night, but this feat meant that the rest of the weekend was spent napping in the chair by the electric fire. Juliet had once suggested that the nap might be more restful upstairs in the new bed she'd persuaded her parents to purchase, but Mrs Greene fixed her daughter with a look of disgust declaring, 'Only babies, women during their confinement and old people take to their beds in the afternoon.' Juliet said nothing more, glad that her mother still had her vanity and pride. The young doctor's diagnosis had not been good and he was banal in his sympathies: 'It's a shame, but your mother's had a good life and a full one, and it comes to us all in the end.' Juliet and Mr Greene had decided not to tell her. They expected that she knew without it being said and the truth was she'd rallied over the last few months – there was less forgetting at the grocer's and she'd been making an effort to eat a bit more herself as well as urge cakes and *latkes* on her great-grandchildren. The colour in her cheeks wasn't just rouge from Woolworths.

Mr Greene dared to hope. As the years passed he'd learned to put more faith in his God – touchy and cankerous as he was, the aged ruffian and he were old pals and, frankly, Jehovah owed him one. He prayed at home every day, pretending he was singing in the shower when really he was wearing his *yarmulke* instead of a shower-cap and his *tallis* instead of a towel. God didn't mind his nakedness – they were old men together and he pictured God much like himself – a bit of a paunch, inconveniently old, struggling to pee. Mr Greene put down the improvement in his wife to these acts of bathroom devotion, although he did not mention this to anyone. His daughter and granddaughter would give him that look of fond indulgence, as if he was a doolally old fool who mustn't be contradicted. He preferred to say nothing. What did it matter? He didn't need to be right; he just needed his Edie to be all right.

Juliet and Frieda did suspect other reasons for the change. Without having discussed it, they were both quite certain that Mrs Greene was waiting for her great-grandson's *bar mitzvah*. She took tremendous pleasure in Frieda's respectability and her marriage into the Cohens. Whenever her friends enquired after Juliet with one of *those* looks, Mrs Greene liked to reply, 'She's perfectly well, and so is my granddaughter, you know, Frieda *Cohen*,' as though the blot from one generation had been washed away by the respectability of the next like an intergenerational stain remover. The *bar mitzvah* was to be the culmination of it all. Paul Cohen, thirteen, acne ridden and so shy he'd taken to hiding in his bedroom during his own birthday parties, was to recite the Torah before three hundred people, give a witty and devastating speech during a four-course luncheon and be the pride of two families and three generations of assorted Greenes, Montagues and Cohens. Privately Juliet wondered whether her grandson would be the next in his family to vanish.

'How are Paul and Jenny managing?' asked Juliet.

'We haven't told them yet. It didn't seem fair. Not until after the *bar mitzvah*. Paul has enough to worry about and we couldn't tell Jenny without telling him. You know she can't keep a secret.'

Juliet sipped her tea and thought about her granddaughter, eleven-year-old Jenny, and decided that concealing the divorce of one's parents wasn't something that a child should be asked to do. But she supposed that it was she who had taught Frieda that children must keep secrets.

Frieda gave Juliet an invitation for Max to come to the *bar mitzvah*. They both knew it was a safe offer – he would never come – but Juliet appreciated the gesture nonetheless. She wanted to take Paul with her to the cottage for a rest before the big event, to meet Max. It had been unconscionable before Frieda had told her that she was going to leave Dov. Juliet had never even mentioned Max in front of the children. She wondered if they knew about him anyway, but she supposed not. Grandchildren rarely suspected grandmothers of having illicit lovers. But Frieda still wouldn't let Paul go, she was only starting to escape the yoke of respectability and couldn't let her mother take him, not yet. 'Perhaps later,' she'd said.

'After the *bar mitzvah*?' Juliet had asked.

'Yes, after the *bar mitzvah*,' Frieda had answered with some relief. Juliet had said nothing more, only considered the watershed that this great event represented in all their lives.

Max was not disappointed that the boy hadn't come.

'Why would you bring him here?' he asked, genuinely perplexed. 'I've never liked children.'

'You liked mine,' said Juliet.

'Yes, I suppose I did. Especially Leonard. You must bring him again. I should like to see Leonard.'

'Leonard is in his thirties. If you want him to come and visit then you must ask him yourself.'

Juliet sighed. It was as though for Max people remained stuck at the age they were when he'd lost his sight. Leonard would forever be a promising adolescent and Max always appeared surprised when Juliet read aloud a review or a snippet about him in the press, jolted that the boy had grown up. Everyone and everything changed but Max and the wood at Fippenny Hollow, which altered only with the seasons. The hawthorn and blackthorn bushes bloomed and withered, put out green leaves, lost them and then dangled with scarlet thorn apples or black sloes, which Max gathered up, shoved into foul-smelling bottles and drowned in cheap gin. The rhythm of his life was steady, measured out by sun and snow and the time it took to brew plum wine or for bread to rise. In the last few years he had become almost totally blind, able only to glimpse shadows, all colours lost to him.

Juliet sat in the kitchen, the windows thrown open to the wood, and chattered as Max cooked. He moved as quickly and easily with the knife as ever, never seeming to cut his finger or scald himself as he put a match to the stove. He peeled the skin from a rabbit, slitting the stomach and then slowly pulling off the fur which he placed on the table, raw and bloody, an empty rabbit sleeping-bag. Juliet shuddered and thought again that she really wasn't country girl – things that wriggled and slithered appalled her. However, she knew that as soon as the stew started to bubble and the kitchen fill with the scent of herbs and wine and cooking she'd be hungry and ready to eat.

'Leonard has a new show. It's up north but I shall try to go. Things are very busy with the *bar mitzvah* preparations and my mother is still so frail, so I might not manage it,' said Juliet.

They both understood that this was a lie. No matter what happened, Juliet would be there. Leonard always ensured that she received an invitation to the show. She wished he'd exhibit at Wednesday's but she was afraid to ask him in case he refused – Leonard had never suggested including so much as a sketch in the summer exhibition. In fact, he'd not asked her opinion on anything he'd produced since the day he'd left home. He hadn't asked for her help and, unwilling to interfere or face being rebuffed, she had not known how to offer it. No, that wasn't quite true – she'd written to a dealer friend in New York a few years after Leonard had left college, asking him to look at a few pieces, and he'd responded with great enthusiasm and he'd sold Leonard ever since. It was a strange sensation during her sporadic trips to New York to view her son's pictures on the vast white walls, as a stranger might. Once the dealer had even forgotten that Leonard was her son, and she listened politely to his *spiel* as he described the young British artist and his use of colour and collage while she studied the pieces on the walls, relieved that even without the labels she could pick Leonard's out of the crowd, like distant cousins who still sported the family nose.

The following morning Max surprised her by asking her to come with him to the painting shed. She traipsed behind him, trying to swallow the waves of melancholy that rose in her throat. Max had kept to his word and his portrait of Juliet had been his last. Every now and again he discovered an old picture in the back of a cupboard or beneath the eaves and gave it to Juliet. He had no use for pictures he couldn't see. Relieved of the burden of selling them, Juliet hoarded them all in the Chislehurst house, stashing them in her bedroom closet. She was greedy for Max's paintings and did not want to share them.

Max ushered her inside the shed. It still smelled of linseed, it had seeped into the woodwork and she experienced a pang of nostalgia, sharp and clear. Early sunshine spilled into the room bright as egg yolk.

'I'm not painting,' he said.

'No.'

He sat down at the workbench and Juliet noticed for the first time a shape under a scrap of sheet, like a child's drawing of a ghost. He pulled it off with a magician's flick, and Juliet saw it was a sculpture of a girl lazing in the bath, a nice leg stretched out, the other knee poking from beneath the surface of the water. As she looked again, she realised the woman was her.

'It's me,' she said.

'Of course.'

'But you've made me far too young. She doesn't have a single wrinkle,' Juliet laughed.

Max shrugged. 'But do you like it?'

Juliet leaned over and kissed him, inhaling the earthy scent of clay on his skin – something new. His beard was dappled with white and in the sunshine she could see the pink of his scalp beneath his hair. He kissed her back with pleasing enthusiasm, reaching to unclip her bra strap with familiar ease and nimble fingers, and Juliet smiled into his mouth thinking how good it was that the young don't have a monopoly on love or sex and that there are advantages in having a blind lover.

Leonard felt sympathy soft and sticky as treacle as he watched his nephew sitting in the front row of the *shul* sandwiched between Grandfather Cohen and Great-Grandfather Greene, a black bird between a pair of white gulls. The boy's father stood at the front mumbling through his blessing, looking as alarmed as any *bar mitzvah* boy himself. Leonard snorted – even after all these years he'd never really come to like Dov. Frieda's husband had grown from a young man with damp palms to a middle-aged man with a shining forehead. Leonard watched Paul fidget in his seat knowing the awful moment approached and sighed, his own guts going on a spin cycle in sympathy. He was glad he'd bought him a decent present to make up for it – an all metal Sony Walkman in blue with several cassette tapes, Van Halen, *Thriller*, Tom Petty, all sent over by his dealer in America. Hopefully that would make up for the inevitable half dozen Corby trouser presses and seven radio alarm clocks the kid would receive. Leonard's own *bar mitzvah* had been too overshadowed by his family's shame to be much of an event. Even Mrs Greene couldn't bear to do much more than a bagel lunch for forty. And of course he'd had no father to stand up beside him on the *bimah* as he read. His grandfather had done his best, but like a tear in a woollen sweater, the gap left behind by his father had stretched to gaping that day.

The rabbi cleared his throat, the grandfathers slapped the boy's back and Paul stood, made his way up to the front. Nerves paled him to a nasty shade of chalky white, making his acne shine. The boy stood at the front swallowing. The silence stretched, grew elastic. The women in the gallery shifted, wriggled on sweaty behinds. Everyone was waiting. Paul closed his eyes. Swayed a little. The rabbi peered forward, starting to fret. And then, the boy began. He didn't speak the words but sang them slow and clear in his new tenor. His great-grandmother reached into her pocket for a tissue. Juliet muttered something in relief that wasn't a prayer. The furrows in Frieda's forehead relaxed and she gave a peaceful smile. Only Leonard grew sadder as he listened to the boy. He watched Paul, small beside his father, *yarmulke* balanced precariously on top of messy black hair, the surprisingly sweet voice swelling into every corner, musical and soft and slow. *He knows*, decided Leonard. *Children always do*. He's standing

318

up there singing and singing and not wanting it to end because he knows that sometime afterwards when lunch has finished and the speeches have been made and the trouser presses unwrapped and the cheques opened and the aunts dutifully kissed, his mother will draw him aside to the corner of the hall and tell him that she's leaving his father and life will never be the same, and soon afterwards, a day, a week or a month, his adored grandmother Edith will take to her bed again and this time she won't get up, and childhood will be at an end. Leonard pictured the Sony Walkman and the cluster of tapes in their Ferrari wrapping paper in the boot of his car and felt sadness heavy as a fever stick in his chest.

Juliet 'Fidget' Montague, My Mother,
Leonard Montague, Oil on 34 Canvases, 130 x 384in, 2006

MAX DIED JUST before Christmas. Up until the end, Juliet continued to stay with him at the cottage. In over forty years together he never visited the house in Chislehurst. After a while she'd found the journey to Dorset rather tiring, the lack of heating was a bit of a bore and midnight trips to an outside loo at seventy-six lacked romance. Max didn't notice the petty inconveniences of the cottage. He'd aged slowly – only his thick wheat gold hair was replaced by thistledown – but then suddenly he became frail. A carer was mentioned. Meals on Wheels. He listened patiently and then told Juliet he was going to die – it just seemed less bother all round. He was quite matter-of-fact about it and it took her a moment to realise he wasn't asking her to bring some more milk or tobacco with her during her next visit. 'Don't come next week. I'll be dead. It'll be a waste of a trip.' She'd thought he was joking, but sure enough a nice lady from social services telephoned to say that she was terribly sorry etcetera and Juliet fumbled and replaced the receiver, cutting her off. She cried a little, but most of all she missed him. Suddenly there was no one to save up the stories for. There was nothing particular to tell, only the debris of the week. She'd always supposed that those elderly women who wandered along the high street were muttering to themselves, but now she wondered whether they were, in fact, confiding to their dead lovers. Leonard was terribly kind and brought round hot meals (grief must be fed like a cold, apparently) and reassured her that the pain would lessen in time. Juliet ventured to hope it wouldn't take too much time, as she was running a little short. Worrying that she might be depressed, Leonard and Frieda colluded and agreed that one or other of them must visit most days.

Frieda knew that something had happened as soon as she called round. She rang the doorbell before letting herself in – Juliet hated it when Frieda simply unlocked the door and wandered into the kitchen.

'I could be doing anything. *Anything*.'

'In the kitchen? You're nearly eighty.'

Juliet had frowned and said nothing more.

Frieda pushed open the door and found her mother dressed in her Jaeger jacket and smart Hermès scarf, seated at the kitchen table drinking a glass of sherry even though it wasn't quite half past nine in the morning. Frieda could barely recall ever having seen her mother drink, and leaned against the door for a moment, wondering if grief had prompted the foray into the cupboard.

'Are you all right?'

'Perfectly, thank you.'

'Is it Max?'

'No. It's another man.'

Frieda pulled out a chair and sat down opposite her, wondering if her mother was starting to go dotty like so many of her friends' parents. Perhaps she ought to telephone Leonard.

'Care to join me?' asked Juliet, gesturing to the bottle. 'It's not terribly nice, but I understand that it's the appropriate response under the circumstances.'

Frieda sighed. She'd been in her mother's company for less than five minutes and already she was irritated. Despite Juliet's breeziness, she noticed the hand holding the sherry glass shake. She took a breath and willed herself to be patient.

'What circumstances?' she asked, waiting for one of Juliet's usual cryptic replies.

To her surprise Juliet did not evade the question but slightly wearily pushed back her chair and retrieved a large round cardboard tube from the draining board. She placed it on the table in front of Frieda.

'It arrived this morning. It's from your father.'

Now it was Frieda's turn to sit and reach for the sherry. She poured herself a good measure into a teacup. She stared at her mother, but Juliet said nothing, only sat with her hands folded in her lap waiting for Frieda to look at the parcel.

'Have you opened it already?' asked Frieda.

'Yes.'

Frieda took a swig and eased open the lid of the tube. Inside was a roll of fabric; carefully she eased it out and placed it still coiled on the kitchen table. She stared at it for a full minute, oddly reluctant to unfurl it and look properly. Finally, Frieda stood and uncurled the fabric, feeling it crackle beneath her fingers. It smelled of attics and long journeys.

'Oh, it's a painting.'

Juliet nodded, almost smiled. 'Do you remember it?'

Frieda looked down at the painting and weighted it at one end with a jar of marmalade, with the salt-shaker at the other. She took a step back and saw the face of a young girl with pale brown hair and green eyes. Her legs were folded awkwardly, and she sat on her hands as though to stop them fidgeting. The child glared at the viewer, neither angry nor smiling, merely interested. For a moment Frieda thought the girl in the picture was herself and then she realised.

'I do remember. It used to hang in the house. In the sitting-room, I think. Then one day, around the time Dad left, it disappeared.'

'He stole it when he vanished,' said Juliet, voice tight, still angry after all these years.

'And now he's just giving it back?'

Juliet reached out across the table and took Frieda's hand.

'He died, darling. The parcel was sent by his lawyer.'

To her own immense surprise, Frieda began to cry. Sobs rose in her chest like a spring tide and she bobbed around on the waves of unexpected grief as Juliet moved round to hold her.

The two women had barely touched in years – fingers brushing across the table when passing the potatoes, a kiss hello and goodbye – but now Juliet clasped her daughter close, feeling the damp of tears and snot on her blouse. She stroked her back and rubbed her head, noticing the grey hair at the base of Frieda's scalp like unripe corn. Juliet didn't attempt to hush her. It was perfectly sensible to cry. She had done so for a full half-hour herself before wiping her eyes and rooting in the cupboard for the sherry. It had been more than fifty years since George had disappeared and she'd been long resigned to never seeing him again. And, yet his death startled her. As far as anyone was concerned she was no longer an *aguna* or a living widow, but merely a widow. An unremarkable grey and white old lady who'd lost her husband. No one was interested enough any more to enquire exactly how she'd lost him or to accuse her of carelessness. Only young women in scarlet lipstick misplaced husbands. Elderly ladies like her merely surrendered them to death in his nightshirt. But she supposed that somewhere her poor mother was relieved that her shame was at an end.

Frieda dried her eyes and smiled.

'I'm sorry. I don't know why I made such a fuss.'

'Don't be silly. He was still your father.'

'Yes, but I never knew him.'

'And now you can't. It's the end of a possibility, however unlikely.'

'Don't. You'll make me cry again.'

Juliet shrugged. Frieda pulled a packet of tissues from her handbag and dabbed her eyes, then rooted around for a comb, fussing in front of her compact mirror. Juliet sighed, wishing that Frieda could replace tidiness with sadness for just a little while longer. After divorcing Dov Frieda was supposed to have been liberated from propriety, but she remained far too concerned with what other people thought. Juliet supposed she ought to care a little more and her daughter a little less.

'What did you say, Mum?'

Juliet looked up, not realising she'd spoken aloud.

'Nothing, darling. I said nothing.'

'I suppose he was an awful good-for-nothing and I should be glad I hardly knew him,' said Frieda.

'No,' replied Juliet. 'He was charming and could be terribly funny. He adored you and Leonard. But then he left and that cancelled out everything good that happened before.'

Frieda laughed. 'You're not supposed to say that. You're supposed to say he was a thief and a drunk and a gambler and a liar. You're supposed to make it better.'

Juliet frowned. 'Well, that is what everyone used to say about him. But it's only partly true. He was a gambler and he did steal my picture, but he wasn't a drunk.'

About his being a liar, she made no remark.

Frieda leaned back in her chair and watched her mother, remembering the photographs in the bedroom closet with her father's image cut out.

'There was nothing else in the parcel?' she asked.

'Just the picture,' said Juliet.

She knew she ought to feel guilty about concealing the letter but it had been addressed to her alone, and even at seventy-six one needed to keep some things secret.

The arrival of the painting marked a change in Juliet. Leonard noticed it first. She caught flu after Christmas, which settled into pneumonia and then progressed into a seeping melancholy like endless spring rain. Frieda put it down to age, 'Oh, she's just not as young as she was.' But Leonard knew it was something else. She seemed indifferent to getting well and while she hadn't exactly started to forget things, she didn't care to remember them. Her seventy-seventh birthday passed without remark when usually she was steadfast about celebrating, no matter how inconvenient it might be for the rest of her family. If Leonard or Frieda or one of the grandchildren suggested that perhaps the celebration could be delayed until the weekend, Juliet would sulk. 'I can't change my birthday any more than I can change the day of my death.' Leonard and Frieda would sigh and agree that 'Mother is getting very difficult, even more difficult' and purchase (Leonard) or bake (Frieda) the necessary cake. But this year the eighth of April drifted past unremarked and it was only on the ninth that Leonard noticed the birthday had been forgotten and telephoned Juliet.

'I didn't forget. I ignored it. I'm too old for birthdays.'

Leonard frowned. This was a logic he might have accepted from someone else but not from his mother. He couldn't quite see that while seventy-six required a picnic in Hyde Park and a walk along the Bayswater Road inspecting every indifferent painting strung up on the railings, seventy-seven was marked by sudden restraint and indifference. He was confident that something was wrong and pondered what to do. He opened his eyes and smiled. Suddenly, he knew.

Later that evening he brought a birthday cake round to his mother, appearing in Mulberry Avenue uninvited. Like his sister he possessed a key, but unlike her it never occurred to him not to ring the bell. He waited on the doorstep until Juliet answered, observing how her face brightened into a copy of her old self as soon as she saw him.

'Oh, it's you,' she said.

'Yes,' agreed Leonard. 'I brought you birthday cake from the deli. I thought we could eat it together.'

He trailed her into the too clean kitchen. It didn't look as if a meal had been cooked here for a week and even in the gloom she looked too thin.

'Is it poppy-seed?' she asked.

'Yes.'

'Did you bring sour cream?'

'Yes.'

'The proper stuff from the Yiddishy deli, not the supermarket.'

'Yes.'

Juliet sighed but it was a sigh of happy anticipation. In the last few years she had started yearning for the Jewish treats of her childhood – the chicken schnitzels and chopped fried fish and cinnamon *rugelach*. She almost wished she'd paid more attention while her mother had been baking. Leonard retrieved plates from the cupboard and cut her a large slice of cake and scooped out a significant dollop of cream.

'Happy birthday, Mama,' he said and kissed her softly on the cheek.

He glanced behind her to the dresser and noticed a pile of unopened post.

'You can't ignore your mail,' he said gently, trying not to reprimand.

Juliet shrugged through a forkful of cake. 'They're only birthday cards. I pay the bills. I'm not gaga yet.'

Leonard retrieved the cards and placed them on the table. 'Let's open them anyway.'

He waited a moment but Juliet made no move to pick up an envelope and so he started to open them.

'This is from Charlie. I think he drew it himself.'

Juliet peered at it. 'Yes. It's a self-portrait. I have one for every year since we met. Well, except for the year we fell out. I was so pleased when he sent a card just the same for my next birthday.' She frowned. 'He's made himself much too slim. He's become rather fat. I can't blame him. His latest wife is a wonderful cook.'

'And here's one from Philip. It's postmarked Santa Barbara.'

'Yes, he spends most of the year there. They're always telling me to come and visit.'

'Well, why don't you? The sunshine would do you good.'

Juliet pushed away her plate, avoiding Leonard's eye. 'I've been to California. I can't go back.'

Leonard toyed with his cake, thinking that now he was actually sitting with Juliet, he didn't know quite how to start the conversation. His mother always did this to him. Earlier he'd been so certain that it was the right thing to do but even in the car on the way over his confidence had evaporated like a puddle in the sunshine. He stood and slipped upstairs pretending he needed to use the toilet. The stairway was crowded with paintings of Juliet – there must have been at least fifty portraits lined up in neat rows like children in the annual school photograph. His mother stared down at him, sometimes smiling, sometimes not. Another twenty Juliets watched from the landing, crammed frame to frame, shoulder to shoulder. A kaleidoscope of women. There were no family photographs – not one of the usual snaps of ice-cream-smeared grandchildren or black and white shots of babies snoozing in Moses baskets. The only photographs were portraits of Juliet – one taken by Cecil Beaton and another by David Bailey. Leonard had never liked either. She looked impossibly beautiful in Beaton's and in Bailey's she was just another of his unhappy, cigarette-smoking women. At the top of the stairs was a mirror and Leonard wondered what it was like for Juliet to look in it and see, in addition to her current face, so many decades of herself reflected back at her. Didn't she lose herself in the collage?

Apart from the portraits, it was such an ordinary suburban house. The brown carpet had been updated from the nasty fifties mustard to an equally dubious eighties green and a dozen years ago the wallpaper had been stripped and changed to a Mulholland blue in order to better display the pictures, but Juliet had shown no interest in either moving or further re-decorating. The London gallery was bright and modern and the exhibition space re-painted every year, sometimes twice. Until her flu last year the colour changes were always overseen by Juliet – she'd insisted that the decorators redo the entire gallery when the shade of red was a single grade too dark. She was the first curator in London to reject the glare of white walls and soon the National and the Tate were asking her to consult. It puzzled him, how this determined woman with all her panache still chose to live in this cramped, indifferent house in a suburb filled with the echoes of old disapproving sighs.

Even now, worn and grey from illness, Juliet wore high-waisted herringbone trousers, an emerald silk blouse and knotted Liberty scarf at her throat. Leonard was often asked, out of the many beautiful women he'd captured, whose style he admired the most. Over the years he'd given a variety of names – sometimes the woman he was sleeping with, sometimes the woman he wished to be sleeping with – but the truth was it was Juliet whom he most admired. And yet, he supposed she didn't count – he'd never painted her so he wasn't allowed to include her in his answer. The house was filled with Juliets, but none of them by him.

When he came back downstairs she was sitting at the kitchen table perfectly still, hands folded in her lap, staring into nothing like a heron poised by a goldfish pond. Her calm unnerved him. She was a woman always in motion, and this recent quiet irked him. Resolved, Leonard took a breath and reached up to clean his glasses, a boyhood habit that still caught him even though he'd worn contacts for years.

'I'm sending a taxi to collect you tomorrow at nine. It's taking you to the studio. I'm going to paint you.'

'Another tea?'

Juliet shook her head. She could tell Leonard was nervous and she was relieved as she had the same tingling, half-fearful excitement herself. She so wanted to like the picture. Most of the time with the others she was only curious to discover how they saw her. Their versions rarely coincided with how she imagined herself but it was always interesting, if sometimes disconcerting. With Leonard it was different. Few mothers have the opportunity to discover how their sons really see them. She knew Leonard loved her – that he couldn't help. But did he like her? She watched as he fumbled with his brushes, set out jars of water, mixed and remixed paints and then finally reached for a pencil. She presumed he wasn't always this unsure how to begin and decided to be pleased by his fluster. She wondered if he wanted her to talk as he worked, some did, some didn't, and with a pang she realised that this was yet another thing about her son that she did not know. It was strange how unfamiliar one's children become. When she thought about Leonard she pictured the small and earnest bespectacled boy of ten, not this man in the expensive sweater with creases around his eyes. Though she was pleased to observe that the creases went in the right direction – Juliet made it a point to like people whose lines curved up from smiling rather than down.

Leonard gave a tiny sigh and set down his pencil. It was useless trying to force it. The picture would come if he relaxed and thought of other things.

'Let's just talk for a while.'

'Whatever you like, darling.'

'Why didn't you ever leave Chislehurst? You must have made enough money over the years.'

Juliet gave a tiny smile. 'Yes, I did. First I bought out the investors and partners. That took some time. And afterwards, well, despite everything I'm still the girl from the *shtetl* in the suburbs. It was easier not to fit in at home than anywhere else.'

Leonard studied her for a moment in silence before asking, 'How many portraits do you have now in your collection?'

Juliet frowned, trying to think. 'I believe nearly a hundred.'

'Why haven't you shown them? You must have been asked.'

'They're painted just for me. No one else.' She reached for a biscuit set out on a low table.

'But I'm sure people would like to see them. You always took us to galleries. Said the best paintings must be shared.'

Juliet re-crossed her legs, brushing crumbs from her trousers. 'You can have an exhibition after I'm gone. Write a proper catalogue and a pompous foreword. You know the sort of thing . . . *"For fifty years Wednesday's Gallery and its icon-oclastic curator, owner and navigator, Juliet Montague, have been part of the fabric of Bayswater. She chartered the gallery from the early sixties through the perils of Pop Art and abstraction, remaining resolute in her passion for figurative painting . . ."* I'll have an exhibition instead of a funeral. But you're not to do it till then.'

She waggled a finger at Leonard, who forced a smile.

'Tell me about the first time you were painted,' said Leonard pulling out a sketchbook and a stump of charcoal.

Juliet smiled and stretched. 'Ah. Well. I was nine years old and it was the most exciting thing that had ever happened to me. But I found it frightfully hard to keep still. To help distract me, Mr Milne told me stories of the Mediterranean and it sounded impossibly hot and blue, like something from the *Arabian Nights*. Each evening I'd go home to Victoria Avenue and spend hours in your grandmother's linen cupboard. It held the ancient boiler and was the hottest room in the house, so I'd tangle myself in her sheets trying to imagine Spanish heat. He told me about catching lobsters and eating them with gulps of white wine in the sunshine and in the company of beautiful women. I always think of my old friend John MacLauchlan Milne whenever I eat lobster. You have to understand the littleness of my life until then, Leonard. London was a worn-out grey. Exhausted. There was no colour left after the war – they rationed it all away. And then this old Scotsman came into the Greene & Son workshop to barter for a pair of spectacles and I discovered that the whole world wasn't like this, that there was something else. He painted me and he painted a window for me.'

'But you never wanted to be a painter?'

Juliet laughed. 'Never. I don't have the talent. But it's more than that. I'm terribly nosy, darling. I like to know how other people see the world. Is your blue sky different, bluer than mine? That's how I know that I love a picture, when I love how the artist sees the world. I return to my weekday morning quite refreshed, seeing a little better and right into the heart of

things. I think, ah, so that's a sunflower. I never quite understood before.'

As she spoke, Leonard quietly set down his pencil and drew
out his brushes and started to paint. He didn't paint his
mother but the window over her left shoulder. In it appeared a
Mediterranean afternoon, sunlight casting short, hot shadows against a harbour wall where at a table covered in a
scarlet-chequered cloth a man ate lobster with a girl. Beside
them, a child swaddled herself in sheets like a toga. A pair of
spectacles rested on the ground, and reflected in the lenses was
a fat yellow sunflower.

The portrait was supposed to take a week, perhaps two.
Leonard had never spent more than a month on a picture
before, but then one month stretched into two and then three
and then a year had passed and still it wasn't finished. More
and more scenes appeared outside the window in the painting
– a pair of naked young men dived into a black swimming
pool, white moths flapping against the dark. At the end of
each month Leonard's assistant helped him make the canvas
bigger, strapping another one beside it, then another, until
soon the painting was the size of the studio wall. And still he
had not started to paint Juliet herself. Her life crowded about
her but he left her as a white space in the centre of the picture.

*Today, today I'll paint her. Leonard knows that he says this
every morning, but this morning he means it. The taxi brings
her at nine-thirty and they make tea together and then he
listens as she talks. She tells him about a lost fur coat and a
pair of sapphire earrings, blue as the Aegean and lost too. He
studies her face, the soft creases, the lived-in skin, tiny blue
veins cross-hatching her cheeks, the eyes still sharp and green,
and picks up his brush and paints. The morning ticks, ticks,
ticks and at last he sets down his brush and Juliet yawns and*

declares 'luncheon' and he looks back at the portrait and sees
the earrings, so blue, and the back of a young woman in a fur
coat with a pawn ticket pinned to the sleeve and a flock of
pink-footed geese crossing a fat Dorset moon and he realises
that there is still an empty white space at the centre of his
portrait. After lunch, says Leonard to himself, I'll paint her
after lunch.

They returned to the studio, pleasantly warm after sharing a
bottle of Chianti. Juliet settled in her chair and waited, in no
apparent hurry to begin. Soft sunlight trickled through the
windows and caught the down on her cheek. Leonard considered her for a moment and then instead of reaching for his
brush opened a drawer in his desk and handed her a worn
sketchpad.

'Do you remember this? Tibor gave it to me that summer in
California.'

Juliet frowned. 'Yes. I think I do.'

She opened the front page to discover the newspaper photograph of George Montague cut from the *Jewish Forward*'s
'Gallery of Vanished Husbands' glued to the inside cover.
Underneath it there was written in a neat childish hand 'My
Father. George Montague. OR sometimes Molnár.' She turned
to the next page and saw a sketch of a man clearly intended to
be a copy of the photograph. It was crude and the lines wobbly
but the similarity was there. On the following page was
another drawing, another George. She turned again and again
– different Georges stared out at her. Some smiled, others
were more serious. One wore spectacles. As she neared the end
of the book, the portraits became more sophisticated. Here
was George in oils, there in the style of a Georgian
miniature.

'Are any of them like him?' asked Leonard quietly.

Juliet set down the book on her knee and returned to the beginning, turning the leaves slowly, studying each George one by one.

'Each has a little piece of him. None of them has him entirely, but taken altogether, you could find him.'

The following morning marked the first day of real summer. The curtains were open and a cabbage white butterfly flitted in through the open window, wafting on a wave of sunshine. Outside the street hummed with the bustle of school mornings, the knock of lunch boxes and a smell of dew-damp grass. A hose creaked and hummed. A car reversed into a dustbin with a metallic clatter. The taxi would be here in half an hour but Juliet was tired and decided to lie in bed just a few moments longer and listen to the morning. She fumbled in her bedside table and drew out a letter, worn along the folds from re-reading.

Brooklyn, January 2005

Dearest Juliet,

I almost didn't write this letter at all. I was going to ask my attorney to send you a note with the painting but then I decided that was a coward's way out and I've been a coward for goodness knows long enough. I'm sure you hated my guts for a long time and, my God, I deserved it and more but now, well, time softens and slackens all things. I thought of you and the kiddies a great deal. At first it was a pain that nothing could take away. Not booze, not sex, not even a game of chess or a big, big win. Nothing. But truth is, give it long enough and everything fades in the end.

You're all stuck in my mind the way you were the morning I left. I'm probably a grandpa but I think to myself – how can that be true when my serious-faced girl and my little boy aren't much more than babies. But, my God, they were babies half a century ago.

You knew that I was married in Hungary before the war. I never told you but somehow I believed you knew or suspected enough of the truth. Though maybe I was just kidding myself about that too. I thought they were dead, all of them – Vera and the children. When I married you, I believed they'd all gone. I truly thought I was a widower. It wasn't a lie then because I didn't know and you can't lie if you think it's true, can you?

Perhaps this will make you despise me all over again, but really, what do I have to lose – I can't regret marrying you, Juliet. Not then and not now. And aren't you the least bit glad because we were happy for a while, weren't we?

I'd heard rumours before that some of my family were alive but I didn't believe it. That's how a man goes mad. Hankering after shadows and I had, we had, a good thing here. I ignored the whispers and I didn't go looking, I swear. Then one day, about five years after we were married, an old friend arrived from California. I hadn't seen him since before the war, and in truth I never really thought about him. If you'd asked me about him, I would have told you that he was probably dead. But then he walked into the cafe and he leads me to the bar and he asks for glasses of schnapps and he tells me Vera and Jerry are alive. Just those two. Not the others. I tell him he's a liar. And he's calm and he drinks his schnapps and he lets me shout, and then quietly he says, 'I know because I've seen them. They're in California,' and he hands me an address on a scrap of paper. What could I do? I have to go to them and I can't leave. I must choose between families. If you can, spare a snifter of pity for a dead man. What I did to you was a terrible thing and I know that, but at least you had no choice. I lived with mine for fifty years, more or less.

Nothing I did before or since could make up for it. I tried to forget them at first. Tried to throw out the address. Tried to be happy with you and Frieda and our new boy. But when I watched Leonard I saw Jerry. He was starting to crawl when I saw him last and I'd spent so long thinking he'd gone that I'd given up on grieving. But he was alive and I had his address in California and I had to go find him.

Things weren't so good for me in London and I loved you but I knew you'd come through in the end. You're one of those girls, Juliet; you manage. And I was right. Look what you've done for yourself. The gallery. The kids. Quite a name you've made. I've followed you. Scraps in newspapers. Bits of gossip from those passing through. It's funny what you pick up when you're always listening. I heard that you came looking for me and found Vera. I always imagined the two of you would get along. She and I never did. I thought, I left Juliet for this woman, the least I can do is stick with her, but I couldn't do it. I was a better man with you. Over the years, the good bits have been chipped away until only the weak and rotten bits are left. But, ah, I wished I had seen you when you came looking for me. Well, I like to tell myself it was me you came to find, but I guess I've always known it was the picture you wanted. Did you ever forgive me for that? No, I'm sure you didn't. Everything else, perhaps, but not that.

The morning I left, I meant to just go. Take nothing. Not a photograph of you or Leonard or Frieda. If I was leaving there was no point tormenting myself, so I thought. But then there was the picture. You. On the wall in that awful brown living-room watching me getting ready to go. Neither approving nor reproachful, just watching, waiting to see what would happen next. And I don't even remember doing it, but I couldn't leave you behind. I slid your picture out of the frame. That other stuff pinned to the back, the money and the like, I didn't even notice was there till later, though I won't lie – it was handy in a tight spot. But it was the picture I took. I had to have you with me. And you have been for all these years. Some adventures we've had, you and I, and more than one man, more than twenty offered to buy you and there were times that I was tempted but no matter how tight things got, I couldn't do it. I don't have much now to leave, but I do have the picture and she's not mine to give away.

George Montague

Juliet re-folded the letter and lay back against the pillows. The portrait had been reframed and now hung opposite her bed, and the two Juliets, one nine, one seventy-eight, watched one another. George hadn't said sorry. She'd read the letter several times when it first arrived just to check. Sometimes she almost thought he had, but he hadn't, not once. But then if he hadn't gone, if he hadn't stolen the painting, her other life would never have happened. She would have lived quietly in this house and one day surrendered and learned how to make strudel and *knishes* and joined some committee to help with the *shul* flowers and lived through her children and then her grandchildren and her solace would be snippets of gossip and news.

'I'm not grateful to you, George,' she said aloud, not wanting him to misunderstand this realisation. 'You were a shit. And I spent a lifetime keeping secrets because of you, and so did your children. That, as well as the painting, I can't forgive.'

A breeze fluttered the curtain and outside a song thrush began to sing.

'The thing is, George, you didn't marry me. It was only pretend. Vera was your wife, not me. I'm not your widow, living or dead, I never was. It doesn't matter to me. Not now. But it will to others.'

Juliet thought of her respectable daughter, so concerned with the world's good opinion.

'You made our children illegitimate, *mamzerim*. The rabbis say that the stain will last seven generations and I don't think poor Frieda would like that at all. I shouldn't imagine Leonard would be too fussed, but all the same. The easiest secrets to keep are the ones you know nothing about.'

She reached into her bedside table and fumbled among the spectacle cases and packets of tissues for a small silver cigarette lighter, engraved in curling letters with *Max Langford, War Artiste Extraordinaire, from your pals.* It was nearly out of paraffin and she had to flick it three times before the flint caught. Doing her best not to singe her fingers, she let George's letter burn, fragments of paper falling onto the counterpane in a flurry of grey snow. It made rather a mess and she supposed that later she ought to wash the sheets but now she was so very tired. She threw back the covers, scattering ash. 'Really I must get up. I'd very much like to see Leonard's portrait.' Until now she'd avoided looking at it, declaring at the end of each day, 'I'll wait until it's finished, darling. I'm sure it's wonderful.' Both of them were equally and privately anxious that she like it and quietly relieved that the moment was delayed. But, Juliet decided, it was getting quite absurd – this morning she would look at the painting.

'It ought to be my last portrait. The final piece in the collection. It's only fitting. Once Leonard's quite finished, I'll tell him.'

She yawned and slid back against the pillows. The street was quiet now, the half hour of stillness before the fleet of cars returned from the school run. There was only the chatter of the birds and the rustle of the larch tree. She could almost imagine that she was lying in a cottage bedroom listening to the sighs of a dark wood. Juliet closed her eyes. There was still time for a few moments' sleep before the honk of the taxi.

AUTHOR'S NOTE

Before my husband David and I got married, we upheld a long-standing Jewish tradition and visited the grave of his grandmother Rosie and invited her to our wedding. One dreich afternoon we went to the cemetery in Glasgow on one of those bone-damp December days when rain surrenders to dusk shortly after lunch. The idea was that Rosie would then join us in spirit under the *chuppah*. No one wants to risk offending a Jewish grandmother.

Rosie was particularly special. In 1948 her husband disappeared. He left her with no money and two small children, but Rosie was determined to provide a better life for her family – no mean feat for a single mother in the Gorbals. She started a popular hair salon, Rosie's, and her son was the first in the family to go to university.

But Rosie and her husband never divorced and she remained an *aguna* until his death. On the day he died, Rosie's daughter-in-law, Maureen, called round to pick her up and take her to work. She discovered Rosie sitting at the kitchen table in her hat and coat drinking a small glass of sherry at half past nine in the morning. Maureen suggested that perhaps Rosie ought to take the day off work – an almost unheard of event. Rosie agreed that it would be best. Despite all he had done, the knowledge of his passing still perturbed her.

Suffering from cancer, she'd stayed alive through sheer force of will in order to witness David's *bar mitzvah*. While I never met Rosie, the stories itched away at me, and I decided to write about a woman inspired by her. Juliet Montague is a fictional creation, but I hope she possesses a dash of Rosie Solomons.

© Ross Collins

ACKNOWLEDGEMENTS

Thanks to my fabulous editor Carole Welch for her patience, endurance and willingness to surrender a Sunday afternoon to the double-checking of timelines instead of doing the cross-word, as well as to the brilliant team at Sceptre. As ever, a big thank you to agent Stan for his enthusiasm and good humour in the face of authorial neediness.

Heartfelt gratitude to my expert readers: painter Charlie Baird, Kelly Ross of my favourite bijoux gallery 'The Art Stable' in Child Okeford, and Leah Lipsey. Any remaining errors are entirely my own.

Huge thanks to Jeff Rona (again) for telling me the stories of his uncle, Tibor Jankay, and permitting me to fictionalise him here. I'm indebted to Bluma Goldstein and her book on the plight of the *aguna*, *Enforced Marginality: Jewish Narratives on Abandoned Wives*, which first introduced me to the 'Gallery of Vanished Husbands'.

Last thanks go to my collaborator, co-conspirator and co-parent, David. I couldn't do any of this without you.

Join a literary community of
like-minded readers who seek out
the best in contemporary writing.

From the thousands of submissions Sceptre
receives each year, our editors select the books
we consider to be outstanding.

We look for distinctive voices, thought-provoking
themes, original ideas, absorbing narratives and
writing of prize-winning quality.

If you want to be the first to hear about our
new discoveries, and would like the chance to
receive advance reading copies of our books
before they are published, visit

www.sceptrebooks.co.uk

Follow @sceptrebooks

'Like' SceptreBooks

Watch SceptreBooks